THE WHIMSY WITCH WHO WASN'T

TALES OF XEST #1

DONNA AUGUSTINE

1

Dead leaves blew across the ground, looking like small creatures scuttling by, spying on the neighborhood, its occupants, its tourists. The wind whistled and howled, and I would've sworn it was saying, "Tippi."

"Shut up," I told it.

Of course, the wind ignored me and continued to call my name. A tingle spread over my flesh like a low current was charging my body. It felt so real, as if I could reach out my hand and touch the magic. I ignored it the way I always did. Most of me was sane, even if I had a toe or two over the line. I could attest to this because whenever I *did* do something crazy, I knew enough to hide it. True crazy was when you had no idea. One day, I might completely succumb to my mother's sickness, but for now, I still *knew* none of it was real.

It hadn't always been that way, though. When I'd been a child, I'd look around and think that there was something more lurking beyond the visible. My mother would tell me it was all real. Believing her, I'd hide in the closet, waiting for gremlins to come and fetch me in the dark of the night.

I'd wake looking for monsters under the bed she swore were real. But that was all in the past. I wasn't a child anymore and had ceased to be one way before most people. I shoved the bad memories from my mind as best I could and got on with what I was here for.

I took the cupcake out of the small pink-dotted box from my mother's favorite bakery and put the candle on it. Shielding it from the wind, I lit it and placed it down.

"Happy birthday, Mom."

Silence greeted me. I'd pretty much expected it. Although she had told me if she ever died, she'd find a way to talk to me from the other side, I didn't fault her for failing. It was hard to talk when you were six feet under. If there was anyone who might've been able to achieve it, though, it would've been her.

As far as mothers, she hadn't been the best. I didn't blame her entirely. Mental illness didn't make it easy. Refusing to get help made it worse.

"So, we haven't seen each other in a long while," I said, filling the silence. Our one-sided conversations were actually an improvement on the ones we'd had when she was alive.

There was one conversation we needed to have that I would've dreaded if she were still around. As it were, I still wasn't looking forward to it. I reached my hand behind me, to the top of my spine, right below my neck, the skin sore.

"I guess I should tell you I got rid of it. Or almost. The doctor said after this last treatment, it should fade completely in the next few weeks."

Silence. That in itself proved she couldn't communicate from beyond.

"I know what you want to say, but it's not true. None of it," I told her.

I'd never wanted it. Had cried every time she'd refreshed it. Now it was gone, this thing most people would've called child abuse, and I somehow felt guilty.

"Hey!" someone yelled.

I jumped, thinking she'd figured out a way after all, before realizing the voice was nothing like hers. I looked about the cemetery, and a twenty-something girl with long locks of purple and blond hair walked toward me. I'd noticed her roaming around before and assumed she was looking for a grave.

"Do you have some salt on you? Mine leaked, and I don't have enough to make the jump. I've only got a couple of grains, and I don't want to end up in Greenland or something."

"Salt?" I looked up at her from where I was sitting cross-legged in front of my mother's grave. Who went around asking people in a cemetery for salt?

"Yeah, for the jump?" she said, mirroring my look of confusion.

"Why do you need salt to jump?" Now *this* was crazy. I'd thought spending ten dollars on a cupcake, which would never be eaten for a birthday party of one, had been the strangest thing I'd do today. This conversation was quickly topping it. People like this were the reason I could claim sanity.

"How else would I do it? Do you know a way to jump without it?" She leaned over a little, as if I had the secret to the universe. "Wait, you're not a..." She leaned closer, staring awkwardly at me. "Or are you?"

"Am I what?" I asked.

"What are you doing here?" she asked, looking about the place.

"It's a cemetery. I'm visiting. What are you doing?"

The more I said, the farther her jaw dropped and the bigger her eyes opened.

"Whoa. This place is *so* weird." She shook her head and took off, jogging away from me.

This was turning out to be a stranger than normal day, which was fitting, considering what my mother had been like.

I looked down at my watch and stood up, wiping the dirt from my pants.

"Sorry to cut your party short, Mom, but I gotta go. I'll try to stop by again in a…" I didn't know when I'd be back. I hated coming here. Would probably always dread it.

"I'm not sure when I'll be back, but I will be." I had a hard time making promises to the dead, just in case they *were* listening. That would have to do.

I leaned down and blew out the candle. "Enjoy your cupcake."

I gave the top of her flat tombstone a pat, the way I used to give her hand a pat when I'd visit her at the asylum.

I opened the door to the shop and Loris called out from the back, "Welcome to Magic, Mayhem and Mischief. Be right with you."

"It's just me," I called back, slipping out of my jacket.

A head full of white hair popped up from behind the one of many shelves that held merchandise and partitioned off different areas.

"Oh, good! I was worried about when you'd be in. I need to run some errands."

For some reason I'd yet to figure out in my three years working here, Loris seemed to always assume I'd be late. I was there before her nearly every day and opened up the shop. The thing that kept it from being annoying was that she was always so happy to see me, as if grateful and surprised I showed up at all.

She walked around the counter, her colorful skirt and scarves sashaying around her. I pulled off my dark grey hat and tucked some black strands back into their bun.

I'd barely gotten myself together when Loris was giving me her usual morning hug. She was big on hugs, love, happiness, and pretty much everything light and bright.

I, on the other hand, grinned and bore it.

"Bun again?" Loris asked, her fingers tapping on it, as if it were a little monster attached to my head.

"Yes," I said, as we went through our typical morning ritual, which was every day but Monday, when the shop was closed.

"How are you going to find a boyfriend if you don't ever doll yourself up a bit? Put some shadow on those..." She squinted, trying to decide what to call the color of eyes that had greys, greens, and amber. "Whatever that eye color is, you should do something with them."

I tucked my purse under the counter. "I'm not trying to find a boyfriend, and you know that." She knew because I'd told her yesterday, and the day before, and the day before that.

"Well, what if one is looking for you? How's he supposed to find you?"

"Maybe I don't want to be found?" I didn't wear black and grey because I wanted to stand out. I wore colors that blended into the shadows, where I liked to hide.

She lifted her shoulders and said, "Okay, I guess I'll leave it be."

"Thank you." She never let it be. Ever. That wasn't Loris.

What was going on? Why was she standing still? Oh no. Not again.

"What?" I asked, knowing it was something I wouldn't want to hear.

"I've got a favor to ask." Loris gave her biggest grin, which meant it was going to be a bad one. "I need another body at a séance tonight."

"Loris..." I groaned, already knowing I'd say yes because I always said yes. I couldn't say no to Loris. When no one else would give me the time of day, she'd given me a job. She'd helped me find a place to live. If it wasn't for Loris, I might've been living in a box in the alley.

"I know you hate them, but I really need you this time. The client is coming by herself, and I don't like two-person séances. They're very awkward."

"I hate séances," I said, because it deserved to be mentioned at least once more before I caved, and we both knew I would.

She walked over and patted my arm. "It's all right to be cautious. There are things in the universe that no one knows about, but I'm confident in what I'm doing. It will be fine."

The saddest part of this was that she believed what she was saying. None of that was why I hated séances. What I truly hated was the sadness that typically came with them, people trying to talk to their lost loved ones. The whole thing brought me down. I really needed to find a different job. This place had been perfect when I was fifteen and everyone else wanted to run my paperwork. Now? I could go somewhere else.

Except who would take care of Loris? She needed me more than I needed her at this point. Every person that walked in the door tried to scam her, and I was often the only one who stopped them.

"You'll do it for me?" She was holding her hands together in front of her.

"Fine. If you really need me."

That problem solved, she was in motion again, heading to the register and taking out money. "We're out of rue. I've got to go down the street and see if Amanda has any. Although she'll probably lie, and then I'll have to go beg Meg, who'll tell me how I do everything wrong."

Amanda and Meg had competing magic shops the next block over, which could only happen in Salem, or perhaps New Orleans. Although I'd never been more than a hundred miles from here, so I couldn't really be sure.

"You don't have any in the deliveries?" I asked, pointing at the boxes, knowing that Amanda and Meg would both overcharge her.

"I didn't order any. Didn't realize how low I was," she said.

"Don't pay more than..."

I gave up, as she was already gone. A strong gust of wind held the door open longer than it should, blowing in all sorts of leaves and debris with it. I'd have to sweep it out, but that could wait until later. First I had to go through the bills and see if she'd paid anyone too much while I was gone. It was easier to rake people over the coals when their crimes were fresh than later in the day, when the dirty deed would be buried under a mountain of other sins. This was why I hated coming in late. The vultures all seemed to know when I was gone.

I grabbed a ceremonial knife from the desk and started slicing open the various boxes, unpacking deliveries, and matching them to receipts, thinking of how awful the séance would be tonight. If there was crying, I'd have to leave, even if just for long bathroom breaks.

I sliced another box open, and the candles in the place flickered with the gust of wind from the door opening.

A man stood right within the door, taller than average but not monstrously so. His shoulders were square, his eyes deeply set in a chiseled face that might've been a little too angular to be called common. Some might even think he had a handsome face, if he didn't seem slightly off-putting in his intensity. He might've been in his late twenties or thirties, but his stare felt like he'd seen it all.

Except perhaps for me? There was definitely a look of shock as he took me in. I ran a hand over my face, wondering if there was some chocolate on my face from the taste of icing I'd had.

I looked down at my fingers. Nothing there.

"Can I help you?" I asked.

He didn't answer. He scanned the room with eyes so grey they seemed nearly silver in contrast to the darkness of his skin and brows, until they settled on the counter, where a single black feather lay. I hadn't noticed it, but it must've blown in when Loris left.

The more he stared at it, the more I wanted it away from me. The feeling didn't make a lot of sense, but I just wanted the thing gone. I leaned down and blew it off the counter. It drifted off and then was taken up by a draft in the room until it circled back and landed in front of me.

I blew on it again, and it wouldn't budge. The less it moved, the more I wanted it gone.

I had to forget the feather. I'd deal with that after I figured out what this guy wanted.

"Are you looking for something?" I asked.

He still didn't answer as his stare landed on me. He walked closer and picked up the stray feather.

Between it being my mother's birthday, the unsettling

girl in the cemetery, and the now-looming séance, my nerves were on overload. This guy standing silently in the room, no matter how attractive, was working the last one I had.

He scanned me again, and for all his good looks, I was getting a little nervous with the perusal and the way he wasn't talking. Although I got the strange impression he was more stunned than aggressive.

"If it's the feather you want, take it and go. It's not one of ours." We did carry a line of feathers, but they were much fancier than this common crow one.

"Is there anyone else here?" he asked.

Perhaps I'd ruled out "aggressive" too hastily. "Yes. There's a few people in the back," I said. I dropped my hand below the counter, blindly digging around until I touched my phone.

"You're lying, and not very well." He held up the feather. "When did this get here? Was someone else here when it arrived?"

"I think you need to leave."

He edged closer. I was glad the counter was between us as I stepped back, taking my phone with me.

"Tell me everyone who was here when the feather arrived." He leaned his hands on the counter, his broad shoulder blocking out the rest of the light as the room grew darker. "How did you get the feather?"

"You need to leave right now."

He reached forward lightning fast, grabbing my wrist in a firm grip. The phone I'd picked up dropped to the floor, and even with the excess fabric of my sweater, I couldn't pull free.

"Who was here when this came?" he asked.

What the hell was he talking about? We got some

whackos in here, but this man was insane. He made my mother look normal.

"You need to get your hand off me, now."

"Answer me."

"It was just me and the owner, I think."

He dropped his hand, and I scrambled to the floor to retrieve my phone. I tried to dial nine-one-one, but the screen wouldn't light up. Should I make a run for it?

"You need to leave or I'm calling the police."

I held my phone so he couldn't see the black screen of my dead phone.

He shook his head before turning and walking out.

I sagged in relief as the door swung shut behind him.

2

Loris called from the back room, "Tippi, are you coming?"

I glanced down at my phone that had decided to start working again. It was six o'clock and Loris was in back with the client already, completely unworried about the earlier confrontation I'd told her about. The séance I didn't want to partake in would eat up a good hour or two. This was officially the day that wouldn't end.

I hadn't the heart to leave after telling Loris I'd help. Part of me—actually, all of me—had hoped she'd start the séance without me.

"Just locking the door," I called, even though I'd done that already. There was no getting out of here until this was done, so I headed back.

The room was ready, the smell of herbs in the air. Loris believed electronics interfered with her gift, so the place was lit by candlelight. I loved Loris dearly, but wasn't so sure the electronics were the true issue. But she believed in what she did. So did her customers, so that was enough.

I sat at the table, taking Loris' hand and the customer's. She was a smiling older lady who already had tissues ready beside her. Getting here late had cut back on the small talk, as I'd hoped. The questions, anything from "how long have you been speaking to the dead" to "how long will they stay and talk" made these occasions even worse than normal.

Loris began chanting as I closed my eyes, thinking about how much laundry I needed to do. It was a lot. I had one outfit left for tomorrow. My building had a few coin-operated machines in the basement and several tenants who didn't like to remove their clothes in a timely fashion. The math didn't work out to my benefit. If I had to dump their clothes on top of the machine tonight, I would. I'd had enough of this laundry rudeness.

"Who are you?" came a deep, gritty voice.

Hmmm. Loris was really working on her voice effects lately. That was a new one. Little on the rude side, but definitely spooky. And had she set up a remote-control fan in here or something? I felt an uncomfortable draft.

"Wh-what?" Loris asked, as if she hadn't been the one to ask in the first place.

She was really giving it her all tonight.

"Who. Are. You?"

My fingers were about to be broken by this customer if Loris didn't chill out soon. I was going to have to shoot her a silent signal and let her know she was taking it too far. I opened my eyes, with the intention of getting Loris' attention, and all words, hints, and signals fled from my mind. In front of me, hovering over the table, was a genuine ghost. Like, a legitimate form in transparent white. Considering Loris couldn't use her cell phone reliably, this had to be the real thing.

"Who are you?" it asked, looking solely at me.

Loris and the client were staring at the ghost, stunned.

"I wasn't paid for a call. Who are you to summon me?

You better be paying for this!" the ghost continued, her face wavering in and out. She was still clear enough to see the angry lines of her expression.

"I did pay her!" the customer said, thinking the ghost was referring to Loris.

I didn't know who was supposed to be "paid," but I'd bet my rent it wasn't Loris. This ghost seemed to think I was supposed to pay her.

Loris was chanting some "Oh, great spirit" crap beside me.

"How much do you want?" I asked. I had some coffee money in my purse if it would make her feel better.

"You didn't pay," she said, almost too clearly for someone who was supposedly dead and talking from the other side. The ghost looked like a bitter hag as she shoved her finger in my face. "Don't call us again without a negotiated deal, jerk."

Jerk? Did that ghost really call me a jerk? I'd heard of nasty ghosts that would haunt your house or possess you. But this? What was this?

"Wait, I have to talk to Mama!" the customer yelled from beside me, grasping at the now-empty space.

The ghost was gone. The customer was screaming, "Come back!" Loris had her hands clasped in front of her chest as she repeated something about thanking the mother.

Me? I was sitting there, not talking, not moving, except for the trembling in my hands as I thought about how the wind had whispered my name, and the leaves had looked like little trolls scurrying across the ground, following me.

It had all been in my head. That was what I always told myself. But if that was the case, what had happened tonight?

I had two witnesses that could attest to this not being a delusion.

I leapt to my feet.

"I gotta go," I said, not caring if anyone heard me.

Loris was still busy thanking the mother while the customer was walking around the room crying for the ghost to come back, waving her hands in the air.

I shot into the front room, grabbed my purse from under the counter, and hustled out of there. I needed to get to a tattoo shop, and there was only one that stayed open late enough on a Sunday to get this done for me. I walked a few steps, then jogged a few feet before I ran the rest of the way.

I burst through the door of the Ink Well. A single tattooist was leaning over, tattooing a tiger onto a girl's outer thigh as her male friend watched on.

"Can you fit me in tonight?" I asked, winded.

"Sorry," the tattooist said, not looking up from his work. "Won't be done until late. I can fit you in tomorrow, though. Nothing scheduled for the morning."

Tomorrow? What if that ghost came back? No. I needed this tattoo back tonight. "I really need it done now. It's sort of an emergency."

"Yeah, well, you'll have to somehow survive your tattoo emergency until tomorrow." The tattooist rolled his eyes, and the three of them chuckled.

"You don't understand. This is really important," I said.

"And mine isn't?" the girl lying on the bench asked, looking at the outline on her leg.

The tattooist stopped and looked up. "Like I said, come back tomorrow. She was here first." He went back to his tattooing as if I weren't there.

"I can't," I said. "I'll wait until you're done."

He leaned back, this time putting his needle down.

"Look, I'm not doing it tonight. Now get out." The tattooist looked at the male friend. "Can you show her out so I can get back to work?"

The male, all six foot something of him, nodded, stood, and took a step toward me.

I backed up. "I'm going."

I jogged home, worried I'd see something else.

I'd call in late and get the tattoo in the morning. It was just a tattoo, and getting rid of it might've had nothing to do with what happened. But still, the timing was too weird to ignore. I'd spent the last several months removing a tattoo that now I couldn't wait to put back on.

In the meantime, I took my kitchen table and moved it in front of the door of my apartment. It was from a second-hand store. It showed its age, but the solid wood was heavy as hell. That wouldn't stop a ghost, but it made the craziness that had been drilled into me by my mother quiet down a bit.

I showered, put on my last clean outfit, and then lay in bed while the stories my mother would tell me ran through my head. Most kids had bedtime stories of princes and princesses. Mine were about monsters and goblins that would come for me while I slept. My hand went to where my necklace lay against my chest, one of the last things I had from my mother.

I wrapped myself in three layers of blankets, closed my eyes, and tried to clear my mind of all the crazy thoughts trying to intrude, all the horrible stories I'd been told. I tried to obliterate all the memories of my childhood, praying that there wasn't some grain of truth in them.

"I didn't bring enough salt."

My door hadn't opened. How was there a voice inside my apartment? It had to be another ghost. I clenched my hands on the comforter. *Don't open your eyes. Pretend it's not there. It'll go away.*

"You're kidding me, right? You didn't bring it again? How do you keep a job? If I wasn't with you, you'd be thrown out on your ass."

"Why didn't *you* bring the salt if you're such a professional?"

"Because I asked you and you said you had it. Just go find some. These humans always have salt."

"Not sure I'm going to find anything in this barren wasteland," a guy said. His footsteps shuffled away, and my bedroom door creaked open.

My heart was pounding. One left. If I could stab him with the knife under my pillow before the other one came back, I had a chance.

I turned, located the man, and swung in his direction. Before my arm completed its arc, the knife was knocked out of my hand. The guy had barely moved, but the knife was lying across the room. I stood defenseless in a worn sweatshirt with holes and faded leggings that had been black once upon a time.

The guy squinted as we took each other's measure. He had a shaved head except for a single braid that sprouted from the top of his head. There were goggles strapped to his forehead, and he wore a studded black leather jacket.

"She's awake! Can you hurry up with the salt?" Braid yelled toward the door.

"Who are you?" I asked.

"Bounty hunter," he said.

The other man walked in, this one with a full head of

purple hair that formed spikes, wearing a silver jumpsuit that was nearly blinding.

Spike glanced at me where I'd pressed my back against the wall, before holding up salt packets to his friend. "She had some fast-food packets. Little stale and crusty, but they should work."

"It'll do," Braid said, pulling a flask out of the interior pocket of his jacket. He opened it and made a puddle on my floor, and for some reason, all I could think about was the water stain it was going to leave if I didn't clean it up soon. There went my security deposit. It wasn't the sanest thought, but this situation wasn't sane.

He kept pouring until it was large enough that the puddle hit the tips of my toes. He then ripped open the salt packets and sprinkled them onto the puddle. With a smile in my direction, they both stepped onto the puddle and then they were gone.

And so was I.

3

It felt like I'd been tossed out a window and dumped in the middle of a darkly lit room. The two men who'd been in my bedroom were there, as well as an older man that reminded me of a picture I'd seen of Einstein once. If anything was normal, that was the extent of it. This place looked older than most of the historical buildings in Salem, with stone walls and floors and a fireplace big enough for me to stand in. I didn't recognize it either, not that I'd been in every building in the area.

Where was I? How had I gotten here? I peeked out the only window and my breathing halted as my heart raced. This was *not* Salem. It looked like some medieval place, with stone buildings lining the lane, and streetlights that appeared to be gas.

"What did I tell you about showing up without warning?" Einstein asked.

"This is the pop-up who had a price on her head," Spike said, throwing a thumb in my direction.

"Where am I?" I asked the three men.

Einstein glanced at me and then back to Spike and Braid. "I'm not paying for her. I can't feel any magic."

"You said bring anyone in that has a price on their head and they'd be worth ten to you. Well, here she is." Braid took a step closer to me and pointed.

"I'm not paying for her. She feels weak," Einstein said.

I felt weak? Paying for me? What was wrong with these people? Was I awake?

"You didn't even test her," Braid said.

"Screw him," Spike said.

"We'll take her down the road. I heard Rottie was looking for someone," Braid said.

These people were trying to sell me? They'd kidnapped me through a puddle and now they wanted to auction me off? This couldn't possibly be real. I was losing it. I was ending up just like my mother. Insane. But if this was a delusion, it was a really good one.

"I think there's been a mistake. I'm not supposed to be here. That's why I'm not screaming magic. I have none. I don't know who you people think I am, but I'm not that person. This is a huge mistake."

They all looked at me, staring like I was crazy. Just for the heck of it, I patted myself on the cheek to see if I could wake up.

"I think she might be crazy," Spike said softly to Braid.

Braid elbowed him and gave him a look that clearly told him to shut up.

"See? No magic and crazy," Einstein said.

They stared at me for another half a second before Braid turned back to Einstein. "If you're saying you don't want her, fine. We're taking her down the street."

Braid grabbed my arm, tugging me toward the door. Spike followed us.

Einstein threw up a hand. "Just wait a second there. She's not screaming 'magic,' but she might be useful on some of the factory floors."

Braid tugged me back in the room.

This seemed like a dance these three had done many times before. I just wish I knew the steps as well as they did.

I tried to tug out of Braid's grip, but his fingers wouldn't budge. "I really don't think you understand. I'm normal. I don't have magic. I don't know where I am, but I do know I shouldn't be here. If you let me go, I won't say a word about this place to anyone, ever. Just put me back where I was and we're cool."

"No one is talking to you. Shut up," Braid said.

"I'll test her," Einstein said, shaking his head as he walked back behind the massive wood desk, one of the few pieces of furniture in the room. He opened a bunch of drawers. When he got to the bottom, something jumped out with a puff of smoke and hopped across the room with a fluffy grey tail, leaving a trail of dusty paw prints in its wake before it escaped into the hall.

Einstein waved a hand in the air, coughing. "Damn dust bunny," he said before he went back to searching. "Where is that tester?" He moved to the door and yelled, "Mertie! Did you take my tester?"

"Bottom drawer on the right," a female yelled back.

He walked back over, grumbling as he looked through the drawers again. "There it is. Blasted woman, always moving my stuff."

He pulled out a small strainer, something that looked like you'd run orange juice through if you didn't like pulp. It had a small jar that was stuck on the other side of it. He walked over, holding the strainer up in front of me.

"Take a deep breath, hold it for as long as you can, and then blow into here." He tapped a long black nail on the jar.

As little as I understood, magic seemed to be what they were after. If I *did* have magic, and this thing proved it, what would happen to me then?

"I told you, I don't have magic," I said, trying to back away but stopped by the ever-present hand on my arm.

Braid lifted my arm, bringing me to my toes. "If you don't have any magic, we don't need you, and we aren't going to waste our time taking you back. If you do have magic, you live, so I'd think hard on that."

"You sure you don't want to blow into the tester?" Spike asked.

"I'd do it if I were you," came a small, squeaky voice. I searched the room and saw three *see no evil, hear no evil, speak no evil* monkey statues on Einstein's bookcase.

The monkey covering his mouth dropped his hand and said, "If you don't have magic, you're not here. If you're not here, you're not *anywhere*."

The *hear no evil* monkey nodded as the *see no evil* monkey stared at me, eyes wide open.

"I'd listen to them. They never lie," Spike said.

All three monkeys nodded this time.

If I'd needed a sure sign I wasn't in Salem, besides a puddle sucking me up and spitting me out, and the view of a medieval city out the window, these monkeys had hammered the last nail in the coffin.

If this tester thing said I didn't have magic, I was as dead as Spike's eyes were. I didn't know how many deaths they had on their hands, but I could almost see the blood dripping from their fingertips. My fate if I had magic was iffy at best, but my fate without magic had been spelled out all too clearly. I took a deep breath and blew into the strainer, while everyone watched on, including the monkeys.

It did nothing until I was nearly out of air, but then finally something happened. The last of my breath went through the strainer and the glass jar filled with a purple dust that shimmered and moved about like a strange sort of snow globe.

The monkeys on the desk snickered. "Just another Whimsy witch," Speak No Evil said.

"See? Magic. Now pay up," Braid demanded.

Einstein held the glass up, shaking it. "There's plenty of Whimsy work to be done in the factory, so I guess I'll take her."

"That'll be ten coins."

Braid finally released my arm in order to hold out his palm toward Einstein, who flipped him a shiny gold coin.

Spike tipped his head. "Pleasure doing business with you," he said.

The duo left through the door. I didn't follow. It was clear I'd been bought and paid for.

I turned to Einstein. "Can you tell—"

"Mertie!" Einstein yelled over me. "Have a new one!"

Mertie appeared in the door less than a second later, slender with long black hair, bright red skin, and two horns on her head. "I heard you, boss. You don't need to scream."

My jaw dropped as I backed away. "I'm already dead, aren't I? I'm in hell."

Mertie rolled eyes that were nearly all black before turning to Einstein. "They all do the same shit. It's getting old. When is this going to stop?"

"It's not my fault you look like a demon," Einstein said, settling back down in his chair.

"Then you're not a demon?"

She groaned loudly. "*Of course* I'm a demon. Look at me! But I take offense at being called one. Now, come on, I don't have all day." She turned, waving at me to follow her. I went because at least she'd spoken directly to me.

She clomped down the hallway, her black leather miniskirt showing off kickass red legs and unfortunate hoofed feet that didn't require shoes.

"I'm sorry. I didn't mean to insult you," I said, catching up to her. This was not the time to acquire enemies. I needed friends, even demon ones.

"It's fine. I'm used to it." She let out a little huff, the smell of smoke following it.

We walked down the long, narrow hallway, also built of stone. Then a circular staircase, also made of stone. There seemed to be nothing that wasn't made of stone in this place.

After giving her a minute or two to calm down after my apparent insult, I asked, "Where am I, exactly?"

"You're in Xest."

"Xest?"

"No. Not Zest. Xest. I can hear the X when you pronounce it." I nodded, even though we were both pronouncing it the same way. I had much bigger problems than her hearing a hidden X in my pronunciation.

She stopped and snapped her fingers at me when I'd lagged behind for a second. "Hurry up."

"Where is Xest? I've never heard of it." If I could get my bearings, I could get back home. Right now I didn't know what direction to take if I did run.

"Xest is Xest. It's north of North and west of West."

"Do you know where Massachusetts is?"

She groaned. "Of course I do. It used to be part of my

territory before I changed—I know where it is. It's in Rest, like everything that isn't in Xest."

"Where is Xest in regards to Salem?"

"It's Xest of Salem. It's Xest of everywhere, that's why it's Xest. North, South, East, and West is the Rest. See, this is the thing that's so annoying about humans, or even fake ones like yourself. They can only go north, south, east, and west. For some reason that is beyond me, they can't travel to Xest, where all the important things happen."

I wanted to have that light-bulb aha moment, but as she talked, the lights faded more and more on my understanding. Where the hell was I?

"Is there anyone else I can talk to about leaving? I don't belong here. I'm not a witch or Whimsy or a whatever it is that lives here. I should be where nothing important happens."

"The magic mist, although unimpressive from what I saw sitting on the table, would say otherwise."

She pushed open a wooden door on the bottom landing, and a blast of frigid air shot through my thin clothes. I got a clear view of this place, and it only made things worse. I'd wondered if I'd imagined what I saw upstairs. Now my bare feet were standing on a cobblestone street and I could see the gas lights up close. The few people that passed could've been human if it was Halloween and everyone had a costume on. This place looked like someone had taken medieval England, wrapped it up in a steampunk novel, and then sprinkled it with some fairy dust to see what would happen.

"Come on," Mertie said, walking across the street to a row house. "This is where the Whimsy witches stay. The Whimsy warlocks are a door down, but don't let me find you in there. We don't have time for babies. Too much work to be done."

Mertie opened the door to a large room that hadn't seen a coat of paint since before I'd been born. Two mismatched couches with stuffing poking out of the arms took up one half of the large room. A long table that would've been at home in a military school cafeteria took up the other. There was fire burning in a small stone fireplace that shed a little light into the room and even less heat. From the girls scattered about, some in orange-striped clothing, it had the distinct feeling of a dormitory of sorts.

Could've been worse. It could've had bars instead of walls. From the lack of beds, and the amount of doors, those must have been bedrooms lining the main room.

"Rabbit!" Mertie yelled, making my ear closest to her ring. Was that screeching a remnant from her previous occupation as well? I could see how it would've come in handy.

A girl with full cheeks and blond ringlets popped her head out of a door. She saw me and smiled, as if I were an expected guest she'd been hoping for.

A few more heads popped out of the open doors lining the room, all checking out what was going on. None of them appeared to be as happy about my arrival as Rabbit, who nearly bounced her way over to us.

"This is..."

"Tippi," I said, when Mertie looked at me like I was milk past its expiration date.

"She's your new roommate. Show her the ropes and get her a uniform," Mertie told Rabbit.

"Got it." Rabbit beamed a smile that would've made a supernova turn green.

Mertie scowled, as if the cheeriness grated on her last nerve, before she turned and left the building.

The second she was gone, Rabbit rolled her eyes.

"Not sure you figured this out yet, but that woman is *not nice*. I've been trying to kill her with kindness for years, but it doesn't seem to be working. I think there's something wrong with my spell. I can't figure out if it's because my magic is too weak or if she's already dead inside, and therefore can't be killed."

I smiled and nodded, pretending I didn't notice the stares, as I tried to figure out if that was a joke. She wasn't laughing, though, and neither was I. I needed to get back to Salem.

"Come on, I'll get you some clothes and show you our room. Don't mind the stares. Everyone always likes to check out the new witches."

Most of the other women there eyed me up and then turned away, as if they hadn't seen me at all. No hello, or who are you, or where are you from. The lack of all those questions made me fairly certain that this happened at least somewhat often.

Rabbit led me to a small room that was twelve by ten at most. The wide-planked wood floors were bare and bunk beds were on either side of me. A chest of four drawers was in the center.

"This is my bed, but the bunk over me is free." She patted the thin mattress.

"Thank you, but I don't think I'll need it. Is there someone I can talk to? The thing is, I'm not a witch. There's been a huge mistake. I really shouldn't be here. I need to go back home to where I live."

"Did you talk to Marvin? The guy with all the white hair? Old dude?"

"Yes, I did, but he wasn't any help. He doesn't understand that I can't stay here. I have a home. They just *took* me."

Her head tilted to the side. "That doesn't sound right. They need a bounty to take you. I've dealt with a lot of pop-ups and there's always something. What happened before you got here?" She tapped a finger to her lip.

"A lot of stuff happened. Some guy yelled at me, and then there was a séance and a ghost came. Then the ghost yelled at me, saying something about not paying. It was a horrible—"

"Wait, the ghost said you didn't pay?"

"Yes." It was something that would be crystal-clear in my mind as long as I lived.

"I think I see what happened," she said, taking a seat. "You called in a service and didn't pay. You're probably indentured."

I took a seat beside her. "What service? I didn't call in anything."

She bent her knee, turning toward me. "It was the séance. Your magic summoned someone from here. They probably filed a claim when they showed up but didn't get paid. It doesn't matter if you weren't the one who called. You were the one with the magic, and it wasn't paid. You owe the debt."

"What does that mean, exactly?" I looked about the room, the bunk beds, the coarse grey blankets that added to the overall bleakness.

"It means you're stuck in Xest until the debt is paid. Since it wasn't negotiated ahead of time, you can't haggle on the amount."

How long would I be stuck here? Would I ever get out? This could not be my life. *Mom, why didn't I listen to you?*

"You get used to it here. It's not so bad once you do, and I'll be your friend."

The one thing I hadn't seen in this crazy place was a guard.

"Do you know how I can get back? Do you have a map or something?"

"You're only a Whimsy witch. You won't have enough magic to jump puddles back to Rest. You'd need at least a strong Middling witch or warlock to do that, and you're only a Whimsy witch or you wouldn't be here."

"What's a Middling witch or a Whimsy witch?"

"I'll try to explain, but coming from Rest—you know, north, south, east, and west—as you are, it's going to be a hard thing for you to grasp right out of the gate."

"Just do your best." Any information beat the big, fat nothing I currently had.

She sat on her bed and patted the spot next to her as she continued. "There's many levels of magic." She dropped her hand low. "You've got your lowest-level magic, which is called Whimsy, which is what we are. So, you could have a Whimsy witch, Whimsy warlock, a Whimsy variety of another type."

"What other type?" I had to leave here, like now.

"Well, obviously there aren't just witches and warlocks, but..." She waved a finger. "Let's skip that for now. It might be too much all in one night. I've talked a lot of pop-ups through their first times, and it's better to take this in small pieces, chewable morsels that are easily digested. Let's just leave it that there's pretty much everything imaginable here but your run-of-the-mill human. Not that we haven't had a couple accidentals, but they die within hours, having less magic than even a Whimsy."

Dead in hours? Where had I landed? I was in some sort of magical hell.

Rabbit must have read some of the horror I was feeling, because she continued, "But let's move on to something else. So a Whimsy witch or warlock has the least amount of magic you're born with to be considered magical. It's like a hop, skip, and a jump above a regular old human, or Rester, as they're sometimes called. If you're Middling, it's just how it sounds. You've got some magic, but you're not blowing anyone's bangs back. Above them, you've got Braws. It's best to steer clear of them altogether, not that a Braw would have anything to do with a Whimsy, but I don't want you to make the mistake of approaching one. That would be pure foolishness. If they didn't kill you, you'd never live it down."

"So Braws are the strongest?" Then a Braw could definitely get me out of here, and probably a Middling too. I was new to this system, but I'd bet there was no way that the two thugs who'd brought me here were more than Middling.

"No, Makers are the strongest, but I've never met one of those myself. They're called Makers because they're so strong that they can do or make anything they want. They rule the roost, so to speak—if they exist, that is. I've only heard of people, who've heard of people, who thought someone might've met one once a long time ago."

Okay, some Middling, all Braw, and definitely Makers. There was going to be someone in this place that would get me out.

"You said there were other pop-ups, like me? Are any of them here?" Having an alliance couldn't hurt. I wasn't sure anything could hurt right now. All help would be good.

Her mouth opened but she couldn't seem to get the words out of it. The silence stretched on for a bit as she looked at the floor and her shoes and anywhere but me before she finally said, "No, there aren't."

"But I thought you'd said you talked a lot of Whimsy witches through their first days?"

She nodded. "I have, but they don't tend to last long. Magic usually runs in families, so you don't get strong magic popping up out of nowhere. Hence, pop-ups, if you haven't figured out the name. It's like a blip that occasionally happens. They come but burn out fast."

Just as I thought this couldn't get worse.

"How long do they usually live?" I asked, so I knew how long I had to get out of this place.

"Six months, sometimes. This girl, Cassie, she made it to a year. She was the longest, though," Rabbit said, dropping her head and toying with the laces in her shoes.

The silence stretched out. "You could be different," she said. "It's always possible."

"It's okay," I said, letting her off the hook. It didn't matter because I wouldn't be here that long. I was getting out of this place and back to Salem way before six months.

She looked up at me through her lashes, as if afraid to look straight at me in case I exploded.

"Really, it's not your fault. I'm not going to die here."

She nodded, not believing me for a second.

4

I woke to the sound of a weird rooster alarm clock, only to open my eyes and realize there was an actual rooster sitting on the top railing of the bunk.

I squinted at it. I would've sworn it squinted back before it screeched in my direction.

"Get out of bed already!" I heard someone scream down the hall.

Rabbit's head popped up. "It's going to keep doing that until you get up."

The rooster nodded in agreement before it let out a screech.

"I'm up," I yelled at it, then jumped from the bunk before I lost my hearing.

The second my feet hit the ground, orange-striped clothes were thrust into my hand and I was shuffled into a bathroom by Rabbit.

"We can't be late," she said.

I was too afraid to ask what would happen if we were, so I hustled along. There was a line of girls all bustling about in and out of the bathroom, and it seemed we were last in line for everything. Still, not one hello.

A brunette using the sink in front of me looked at the girl at the next sink over and said, "Rabbit finally got another friend."

"Only one she can get," the other girl replied, before they both laughed.

Rabbit looked at the other side of the room, as if she hadn't heard any of it.

I waited until we finally got our turn as the place emptied out before saying, "They're a mean bunch, huh?"

She shrugged. "It's not them. It's just the way it is here. Even for a Whimsy witch, I don't have much magic. Magic levels stick together."

That was all the time we had for talking before I was hustled out the door, crossing the street toward the building I'd been in last night, another line of young men joining in as we melded and made our way inside.

I caught some glances from some of the guys, but they were wasting their time. I wasn't going to have time for anything other than getting out of here. There was only one way I'd be interested in talking to any of them.

"Are they all Whimsy too?" I whispered to Rabbit.

"Yes."

Yep. Not interested.

"Where are we going?" I asked, as we all filed down a hallway.

"We have to punch in first to find out where we're working. We do it once a week because Marvin likes to get his money's worth. There's an ebb and flow to everyone's magic. Like, a Whimsy witch might have one week a year where her magic flows stronger and she's Middling. A Middling might also drop to a Whimsy every so often if she's sick or whatnot. If we get sick, we might lose all of our magic for days, so you need to take care of yourself. It's very dangerous to have no magic here. It can kill you if you ever go completely empty."

"Could a Whimsy ever surge to Maker?"

"Oh no, they never get a surge that strong. Makers are something special. They have more than double the magic anyone else has. You don't surge into a Maker, not even for a day."

But I might surge to a Middling, and that would be enough.

Somehow, even though we'd been last for everything else, the crowd parted for us this time. We made it past a single-file line that was fifty people long. Rabbit walked up to a clock on the wall and punched it in its dial. The clock's mouth opened and said, "Dandelions."

The line grew quiet as I approached. The people yet to come were breaking ranks and standing on tiptoes to get a better view.

I stood in front of it, taking a deep breath.

"Well? Come on, sissy! Punch me already," the clock said.

I swung my arm back and punched the thing in the center.

"Dandelions," the clock said.

There was a general murmur of non-interest. "Eh, just another Whimsy witch," someone a few people down said.

"I told you so," another said.

The only one who seemed happy was Rabbit. "Great! We can sit together," she said, waving me along. We climbed a couple of flights up, and she urged me to one of the long tables, close to the windows and about as far from the heat of the fireplace as you could get.

"Can't we go sit over there?" I said, rubbing my hands together.

"The stronger Whimsy witches and warlocks sit there." She sat on the bench in front of a heap of dandelions. "But it doesn't matter. Better view from here anyway."

I sat down beside her but wasn't sure I was sold on her view. The window was drafty, and I was beginning to fear this place was never sunny, not even during the day.

"So this is what you do." She picked up a dandelion from the pile in front of us, held it in her hands, and then blew gently on it. The dandelion sparkled for a minute before it vanished.

"What was that?" I asked.

"I gave it some of my magic. That dandelion will replace a dandelion somewhere in the world. Once it goes to seed, if someone blows on it and makes a small wish, it'll happen. Marvin has the wholesale contract on a lot of these things. You know, dandelions, clovers, blowing on dice, eyelashes. All sorts of odds and ends. That's why he's so rich. He got in on the market when no one wanted to bother with the small stuff." She pointed at the pile. "We've got a lot of dandelions to get through, so you better start trying."

I lifted the flower up and blew. It glittered and disappeared from my hands.

"See? All good," she said loudly, as Mertie was poking her head into the room and the other tables were filling up. Then Rabbit whispered, "Try to blow as little as you can on each one. You want to conserve your magic. You need to figure out how little to give it."

"What do you mean, conserve?"

"It's not endless, or not for most people. The more magic you spend, the faster you burn out. Why do you think pop-ups only make it to a year if they're lucky? Most aren't born with much magic. It's why everyone here is young. Whimsy witches don't last long. This job has a high burnout rate. Most of us don't last to forty."

I looked around the room, realizing no one looked older than maybe mid-thirties. Man, woman, didn't matter. There wasn't a lined face in the bunch. "Do all witches die young?"

"No. Some live forever. Just depends on your magic. Some people are lucky enough to have infinite magic, but that's rarely the case with Whimsy witches. We're born with whatever we have, and it's not much."

Mertie was across the room, scowling.

I turned, going back to blowing on dandelions as the heaviness of this situation settled onto my soul.

A few hours in the factory doing dandelion work was beginning to feel like I was strung up on the rack, my insides getting torn apart. It wasn't that I was struggling with it. As weak as my magic was, there seemed to be a constant flow with which to do my job. The problem was how was I ever going to get out of this place if I never came in contact with anyone stronger than a Whimsy?

Working beside Rabbit was making me feel even more desperate. She was a poster child of why I didn't want to be here. Each blow on the dandelion had begun to sound like a death rattle from her chest. Her skin, which had a normal hue this morning, now seemed to be turning ashen, her cheeks more sunken in by the minute.

I glanced around, making sure no one was paying attention, before I leaned in. "Are you all right?"

"Don't worry. I'll be fine as soon as I stop for the day. I'm always like this while I'm working." She nodded, trying to look cheerful, but the cost was clear in her lopsided smile.

Fine by the end of the day? She didn't look like she'd be alive by the end of the day.

"Rabbit, I'm getting out of this place. You need to as well."

"Even if we found someone willing to jump us back, I have nowhere to go. My mother was a Whimsy worker, her mother, and her mother before that. This is all we are. And it's okay. This is what life is, and I know it."

Nothing about her bent shoulders and wheezing breath agreed with that statement.

Rabbit had so much of my attention that I nearly missed seeing *him* as he stood in the doorway, scanning the factory floor. It was the guy that had come into the shop, who'd been obsessed with the black feather.

The room hushed, including the table of witches by the fireplace who'd been laughing loudly a few seconds ago. How was he here? Did he have something to do with my being here? There was no way this was coincidental. One thing was clear: he was strong enough to jump.

His eyes stopped on me, as if he'd found what he was looking for. They narrowed, and for a moment, I thought I saw annoyance flare in his gaze. Annoyed with me, or that I was here? That I couldn't begin to guess at, but I was going to find out.

"Who is that by the door?" I nudged Rabbit, the only person in the room who hadn't noticed him.

Rabbit lifted her head, catching a glance of him right before he left. "You mean *Hawk*?"

"I've seen him before."

I began to stand, afraid I'd lose him. Rabbit grabbed my arm, tugging me back down.

"Don't go after him. Hawk's the broker. He'd never talk

to a Whimsy witch, and it could be dangerous to approach him."

She could say whatever she wanted. He'd come here for me. I could feel it in my gut and see it in the way his eyes had stayed on me. The thing I didn't know was whether that was a bad or good thing. My first meeting made me hesitate long enough to hear her out.

"What do you mean, he's the broker?"

"He owns the broker shop. He's in charge of most of the big deals between Xest and Rest—you know, the place you came from."

"I don't understand. What deals?" I asked.

We both fell silent as Mertie walked into the room. She passed by our table, pausing and looking down at us as she did, before walking around the rest of the room and leaving, her hooves echoing down the hall.

"Could he get me home if he wanted?" I whispered.

"Yes, but it doesn't matter. You don't want to talk to him or even look at him."

"But I saw him in Salem. He came into the shop I was working at. He talked to me there."

Her chin dropped as she leaned back. "He did? About what?"

"Honestly, nothing that made much sense, but the point is I'm still alive." And he might be my way out of here. It was the only option on the table, and I wasn't letting him go that easy. "I've got to talk to him. I think he can help me."

She shook her head again. "I've heard bad things whispered about him. You're setting yourself up for trouble. He's not like everyone else."

"Just cover for me if anyone asks, okay? Say I went to the bathroom." I stood up. She could've said he was the devil himself come to take me to hell and I'd still have followed him. I was getting out of this place.

Rabbit was chewing on her lip like it was lunch, her hair frazzled from swiping it away from her face, as if she were already preparing for an interrogation. That girl would not hold up under pressure.

I made my way toward the bathroom and then did a quick dodge out the door. Hawk was nowhere to be seen in the hallway, and I didn't know where to look. There was only one thing to do: make my way to the entrance and hope I hadn't missed him. I ran down the steps, surprised at how easy it was to get out of this place.

I was out the door and behind a few tall bushes. The idea of running occurred to me, but run where? I had a bad feeling that Rabbit was right. The only way to get out of this place was to have someone get you out, or jump you out, as she'd called it. There would be no running anywhere. It was probably why they didn't need to guard the doors.

The wind was whipping around, and I wished I had a jacket while I waited.

Hawk finally walked out the door a few minutes later. I let him get across the street before I ran after him. A discussion on the front stoop of the factory could turn bad fast. I dashed across the street and planted myself in front of him, stopping him with a hand on his chest.

"Did you turn me in?" I asked. If he had, getting him to jump me out was going to be a hard sell.

He looked down at my hand, pausing as if he wasn't used to someone approaching him or touching him. It reinforced the way Rabbit had spoken of him. Desperation had its own set of rules, though.

He grabbed my wrist, moving it off his chest and then releasing it. "I didn't turn you in."

He stepped around me and began walking.

I chased after him. "You're saying you had nothing to do with me being here?"

"I'm pretty sure that's what I said." His jacket flared as he walked briskly in front of me, and I nearly had to jog to catch up.

"I don't believe you."

"I'm devastated." He continued to walk, not bothering to look at me.

He walked away as if I were of no consequence, but he wasn't getting out of this that easy. I ran in front of him, grabbing his arm.

He looked at my hand gripping his sleeve. "I don't know who you are, and I don't have time for you or your problems."

"Did you turn me in because of your feather?"

His gaze shot to the surrounding area, to who might've heard me, and I knew I was onto something.

"Don't mess with me, Whimsy witch. You won't like the outcome." The indifference in his voice turned to a growl.

He wrapped his hand around mine. I thought he was going to throw my hand off him, but he paused, his fingers stilled. It was the first time we'd had skin-to-skin contact, and I could feel a sizzle where our flesh met. I was the one who pulled back this time, ending the sensation.

"What are you playing at? Who are you?" he asked, stepping closer, the prey becoming the predator.

I was running out of time. He would either help me or not, and at least he was finally paying attention. "I'm no one. I'm a human, and I need to get back home. Can you help me? I'll pay anything."

He scanned me again, and I would've given anything to crawl into his mind for one minute.

"What are you doing out here? Why are you talking to him?" Mertie called out from across the street.

She was walking toward us. I didn't know how I'd missed the sound of her hooves on the cobblestones. My best chance of getting out of here was about to disappear. I choked on my words, scrambling for an excuse that might buy me a few more minutes with Hawk.

With another long stare, Hawk turned to Mertie. "*I* called her over. Now mind your business."

Mertie ducked her head, nodding, and walked back to the building. She didn't go in but hovered by the door, watching.

"Don't look, but there is a large tree down the way." Hawk lowered his voice as if he wanted to make sure it didn't carry to Mertie.

I knew which tree he was talking about. I'd been staring at it all day from the window in the factory. Its trunk was whitish grey and its leaves were all black. The thing was huge, and appeared to be some kind of cross between an oak and a weeping willow if it had been grown in hell.

"Be there at two a.m."

"You'll help me?" Adrenaline mixed with hope and shot through my veins. I swallowed hard, trying to keep the excitement from spreading to my face and tipping off a spying Mertie.

"Maybe." He was back to sounding indifferent.

My heart jumped as I forced the rest of my body to stay languid. He was going to give me a chance. I had a chance.

He walked away, and I turned back to Mertie, planting a contrite face on as she watched my every step. I walked in the factory, and Mertie followed me, yelling, "Get back to work, you lazy Whimsy witch!"

"I'm sorry. I got woozy. I'm not used to all this strong

magic. I thought the cold air would help, and then Hawk called me over." I tried to muster up a few tears for her benefit. I failed miserably. I'd never been good at crying on demand, or crying at all.

"It wasn't break time," Mertie said. "You're not getting your dinner now." She stopped outside the factory room I'd been assigned to, pointing. "Get back to work and don't let me see you out of that chair again, or Marvin will be hearing about it, and you won't like what comes next."

I nodded, keeping my head down until I took a seat by Rabbit.

"What happened? I saw you talking to him," she whispered as soon as Mertie disappeared.

"Nothing. He didn't want to talk to me," I lied, watching as she chewed on her lip and fidgeted.

5

The room was filled with soft snores at one thirty as I climbed down out of my bunk, pausing every time the metal creaked or there was a hitch in someone's breathing. I had a feeling Rabbit would try to keep my secret, despite my lying to her, if she woke, but the other two girls in the room hadn't even introduced themselves. They were part of the clique that sat near the fireplace, and I had no delusions about how loud they'd scream if I got caught.

I tiptoed out into the common room, then made my way to the bathroom. I'd opened the window earlier tonight to see if it would set off any sort of alarm, or if it would open at all. With the lack of security in this place, it was surprising anyone stayed.

As soon as I climbed out of the window, I broke into a jog. Hawk was there already, leaning against the tree, waiting.

He straightened before I finished getting to him and began walking.

"Where are we—"

He spun, putting a finger to my lips, and then took off

walking again at a pace that was brisk enough that I was winded. If I'd met a strange man like this a few days ago in Salem, I would've been afraid of where he was taking me and what he might do to me. I'd had to nearly stalk him to get a meeting, but fear of him trying to abduct me had vanished. Even now, he didn't seem overly concerned about me having second thoughts. What was the worst thing that could happen? Maybe he'd abduct me and dump me somewhere I wanted to be more than here? If he took me somewhere other than Xest, my odds of survival increased. Made me wish for abduction.

Then he took a turn down a dark alley. I paused. Maybe abduction *wasn't* such a good idea. I glanced back down the road, in the direction of the factory and barracks.

He was almost out of sight, absorbed by the dark as I weighed my decision. Abduction. Factory. It wasn't even close. Even with the dark alley thrown in, abduction won all day long.

I ran to catch up, not wanting him to get too far ahead of me. Losing my abductor wasn't in the plans for tonight, and as far as abductors went, he really wasn't on his game.

We continued down a maze of alleys. He didn't stop walking to check on me or even throw a casual glance back to make sure I was there. He ignored me completely until he was swinging open a door and motioning me in.

The room was lit by a few candles and a roaring fire, and I was beginning to realize that there wasn't anywhere in Xest that had electricity. I walked inside, grateful for the warmth as I turned around and took in the room. It wasn't that small, but the shelves of books and knickknacks made it feel cozy. There were a couple sofas and chairs, and it had a strangely warm and homey feeling, considering who it must've belonged to. I'd barely taken a look at the place when there was another knock at the door. Hawk opened it without asking who it was.

Another dark-haired man walked in. He looked at me and paused, taking my measure.

"Did you bring it?" Hawk asked, dragging the man's attention back to him.

He dug into his pocket, producing a box. "Of course."

"Thanks, Oscar."

"This is the girl?" Oscar asked.

The look on the newcomer's face reminded me a bit of the way Hawk had looked at me the first time he'd seen me. Was there something wrong with my hair or face I didn't realize?

"Yes." Hawk took the box and walked the few feet over to me while Oscar took a seat on the couch, watching intently.

He opened the box and held it toward me. "I need you to hold this gem for me."

I stared down at what looked like a pale, cloudy diamond that was the size of a lemon and sat on a bed of velvet.

"What is this going to do?" Just because it looked like a bad-quality diamond didn't mean anything. I was learning fast that nothing in Xest was what it seemed.

"It'll give me your measure. Tell me if you can do what I need. If you can, we'll have a deal."

I'd never heard a sweeter phrase. A deal. I might be able to get out of here.

I reached out but paused. "That's it? Like a scale or something?"

He raised his brows, as if silently mocking my concern. "Yes, like a scale...or something."

Oh yes, he was mocking me. Didn't care. I passed this and I was on my way home.

I rubbed my hands together, afraid the chill in them might throw off his tester, because I needed this thing to measure me as good. Better than good. Awesome. I wanted to register as awesome. So far, this Hawk guy was the only one who might be able to help me, and I wasn't spending the rest of my life in Xest, blowing on dandelions until I died an early death. Having nearly rubbed a layer of skin off, I picked the gem up.

It glimmered for a second before dulling again. I didn't have to ask how it had gone. The guy on the couch made it clear.

"A flicker at best. Can't imagine how she could help." He stood as if preparing to leave. "Well, this was a waste of time."

Hawk was staring at me still, as if he'd had expectations of a different outcome. He held the box out to me to place the gem in, but he still hadn't said a word.

"Does this mean you won't help me?" Clearly things had taken a turn for the worse, but until he said so, I was going to keep hoping.

He grabbed my hand, the sizzle between us flaring in our flesh-to-flesh connection.

His gaze burned into mine as he dropped my hand. "If you're holding back somehow, this isn't the time to do it if you want my help."

"She's not it, Hawk. She's just another Whimsy witch." Oscar, who'd seemed very interested before, was now reclining back against the couch.

Hawk wasn't paying attention to him, though. His stare hadn't left me, as if he were waiting for something.

"I want to try again," I said.

Hawk lifted the box. "Then try."

I lifted my hand and rubbed the back of my neck. "May I use your bathroom first?"

His eyes hardened. "No. You do it now or go. No secrets and no tricks."

It was do or die, and I wasn't sure why I felt so strange about what I was going to do. Maybe it was years of my mother rattling off her absurdities in my ear, building layer upon layer of paranoia. Now that her hysteria seemed to be founded in some truth, all her warnings about never trusting anyone were nearly choking my voice.

"Promise me I can trust you?" That question from me was the epitome of desperation. It was a Hail Mary from a person whose faith had been destroyed years ago.

He stared at me, and it seemed we were the only two in the room. "Promises from people you don't know mean nothing. It comes down to instinct. Are you going to decide to trust me or not?"

True to form, he wasn't an easy sell. I either did this or walked, but he wouldn't be barring the door. It was up to me.

"He might be a bastard sometimes, but you can trust him," Oscar said. "I'll vouch for him if it gets this show rolling."

That didn't help even a little.

"If I can help you, you get me out of here. That's the deal," I said, holding out my hand to shake on it.

"Yes." He shook my hand. "Now, if you don't mind?"

It was time to take off the coal necklace I wore. If everything else my mother had said were true, then why wouldn't that be as well? I had to try. I might not get another opportunity.

It was a stupid rock hanging from my neck, but taking it off now suddenly felt like stripping naked with an audience.

Whatever. This had to happen.

I put my fingers to my striped orange shirt and undid the first button.

Oscar said, "Honey witchy pie, I don't think you know how many pairs he's seen. You're way off the mark. I wouldn't mind seeing a glimpse if you insist, but it's not getting you out of—"

"Oscar," Hawk said, which stopped Oscar's flow of words.

I gave Oscar a glare, which only encouraged laughter. Hawk wasn't laughing. He was watching as I pulled on the thin chain I wore around my neck. It would've been better if he was laughing, because something about this moment felt too personal, like he was seeing into part of my soul as I stripped my final defense away.

The small nugget of coal finally came out of my shirt, and the laughter from Oscar stopped completely.

When my mother had been alive, I wore it because she'd made me. When she was taken away, I hadn't taken it off for some reason or another. When she died, I'd found I didn't have the heart to take it off. Crazy or not, misguided or not, she'd believed that this coal would protect me. And I was beginning to believe it had. I was starting to realize that a lot of the things she'd done had saved me. She'd been given shock treatments and thrown into a loony bin until she'd died in that institution, and she'd been right all along. If I could only have her back for a day, the questions I would ask...

Both men stared at the coal dangling from my fingers like humans would've stared at the Hope Diamond. I fisted it in my hand, and their gaze switched to me.

Forcing my fingers to loosen, I let the necklace slide from my fingers and onto the table beside me. A whiz of energy whooshed toward me, like a vacuum sucking up a glitter bomb.

"Oh shit," Oscar said. He took a deep breath, leaning forward.

Hawk said nothing as he continued to watch.

I lifted the gem from the box. This time it flared to life, a rainbow of light exploded into the room, the gem almost sun-bright and hard to look at.

"Holy shit! Look at that color! No way she's a Whimsy witch."

"Put it down," Hawk said.

I dropped the gem back onto the box. "Did I do something wrong?"

"Oh, you did something, all right," Oscar said. "Maybe too right. I've never…"

I looked up to see Hawk staring in his direction.

"How did you manage to keep all that magic hidden for so long?" Oscar asked. "Even coal isn't foolproof at blocking it."

"I don't know. I guess I lucked out." I'd revealed enough tonight. I wasn't getting into the tattoo or any of the other rituals my mother had made me do.

"That was a whopper if I ever heard one," Oscar said.

Hawk reached down and picked up my necklace. "The only thing that matters at the moment is that you keep this necklace on at all times. You don't take it off, not even to sleep, and you don't let anyone see it. If they find out how strong you are, they'll make getting you out a lot more difficult." He placed it in my hand, then watched as I put it over my head.

"So you'll get me out?" I asked, again, fearing that at any moment he'd go back on the deal.

"Yes. I'll be getting you out. For now, go back to the barracks."

"Don't worry. He's getting you out," Oscar said with enough attitude that I believed it.

"Why can't I just stay here now? Why bother going back?" Was this a setup? Maybe my gut, which told me to believe him, was wrong. People had bad guts all the time. Loris had a gut so bad that I'd often told her to do the opposite of whatever she thought it was saying.

"You can't until I negotiate your contract. If you disappear, they'll be able to track you down and take you back."

"What contract? I didn't sign anything." I was beginning to hate learning anything new in this place, because it was almost always bad news.

"You incurred a debt. You didn't have to sign."

I should've known it wasn't going to be easy getting out of here. No wonder there weren't any guards. I could've strolled right out the door and still been screwed. They had me on some invisible house-arrest magical crap.

"When you see me next time, you act as if you only spoke to me that first time outside the factory, and only if it comes up. You tell no one until I come for you. Now go," Hawk said, grabbing my shoulders and setting off that little magical tingle as he steered me out the door, gave me vague directions, and then shut it, as I was still standing there hoping I didn't have to go back.

6

I blew on a dandelion, watched it glisten with a dollop of magic, and then disappear in front of me. It was my third or fourth hundredth, if I had to guess. I'd stopped counting after the first fifty, when I'd switched my preoccupation to the clock. Would Hawk come today? Would he come at all? Was I stuck blowing on dandelions for the rest of my life? Or wait, maybe clover? Or eyelashes? Turned out there was a floor for just about all of them.

Rabbit was sitting next to me. The way she kept glancing over told me she knew something was up. Hawk had said not to tell a soul, and I was going to stick to that, as long as he showed up in the next few days. Or a week. I'd give him a week. I could give him two weeks. Point was, I wasn't breaking my end of the deal, not when it was the only way I might get out of here.

"Did you slip out last night?" Rabbit whispered, finally caving to the curiosity that had been driving her attention my way all day.

I didn't like to lie to anyone, especially not Rabbit, the only person who'd been kind to me since I got here. That was what living a childhood built on lies did to you. You either became fluent in bullshit or you gagged at even a whiff of it. I had a fast gag reflex, myself.

"Why do you ask?" That was another thing I'd learned since my aversion to lying grew. If you can't answer, don't, in the nicest way possible. Sometimes that did the job for you. She'd assume my answer was whatever she wanted it to be, hopefully.

"Tippi, I know we've just met and all, but I hope you'll trust me when I tell you that there are places in Xest that you don't go. People that you don't want to be around that might live too close to the edge. You have to be careful. There's a darkness here. No one talks about it, but everyone can feel it. You need to be careful who or what you associate with. There's much worse things than the factory —" She might've kept going, but she launched into a coughing fit.

She might think there were worse things than the factory, but she didn't see what it was doing to her. It wasn't only her, either. I'd paid closer attention today, and there was a reason that the laughs dwindled by the afternoon. This place was taking something out of every person in here, slowly leeching their life away. She could say whatever she wanted about what was out there. At least it was an unknown, as opposed to what I saw happening here. Whatever might come of it, I'd take my chances, because this place was death.

"I'll be careful. I promise."

She nodded, but she was chewing on her lip, as if she thought her words meant nothing to me.

"Rabbit, I mean it. I'll be careful."

"It's just..." She blew on another dandelion, looking away as she chose her words. "Look, it's hard to make friends here, and I think we could be good friends. I don't want you to disappear or get hurt."

I looked around the rest of the room and could see the cliques, the different groups sitting closer and chatting. She wasn't only dying. She was dying alone.

"I won't do either of those things. If I disappear, you'll disappear with me."

She hummed but didn't say anything else. It was clear what she was thinking: we'd both probably die here. That was not going to be my end. And if I had any strength in my body after I crawled out of this hell, it wouldn't be hers either.

I went back to blowing on dandelions, hoping this would be my last time.

Rabbit kept watching. "You know, for someone who doesn't have a lot of magic, you've got especially good endurance. By midday, I put out more duds than wishes. Not you, though."

"Seriously, she's right," someone said from behind me. "You might have low magic, but you've sure got endurance."

I turned to see one of the girls from the barracks who hadn't spoken to me yet, which included pretty much everyone but Rabbit.

"Thanks," I said, before turning and going back to work.

"Hey, do you want to come sit at the other table with us? It's warmer there," she said directly to me, as if Rabbit weren't sitting beside me.

"No, thanks. I like it over here," I said. I'd rather freeze from the window than get frostbite from the company.

She shrugged and walked away, as if no skin off her nose.

"Thanks," Rabbit said.

"You don't need to thank me. I *do* like it better over here. The company is much nicer."

She was still smiling at me when "Tippi, to the main office" filled the air around us. Every set of eyes in the room swung to me. It was obvious from the expressions of angst and curiosity that this didn't happen often. What if they knew I'd snuck out last night? What if Hawk was full of shit and had sold me out?

"Is this bad?" I whispered.

Everyone in the room was talking and looking at me. When I finally looked at Rabbit, she looked worse than she had when I'd "escaped" to the bathroom.

She shrugged. "I don't know. No one gets called. Mertie usually handles things."

"What do I do?"

She stopped chewing on her lip so her jaw could drop open. "You go. You don't have any choice. But you're new. Whatever you did wrong, you'll probably just get a warning. Tell them you didn't know any better. That you're really stupid."

I nodded as I got up, knowing the only plan I had was Rabbit's "I'm stupid" option. At least she had something, which was more than me.

Everyone followed my path out the door with their eyes, as they whispered behind their hands.

Marvin must've known I'd snuck out. I would say I was feeling sick and needed air or something. I'd come back, though, and they probably didn't know where I went. And like Rabbit suggested, I was too stupid to know better.

What if they tortured me? What if they had some witchy way of knowing lies? What did I do then? Panicking was no good. If I walked in the office with sweat pouring off me, it would be akin to an admission of guilt.

I made it to the hall, and a few people that I'd seen working on clovers earlier in the day walked past me. They all had curious expressions and were looking at me as they talked. The entire factory must've heard me getting called in.

By the time I got close to the office, my palms were soaked but my forehead was hanging in there.

Mertie was sitting at the desk outside the door, her hooves crossed on top of the desk as she puffed on a cigar that she lit with her finger. "They're waiting for you."

They're? There was more than one?

I didn't bother asking her who was with Marvin. I swallowed the boulder lodged in my throat and opened the door.

Einstein was sitting behind his desk and Hawk was leaning on the windowsill with his arms crossed and a harsh look on his face.

"She's the new pop-up. She's only a Whimsy but she should suit your purposes, and she's fresh, as you requested." Marvin flipped through a folder that I presumed was about me. "You can buy out her contract for fifty coins."

Fifty? He was worse than the dealers Loris dealt with.

"Fifty is a little steep, don't you think?" Hawk asked.

Damn straight it was. He'd only paid Spike and Braid ten. Yes, they might've been arguing over my monetary worth, but years of haggling to get Loris a better price was scarred into my brain. I'd take affront to being sold later.

"I thought my contract was ten coins? Isn't that what you paid?" I asked as if I were clueless to what I was doing.

"Ten, huh?" Hawk gave Marvin a stare that said fifty was a joke.

Marvin sneered at me and then looked at Hawk. "I've also had transport and training costs."

Training? What training? What a load of bull.

Hawk looked me up and down as if he'd never seen me before. "Can you light a fire?" With a flick of his wrist, the fireplace went out.

"I'm not sure," I said. Hawk hadn't said anything about auditions. What was this crap? This better be part of the negotiations. If he left me here because I couldn't light a fire, I'd... Well, I'd probably do nothing.

"Can you do it or not?" Hawk asked.

I walked to the fireplace and blew at the logs, the way I did with the dandelions. The only thing that burst into anything was Hawk into laughter.

"We've only just begun her training," Marvin said.

"Training? A toddler knows how to light a fire. What kind of sham are you trying to foist on me?"

Einstein dropped the folder on his desk. "Okay, look, I'll cut the price to help you out. You can have her for twenty coins."

The three no-evil monkeys decided to chime in and giggle.

"Twelve, and only because I need a maid. I'd take it if I were you. I could walk out of here with her and give you nothing, and there wouldn't be a damned thing you could do about it."

The no-evils' heads swung to Marvin, nodding in unison. "He's right," Speak No Evil said.

"Fifteen," Marvin countered.

"Deal," Hawk said.

The monkeys turned and shook each other's hands.

"But don't come looking for a refund if she's dried up in a month. Not my problem." Marvin turned to me. "Go. You're his now."

7

Hawk walked down the hall. I was right behind, not letting light in between where he ended and I started.

"That's it? I'm out of—"

"Not here."

Okay. I could wait. Not a problem. There was only one issue with leaving, and it was approaching fast on the door on the left. There was no way I'd disappear on Rabbit. Not only was I saying goodbye, I wouldn't be saying it for long. I'd figure out what Hawk needed from me and then I'd leverage it to get her out of here, too.

"I need to make a quick stop."

He paused, glancing over his shoulder. "Fine. You've got five minutes to meet me in front." Hawk left, without even a glance over his shoulder.

I dipped into the dandelion room. Rabbit's face lit up like it was Christmas and I was Santa. She waited until I got close, past all the listening ears who were watching me as if surprised I was in one piece. The bounce in my step flattened out before I took the seat next to her again. This was going to suck on an epic scale.

"What happened?" she asked.

I'd known Rabbit for barely a day and part of me already wanted to stay so she wouldn't be alone. That wouldn't do either of us any good, though. If I didn't get out, I'd never get her out either. Now to deliver the news.

The longer I remained silent, the more the lines around her eyes crinkled up with worry. I had to get it out, no matter how hard.

"Something very good happened. That guy Hawk, the broker? He bought out my contract. I'm leaving."

"You're leaving. That's good." She forced a smile, even as her skin looked pale with a greyish hue.

I leaned closer, knowing the room was trying to listen to every word I said. "I'll come back for you. I'll figure out a way, okay? I'll make him buy out your contract too, so you need to hang in there."

"It's all right if you can't." She nodded, but her eyes kept dropping to the floor and the smile trembled. I was one of many pop-ups that had passed through here. How many people had she lost?

"I will. Just give me a little time. I'll figure something out." I took her in a hug, wishing I could drag her out of there with me right now.

"You better get going. I don't want you to lose this chance."

She didn't believe me. There was absolutely no reason for her to think I'd be able to help her. I didn't know how I was going to pull this off either. I did know I would, though.

"I'm coming back for you. I'm making you that promise." I put as much force as possible behind my words, without raising my voice, in an effort to convince her.

"I know."

She kept nodding but clearly didn't believe me. With a

last smile, she turned back to her dandelions. It wasn't to be hurtful. She was trying to keep it together. I'd been there.

I left, wishing I could've brought her with me right then and there. And why couldn't I? How hard would it be to buy her contract as well?

Hawk was standing in front of the factory, his back to me as I walked over and stopped beside him.

"I need you to get someone else out before—"

"Not here." He began walking.

"But—"

"Not. Here."

Okay, fine. *Not. Here,* I repeated in a mocking voice as we walked away from the factory. Of course, he couldn't hear it because I said it in my head. I couldn't afford to piss him off too much, not yet. I needed him to get me back to Salem and Rabbit out of that factory.

Once we were a good block or so away, Hawk said, "Now you can talk."

"There's another person I was working with who I need to get out." I'd planned on working up to this slowly, after I had more details of what he needed. That plan had crashed and burned with Rabbit's expression when I said goodbye. She didn't have time. She needed out, and the sooner the better. That place was killing her on every level.

"I suggest you worry about fulfilling your obligations to me before you ask for anything else." He didn't slow his step.

It was a fair request, and if it was for anything else, I'd hold my tongue. I'd wait until I got some leverage. But I couldn't.

"We have to work out something in the meantime. That's a bad place, and I need to—"

He stopped walking. "It's not possible. Not right now. It would draw too much suspicion. After you're done, I can try to do something about this friend, but there are too many obstacles right now." Without waiting for a reply, he started walking again.

I knew a hard no when I heard one. This was going to take a little work, but I'd never shied away from digging in. I'd figure it out. In the meantime, I needed to get my bearings. If I was going to help her, I had to help myself first.

As we made our way to his place, I took Xest in for the first time in the daylight, up close. We walked past lines of shops and stores, and nothing looked how I'd imagine. Even the butcher, or what I guessed was the butcher, had strange purple meats hanging from hooks in silhouettes I'd never seen before. It could've been a carved-up dragon for all I knew.

There were shops with nothing but bottles lining the walls. Other shops had nothing but plants, the likes of which I'd never seen. And the people—what I could see of them, as they tended to cross the way when we approached —were even stranger. The hair colors ranged from natural to rainbow. The colors they wore were either brighter than bright or all black.

We didn't stop walking until we got to a building with a shingle over the door with "Broker of All" carved into the wood. There were large picture windows comprised of many tiny, wavy glass panes on either side.

The place was packed with people who appeared to be waiting to speak to one of three workers who sat behind desks.

The wall above them was at least two stories high and was covered with strange levers and wheels that seemed to rotate and grind to no rhythm I'd ever heard. The gears would begin and then stop, only to start up two seconds later, pause for a split second, and then grind faster. At the far-right corner, slips of paper shot out of a slot to pile up into a woven basket that was nearly five feet tall and spilling over.

The entire place, other than the machine wall, ground to a halt as all eyes turned to Hawk and me as we entered. Even here, the crowds seemed to part for him. Everyone continued to stare until he opened a door on the other side of the room. He had me precede him into the next hallway, the buzz on the other side of the closed door kicking up even louder.

Beyond the door, there was a landing and two sets of stairs—one to the left, the other to the right.

"Don't use those unless you want to die," he said while pointing to the stairs on the left, as if that were normal conversation.

He climbed the stairs to the right. They led to a platform and a door that he opened.

"This will be your room while you're here."

It wasn't Shangri-La, but it was better than the barracks by far, even better than my apartment bedroom, with a cozy charm, a comfy-looking bed, and white bead-board walls. He flicked a wrist, and a flame ignited in the wood-burning stove. That would take the chill out of this room quickly and keep the place comfy on the coldest nights. I had a feeling they might have some doozies in Xest that would put a Salem winter to shame. I still wasn't sure how long I'd be staying, but I hoped I'd be gone before January, when things would get even colder, if their seasons worked the same.

"Belinda will get you some clothes. If you need anything else, ask one of them below. We'll work in the evenings, starting tomorrow. I'll need you to keep up the pretense of being help around the place during the day. Zab, Musso, and Belinda will know, but I don't want to draw any outside attention."

Since I didn't know exactly what business I'd be helping with, that was going to be exceedingly easy to accommodate.

"What do you need me to do, exactly? And can it be done fast? I'm fairly certain that this isn't somewhere I should linger too long. Plus, I'll be missing work while I'm here, not to mention my boss is going to be a wreck, since we're more like family at this point. If I get back to Salem in the next few days, I won't be late with my rent, either. Of course, I have to get Rabbit out first."

The less he talked, the more I continued. I'd never been a nervous rambler before I'd met him, but something about this man put me on edge.

"But back to my landlord. I've never been late before, so he'll probably be okay even if I am. Point is, if I can get back home in the next few days, it would limit the damage to my life. I could figure out some excuse for Loris. It'll be manageable." I nodded as I added up the tally of damage. I'd be out of here soon and mitigate most of it. It would be okay.

I'd stopped watching him watch me as I'd run on. But now, as my brain was finally quieting, silence was becoming suspicious. The dead, heart-wrenching silence. Something wasn't right.

I pulled my gaze up from the floor, where it had gotten stuck, and turned all of my attention back on him. He was relaxed enough in form, but his steely eyes were a whole other matter. They didn't look like they ever relaxed.

"This is going to take more than a couple of days, isn't it?"

He nodded, his expression flat. No clue as to how long I'd be here.

"A couple weeks?" I asked. Weeks would still be okay.

More damage to go back to, though. Loris would be sick, thinking I was dead. She'd probably be robbed blind, but not too badly. My apartment might still be there. Not optimal but still doable.

"Considering you couldn't light the fire?" Hawk asked. "I'd say closer to three, but maybe more. You've got the magical ability, but you're raw. You don't know how to use it. Magic is like a muscle, and yours is atrophied. It's as if you have two working legs but never learned to stand. Getting you out of the factory was easy. Getting what I need out of you isn't going to be as simple."

He watched me in a way that made it obvious he fully intended to get what he wanted. He looked the type that always did. I'd always had the reverse experience in life, so I could spot my opposite easily. I'd studied them for years, trying to figure out where I'd gone wrong. I was still studying.

"What exactly am I going to be doing for you?"

"A spell. I'll tell you more as I can."

"What's the spell for?" I asked.

"I'll let you know when it's time to do it."

Really? That was all I was going to get? There was nothing to be done about it now. I wasn't going back to the factory, and I couldn't go home. There should've been more negotiating on my part before I'd come here, except it was hard to bargain when you were climbing out of a ditch of nothing, nothing, and more nothing.

If I could convince him to get me back home, though...

"Couldn't I commute while I learn this spell? Why can't I do whatever this is back in Salem? Why do I need to be here? You can get me back. I won't go anywhere. You'll know where I am."

"Because we can't do what needs to be done there, and jumps can be tracked in the ether. They leave a trace."

How many times had I jumped in puddles when I was kid and had no idea of what might actually lay beyond? If I did ever get out of this place, I'd never step in a puddle again. Dry land only.

I dropped onto the bed, sitting down before I did something crazy, like try to jump out the window or yell like a maniac.

"I'll have your rent taken care of," he said, with no discussion of how much or where to send it.

"It's not just the rent. It's my life." Having a place to go back to was on my mind, but not the beginning and end of my issues.

"Then you're going to have to make this work, because it's the only way back. You made a deal. I got you out. You could be looking at a lifetime in the factory. I'd say a month is a fair trade-off."

He walked out of the room as I watched his back. It was becoming a trend, and not one I liked.

8

Hunger and darkness drove me out of my room. I walked downstairs slowly, hesitating by the door, listening for sounds and trying not to look at the other set of stairs. I wished Hawk had never mentioned the other stairs at all. Then I would've assumed they led to some storage area or something equally mundane. Might never have looked twice at them. Now all I was going to do was stare and wonder if something was eventually going to climb down from them and try to eat me, and it was his fault.

I pushed the stairs from my mind and planted an ear to the door, making sure I was facing my stairs as I did. Someone was definitely moving around in there, but the hordes were gone. Hawk had told me to come down if I needed something. Well, I did. I needed to get out of that room for a minute.

I cracked the door open slowly, listening to the gears on the wall moving around.

"Hey! I'm Zab."

I spun around and saw the guy who'd been behind one of the desks earlier. He had spiky hair that was black at the roots with lavender blue tips that fit his youthful face. He couldn't have been more than a few years older than me. But unlike me, he seemed very happy.

He waved a little too vigorously, as if an abundance of friendliness could overcome any uncertainty on my part.

"Hi. I'm Tippi," I said a little less enthusiastically, but not for trying. It'd been a long day and his energy was hard to match. I held out my hand to shake, trying to make up for my lack of zest.

He stared down at it, confused.

I dropped it, wondering where I'd misinterpreted something. He'd seemed friendly.

He motioned to my hand. "That's a Rest thing, right? We don't do that here."

"I'm sorry. I didn't know."

"No need to apologize. It's a magic thing. Sort of personal."

Like the way Hawk's flesh had tingled on mine. That was what he meant. Once he'd said it, it made sense. No one really touched around this place, now that I thought about it.

"Things are a lot different here." I crossed my arms so I wouldn't accidentally make another gesture.

"There's going to be a learning curve, I'm sure. Are you hungry?" He moved over to the back shelves, where he pulled a cover off a dish. "I was going to bring this up if you didn't come down soon." He put the dish and a fork on the other side of his desk, where I'd seen clientele sitting earlier in the day.

"Actually, I'm starving. Thanks."

I took the offered food and seat as he continued to watch me, as if I were some freak of nature.

Pretending not to notice, I dug into the shredded meat of

unknown origin. It was heaped over something that might've been rice, if it wasn't red and twice the size. Whatever it was, it was tasty.

He sat on the other side of the desk, staring as I ate, waiting.

"It's good. Thanks," I said, smiling as he watched me.

"I wasn't sure what to order you, coming from Rest. I've never even talked to someone from Rest before." He planted his chin in his hand, watching me like he'd never seen anyone eat before. "So what's it like over there?"

"The factory?" I asked between bites.

"No, in Rest. Do you like it there? I've never been. Heard it's crazy, though. Lots of weird people and almost no one can do anything magical." His lips parted as he shook his head.

"It would probably be as weird to you as this place is to me."

The wall took that moment to grind into overtime, the candles glittering off its golden metal parts. Shelves lined the rest of the room, filled with bottles and books that looked old enough to belong in a museum. There were all sorts of other knickknacks as well, from lamps that looked like they'd spew smoke and strange dice carved of stone. It was an odd blend of what appeared to be antiques, toys, and machinery.

He looked around. "Yeah, I guess I can see that."

"So what do you guys do here, exactly?" I spooned another couple of bites in while I waited.

He shrugged. "Broker magic. You know, the usual stuff."

There was nothing usual about any of this. "How does this stuff happen?"

"It's pretty simple, actually." He pointed to the large wall of gears and machinery. "See this thing? It's called the

Helexorgomay. It runs on the energy created by the hopes, dreams, wants, and fears of the people in Rest. If they give them enough juice, so to speak, that request shoots out there."

He walked over to the basket I'd seen earlier that was overflowing with slips of paper. He grabbed the first one off the stack and read, "'Please let me pass my science quiz.'" He held up the paper. "This goes right in the shredder because there's no payment offered." He tossed it in another basket. "Lots of requests don't offer payment that's worth anything. If they don't, there's nothing we can do. Everything costs something."

"What kind of payments are offered?"

He riffled through the basket. "Here's a good one. This person is asking for their daughter to get better, and they're tattooing something on their arm. That's basically offering a pound of flesh. This we can do something with."

He moved the slip to a basket beside his desk.

"So you take the flesh as payment?" I suddenly wondered what exactly I was eating as my fork hovered over my strange meat.

He let out a deep laugh. "We don't take the actual flesh. That sacrifice is converted. The list of commodities we deal in is very long. Some pay in time, some in energy, happiness, you name it. See that board?" He pointed to the wall behind me on the other side of the room.

I'd been so busy taking in the things at eye level and the machine that I hadn't looked behind me. There were all sorts of emotions, dates, lengths of time, and numbers jotted down on a huge gridded chalkboard.

"What does that all mean?"

"It's exchange rates. If the request isn't paying in a form the supplier is accepting, we can convert it for them for an additional three percent rate, unless it's loneliness. No one wants to touch that, so it's a twenty percent surcharge.

"We make the deal. I'll call in a witch or wizard who can handle it. Once the order is filled, it'll be fed back into the Helexorgomay machine—or Helen, as we call her." He pointed to a slot that looked more like a mouth with grinding teeth above and below the opening.

"So people wish, pray, ask whatever god they believe in for something, and you guys connect the dots, getting them what they want?"

"Pretty much. Like I said, business as usual." He sat back down, rocking in his chair as if this were just another day at the shop, and for him, it was.

I looked at that basket, wondering how many times my deepest wishes had ended up as a slip in the basket. However many had made it to the basket, they'd ended up shredded every time.

"Can they wish for anything? Or are there certain parameters to what ends up here?" Maybe I hadn't ended up in that basket, another scrap among the desperate.

"Yes and no. There's limitations, mostly in what can be paid for. Like, say you have some whack job wanting the end of the world?" He waved his hand as if that were the only thing crazy about this situation. "They'd never be able to fund that kind of request. It won't even make it to Helen. It'll go right to the spam box."

"Was that what I was doing in the factory with the dandelion wishes?" I asked.

"Nah. Marvin is a hack. The factory you came from has a wholesale deal that they've had the contracts on forever. Lots of cheap magic that's been spread pretty thin at this point. Mass-produced garbage that doesn't usually produce."

"Wholesale deal?"

"You know, like wishing on an eyelash? Some of the stuff Marvin is supplying was negotiated a long time ago. He gets a steady trickle of income, but not the big orders like we do. And now that we're nearing the holidays, it'll really be booming. Lots of transactions to be made."

"Do you live here too?" I wondered if there was a barracks for the workers here, similar to where I'd left.

"Nah, I got a place down on the other side of town. I like to have company over, and Hawk's real funny about who he'll let overnight here. Too much sensitive information."

"I'll be alone here at night?"

"Hawk's in and out of here sometimes."

"Does he live here?"

"Sort of." He hummed and shrugged, just enough to tell me to stop with that line of questioning. "If you're worried about being bored, there are a ton of books if you want to read. No one ever touches them. Not sure where half of them even came from." He motioned to the half wall that lined the other part of the office. "Plus, there are more in the back room, and a tea and coffee station if you like that. There's cocoa, too. Nothing like they serve over at the Sweet Shop, but good enough in a pinch. Oh, before I forget, there's a bag of clothes Belinda left for you." He pointed to a sack in the corner.

"Thanks!" I couldn't wait to lose the orange stripes that made me feel like I'd broken out of a magical jail.

I ate a couple more bites as he kept glancing at the clock on his desk.

"If you have to go, it's okay. I'll be fine." More than fine. Somewhere in those books, somewhere in this office, I might find an explanation of how to jump puddles.

He got to his feet. "You sure? If I'd known you were

coming today, I would've canceled, but I've got this date, and..." He was grimacing and shrugging.

"Go. I'll be fine. You've helped me immensely." He was already grabbing his jacket as I said, "And thanks for the food!"

"I'll see you tomorrow, right?"

"Yep." I tried to keep the smile strong.

He walked about, snuffing out all the candles one by one. He took the final one and handed it to me. "Here, take this with you. Can't read in the dark."

As soon as he was gone, I was off to scanning titles, half of which seemed like gibberish. I grabbed anything that was readable and contained the word *magic* in the title, flipping through them.

After skimming the first ten books, I decided I'd just try it out. If they could get me here with a puddle, I'd get myself out with one. If I could make that gem glow, I had to be at least as strong as those losers who'd brought me here.

I made my way to the back room, where there was a little area set up in the corner with a teapot and some other odds and ends, as Zab had said there'd be.

There was a shaker of salt and water in the teapot. The mess on the floor would be unfortunate, but it would have to be done. It wasn't like this could happen outside, with an audience.

I poured a puddle in front of me and then scattered the salt over it, the way Braid had done. With a deep breath, a thought of my little apartment in Salem, I did a quick click of my heels just for good measure. Had to give it all I had. I stepped into the puddle.

And there I was. In the back room, except now I was standing in a puddle. Maybe I hadn't jumped firmly enough.

I took a step out of the puddle, and then jumped with

purpose, leaving out all *The Wizard of Oz* stuff, since clearly it wasn't working in my situation, and closing my eyes as I did.

I opened them again.

Yeah, still in the back room. I looked around, wondering where they kept the towels.

9

I made my way downstairs in the least hideous outfit I'd found in the bag, red polka dot pants and a white sweater, with only a few moth holes. Either Belinda had really bad taste or she hated anyone from Rest. Either way, it was all I had, so I tried to wear it proudly, bringing along the candle that wouldn't go out no matter what I did. Even the wax seemed to keep regenerating. Not that it made much of a difference. There had been little to no sleep going on last night anyway. I skimmed half of the books on magic, but none of them talked about jumping puddles.

I was still looking at only one way out of this place, and I had to deliver in order to get that ticket back to Salem. If I couldn't do what Hawk needed from me, couldn't hold up my end of the bargain, forget getting Rabbit out of the factory. I might be back there with her. When Marvin had told Hawk he didn't take refunds, I'd been insulted. Now it was the only thing offering me any peace. Hawk was stuck with me. Or at least it wouldn't be that easy to unload me, I hoped.

I walked into the main room of the shop that hadn't opened its doors for business yet. There were two other people with Zab, an older man with a gruff look and a scraggly beard, and a woman who was maybe late twenties, with the most glorious head of red hair I'd ever seen, and a body that rivaled it.

Zab nodded to the man. "Tippi, this is Musso."

Musso nodded in my direction. Not quite as enthusiastic as Zab, but he didn't seem the type to waste emotion for no good reason.

"And that's Belinda," Zab said, waving toward the redhead.

"Thanks for the clothes," I said, smiling, but also taking in the nice jeans she was wearing with the pretty, fuzzy sweater. So taste wasn't the problem. It was me for some reason.

"Of course." She smiled back, but hers dropped the temperature in the office a few degrees.

Zab was looking at my outfit when I turned back to him. I pretended there was nothing amiss as I held the candle out to him.

"I can't seem to blow this thing out," I said softly, hoping not to draw Belinda's attention. She already didn't like me. She didn't need to know I was an idiot to boot. I had to survive with these people for a while.

"It's all right to reabsorb small amounts of other people's magic. It won't hurt you. Just don't do large amounts. That's when it's a problem," Zab explained, obviously not realizing quite how clueless I was.

I hadn't known any of it was a problem to begin with, but decided that didn't need to be shared either. How the hell did I reabsorb magic?

Musso walked over. "Zab, she's not afraid to suck in the magic. She doesn't know how."

Well, there you go. At least one of them realized the extent of my ignorance.

Zab gaped but shut his mouth quick enough.

Belinda was watching. She didn't have to say anything. Her expression called me a thousand kinds of idiot, and her soft giggle rubbed salt into the wound.

"Don't feel bad. I don't know lots of things." Zab hooked his thumb at Musso. "He, on the other hand, never has the problem of not knowing something."

Musso raised a hand toward Zab, like he'd like to smack him, but neither of them seemed to be serious.

Musso pointed to the candle. "Touch it and imagine your finger is a straw, sucking up a warm drink on a cold day."

I placed my finger on it and imagined the straw. Nothing happened. I moved my finger closer to the flame and tried again.

All three of us stared at the candle, Zab and Musso seeming as stumped as I was.

"How old are you?" Musso asked.

"Nineteen."

"And you've never done magic before?" Musso asked.

"Just at the factory."

"She's probably just too full. She's got to unload some magic. It's like eating too much. A few days with Hawk should fix that." Musso waved his hand in the air, seeming to call the matter solved, and went back to his desk.

"Or not," Belinda said, as she raised her eyebrows and flipped through a magazine on her desk. "Maybe you won't be the savant Hawk thinks, but I'm sure he'll let you stay on as a maid or something. Always garbage to be emptied and floors to be mopped, after all."

Zab leaned closer. "Don't mind her. She thinks she owns the place because she sleeps with Hawk."

She looked like the type of girl a man like Hawk would date. Perfect hair, perfect clothes, perfect nails. The works. While I stood here with hair that wouldn't lie flat no matter how many irons I took to it. My wardrobe, which had never been good, had taken a nosedive, not that she'd had to pick out such horrendous clothes. No one would ever notice me standing beside Belinda. The only person who seemed to think there was a reason to feel threatened was her. Maybe she'd had to grow into her looks? Ugly-duckling syndrome or something? Didn't matter. She'd soon realize we weren't in competition and things would be fine.

I looked about the place, eager to move on from the candle issue.

"Is there anything for me to do? I'm supposed to help out."

"Yes," Belinda said. "There's a broom closet over there. After you're done with that, the shelves need dusting."

I kept on smiling as I made my way to the closet and took out the broom. This was going to be a long few weeks.

I was drinking tea in the back room, blissfully alone. It was the same place Hawk had brought me to test my magic with the gem. Now it would act as my sitting room while I was here. Zab had lit the fireplace for me before he left, and the place was quite cozy. Musso and, more importantly, Belinda had left shortly after him.

I'd been alone here just long enough that I was beginning to think Hawk wouldn't show up at all. I wasn't certain if that was good or bad. If I didn't get this thing that he needed done, I'd never be free of this place, and Rabbit's fate was tied to mine. But boy was it nice to get a second alone where I could pretend things were still normal.

Plus, I had some interesting reading: *Advanced Spells Made Simple Enough for Even a Whimsy*. Besides the title being insulting, it might be useful. If Hawk wasn't going to show up and train me, there was some training I needed to do on my own.

I scrolled through the list of spells: warts, bad luck, good luck, love, hate, greed, happiness. Still no puddle jumping. What was the problem with these books? I needed to puddle-jump. I continued to scroll and paused on "eaves-dropping." Now *that* might come in handy, considering my current predicament.

I flipped to the page and read the spell. That was it? I could remember this. Maybe the title was fitting. This was pretty simple.

The back door opened, and I slammed the book shut as Hawk stepped inside.

The moment he walked in, he brought that energy with him. The kind that filled the room. It made sense why people avoided him. There was something altogether unsettling about it, almost as if it put you on the edge of your seat. For some reason I couldn't begin to fathom, I sort of liked being there, hanging on to the edge, not knowing what would happen next but always feeling like something would. Maybe it was growing up with chaos? I'd thought I longed for peace. I'd made my life as calm as possible. But being near him, it was like taking a shot of adrenaline. Hawk called to something fundamental in me that needed to die for good.

"You're not going to find it in those books," he said.

"Find what?" I watched as he walked to the side of the room where the tea and coffee were, and I might have taken in the line of his back. Where was his coat? Had he taken it off before he came in? Had he not worn one? Maybe he'd been close by and forgotten it? It was frigid out there, but you'd never know from him. It was probably like living in Antarctica. Your blood got thick like molasses.

He poured himself something from one of the pots. Something that steamed. See? He was normal. He'd just forgotten his jacket and now wanted something warm, like normal people did. Nothing odd about it.

"Puddle jumping." He walked over, sipping a tea or coffee. "It's not a spell. It's innate. If it didn't work the first time you tried, it's not going to."

Shit. He was truly the only option to get out of here. I wanted to stomp up and down, cursing, instead of sitting there calmly.

"I didn't try," I said, looking back down at the book because I could never keep the lie from my expression.

"I guess the saltwater splatter on the rug must've been from Musso," he said, and sipped his drink. The smell of coffee wafted over, along with a woody scent of his own.

I dropped the book to the side. "So, what are we doing tonight?"

"Learning how to control your magic. You're no good to me otherwise. A witch who has no control is a danger to everyone around them."

If I'd been asked what magic lessons would be like a year ago, I would've envisioned something with more of a Loris flair—not a lecture.

"You know, if you're really concerned, you can always send me home now."

"Not likely." He smiled, but without teeth or happiness included.

"Yeah, I guess you want to make sure you get those fifteen coins' worth out of me. Well, lay it on me. I'm a quick learner. I did the dandelions with no issue." If I was doing this, I was doing it fast and efficiently. This was not getting dragged out for weeks or months.

"We'll see about that. I need a sprinter. Lighting up dandelions and clovers is the equivalent to magical crawling." He grabbed the book that I'd placed on the table and pushed it even closer to me. "Let's start simple. Push that off the table. Flick your wrist, like it's in your hand and you're tossing it."

That was it? I could do that. I imagined the book in my hand, down to the feel of the leather on my fingertips. I threw it. Nothing happened.

He walked over to me, but instead of instructions, he grazed my neck with his fingers. I shivered slightly as he lifted the chain.

"Your hands are cold." I wasn't usually a liar but couldn't have him getting any weird ideas. This was a business relationship. Plus he had a girlfriend who already wanted to stab me with no provocation. If she caught a sniff of something, *anything*, she'd surely break out the meat cleaver.

He took my chain and put it on the side table, by the tea and coffee pots.

"Try it again."

I imagined the book in my hand again and then throwing it. Instead of the book flying, the couch I sat on bounced up, dumping me on my ass in front of it.

Hawk walked over and looked down, not bothering to offer me a hand up. "I thought you were a quick learner?"

I got off the floor, with no help from him, and brushed

off my pants. "I was infusing dandelions with wishes and magic like I'd been doing it my entire life."

"Glad you know how to crawl well." He walked back to the other side of the room, shaking his head, the vein in his neck twitching.

"I will learn fast. You'll see."

"You'd better, because I can't afford to waste time."

"Why? What do you need, anyway? What kind of spell?" I asked, annoyed that I was working toward something he hadn't bothered to disclose yet.

"Nothing you're capable of giving me at the moment."

Talking was getting me nothing but high blood pressure. I ignored him and his scowl and focused on the book again. I flicked my wrist, concentrating on knocking the book from the table. The book fell off the table. *Everything* fell off the table, because it flew across the room and landed a few feet short of where Hawk stood.

We both stared at the table for a minute.

"Maybe we should try something simpler. Come over here." He put a hand close to the fire and the flames disappeared, and then even the burning embers went out.

I got as close to the fireplace as I could. If things went wrong, I wanted to limit what I might burn, since this was currently my home.

"Imagine heat building in your hand, your fingertips, as if your hand was on fire. Then fling it toward the logs."

Hand on fire. Boiling heat. Sweltering heat. I could feel it. I threw all that energy toward the logs. Ashes and dust flew up, blowing out and filling the room. My eyes burned and I coughed on ash. The only thing that happened to the logs was that they now sat in a clean fireplace.

I looked at Hawk. He had ash all over his shirt and pants, but not quite as bad as I did.

He shook his head. "I'm not sure how you can have this much magic and also be *this* bad. This is going to take longer than I imagined."

He walked out of the room. I knew practice was over when he didn't come back. This night had gone to shit, and now worse—was I supposed to clean this all up on my own?

10

I'd swept, dusted, dusted again. Then swept again. Belinda was making the factory look good. Luckily, Zab kept taking pity on me and needed me for things, which were often tea breaks in the back. But then more clients would come in, and Belinda, not one to overlook idle hands, would send me to clean the windows for the third time.

By the time Hawk showed up and was ready to torture me, I was already exhausted.

I sat slumped in front of the fireplace, face covered in ashes, realizing that even failing at magic could take a lot out of you.

"You're. Not. Trying." Hawk glared at me from the other side of the room like I wasn't killing myself to light the logs on fire. As if I hadn't already tried ten times since he'd called me back here.

"Yes. I. Am." My jaw barely unlocked as I spoke. "Do you think I'm trashing this room for shits and giggles?" I waved a hand about the place that was indeed a mess and, I was fairly certain, I'd be cleaning up alone. "That this is fun for me?"

He shook his head. It seemed to be a trend with us. He'd tell me to try something. I'd fail. He'd shake his head and act like I was purposely frustrating him. Not that I wouldn't at this point. If I could knock him upside his head, I'd do it. What did he expect? I was new at this, and clearly something was going wrong.

"This, what you've been doing, is not *trying*. If you were trying, we'd be getting somewhere. I ask you to move the book, you knock over the bookcase. I ask you to light the fire, and you do everything but." Hawk stepped closer. "Let me ask you something, Tippi. Are you even here by accident, or was this a setup?"

Now he was going too far. Did he think I was some sort of spy? Here to read his books at night? I didn't even know why I was here in the first place. A spell, he'd say, with no other explanation. Anger drove energy back into my limbs as I got to my feet.

"A setup for what? To make your back room a mess? Beg you to send me home? I must be a genius spy." I was barely under a yell. The only thing that stopped me were the people still in the office who might be listening.

"I'm finding it hard to believe that you're quite this bad. It's not natural." He was crowding me, standing so close that I could feel some sort of electricity that fizzed from him. He had an energy that somehow called to mine, made me want to reach out and touch him, just to see if that tingle would be there. But if I did touch him, there was a very high likelihood that I'd kill him, or attempt to, anyway.

I looked up at him, wishing I was a foot taller. "Then why don't you get rid of me and send me back to Salem?"

"Because you're bought and paid for, and damned if I'm not getting what I want." His voice was deep and growly, nearly vibrating through the room.

"Then you better figure out another way to teach me, because this isn't all on me. You need to take some of the blame here. Maybe it's *you*. Have you ever even taught anyone before? Because I hate to tell you, but you suck at it."

There was a flicker of light in his eyes, a sizzle of energy that notched up. If everyone here in Xest had magic, why did no one feel quite the same as he did when I neared them? There was something wrong here. Or something different, at least.

I lifted my hand, as if I were about to touch him, my curiosity getting the best of me. I caught myself in time and pointed instead.

He finished the connection, wrapping his hand around mine. "You *are* going to do this."

Our flesh connected, and I barely paid attention to his words, my concentration on the feeling of where our skin touched. I felt a surge of power flood from him. I didn't need to know magical scripture to know what I felt, and it was something immense. There was no more doubt.

"You're not a warlock. What are you?" I asked, pulling my hand back even as I could feel his magic surrounding me.

And then the magic was pulled back, like it hadn't been there. He took a step back, as if he'd caught himself.

He'd slipped. Whatever he'd just shown me was an accident.

"Hawk, are you ready?" Belinda asked from the doorway, her tone pure sugar instead of the acid I'd gotten all day.

"Yes. We're finished."

Hawk walked out.

I surveyed the damage. I should just leave it. I was doing this for his purposes. One would think he'd offer to help straighten up with me. The first time he left, I'd thought it was an oversight. He'd been aggravated and hadn't thought of it. But what about this time?

I went to the corner, dumped ash out of a cup, wiped it with my shirt, and then made tea while I waited for the sounds of the office to quiet. It was one thing to be the maid all day, but tonight I preferred to do my cleaning without an audience.

I took a seat on the ash-covered couch, waiting until the noises died down before I made my way to the turned-over bookcase. The thing must have been made out of some wood never heard of in Rest, because it weighed as much as a mountain of granite.

"Hang on. Let me help you," Zab said, walking in.

"Thanks," I said. "I thought everyone was gone."

"I was going through a couple last-minute slips." He got on the other side of the bookshelf and righted it with me, then began replacing books. "Not going so well?" he asked, already knowing the answer from the look of the room.

"Nope. Not going well at all. The only thing my magic seems to be good for is doing the opposite of what I need. Worst part is I don't even know what that spell is, because he's not telling me." By the time I'd finished talking, I was already sweating, streaks of ash on my arms, and it wasn't just from the bookcase.

Zab looked around, like he'd considered sitting but continued standing. "I understand why you'd be upset, but you can't tell someone something you don't know. I don't think he's trying to make you miserable. He just doesn't know himself, and he's never been long on patience."

How much did Zab know, exactly? Why had I assumed he wouldn't know what Hawk was up to when he was here all the time and Hawk clearly trusted him to some degree?

I let out a long sigh, as if all my aggravation was draining when it was ratcheting up. I grabbed some more books and shoved them back on the shelf. "It's hard to understand how he has no answers for what he needs and yet knows so surely that I'm the one who needs to do it, you know? I guess coming from Rest, as I do, it's hard to wrap my head around the whole thing. Maybe if you could explain it all better, I'd understand."

Zab moved his weight from foot to foot and looked at the clock again. "You know, I totally forgot I had to be somewhere. I'll see you tomorrow, all right?" The entire time he was talking, he'd been easing back toward the door.

I barely had a chance to say bye before he was gone. I'd pushed too hard, and now not only did I not have any more information, I'd have to finish cleaning on my own.

11

I went through the entire bag of clothes I'd gotten. Belinda had handpicked the worst possible outfits imaginable. Anything that would make me look ugly and frumpy was in the heap.

The lime-green pants that were two sizes too big were at least unstained. I also did have a belt, like she knew how bad she'd screwed me but didn't want my pants to fall down. The tops were no picnic either. Did I pair my glow-in-the-dark green with brown polka dots or a sweater with moth holes? At least the eaten-up one was a tolerable grey and would possibly tone down the green. I threw it on. Nah, there was no toning down this green.

It didn't matter. "Get through the day" was my motto of the moment. If it didn't kill me, it didn't matter. I wasn't so optimistic to say it would make me stronger. "Didn't matter" was as full as my glass was getting today.

I forced on a smile, walked downstairs, and stepped out into the buzz of the office in the morning.

Zab and Musso both stared a little too long at my attire. Belinda kept talking to the only client in the office at the moment. I wasn't fooled into thinking her smile was for the client, though. She was enjoying my distressed wardrobe.

"So, tonight?" the short, stout woman said to Belinda.

I typically let my eyes pass over Belinda's general vicinity, but my head jerked back in that direction at the familiar voice.

"Yes," Belinda answered.

The woman stood and turned. "You!" she said, pointing a stubby finger at me.

I had the exact same reaction.

"You got me stuck here," I said.

"Of course I did. Try to order a séance and not pay." She sneered and turned for the door, muttering something about the kids these days.

"I didn't know," I yelled after her.

She didn't reply as she made her way out the door. I was still watching her leave when Belinda stepped in front of me.

"Here. This is a list of things we need. Tell the shops to charge everything to the broker, and don't take all day about it."

She thrust the list toward me when I didn't take it right away. It was at least fifty items long. As soon as I got over the shock of what she was sending me to do, the pluses quickly kicked in. It would get me out of here and away from her for the day, so maybe not so bad. Plus, with a list like this, I'd surely end up somewhere near the factory, and I could stop in and check on Rabbit.

I plastered a gloomy expression on as I made a show of looking at all the different items. I shook my head as I grabbed my jacket, as if every step was torture. If Belinda caught the scent of happiness, I'd never get out of this place.

I took my list and headed off.

Zab walked out of the shop after me. "Hey, I wanted to go grab a chocolate at the Sweet Shop. Come with me before you start. It'll give you some sustenance." He nodded in the direction of the store.

I looked beyond him to the shop he was talking about. I'd caught glimpses of its pink and white striped awning. Even from here, you could see sugar sculptures of all different colors in the window.

"Sure. That'd be nice." I glanced back at the shop, wondering who he wanted to avoid hearing this conversation. I'd find out soon enough, as the chocolate place was only a half a block away.

We started off in the direction with Zab pulling his jacket tight around him. "The fifth wind is a killer today."

"Fifth wind?"

"Yeah, it's why it's so cold here."

Figured Xest would have to have even extra wind.

"Look, I wanted to put in a word for Belinda. I know she's been rough to be around, but she's got this complex, and you seem to be making it worse." Zab shrugged, his hands tucked in his pockets.

"But why? What did I do?"

"Nothing you actually did. The thing is, I'm pretty sure that she thinks if she was *more* than Middling, Hawk would want something *more* with her."

"I still don't see what this has to do with me."

He stopped on the side, halting before we got to the shop, but out of sight of the office.

"Well, none of us know your magic grade for sure, but from the look of things, the way Hawk is acting, you're stronger than Middling. He wouldn't be so protective otherwise."

"Protective?" I doubted my ears, but I could think of

another word that sounded closer to what was actually going on with him. Dickish, yeah, that I could get my head around.

"Oh yeah. Definitely. He gave firm orders that you weren't to be given anything dangerous to do unless he approves. He's never cared what assignments Belinda does. It's driving her crazy."

"She realizes he's keeping me here as a type of jail, a forced labor situation, right? He might be protective, but it's the *way* someone protects their property. It's not like he likes me." I'd had sweaters I treated better than he treated me.

"That doesn't count. He doesn't really like anyone," Zab said, walking the last few steps and pulling open the door to the Sweet Shop.

That was the last of the talk about Hawk. I'd always had a sweet tooth, and it was as if the motherland was welcoming me home. There were sugar sculptures everywhere. The walls were lined with candy wells, and in the center, there was a fountain of chocolate. This place almost made the abduction, the factory, Belinda, pretty much all of it okay.

"Amazing, right?"

"Beyond," I said reverently.

I'd just finished my hot cocoa and it was time to get on with things. The list wasn't getting any shorter, and I needed at least a few things before I went to the factory. Now it was time to figure out where I had to go for these things. I walked to the busier part of town, where the roads opened up into a square of sorts, and glanced at the shop names.

Stationery and Sundries was ahead on my left-hand side. I glanced at the list again. There was some sort of paper listed. Stationery, paper. Seemed like a good bet.

I walked into the store that was reminiscent of some of the larger chain stores I was familiar with, or would be with a dark and haunted makeover. Still, there were different stacks of pens, feathers, and papers all about the place.

An old man, with a hunch in his back and eyes nearly black, walked around the shelving. "May I help you?"

"Yes, thank you. Do you carry newsflash papers?"

"Of course." Instead of pointing to them, as I'd hoped. He walked across the store, each step seeming long and drawn out. I slowly followed behind him.

"I haven't seen you around before. Would you happen to be that new pop-up over at Hawk's? The new Whimsy witch?" It had only been a few days. News really spread fast here.

When I was handed this chore, I hadn't been prepared for questions, especially ones that would put me on the spot to make stuff up. And if he was going to ask me questions the entire time it took him to get the newsflash papers, he might know my life story before I got out of here.

Hawk had said he didn't want attention drawn to me. Now what?

"Yes, I'm her. Just another Whimsy witch, doing odds and ends for him. You know, cleaning, errands. I can't seem to do much more."

He stopped, looked over his shoulder, and lowered his bushy brows.

"Never met a Whimsy witch so okay with her position in life before," he said, then nodded and continued his trek across the store.

I'd said too much. He was already suspicious.

Wings flapped, and a large bird with a cat body landed on my shoulder. It settled in, wrapping its body around my neck and licking my jaw with its rough tongue.

"That'd be Sebastian. Seems to have taken to you," the old man said, as he finally picked up a pack of papers.

"Nice...cat," I said, not liking the way the old man was eyeing us up. Something wasn't right. I'd already messed up again and didn't know how.

"He's a Losso. Comes from the Valcan forests in the Unsettled Lands. Sebastian doesn't like that many people. Does your magic lean toward creatures, then?"

I smiled and shook my head. "No. My magic is too weak to do that." I didn't know what magical aptitudes I had, but I was certain that I wouldn't be considered a specialist of any of them.

He hummed and then cleared his throat as he walked back with the papers and placed them in a bag for me. He kept looking up at Sebastian licking me as he did. This wasn't a good thing. *Don't draw attention to yourself.* That was the only rule I had, and I was afraid I was breaking it.

"I'm supposed to charge this to the broker?" I said.

As soon as the shopkeeper turned his back to open up a large leather tome, I picked Sebastian off my shoulders, in spite of him trying to hold on with claws in my coat, and put him on a nearby shelf. He immediately flew back to me and perched on my shoulder again, licking any piece of me he could get his sharp tongue on. I tugged at him again, but he dug his claws in, refusing to leave.

I dropped my hands as soon as the shopkeeper turned around. The last thing I needed was for anything to add to his suspicions.

He looked at his cat-bird again. "So, Hawk took you to work for him out of the blue? Did you know him at all?"

"He needed a low-level Whimsy witch to run errands for him, so he went to the factory. Luck of the draw, I guess. Well, thanks!" I grabbed the bag he'd placed on the counter and tipped sideways, hoping to encourage Sebastian off me.

"Bassy, come here, now." The shopkeeper held out his hands.

Bassy wasn't having any of it as he continued to lick my hair.

"Bassy, boy, come on." The lines on the shopkeeper's forehead were deepening.

When Bassy still didn't listen, the shopkeeper made his way around the counter, trying to lift Bassy off me. Sebastian tried to resist again, but the shopkeeper eventually got him off my shoulders after some hissing and growling and disgruntlement.

The second I was free, I made for the door. "Thanks for the help." I got out of there before he could ask any more questions.

I stepped out of the building, dodged some people, witches, warlocks, and the like, as I walked down the street until I was a safe distance from the stationery store. Definitely not going back in there while I was here. That guy was way too nosy.

I tucked myself close to a building and tried to become invisible as I scanned the list for my next stop.

Oil of Newt
    Essence of Evil Vapor
    Shavings from a three-headed turtle

.   .   .

Once again, it was hard not to wonder what I'd done so wrong to end up here. Some people were meant to have blue eyes. I seemed to be destined to live with crazy people.

With a glance to my right, I saw Al's Chemist Shop. Worth a try, and it was a long list. They'd have something I needed.

Unlike the stationery shop, this place was bustling. I moved toward the counter, waiting until one of the few people gathering supplies off the shelves could help me. Other than a few glances in my direction, these people seemed too busy to care much about me, what I was doing here, who I was working for.

Maybe after I got out of here, I could swing past the factory. Rabbit hadn't believed I'd come back for her, and it had been days since then with no word. If she continued to not hear anything from me, she'd surely assume she was forgotten. I had to get over there, and soon.

"Who's lighting the potions? Whoever it is, cut it out. You should know better than to do such a thing in here," one of the clerks behind the counter yelled. He seemed to be the one in charge, or at least the loudest.

The bottles lining the back shelf were all glowing. It might've been the prettiest thing ever, with the various shades of reds and blues, purples and yellows, all lighting up almost to some sort of rhythm, some even twisting about like a lava lamp.

They continued to light as the man became angrier, his eyes searching the crowd until they settled on me. It was probably because I was the only unknown person there. I looked around and realized the entire place was staring at me. The longer they stared, the warmer my face got and the stronger the potions glowed.

"Who are you?" the shop owner called out.

I looked around again, hoping he was talking about someone else, but everyone was still staring at me.

I put my hand to my neck and searched for a chain that wasn't there. I'd forgotten to put the necklace back on. I'd left it on for so many years that I hadn't thought about it. It hadn't occurred to me to make sure it was back on, because I so rarely took it off. So much for not drawing attention to myself. It was game over.

"I'm nobody. Just a Whimsy witch." I took a few steps backward, making my way to the door and brushing shoulders in the tight squeeze.

"Is that the new pop-up?" someone in the crowd asked in a hushed tone.

"I'm not sure, but I think so," another nearby witch replied.

I hurried my steps.

"Tell us who you are," a dark-haired warlock said.

"I'm no one." I turned, pushing through the crowd as they stared. "I've got to go now." I took off in a sprint at the last moment, scared someone would block the door before I got out.

12

I didn't stop running until I was a building down from the broker house. Resting a hand on the stone of the neighboring building, I caught my breath and then straightened. No need to broadcast the issues to a roomful of people. With the bag of newsflash papers in my hand, I walked back in with the only item I'd managed to get off the list.

Belinda's eagle eyes narrowed on my measly bag as I made my way through the office.

"Why are you back here? Where are the things from my list?"

She was not going to make this easy, not that I thought she would. That wasn't who Belinda was. Even in the crazy world of Xest, I'd know her type anywhere. Still, it was better to play nice, or she'd have me mopping the floors for hours.

"I had a small problem. I'm going back to get the rest of the things tomorrow." Or most of the stuff. I couldn't go back to Al's. I definitely wasn't going into the stationery store again. There were so many other things on her stupid list she wouldn't even notice. Most important part was it would all be done tomorrow, when hopefully people wouldn't be looking for me. And I'd go to the factory first this time.

Belinda's face started winding up, like she was about to get into it with me. She could rant all she wanted. Wasn't happening. She could have a fit, but I couldn't be out there, at least until I found less conspicuous clothes and a little time had passed.

"That's not..."

The door swung open and Hawk walked into the office with enough purpose in his step that it was obvious something was afoot. He stopped in the middle of the room. "Everyone out but employees. Come back in a half an hour to conclude your business."

No one made a peep as they gathered their belongings and skedaddled out the door. He waited until the last person was gone before he nailed me with a look that made me afraid to move.

"Were you at Al's Chemist Shop a few minutes ago?"

Oh no. This wasn't going to go well from the look on his face.

"Yes. Belinda sent me out with a list of supplies." I wasn't taking heat for what I'd been directed to do. I had enough issues of my own making.

Belinda sat, and then slid a bit farther into her chair. Didn't matter, as Hawk's attention was still fully on me.

"How many people did you talk to?"

I'd lost count. "I don't know. A couple?"

"Did you go anywhere else?"

"The Stationery and Sundries."

He glanced at my neck before moving his eyes back to my face. My hand automatically went to the barren spot. He couldn't see, but he knew.

"It was an accident."

He looked skyward for a moment before taking a deep breath. A moment later, his veins about to burst, he said, "Don't forget it again."

Hawk walked over to Belinda. "I need a word with you."

"Sure," she said, standing and walking over to the stair door with him. Was he bringing her up the other stairs? What was up there? Today wasn't the day I'd find out, though.

Musso shook his head and returned to work. Zab shrugged and did the same.

I took off my jacket and went to put it in the back room, coming face to face with an odd stone sitting on the shelf. I'd never noticed it before, but now it was there, in my face, calling my attention to it.

Don't do it. Don't.

Was it truly eavesdropping if he wanted me to practice my magic? Plus, it was about me. How did I *not* listen? This conversation practically begged to be eavesdropped on.

I glanced about the room, making sure Zab or Musso hadn't followed me in, before grabbing the odd stone. I didn't know what type of rock it was, but it looked like a natural material. It should do.

I held it to my ear while I whispered, "With the magic within, and the magic around, take this stone and drop it within earshot." I moved myself to a thick rug and let the stone drop. If my understanding was correct, it would act as sort of a tin can with a string between me and them. It was glowing softly when I picked it up again and held it to my ear.

"Why are you sending her on errands?" Hawk's voice sounded softly through the stone somehow. Maybe my magic wasn't so horrible? That had been the easiest thing I'd ever done.

"You said treat her like she's 'no one.' That's what I'd have a 'no one' do, go on errands."

I cupped the stone, trying to muffle it a little as the volume increased. It wasn't that loud, but the shop was a little too quiet with all the people gone.

"Except she's not actually a 'no one,' and you know that."

Were they screaming or was this thing getting louder? I didn't remember reading anything about volume control. There had to be a way to turn this thing down.

I made a shushing noise at it.

"Oh, I'm aware. And while we're talking about it, why does she have to stay here? Why can't she stay somewhere else?" Belinda asked, her shrill voice carrying across the room so clearly that there was no way they didn't hear me in the office.

I shoved the stone under a pillow on the couch.

Hawk's voice came out of the stone, still booming. "You already know. We've discussed this."

I wished they'd discuss it again—if I could get some volume control. Too bad the entire office probably heard, because nothing, not even a pillow, would mute this thing.

"Oh, no you didn't," Musso said.

I turned. Musso and Zab were standing inside the door.

"Why can't she stay with Oscar, then?" Belinda asked.

I rushed across the room, holding the thing out to them. "How do I turn this off?"

"I'm not putting my magic prints anywhere near that thing." Musso held up his hands and backed away before he turned and left the room.

"How do I turn it off?"

Zab shrugged. "I never used that spell. I don't know it

that well. Maybe Musso will tell us, and then we can do it without his magic being on it."

He walked back into the office with me right behind him. I passed the stairs, wondering how Hawk and Belinda hadn't heard themselves. The Sweet Shop down the block probably heard them.

"She's staying here, and I'm not debating it with you. Conversation is over," Hawk said.

"You like her, don't you? Just admit it. That's why you want her here," Belinda said.

"I told you, I barely know her, not that it would matter. You and I are not together. I thought this was a casual thing. That's what *you* said."

I cringed like I'd taken that blow myself. I didn't like the girl, but that was a punch in the gut after a full meal.

"Musso, please, how do I turn this off?" The smell of desperation permeated my words.

"I don't know. I don't mess around with those spells," he said, the words steeped deep in judgment.

Easy for him to judge when he wasn't the one with no way out and no clear answers. I didn't have the liberty of high standards.

"Bel, I told you before we began, I don't have anything more to give," Hawk said.

Ugh. This conversation was not helping my case. I was hoping for a little information to help me out of the situation I'd been thrown into. I never would've cast that spell to hear this.

Musso and Zab were making their own pained faces. The only one privy to this conversation who didn't seem to get the situation clearly was Hawk. Did he really think she was sleeping with him just for sex? That she wasn't utterly in love with him? Thought he walked on water, or whatever weirdo thing their gods did?

I was in a completely different world, with utterly changed rules, and I still would've laid money down on how this had started. Hawk hadn't wanted anything serious, so, the bright one Belinda was, she thought she'd lure him in, saying it was casual. Of course she figured he'd sleep with her and see the light. He'd realize how wonderful and perfect she was. How she'd been the one thing missing from his life and now he was complete. He'd fall head over heels and she'd live happily ever after.

From the sounds of it, this plan was playing out about as well as it did in Rest. He fucked her a bunch, thinking stupidly that they had the same goals—a good time. He continued because it was convenient and now couldn't fathom where all these feelings were coming from. Why? Because the dumb man had believed her.

From the sounds of it, they were definitely hitting the third act of this show, and it wasn't going to have a happy ending.

There were footsteps. I heard a door creak open.

"I know, and I'm fine with what it is," Belinda said.

Sure she is.

There was a pause before she continued more hesitantly. "Why are we echoing?"

I groaned, wondering if lobbing the stone out the door would turn it off. All that would probably do was let the entire neighborhood hear as well. I was pretty sure it was too late anyway.

Musso was at his desk, rolling his eyes. Zab ran to his desk as well, distancing himself from the scene of the crime.

Belinda came into the office first. Her gaze shot straight to me. I might've turned a toasty pink. Yes, we weren't friends, but still, that wasn't well done of me. I would've apologized then and there, but she stormed out of the building before the opportunity presented itself. She took a left turn, walking past the window and disappearing from view.

I was still watching her when Hawk entered the room. My skin went past toasty and into "raging forest fire" temperatures.

He walked over and held out his hand. I saw this all in my peripheral vision, since I was still working up the nerve to look at him. I put the stone in his palm, still not meeting his eyes.

"I guess you learned at least one thing from that book." He wrapped his hand around it, and the thing stopped glowing.

I wanted to ask how he'd done that, but this didn't seem like the right time. He held it back out to me, as if I'd have some need of it again. I took it because I feared not doing so would lead to more conversation.

He walked to the door, and I found I couldn't look away now. He was going to follow her. Maybe things would work out for them. What if he'd only needed an eye-opener?

And then he took a right, the opposite direction Belinda had gone.

I felt bad for her. I definitely did. If there was any happiness in me, it was only because she was probably better off moving on to someone who was into her. Hawk clearly wasn't—not that I cared.

Zab and Musso were staring at me when I turned around.

"Well, that was awkward," Zab said.

"I've seen worse." Musso shrugged.

13

Musso and Zab were gone. I'd pulled up a chair near the front window of the office. If I sat really close and leaned my head a certain way, I could see the top of the factory's roof from here. Even though it was late, there was still a steady stream of glittering smoke coming out of the factory chimney. The only friend I had here was going to die an early death in that place if I didn't figure something out, and soon. People on the street stared at me as they walked past, but I didn't care. There were many things that were bothering me, but what these strangers thought was not among them.

Hawk walked out of the back room. I hadn't seen Belinda or him since the "incident" earlier today, and I was sort of hoping I wouldn't.

He walked through the office, checking a couple of things on the different counters without saying anything.

I *had* to say something. "Sorry" fell a little short, considering I'd purposely invaded his privacy, but there weren't any alternatives.

The silence in the room was heavy as he continued to go

about his business. I might as well just get it out. It wasn't as if I could avoid him. It had to be done.

"Sorry about today," I said, leaving off the *buts* that wanted to follow, like the one about Belinda being an ass. Or the big, fat BUT where she taunted me and tried to make me miserable all day. I couldn't add all those, though, because then *I'd* look like an ass. That was the problem with apologies. No one wanted *buts* with them, even good buts. I had to pretend I didn't have an entire list so long that any jury would've acquitted me of a crime due to temporary insanity from torture.

I waited, my gut churning.

He was certainly taking his time accepting my "no buts" apology. If he was going to be an ass about it, I should've added some buts. Why not?

Or maybe not. I couldn't start a fight, and this needed to get ironed out. I needed to get the hell out of this place, and that took him. I was not going to die in Xest.

I got up and walked over to where he was flipping through some papers, ready to put a little more effort in. "It was stupid. I'm really sorry."

He finally looked at me. "I'm not angry about you listening in. I'm not happy about it, but that's not the main problem. I told you to be careful, and now there's talk spreading about what happened in Al's."

"It was an accident. I don't know what happened. I was standing there, and then they started to glow."

"Which wouldn't have happened if you had your necklace on. You showed your magic, and I'm not the only one who'll be interested in what you can do. Now you might be called on by others."

"What others? Who's going to call for me?" For the first time, the reality that this might be a little more serious than

I'd feared was hitting me. I should've realized a man who barely bothered talking to half the people he saw wouldn't care about rumors.

"There's other factions in Xest who would use your power and not be so generous about allowing you to leave once you were done. I was trying to keep you out of the politics of this place, keep it uncomplicated, but I'm fairly sure you blew that up."

I'd hardly call letting me leave of my own free will one day generous, but I was quickly learning how archaic Xest could be. I had enough troubles. I didn't need more.

"Who's going to call?"

"Raydam, for one."

I didn't know him, and I already didn't want to meet him. "And he's a problem?"

"A definite complication."

I had the sense that a complication for Hawk equaled a definite problem for me.

"But I have no power." I crossed my arms, taking a few steps around the office. This made no sense. I was the worst witch imaginable. No one should want me.

"You have magic. That's power." He watched me, mad but much calmer than I was now.

"That I can't even use without screwing things up," I said, flinging my hands into the air.

He dipped his chin. "Which is a temporary situation."

"What about the whole indentured servant business? That I couldn't leave?"

"There are other possible complications."

I was on the move again, shaking my head. "What's going to happen now?"

"If he hears about the incident and it raises his interest, he's going to call for you. Once you have an audience with him, he'll test you. If he thinks you have power, he'll woo you next."

Woo. That sounded nice, except in Xest, they probably wooed you by hitting you with a club. Nothing was civilized in this place. The entire bunch of them were lunatics, and I needed out.

"And if that doesn't work?" I asked.

"A year ago, it wouldn't have been an issue. Now, I'm not sure."

"Why could it be a problem now?"

"Hard to explain."

"Hard, or you don't want to?" I asked.

"I don't want to," he said calmly, making no bones about it.

I didn't have the answers I wanted, but I now knew why I didn't have them. At least we were being upfront. He didn't trust me. I didn't trust him either.

My hand went to my neck. "If he calls and I keep the necklace on—"

"He'll still sense something is wrong, the way I did when I touched you."

"But you didn't know."

"Yes, I did."

"But when I said I had to go to the bathroom that first—"

"I remember the day well enough. I know what I said, and I'm telling you, I knew. He'll know as well."

"What if I don't go?"

"You can't. An open snub like that would weaken him in the eyes of all. He'd force the issue, and it would make matters worse. If he calls, you have to accept."

I stopped moving around. Stopped fidgeting. The shock of it all immobilized me. Somehow, it had gotten worse. On a theoretical level, you're always aware things can get worse.

But they had, and all because I hadn't worn my necklace. Such a trivial thing when you thought about it.

I was jarred from my little pity party as Hawk moved about the room again. He grabbed a small bag out of a chest on one of the counters. It sounded like it had coins clinking around in it. I watched as he headed toward the door.

"Aren't we practicing tonight?" I asked, not wanting to be here alone after what he'd told me, even if it were to be tortured in the back.

"No. I'm still working on damage control. Don't leave the building." There was no mistaking it for anything other than what it was—an order.

He left.

I went back to staring at the factory. How was I supposed to get to Rabbit now?

14

I came down to the office the following morning in my favorite lime-green pants and grey sweater with holes, wondering how they'd gotten laundered and by whom. Somehow my clothes kept getting cleaned and folded, and I wasn't sure how, but I had too many real issues to worry over. I was about to grovel to Belinda. I opened the door and prepared myself for what was to come.

Zab and Musso were in the office, but Belinda wasn't. She was always here when I came down, as if maybe she slept in the alleyway or something, just to be close. She might've run out on an errand somewhere, but the timing was questionable. I was already a bit behind, stalling as I'd been. Couldn't blame the woman for needing a day off after what had happened.

Zab greeted me with a big smile. "Hawk told me that I'd be in charge of your duties from now on." He waved a hand at a table set up for me.

He walked over to the basket and grabbed a heap of the slips that Helen dumped out. He dropped them on the table, slips flying off and scattering.

"Sort through those for anything that looks reasonable and might have some payment involved," he said.

The pile was huge and the slips kept on shooting out. I might've been better off with mopping. I couldn't be in charge of all these people's hopes and dreams. I had no idea what I was doing. But Zab seemed to think I could, as he was already going back to his duties.

I picked up a slip.

I'll be nice to Jennifer if I can be a supermodel.

Well, that was definitely garbage. I didn't know who Jennifer was, but this person should've been nice to her anyway. Big fail in my book. Into the shredder pile it went.

Next slip:

Break up with Gil if I get drafted.

Jerk. This was definitely going into the shredder too. Gil was more important, and you should know better. Maybe this wouldn't be so hard.

I sorted through a few more slips, but my attention was getting tugged away by the clock and the empty chair.

The clock ticked, and Musso went and opened the door for business.

I turned to Zab. "Where's Belinda?"

"She said she couldn't come today. Didn't feel good," Zab said, and then raised his brows.

I hummed as I nodded, wishing she had. Now I was going to dread apologizing to her all today and tonight, too.

I was back to the slips when Hawk strode in, an air of foreboding spread through the room, as he didn't speak to anyone. He walked through the office, grabbed a bag of coins, and pocketed them.

"I won't be back tonight," he said in my general vicinity right before he was gone again. Now what had I done? I'd been sleeping for the last eight hours. How could I have messed up when I wasn't even awake? Seemed I couldn't even sleep now without pissing people off.

Zab and Musso shook their heads as if they were already aware of Hawk's issue, the ramifications and the final prognosis, while I was still asking the doctor about symptoms.

"Why's he angry at me now?"

"There's been more gossip spreading about the Whimsy witch who works here," Zab said. "They're saying that you're some sort of creature specialist of the Maker level. What did you do there?"

That damned flying cat had been bad news. Him and his licking had sunk me.

"His cat liked me. That was it. I was careful not to say anything or do anything." I got licked by one weird cat and then this? I couldn't stay out of trouble if I tried, and I was, in fact, trying. I'd spent years flying under the radar. One séance and now this.

"The Losso liked you?" Zab asked.

"Yeah, the Losso liked me. Cats like me. Why is that such a problem?"

"That thing is from an area that no one dares set foot in. They're evil creatures. No wonder he thought you were high level. The only reason that old, crazy idiot can keep that thing with him is it's enchanted."

I groaned, leaning forward until my head nearly hit the table. Hawk was going to kill me, and things were already rocky. He already hated me. Now after Belinda and this, it was going to be even worse.

"Don't worry about it. He can't be too angry. He did sign up for this when he sent the finder for you. I mean, when the black feather landed on someone from Rest, you had to know it was going to get tricky."

All my other thoughts vanished, as Zab's words kicked them out so they could run through my head without distraction and take over. After they banged all around, I replayed them at a slow stroll. I let them sink in a little better, afraid I'd missed some nuance that would make sense of this.

When I finally straightened and turned to Zab, his eyelids slowly lowered until there were crinkles at the corners. "You didn't know about that, did you?"

"No. I didn't."

That black feather he'd been staring at the first time I met him. It all made sense now. I'd chased after Hawk, nearly begging for help, and he'd been seeking me out from the beginning.

15

Another night of bad sleep, but this time it was fury that had kept me awake, in addition to the candle I could never put out. I'd been waiting for Hawk to walk in the office all day so I could ream him out, although I'd probably have to race Belinda to get to him first. Her mysterious illness gone, she was back at work. Every time the door opened, the two of us were the first to look over. She reminded me of a dog left at a kennel waiting for its owner. It was almost too pathetic to stomach. On the other hand, I probably appeared like the junkyard dog, ready to rip someone's heart out of their chest after I'd mangled the rest of their body.

The worst was when we both caught the other staring at the door. Then it was some funky combination of awkward and anger.

"Belinda..."

"No." She turned her head.

It was the fifth time I'd tried to speak to her today. She wouldn't even let me apologize.

The door opened, and I didn't look for once. I heard Belinda's chair scrape the ground, and I still didn't look.

I would've trampled him at the door but was beaten out by the stampede that was Belinda. She did her ritual shadowing-Hawk routine. The only thing that made it tolerable was that Hawk didn't seem to notice her as much as he should've.

She shadowed him across the room to where Musso was flipping through some of the work, discussing weird things in hushed voices.

I was barely keeping my head from exploding as I sat and waited for my opportunity to strike. Didn't know when that was going to happen, as Belinda was still tailing him, and Musso seemed to think he had something equally pressing. I crossed my arms, looking toward the windows and the witches and warlocks walking by, trying to hold my patience in check, the weight of which would strain an Olympic lifter.

"Is there a problem?" Hawk's voice carried clear and loud across the room.

If he didn't realize all the problems Belinda had by now, they were made for each other. The two of them were the same, birds of a feather, cut from the same cloth—the sayings could go on forever. Neither of them wanted to see a problem when it was right in their face. Nope. Just kept on going. He should throw in the towel and get hitched to her, because she wasn't going to let daylight in between them anyway. He didn't seem ready to really hammer home that point, though, so maybe he was more into her than it seemed?

"Tippi, is there an issue?"

I swung my head to him, surprised he was aware I was in the office, let alone noting that I was fuming so much I could've brewed tea on my forehead.

Belinda was twitching as she still hung as close as she

could to him, only taking breaks from staring at his back to try to stare my existence right into hell. She didn't realize it, but I was already there.

"Tippi?"

The rest of the room was watching, including customers, as Hawk's attention was solely on me.

"Yes, actually, there is," I said.

He detached himself from Musso and Belinda, and walked until he was standing right in front of me. "Do we need to discuss it?"

Belinda, who was typically begging for any scrap of attention, good or bad, looked beyond words with envy. The rest of the room seemed to step back, giving us a wider berth, as if there would be bloodshed soon and they didn't want to catch an accidental blow or get any on their clothes. They didn't know what I knew. He couldn't kill me, not yet. He needed me, and I was beginning to realize it was a lot more than I thought if he'd tracked me down in Rest.

What the hell was he going to have me do? That wasn't even my biggest issue, though. How dare he let me think I'd chased him down for help when it was the other way around?

I stood. "Oh, do I."

Zab muttered, "Ooooh, noooo," off to the side. It was unclear whether his concern was that he'd been the one to inform me of the finder situation or that I was daring to call Hawk out on something. For some reason, it didn't seem the thing to do in this place.

"Walk." Hawk went to the stair door, leaving it open.

Oh, I walked. I'd been waiting for a moment alone with him for hours. We were going to talk, and I might even need to yell, and it was happening now.

I walked past him and made a right turn to climb toward my room.

"Other way," he said.

I was supposed to use the left staircase? The one he told me not to use unless I wanted to die? Oh no. Maybe all those "uh oh" expressions in the office were right. Any comfort I felt with him might've been delusion on my part. What did I really know about Hawk? Absolutely nothing. I turned to go to the left and then froze. I was being crazy. He needed me. I took one step up and paused again.

Whatever was up there might be really bad. If he tried to kill me in the office, Zab would take pity on me and try to save me. He probably wouldn't succeed, but if Musso kicked in? There was at least a chance. Up there? All bets were off.

"You're not going to die." Hawk's voice was deep, sending a little shiver through me.

"I didn't believe I would for a second," I said, throwing him a look over my shoulder that called him an idiot if he thought otherwise, before I began climbing.

"You might be the worst liar I've ever met. No wonder the shopkeeper didn't believe you," he said as he followed me up the stairs.

So he knew all the details. Didn't matter. I'd wear my crappy lying abilities like the badge of honor they were.

"Yes, I'm not well trained in duplicity," I said, wondering when the stairs were going to stop. I'd definitely climbed more than a flight, and unless I'd gone crazy, I thought this building only had two stories? Where was the landing? But we kept climbing past where the roof should've been.

Ah, there it was, a landing and a door. He waved his hand, telling me to enter. He could say I wasn't going to die, but I wasn't taking any unnecessary risks. Maybe that was why he was so upset about me being out and about. He didn't want too many people to notice when I went missing? He wanted the option to kill me when he was done.

"You should go first." I stepped to the side. If there were a monster about to pop out of that door, maybe it would eat him first, if he was willing to open it.

He looked at me with an expression so dry that the Sahara could've been a rain forest in comparison. He opened the door and then gasped. "Oh no. It's a *sitting* room."

He turned to me, raised an eyebrow and then walked in.

Yeah, it was a sitting room, all right, and he was already making himself comfortable on the only couch in the room. I can't believe I'd bought into that "it'll kill you" bullshit.

"Now what's your issue?" he asked.

After that buildup, I'd almost forgotten why I hated him today, and possibly tomorrow, and the day after that.

"The finder. Care to tell me about that?" If he couldn't figure out the problem from my words, my fighting tone surely invited him into the ring.

"And?" he asked. He stared at me, contemplating something or other I was too dense to discern. If he'd gotten my invite to the fight, it didn't look like he was going to step into the ring.

I walked to the window, refusing to sit next to him. "The finder? The black feather that located me? That's my issue." I lost interest in the scenery, waiting for this to finally click for him. I didn't care what bullshit he gave me. Yes, this world was very different from where I'd come from, but some things had to be the same, like lying and withholding. He'd done both.

"I'm not seeing the problem, so you're going to have to spell it out for me." He waved a hand, signaling that I should continue.

"You were coming for me first. You sent a finder to locate me. You *found* me first. Not Marvin. He might've hired those idiots to bring me here, but you were going to do the same, weren't you?"

"I wouldn't have hired anyone. I would've done it myself. And I'm still not seeing the issue."

As he leaned back on the couch and looked at me, it was painfully clear that he didn't see any problem with what had happened. I was going to have to break it down for him, in the simplest of terms.

"Why did you make it seem like I came to you? That you were doing me a favor?" If he wanted to tell me there was nothing wrong with that, he was a liar.

"A, you did approach me. B, I did do you a favor. You'd gotten yourself in a situation."

I wanted to march over there and beat him until he saw my point. Instead, I broke it down ever further. He was going to see my point at least one time before I left here.

"My point is, you should've told me you were going to come back for me and do the same thing I was asking you to do." I could hear my own exhale as I tried to calm myself.

"You're right. I would have, and at that point, I would've offered more favorable terms. You would've agreed, so what is the problem?" He leaned his head on a few fingers, as if this talk was becoming tiresome.

His explanation was fine and dandy except for one problem. "And when I declined? Then what?"

He plucked fuzz off his pants. "I would've offered you more."

"And if I still declined?"

He let out a long sigh. "You wouldn't have. I would've raised the price until you agreed."

"You don't get it. That's not who I am. I can't be bought. I don't care about money."

He smiled. "You're the one that doesn't understand. When I say price, I don't mean money. And everyone has a price, even you. The fact that you don't know that shows your naïveté."

"I'm not naive. I'm telling you—"

"What if I said I'd bring your mother back?"

I felt like he'd just knocked the air out of my lungs. Was bringing her back an option? Would I want to? To call our relationship complicated would've been a massive under-statement. Unpacking that relationship would take at least five psychologists and several lifetimes. What concerned me most was that he clearly knew something about her, at least to the extent that she was dead. How much digging around had he done?

"What do you know about her?" I narrowed my eyes at him.

"Some, but not much," he said, still calm.

I didn't particularly care for people who didn't fight normally. I'd been ready for a brawl, but as he kept his calm, he made it harder to keep my ire up, especially when he dropped a bomb like that.

"Could you bring her back?" I wrapped my arms around myself, wondering if she'd come back normal or more like something out of a Stephen King novel. She'd already been barely sane to begin with, which wouldn't help matters. But if she could come back, oh, the things I'd ask her.

"I don't deal in that kind of magic. But like I said, everyone has a price."

"You're an asshole." The calm that had been settling over me fled.

"Why? Because everyone has a price, something that

will make them do things they never thought they would? You need to learn that or you won't make it here very long."

"Good thing I'm not staying long, then."

I walked out of the room, leaving the door open. I hadn't gotten any answers, or an admission of guilt, and I was fairly sure I wouldn't in the future.

16

It was such a joy to have Belinda back to work, sitting at her desk, declaring war on me without a word. Couldn't even blame her anymore. I'd pretty much shot a nuke at her with my little eavesdropping scenario, and now her love interest had just taken me away for a little chat when she could barely get his attention. At some point in the future, I might try to lob an apology over her way again. That future had not come yet. If I lobbed anything at her right now, she'd assume it was a grenade and shoot first.

Belinda hadn't attempted to give me anything to do all day, so something must've been said to her about the work as well. I was content. Things had been bad enough when she'd disliked me. The pure rage exuding from her now could make life here unbearable.

I could sense the problem coming even before she stood and pointed at me.

"Zab, should she really be doing that? She's been a witch for all of, what? Two seconds? She has zero qualifications."

"You mean like common sense? I think she can manage.

And they all have to go through us for rates anyway. It'll make our lives easier if they're presorted." Zab went back to work, as if nothing were amiss. Musso never stopped, clearly trying to evade this conversation.

Belinda was strung so tight that I was afraid she'd shatter if a wind hit her wrong. She stood there staring, torn between carrying on and pretending I didn't exist. She could choose whichever made her happy. I was getting back to work.

Destroy the world and become Satan's bride.

Well, this was easy. Shredder pile. Although I silently thanked the wisher for bringing some levity into my day.

Promise my life to God if he could kill my ninth-grade teacher for flunking me in gym.

Really? What was wrong with these people? Maybe you should be asking for some coping skills or better self-discipline. Either way, your teacher would live on, as another request hit the shredder pile.

Will eat every lima bean on my plate until I die if my dog Bingo lives.

.   .   .

Finally, a keeper. What was the date on this thing? We were running behind. I hoped Bingo was still alive.

"Zab? Do we have a priority pile? This needs a fast turnaround."

"What is it?" he asked, holding out his hand for the slip. He looked it over. "Too vague. We could end up with an immortal dog, and the suffering incurred from lima beans won't cover a life. Bingo might make it, but we can't intervene. Shredder."

Belinda huffed from across the room. "A dog is top priority?" she muttered under her breath, as she worked on some form in front of her.

Right there was the proof of why I shouldn't like her. Who *wouldn't* put Bingo in a priority pile? Still, I understood Zab's argument. I mean, lima beans might not taste very good, but was that really a fair price? The kid could've done a little better, but a lot of people really hated lima beans. Perhaps they weren't getting their full due?

My hand hovered over the shredder pile before making a brand-new pile. A "reconsider later" pile. A pile that might be sitting very close to the acceptance pile. I would be very careful that those two piles didn't merge accidentally.

Zab rolled his chair a little closer, looking at Bingo's slip.

"I put it to the side in case you feel differently later."

Zab was trying to figure out the nicest approach to get Bingo on the shredder pile when Hawk walked in. He had a newspaper in his hands. This place had newspapers? Couldn't imagine what crazy shit they'd have in them, but as he walked toward me, I was clearly going to find out.

He dropped a paper in front of me that I instantly recognized. This wasn't a Xest newspaper. It was one of the biggies in the Northeast, even globally.

"Go to page three." He leaned an elbow on the cabinet behind me, waiting.

Zab slowly rolled his chair away.

I flipped the pages. The second I saw the headline, I groaned.

Hawk leaned down, laying a hand flat on the desk, reading, "'Dandelions exploding. Scientists fear it's a rare side effect of global warming. Others say it's a sign of the apocalypse. One thing is for sure, no one can explain why.'"

He straightened, and I could finally concentrate and skim the article. It had happened fifty times in the last day or so. How many had I done? Not all of them had probably been plucked and blown, so that might've been right. Other than some minor burns, everyone was fine.

"You just *took* to dandelions. A natural at them," Hawk said. I understood his motivation. I might've tried to lay my failures on his teaching ability on occasion, but did he have to mock me here? Now?

There was a muffled feminine giggle across the room. I didn't look in *her* direction.

I dropped the paper and looked at him, all pretenses stripped away. "You should send me back. Obviously, I'm not good at magic. You're not going to get what you need."

His eyes crinkled at the corners as he watched me, as if he could read all my inner fears. He had to face it. This wasn't going to work out. As Belinda had pointed out just moments ago, I'd been a witch for all of two seconds and was far from a natural.

"No. I don't think so," he said, walking toward the back room. "Let's go. We have work to do."

Great. Now he was mad again, and I didn't even know why.

"Hawk?" Belinda called, stopping him.

Hawk looked at her. "Yes, Bel?" His voice was softer than he ever used with me. Softer than he typically used with her, even. Was it guilt because he didn't want her? Was there a heart in that cold chest somewhere?

"If she doesn't want to be here, does she really have to stay? If she can't do what is required, it would be kinder to send her back."

Oh yes, kindness. I wouldn't knock her ploy aloud. Her hate could come in handy. She was an angle I hadn't considered. I never thought me and *Bel* would be on the same page of anything.

She walked over and laid her hand on his arm, and I swallowed down a strong desire to rip it off. It wasn't about Hawk, obviously. I just didn't like her.

"You know I can't," Hawk said, his voice calm and patient, like he had all the time in the world.

Who was this man?

He walked away from Bel, heading toward the back room. A second later I heard, "Tippi," when I didn't come fast enough.

I walked into the back room just as he tossed a book onto the table. "You know the drill."

Oh, yes. Too well.

I reached under my shirt, taking off the coal necklace and placing it on the farthest shelf.

I looked at the book for another couple of minutes before asking, "You're sure you want to keep doing this?"

"This is the easiest magic, so yes, this is probably the best way to continue."

He'd confused the actual question, or maybe not. Either way, I had the answer. He was in this for the long haul. I focused on the book, as I had the first time, and the time after that.

A minute later, the teapot went flying across the room.

I sighed. He might've sighed as well, but it was hard to hear over my own.

"Try again," he said.

It might've been the steely determination in his eyes or the tone of voice that sounded as immovable as a mountain, but either way, we were going to be here a long while.

17

I looked up from my table and stacks of requests, watching Zab scribbling on one of the newsflash papers I'd picked up at the stationery store.

He walked to the door and said, "Carry my message," before flinging the folded paper into the air. The paper turned into a paper bird, beat its wings a few times, and then disappeared.

He walked back and sat behind his desk.

"What was that?" I asked, fascinated. I had to admit that some of the craziness that went on here was incredibly cool.

"Had to call someone in for a job. Easiest way to get them here. That'll track them down, and no one ignores a newsflash from the broker's office." He leaned back in his seat and nodded to my stacks. "How's it going? Do you like what you're doing?"

"Oh, yeah, very entertaining." I neatened my piles a little.

"Okay, because you seem a little off, is all."

"I'm good." I could've had a knife sticking out of my

back, but as long as Belinda sat across the room, trying to listen to every word, no way was I complaining.

Zab glanced at Belinda's bent head and then back to me. "Come on," he said, standing and grabbing some coins from the chest. "It's slow. Let's go grab a cocoa at the Sweet Shop."

If there was anything that might've been able to take the edge off, that Sweet Shop cocoa might've been it. Hawk had said not to leave the building, but he couldn't possibly mean going across the street. I grabbed my jacket as Zab waited for me.

The wind hit my skin, and it felt like I was going to get instant frostbite. It still felt warmer than the chill in the office.

Zab didn't waste any time questioning me. "So what's wrong? Is it practice? I know it's not going so well."

"It would be easier if that was the problem. I mean, don't misunderstand me, practice is a mess—*I'm* a mess—but that's not the thing that's bothering me most. I have one friend I met here who's stuck in a factory, which is sucking the life out of her, and I can't do anything about it. I left another friend, who's more like family, back home. She's probably worried sick at this point, and I can't do anything about that either. I just wish I could've given Loris word so she didn't worry. I'm afraid she's going to think I'm dead by now."

"I can't do anything about your friend in the factory, but why don't you write Loris a letter?"

"I don't think journaling is going to help right now."

"I don't mean journaling. I mean write one and send it to her. You can send mail to Rest. We don't get any back. It's a one-way correspondence, but you can send it out. Well, except at Christmastime. Sometimes the miscellaneous letter to Santa comes through. We used to field the big items occasionally, but Hawk thought it wasn't worth our time after a while. Now we just shred 'em if they end up here."

"I can get a letter to her?"

"Yeah. We can do it today if you want."

I turned to run back to the office.

"What about our cocoas?" Zab asked, still standing in the same place.

This was going to be a tough letter. A little cocoa might help.

Dear Loris,

I'm sorry I disappeared, but...

But *what*? I was kidnapped to Xest? A place most had never heard of? Was being held as an indentured servant to a warlock? Sorting slips from Helen, a huge machine that tapped into all the wishes in the world and monetized them? She'd think I was alive but off my rocker if I sent this.

I tapped the pen on the table a few times, staring at the page. This was not a pen letter. This really called for a pencil for the first hundred drafts. I dropped the pen on the table and leaned back, groaning and running my hands through my hair before draining the last sip of cocoa.

"What's wrong?" Musso asked, his voice as gruff as ever. I'd begun to realize the gruffer it was, the worse he felt for you. Was everyone aware of my near-daily crash and burn?

"She's trying to write a letter to someone she's worried about in Rest," Zab explained, before I had to.

"Oh," Musso said. "That never goes well." He followed those words of wisdom up with an ambiguous grunt and then walked back to his desk.

I glanced at Zab. "I can't begin to think of what to write. Everything sounds unbelievable. I'm trying to reassure her, but I feel like an idiot with nothing to say, and I'm the worst liar."

It was Belinda's turn to huff from her corner of the office, obviously agreeing with the idiot part. She didn't make any other noises, but her lips moved as she silently spoke to herself. As long as she kept it to herself, I didn't care. She could think whatever she wanted, including that I was an idiot or the best liar out there.

Zab sat on the corner of my table and bent over my paper, looking at the sparse words.

"Okay, write this. 'Dear Loris, I'm sorry I disappeared, but I received an emergency call in the middle of the night from a long-lost cousin who was in dire straits. As I have so little family, and none close, I felt the immediate need to rush to her side. I hope you received my earlier notice that I slid under the door of your shop. I wanted to follow up with this correspondence so you know how much it pains me that I had to leave you in such a predicament. As soon as my cousin is out of the woods, I shall return. Again, my gravest regrets about leaving you so suddenly.'"

It took me a few more minutes to finish scribbling off Zab's dictation. Nothing about it sounded like me. She might think my kidnapper had forced me to write it, but it was better than my blank page. Maybe if I added just a touch more?

· · ·

To make it up to you, I'll do as many séances as you want when I return.

I read it over again. At least that last bit sounded like me, but maybe...

"Don't overthink it," Zab said, taking the note I'd signed. He put it in the envelope I'd already addressed and tucked it into his pocket, before grabbing his jacket.

"What do I do about the return address?" I asked, putting on my jacket as well.

"No need for that. Come on. Let's get this off."

I followed him out of the shop. "What about postage?"

"What's postage?"

"It's what we pay to have someone send our letter."

"Oh, we don't have that here," he said, weaving through people who seemed to be paying more attention to me than normal. That didn't matter soon, as the building and people spread out farther and small houses popped up.

"Where do we mail this? We're leaving the town?" Town wasn't that big, so it wasn't that hard to leave. "Why isn't the post office in town?"

"There is no post office. There's only a mailbox, and it's not in town. It's on the outskirts."

We continued to walk for another ten minutes until we came to a field. In the middle of it was a blue mailbox, or what used to be blue. Now it was more rust than paint. The snow around it was unmarked by footprints.

He held the letter out to me.

I took it and paused. "Just put it in there?"

"Yes." He waited.

"But it doesn't look like anyone comes to collect the mail from here."

"Because no one has mailed anything recently. Not too many of us have anyone in Rest to write letters to."

I looked at the mailbox again. I wasn't getting Loris a note any other way, and it was already written. Not much point in holding on to it, even if it didn't make it to her.

"Go ahead. Put it in. They'll collect it." Zab pointed at the box.

The handle took some effort, a cloud of dust and rust puffing as it was forced open. The letter slid inside.

"That's it?" Maybe there was some magical spell that might help things along?

"Yep. Come on, let's get back. You're freezing, and a nice spot of tea will help that." He nodded back toward the direction of the office.

Giving the mailbox one last glance, I followed him. As soon as I did, there was the sound of crunching snow under someone else's feet, and it was coming from behind us. I turned, trying to locate the person, but saw nothing. But the crunching continued.

Off to the right, a shadow appeared on the snow as tracks pressed it down. More shadows appeared as the sound grew closer. The tracks became clearer as they walked toward the mailbox and then stopped.

The bottom of the box swung open and my single letter dropped onto the ground. It was lifted, as if by air. It then descended a few inches before it disappeared again, right around the height where a sack might be. The crunching of snow underfoot began again as the steps retreated off in the direction they'd come.

"Someone took my letter," I said to Zab, who'd stopped a few feet ahead of me, waiting.

"Yeah, I told you they would," he said, waving me along.

"This isn't working," I said. After mailing the letter to Loris earlier, I'd been a little more optimistic tonight. That had quickly come to an end.

Both couches were turned on their sides, so I dropped to the ground, perching my elbow on my knee and running my hand through my hair. We'd been at it for four hours, and it showed. There wasn't a piece of furniture still standing, and I felt like I'd been drawn and quartered. Failing at magic was very tiring.

"At least you got *that* right," Hawk said where he was leaning on an overturned couch, sipping a drink. I wasn't sure what he'd poured, but it didn't smell or look like coffee.

I wasn't sure if he was trying to be funny or just honest. It was the only thing I'd gotten right. It was as if my magic did the opposite of what I wanted. At one point, I'd even tried to *tell* it to do the opposite of what I wanted. It still hadn't worked.

Footsteps sounded from the office, which had been closed up long ago.

"I asked Oscar to come. You met him the night I tested you," Hawk said.

Oscar walked into the back room and stopped inside the door, taking in the place that appeared to have been vandalized.

"You weren't kidding when you said things weren't going well," Oscar said.

How many people had he told? It wasn't a secret, but I didn't want my failures broadcast, either.

"I only told him and asked him here because he might be able to help give us fresh eyes on the problem. I trust him," Hawk explained, as if he'd read my concerns.

When had we switched over to looks instead of words? Of all the people in the world, I'd never had that kind of relationship with anyone, not even my mother. Yet Hawk knew my mind without me saying a word? And why was it a one-way deal? I couldn't read his thoughts.

"What exactly is happening?" Oscar asked, stepping over a broken table as he walked farther into the room. "Clearly the outcome is bad, but what's happening to bring this about?"

"No matter where I aim my magic, it goes somewhere else," I said, wondering how I was going to clean up this mess later. It wasn't like Hawk hung around and helped.

"Do you mind?" Oscar asked. "I need to get a feel for what you've got working."

He held out his hand, as if to shake mine. I knew from Zab that this wasn't done in Xest. It was done all the time in Rest, so I didn't care.

I went to take his hand, but Hawk said, "No. That won't be needed. We both know it's not how much magic she has."

Oscar dropped his hand. "Is she consistent?"

"Very."

Oscar reached down, picked up a teacup that had managed to survive thus far, and placed it on the side of the couch. "Push this off the couch."

How many times was I going to have to fail today?

"One more time," Hawk said.

I hated when he answered my unasked questions.

I slumped, turning back to the couch. "It's nothing personal, Oscar. It's just the same thing we've done over and over."

I tried to throw the teacup off the couch, the last unbroken one in the room and my personal favorite. The only thing that made it better was my confidence that I wouldn't break it. I flicked my wrist, and the table on the other side of the room lifted a few feet off the ground before dropping.

"And you were focusing on the teacup?" Oscar asked.

"Yes." Clearly, Oscar had no answers either.

"That's so odd," Oscar said.

"So, no ideas?" Hawk asked.

Oscar's cheeks puffed out a bit as he blew out air. "None you don't already know," he said, rocking back on his heels.

"I'm not looking to do that," Hawk said.

"But you might get answers."

"The idea alone irritates me."

Oscar shrugged. "I don't have anything else, then." He waved his hand toward me. "I've never seen this before."

"I'll see you out," Hawk said.

Oscar tipped his head toward me before he left.

I heard the door shut and waited to hear a single set of footsteps walking back. There weren't any. He'd left me here with the mess alone again.

The couches were flipped, and the table might've been broken. Smashed pottery and china. The bookcase was too heavy to lift alone.

I moved to pick up a book, and had nowhere to put it. I let it drop to the ground with a thud. Maybe if Hawk had to deal with the mess, he'd realize his way wasn't working out finally. Something I knew all too well.

Screw it. He could deal with it for once.

18

I walked downstairs, fearing the dirty looks I'd get for trashing the back room and leaving it a mess. In hindsight, I wished I'd cleaned it up. A couple hours of cleaning wasn't worth losing Zab and Musso's friendship, but that option was gone. Now I'd have to suck it up and hope they took apologies better than Belinda.

I paused at the door, feeling like I was about to start flapping my wings and squawking. Nothing to be done but to deal with it now.

I walked in and braced myself. Zab greeted me with his usual smile, Musso with his normal grunt, and Belinda with her typical avoidance of my life form. I was still being acknowledged by two out of three. That was good. Maybe I could go clean it now and no harm done?

I went into the back room and everything was already back to order. This was so much worse. They'd cleaned it while I'd slept. Without bothering with my normal coffee, I walked back into the office, still stunned they'd smiled at me after cleaning up that mess.

"I'm so sorry about the back room. Did it take you a

while to clean?" I focused my attention on Musso and Zab because Belinda certainly hadn't taken part.

Zab leaned back in his chair. "What do you mean? We didn't clean anything."

I turned to Musso. Unlikely, but it couldn't have been Belinda.

"I don't clean," he said, and went back to work.

Could it have been Belinda? If she'd cleaned it, I was really going to have to apologize, even if she didn't acknowledge me at all while I did it.

I glanced her way. She stared back at me like she smelled rotten milk.

Yeah, not her.

"It was probably the cleaning crew," Zab said. "Hawk must be paying them extra. They were leaving as we came in. I was wondering why they were grumbling so loudly and working so late."

"There's a cleaning crew?" My mouth dropped open. How had I not figured that out? That was how my clothes kept getting cleaned. "And Hawk lets them? I thought he was weird about who was here overnight."

"They're sprites. Totally different," Zab said, as if I should realize this.

"Then why did you help me clean the other day?" I asked.

Belinda started laughing so hard that she nearly bent over. "You've been cleaning, you idiot?"

I didn't bother asking her why she'd had me clean the office. I knew that answer.

Zab cleared his throat, drawing my attention back to him. "I thought you liked doing that, being from Rest. I've heard that some Resters like to straighten up their homes. It's a thing with them, nesting or something."

"Well, it's good that there's a cleaning crew." I tried to sound as pleasant about it as possible. Hard to do when you found out you'd been killing yourself for nothing.

Belinda was still laughing, and I could see Zab's lips start to curl up. If this were a different situation, I might've found it funny too. If I didn't want to go home so bad, if I knew my friend wasn't rotting away in a factory, if Loris wasn't probably worried sick, I might've laughed with them.

But today, I didn't have it in me.

"I've got to go run an errand. I'll be back soon," I said, grabbing my jacket, not caring what Hawk said about staying in. I was so done with this place that if I didn't get out of here for a little while, I was going to burn down the building.

"Tippi, I'm sorry. I didn't—"

"It's okay, really. I just need to do something."

"Just let the crybaby go," Belinda said.

I walked past her, my fists balled as I tried to keep them at my sides.

The wind blew through the narrow streets as I kept my hood up and my head down, avoiding eye contact.

Hawk was right. I didn't need any more attention after what happened the last time I ran errands.

I walked until I got to the factory and then kept walking like I was supposed to be there. With my head up high, I made my way to the dandelion room, passing the other tables of witches and warlocks. They watched me with a skeptical eye. Rabbit was sitting at a table by herself and hadn't noticed me yet, and it tore up my insides like I'd swallowed a bottle of acid. I was so busy feeling bad for myself, and she was still stuck here. I had to get her out. I didn't know how, but I had to.

I saw one of the other witches get up from the table and

head to the door. She might've been going to the bathroom or something, but I had a feeling my time was limited. I took the seat beside Rabbit, who finally turned around.

"Tippi!" She was all genuine smiles and grey skin, looking like she'd aged ten years in the last week. "Are you back?"

"No. I wanted to see you and tell you I didn't forget about you. I'm trying to figure something out."

"I can't believe you came back here just to tell me that."

She really couldn't, and it made it that much worse. I should've been fighting to get her out of here every day, but I was going to make it right.

I leaned forward. "I'm not leaving here without you. That's not some bullshit I'm spewing, either. It's a promise."

"There's no way, but I appreciate you trying. I really do."

"What are you doing here?" Mertie's shrill tone carried across the room.

My gut had been right. They'd run and tattled as soon as I walked in.

"I'll be back for you soon," I said, before standing and facing Mertie. "I was in the area, so I figured I'd say hello. I'm done now." I turned to the door and walked, making it clear I was done with her.

"Don't come back," she said as I walked past her.

"Why are you staring at the factory as if you want to be back in there? Why are you out of the office at all?"

I jumped, not expecting someone to be talking to me, let alone Hawk.

I shrugged and began walking back to the office. "Of course I don't want to go back, but I made a friend there. As to why? It was either leave your office or commit murder."

"Hmmm" was all I got as he began walking back with me.

I didn't expand on my homicidal inclinations, and luckily, he didn't ask. He probably didn't want to hear about his girlfriend.

Although if he did, he'd hear me better than usual. The typical distance between us, which used to be three or four feet, had shrunk to one or two. While I did have favorable proximity, there was something we needed to hash out, and it couldn't wait anymore.

"My friend's not doing well. I need to get her out."

"That might be possible at some point, but I've other concerns right now." He didn't slow his pace.

"She's running out of time."

He continued to walk.

I double-timed it until I was standing in front of him, arms crossed and ready to do battle. "What if I made it part of our deal? Then could you work it in?"

He stared at me with a look of such condemnation that I nearly took a step back. I held my ground anyway. This had to be done.

He dipped his chin. "You've lived as a human for too long. Our deal is set and can't be changed. I bought out the price of your contract. You're lucky I gave you any concessions."

Bought and paid for. The mere mention of it made me want to scream and run.

He picked me up by my waist and moved me to the side.

I watched him walk away, deciding I wasn't ready to go back to the office anymore. He continued walking, not looking back.

It didn't matter if he said no. I'd find a way to get her out, and soon. Rabbit was not dying in that place.

19

I was sitting in the back room with my second cocoa of the day. The extra sugar was feeding my adrenaline in a way that didn't bode well for Hawk—whenever he decided to show, that was.

Hawk walked into the back room with a purpose. Something was up. Today wouldn't be the usual routine of me trying to work my magic and him yelling at me because I couldn't.

"Come on. We're going somewhere." As usual, he made demands and expected me to follow blindly.

"No. We aren't practicing today?" Something I'd dreaded all day suddenly seemed better than the unknown he was about to take me to. This place had way too many unknowns for my liking. For a girl that had lived a predictable life for the last couple of years, being yanked back into chaos at every turn was unsettling.

When I didn't move fast enough, he grabbed my jacket off the hook and tossed it to me.

"We need to go see someone." He moved toward the door.

For a split second, I thought about grilling him about our meeting. Then I thought back to what I was planning on doing tomorrow, the idea I'd come up with after I left the factory, and decided I was going to need as much goodwill as possible. Probably more.

There was a well-known saying: it's easier to beg for forgiveness than to ask for permission. I wasn't quite confident that the amount of forgiveness I was going to be begging for existed inside Hawk's heart of stone. But maybe there would be enough soft and mushy in that chest to stop him from killing me.

He was already a couple of buildings away by the time I walked outside. People scattered like fish in a shark tank as he approached. It seemed that in Xest, even the devil might've crossed the street if he saw Hawk coming. That should've given me even more pause about my plans, but the way I saw it, I had no choice.

"Who are we going to visit?" I asked as I caught up, sounding as pleasant as I could. He needed a reminder that I was a nice person who shouldn't be killed.

"A scholar of sorts. Someone who might be able to shed some light on why your magic isn't working the way it should."

He was back to walking almost four feet ahead of me, and it wasn't because he was making sure the path ahead was safe. Nope, it was because I'd pissed him off today with my deal renegotiations. If *that* gained me an extra foot or two, there were big problems to come.

"What if I don't have good magic? Maybe you should accept that whatever it is you need, I can't do it and you should let me go." Letting me go would be much better than killing me, the way he was going to want to after tomorrow.

"It's not going to happen, so stop asking."

At least he didn't sound annoyed. More determined. *Tomorrow* annoyance might be my best-case scenario.

"Why are you so sure?" I'd never been sure of anything in my life, which made sense when your mother was saying things that were totally insane and the world was saying something different. Who knew insanity would win out in the end? Either way, that kind of childhood didn't breed an overly confident adult.

"Because I am. Finders are almost a hundred percent accurate."

And here he was, in the face of mounting failures, enough that I was convinced I was a total failure, absolutely positive I was the person he needed for his big spell—or thing, or whatever it was. Sometimes I was in awe of his confidence. Sometimes I wished I could take a sledge-hammer to it so he was as messed up as me.

"How accurate? You said *almost*. What amount aren't accurate?" I did a little jog to catch up to his longer stride, closing the gap that would surely appear again as soon as he noticed.

"I don't have scientific data on it, but I guess about one percent."

"What if I'm that one percent?"

"When they're not accurate, it's user error. I don't make errors like that." He stopped abruptly and turned, moving his hand to my neck, his fingers grazing my skin, sending a little tingle through me as he confirmed my necklace was on. "Don't take that off unless I tell you to," he said, and then continued to walk.

I hated when he touched me. Mostly because I *liked* it when he touched me. And I hated that I liked it. It wasn't that he was such a horrible person that I should be revolted. He didn't seem *that* bad. I wouldn't say he was that great, either, or he'd be helping me get Rabbit out. It was a combination of everything.

He was probably still messing around with Belinda, which was wholly unappealing. Plus, he and this entire place were too crazy, and crushing on him would be insanity. So if he could stop touching me and reminding my body that it liked it, things would be much better. I needed to adopt his three-foot-buffer rule. And why was it that he seemed to be the only person in Xest that didn't have a weird aversion to touching?

And why was I even dwelling on him? I had much bigger issues.

"Does this have anything to do with what Oscar mentioned last night?"

"Yes," he said.

"But you didn't want to do that." If Hawk didn't think it was a good idea, I might absolutely hate it. Obviously, there had to be some drawback here, or we would've tried this sooner.

"It's not that I didn't want to go to him. I don't like the cost of what going to him will be."

I stopped walking. Cost? I was already stuck here because of debt. I wasn't getting farther in the hole and never getting out of this place. "Hold up a second."

He turned around and saw my feet glued to the ground. "What?" he asked, his tone as chilly as the weather.

I tried not to take it too personally, annoyed it bothered me at all. Clearly, whatever we were doing was making him not happy, so how was I supposed to be enthused?

"What's the cost that's so bad you don't want to go? I don't have anything. As it is, I'm basically an indentured servant."

He began walking again. "It won't cost you anything.

And if we're going to get technical, you're not *basically* an indentured servant. You *are* an indentured servant."

There was humor in his voice, as if he found my lousy situation funny. Glad he'd gotten his good mood back.

"My life is not a joke," I said, watching him walk.

It didn't take him long to figure out that I wasn't following. He walked a few more steps before turning again. "If we don't figure this out, you're never getting home and you'll die an indentured servant."

I didn't like how amused he still seemed, but I did start walking. I was not having "Tippi, the best indentured servant there ever was" on my headstone.

We got to the farthest point of Xest I'd been so far, past even the mailbox, to a building sitting all on its own. It was made of black stone. The windows were all closed, and there was a large knocker on the front door in the shape of a skull, which Hawk used to announce us. I already didn't like this place or whomever was inside it. What was wrong with having a lion head, like a normal person?

A window on the door slid open.

"We need to see Jasper."

Jasper? That was a solid, normal name. Maybe this meeting would be somewhat normal too?

The set of eyes narrowed on Hawk, then on me, before returning to Hawk.

"He's not happy with you," the man behind the door said.

"I'm aware. I also know he'll still see me, so open up."

The man's eyes turned beady, and I heard a snarl. Then he turned his head, as if someone had called him.

Hawk smiled as he turned back to me. The window closed and then the door opened.

The man who opened the door was only two feet tall

and definitely not all human, from the looks of the ears that were as tall as his head and slightly floppy at the tips. If he had any other abnormalities, it was hard to tell under the thick coat he wore. The inside of the door was lined with a ladder, explaining how he'd gotten up to the window.

The place was like walking into a cave and got even worse after the door shut. Nope, nothing normal about this meeting so far. Should've known.

Hawk closed his hand over mine, the sizzle of his magic meeting my own where we touched, building warmth. Did he feel it too? He was probably only holding on to me because he was afraid I'd run, but there was something very intimate about touching hands with him in the dark.

I need to stop having thoughts about intimacy with him.

I focused on death and dismemberment instead. It was safer that way. As he guided me along with him, I picked up the occasional change in shadows, from pitch-black, to very, very dark. It gave the impression of hallways as we continued to walk. I imagined monsters coming to get me so I didn't focus on how warm and big his hands were.

He stopped walking, and I heard the sound of a large door opening. Finally there was some light. A smattering of candles about a smallish room and a fireplace on the far wall.

Another small man sat in a small chair beside the stone mantel. A gnome, maybe? Was that what they were? Or dwarves? Wait, they lived in stone. Was that a troll? Were trolls big or little? I wish I'd played more fantasy games before I ended up here. I would've been much more prepared for Xest.

Whatever Jasper was, troll, gnome, elf, he was an irritated one. "Can't believe you'd show your face after you failed me on that last job."

"You wouldn't pay the price," Hawk said, with a tone that promised we might be out of here soon if the topic didn't change.

"Because you didn't negotiate it well enough," Jasper said, pointing a bulbous finger with a pointy nail.

"No one works for free."

Jasper sneered and then looked at me. "Who is she? Is this the Whimsy witch they're all talking about?" He leaned closer, large nostrils flaring.

"Before I tell you, I'm enacting absconditum juramentum."

Jasper lifted the corner of his lip and growled. He was little, but he looked scrappy. I edged closer to Hawk.

"What's that?" I asked.

Jasper answered for him. "He's screwing me. He's binding me to secrecy if I accept his terms. Which, of course, I do accept."

There was a flash of light in the room as soon as he said the word *accept*.

"There. It's binding. Now what is the secret? What's up with your Whimsy witch here? She's not throwing off any kind of serious magic that I can feel." He was sniffing around me again.

Hawk motioned toward me. "Take off your necklace." He looked at me as if trying to reassure me this was the right move.

I put my hand to the stone where it hung underneath my shirt. Jasper's greedy little eyes roved over me, and I paused.

I toyed with the chain at my neck as I glanced at Hawk. "That's definitely binding, right?"

"Yes. He's sworn." He turned back to Jasper, as if reminding him of the oath.

If Jasper needed a reminder this fast, was this such a good idea?

"Your little witch here doesn't completely trust you. Does she know what you are, Hawk? Or are her instincts that good?" Jasper asked, then snickered.

His goading wasn't helping my confidence much, but it did drive me to take the necklace off. I might not trust Hawk completely, but I liked him a lot more than the little jerk in front of me.

"I know exactly what he is, and he has all my faith. It's you I don't trust." It might've been the most convincing I'd ever lied. Probably because it didn't matter what Hawk might be hiding. He was my way out of this place. He was Rabbit's way out as well, even if he didn't know yet. Hopefully nothing would change after tomorrow.

I dragged the thin chain upward, my pendant of coal snagging on my shirt before it popped out. Hawk held out his hand for the necklace.

The second it was out of my hands, Jasper gasped, circling me. "Her magic is chaotic and beautiful. So pretty. It lights up like the sun going supernova."

If I was lighting up, he was the only one seeing it. The room was barely lit and hadn't changed.

As Jasper did his second lap around me, I shot Hawk a look that made it clear there would be grave repercussions if this came back to bite me in the ass. What those repercussions were weren't clear, but they'd be fierce, especially if I had a supernova going off inside me.

He raised an eyebrow, silently asking what I'd do. If we weren't on the same side right now, I would've hated him.

"What can she do?" Jasper asked, circling me again, reaching out as if he were touching my glow that wasn't there.

"Nothing good," I said, owning it before I had to hear it from Hawk.

"That's the problem. We aren't altogether sure. We can't figure out her aptitude," Hawk said, in a much kinder way than anticipated.

Our problem was a little worse than not being able to figure out my aptitude. I glanced at him again, not so angry this time.

He nodded.

"I have to feel the energy," Jasper said.

I held my hand out. If I wanted to get out of Xest, we needed answers. The parade of failures was tiring.

Whatever wrapped around me didn't look like the same hand that I could see. It felt like bones and a claws poking gently into my skin. So, another one who wasn't what it seemed.

Jasper shivered, or his body at least appeared to. What was visible didn't seem to be the same as what might've been truly there.

"So much magic here. So very much." He closed his eyes and squeezed my hand. His head dropped back as he asked, "Did you test her with a gem? What color did she shine?"

"Every color. It was like watching a kaleidoscope."

Jasper dropped my hand immediately. The amazed and enthralled expression turned to lower brows and an open jaw, a look of horror crossing his face as he eyed me and then Hawk.

"That's abhorrent."

"I'm aware it's rare, but I wouldn't say 'abhorrent.'" Hawk stepped closer until he was partially in between me and Jasper.

"No, I'm telling you it is. She is." Jasper moved to the

door and held it wide. "It's time for you to go." He left the door open and stepped farther away.

"No. I need answers. You already accepted the deal." Hawk stepped closer to him instead of retreating.

"I'll keep my sworn secrecy and will decline payment. Now you need to go. I can't help you," Jasper said, glancing at Hawk but then training his eyes on me, as if I were the true monster in the room. He took another step back and began chanting in a weird tongue, making signals in front of his chest.

Hawk stepped closer, hovering over him. "What do you know?"

"Nothing other than that's evil and you must leave." Jasper swallowed as he looked at me.

"If you say a word to anyone..."

"I won't. Under the terms of the oath, you need to leave," Jasper said, and then launched into his strange chanting, like it would protect him from whatever I was.

Hawk let out a breath, as if Jasper had just pulled a trump card he couldn't argue.

"Come on," Hawk said to me, motioning to the door. Jasper watched as I moved, afraid I'd lunge for him at the last moment or something.

"Thanks?" I didn't mind leaving. I would've liked to have left under normal circumstances, though, and not like Jasper was exorcising the devil, which he believed was me.

We didn't talk until we were back outside and Hawk stopped me, putting my necklace back over my head. I'd forgotten he had it.

I tucked it in my shirt, using that as an excuse not to look at him as I said, "He looked at me like I was a serial killer. What's so bad about a rainbow? You don't think a rainbow is bad, right? I mean, it's a rainbow. Rainbows are happy— unicorns and pots of gold and stuff."

"I come because Jasper sometimes sees things others don't. Good and bad are relative, and Jasper isn't always reliable. I don't come here for moral advice."

And what Jasper saw in me was evil. Echoes of a life I wanted to forget haunted my mind, and words echoed in my ears, in my head, and worse, in my heart. What if it were true? What if Jasper was right? What if everything *she* ever said was true?

I began walking back toward the office, leading the way for once. I needed to be alone where I could sort this out or shake it off. Find a neat little place to lock it away and never think about it again.

I felt his hand on my arm, stopping me. I didn't fight him, but I didn't turn back around as I felt him close in.

"Tippi, you might be many things, but I know evil. You're not." His hand was still holding me there.

I nodded, and neither of us moved for a few seconds.

"You're not scared of me, right?"

When he didn't answer, I finally looked up at him. "Do I appear to be frightened?" His tone couldn't have been flatter if I'd pounded it with a mallet for the last hour.

Relief surged through me. It might've been unfounded relief, considering everyone seemed afraid of him. Maybe he was more of a monster than I was. Either way, I'd take what I could get and cling to it. If Hawk didn't think I was evil, maybe I wasn't.

I laughed a little, realizing how badly I'd let that small creature rattle me.

"You know, I wasn't thrilled about being a witch. Now that Jasper thinks I'm an evil monster, a witch doesn't seem so bad."

"That does seem to be the way things work," he said, and then resumed walking.

Whatever strange connection we had seemed to pass. Except as we walked, and he took the lead, he was back to only about a foot away. Not so bad.

"So where does that leave us now?" I asked.

"No better and no worse."

He might have felt no worse, but I wasn't going to shake off that meeting as easily. Jasper, the one who saw things, saw evil. The one Hawk thought might have answers feared to be near me. Maybe I wasn't evil but my magic was? That was why, no matter what I did, I ended up destroying things when we practiced.

Maybe *she'd* known my magic was evil all along. They say no one knows you like your parents. That was why she went through such lengths to block what I was.

Did I tell him that my magic might be bad? Then what? Convince him so entirely of my evil nature that he tried to kill me? We might be on the same side right now, but only a fool would trust that it would always be that way.

I continued to walk until we were just a few paces from the office when Hawk stopped again.

"Tippi, don't let what Jasper said get into your head."

"Sure. No problem."

From his expression, I was certain my newfound skill at lying had disappeared.

20

The office was closed for the day. No one was around. This was it. This was the time. Maybe if I had someone else to run the idea by, they'd tell me not to do it but I couldn't talk to Zab. He was too close to Hawk. Belinda hated me. Musso seemed the type that would kill me himself if he thought something was wrong with me. There was only one person I could turn to here—Rabbit. And she was the one I was doing this for, so that wasn't an option.

I looked at the newsflash papers sitting on the counter. In the last few days, I'd seen Zab, Belinda, and Musso all use them to summon someone who could do a specific job. It hadn't been a big deal.

Well, I needed something, so I was going to send a newsflash. I was magical, and even though my magic might be temperamental, chaotic—*evil*—it seemed I had a lot of it, and this was very simple. And Zab had mentioned in passing that no one ignored a newsflash memo from the broker. No one.

I was going to do this. I had to do this. If I didn't get

Rabbit out of there, at least for a little while, she'd die. She was not dying. Not on my watch.

I grabbed a piece of paper from the ones they used, the ones I'd picked up, and jotted down my info, just like they had numerous times. The only thing I didn't do was add a name to the bottom, as they usually did. But what if that had to be there? Like the postal service and a return address thing? Maybe it wouldn't send without one?

To sign or not to sign? What to sign? If I used my name, they might laugh it off. I couldn't do Hawk's. I wasn't willing to push it that far. I wanted them to assume it came from him, but forging his signature? No, that was way over the line. *But* a "representative of the broker" was accurate. It would have to be good enough.

I held it up and examined it for problems. It looked pretty good to me, not that I'd know an issue if I saw it. I folded the paper, folded it again, then again, the way I'd seen the others do. I walked to the front door and peeked through the glass for pedestrian traffic. As soon as the street had a lag, I swung the door open fast.

"Carry my message," I said, tossing the note in the air.

The thing burst into an eagle that nearly spanned the width of the street. It was so big that I ducked. Then a loud pop, followed by a flash. Well, I'd done something, all right.

A man had just turned the corner, and he was staring right at me. Dammit.

I didn't wave or acknowledge the attention. I swung the door shut with nothing left to do but wait to see if Rabbit would arrive.

The first person who showed five minutes later was the last person I wanted to see right now.

Hawk stormed inside the office, and it was immediately

clear that he already knew something by the way he stalked over to me.

"What did you do? It's Offday. Can I not leave you here alone one day of the week?"

Oh no. This was not good. Not good at all. I might've fessed up to what I'd done, but I wasn't sure what that was yet. It wasn't as if my magic was predictable. I was better off waiting to see what he *told* me I'd done. Maybe it wouldn't be that bad?

"I didn't even leave the building." Technically, I hadn't. I'd leaned out of it, but my feet had remained squarely within the threshold.

I edged toward the front door, in case running was going to be needed. I tried to go around him, but he blocked my path.

"You might not have left the building, but you did set off a newsflash from here," he said.

I dodged right, and he followed. I dodged left, and he caught me about the waist, hoisted me onto the nearby table, and then kept me there with a hand on either side.

"What did you do?" he asked.

He was leaning over me, but instead of being intimidated, I felt my stomach getting all squirrely, and my eyes kept going to his lips, as I wondered what it would be like if he kissed me. I'd had a few kisses in my life. None were that good. I'd lost my virginity to a boy that I hadn't liked very much in an effort to get the deed done. I'd never gotten flutters like I did with Hawk.

He was making me so nervous that it was worse than if he was threatening me with violence. Maybe he was threatening me with violence and I hadn't noticed it?

I looked to the floor and kept my gaze there so I'd stop

looking at his face, my skin burning, afraid he'd read these thoughts too. I had no business being curious about him in that way. None. Now I needed to convince my libido of that as well.

"Tippi, what did you do?" He lifted my chin, making it impossible to look anywhere else.

I shrugged. "I mean, I might've sent some correspondence." This way, as I blushed, which I feared from the heat might've been happening, he'd think it was from guilt. That was much better than the truth.

"Correspondence that went off in the middle of the center, demanding Rabbit's immediate presence in the shop or else?" he asked.

I licked my lips as I thought about how to answer that. When I'd scribbled my message, I didn't think everyone would hear it. That wasn't the way it typically worked, from my understanding. I thought it would appear in Marvin's office and prompt him to send Rabbit here.

Now Hawk was staring at my lips, probably because I was biting the lower one as I tried to figure out what to say.

"I didn't think it was going to be that big of a thing." My skin was flushed even worse, and this time it was definitely from some measure of guilt.

His hand grazed my leg. Did he know we were touching? I wished I wasn't so aware. Made it damned hard to concentrate on my latest screw-up.

"You don't understand. I was in a shop off the center when it went off. Word is going to spread that it wasn't me who set it. No one else that works here is strong enough to send out a newsflash that large. You didn't just send a message that you wanted Rabbit to come. You sent a message to everyone in Xest that you have massive amounts of power. The ramifications of what you did are going to be widespread. It's going to have implications even after you return to Rest."

His arms were outstretched on either side of me as he dipped his head.

"It can't be that bad, right?" I said, resisting the urge to run my fingers through his hair. I still wasn't sure what had gone so wrong for him to look this frustrated, but I had to grip the wood of the table to stop from touching him.

"It's done. We'll handle the ramifications." He straightened and then stepped away from me. He ran his hands through his hair as he came to terms with my latest screw-up.

It was probably a little late to ask now, but his words were really sinking in. I crossed my ankles, swinging them to and fro. The deeper his words sank, the faster my legs swung. "What kind of ramifications are we talking about, exactly?"

"Hard to say, but you're not going to be able to go back to Salem. You'll have to go somewhere else. Too many people are catching on to what you might be. A Whimsy witch disappearing wouldn't cause much notice. After the shop incidents, it was bad, but nothing concrete. Now, you might as well have sent out a memo to everyone in Xest stating you're anything but a Whimsy witch. They'll never leave you alone."

My swinging legs came to a complete halt as I gripped the table so hard that it should've splintered. "I can't go back to Salem?"

"You'll have to go somewhere no one knows about."

"I don't understand. Who would bother me? I have zero idea what I'm doing. Everything I touch goes wrong."

There was almost a look of pity on his face at my ignorance. "You were dragged here when they thought you could do almost nothing. You think now that they know you have real power, they'll let you go?"

"You mean Marvin?"

"No. Marvin is nothing. There are others I'm worried about—but you'll find out soon enough."

"You mean that Raydam person?" I jumped off the table. This was definitely a standing conversation. From the sounds of it, it might even progress into a pacing one. Hopefully we wouldn't get as far as a "screaming and running for my life" talk, but it was within the realm of what I was hearing.

"He's only the beginning of the problems you stirred up with your latest decision."

There was a flash of movement right before Rabbit came charging into the office. She had a bag slung over her shoulder and a big smile on her face. At least with her, I'd done the right thing, hopefully.

She dropped her bag and hugged me. That was a big thing from someone from Xest who didn't touch. Then she turned to Hawk, arms outstretched. "Thank you, thank you, thank you!"

He took a step back before she could get her arms around him. "Don't thank me. I did nothing."

"You called for me?" she asked, the smile starting to fall as panic replaced it.

"I called for you," I said, smiling and nodding, trying to convince her that everything was still good. She was not going back. The damage was done now, but it would not be for nothing.

She paused for a moment, squinting slightly. "You did that?"

I nodded, feeling suddenly self-conscious.

"How?"

I shrugged. "I'm not sure, but you're here, and that's all that matters, right?"

It didn't take more than another second for her to snap back to normal. She wrapped her arms around me again as I wondered what I was going to have to do, if there was anything I could do, that would persuade Hawk to let her stay. She wouldn't be going back, no matter what I had to do.

I looked over Rabbit's shoulder to Hawk, who stood behind her.

Please, I mouthed. I'd start off nice, but I wasn't afraid to dig in if needed.

He didn't move an inch. It was long enough to feel steel harden my spine. He couldn't make her leave. I'd walk out right beside her and we'd see what happened. This was my line in the sand, or snow, as that was all that was available here.

Rabbit backed up a bit, looking at both of us and sensing the mounting tension in the room.

Hawk had said everyone had a price. I'd found mine. He wanted to keep torturing me every night with failure? Wanted my full cooperation? This was what I needed. "Our discussion the other night? This is my price."

He crossed his arms, measuring me. "I already paid yours," he said.

"Are you sure about that?" We both knew he hadn't, not really. I'd been biding my time, waiting for an out. I had a feeling that when the truth of what he really wanted from me came to light, there might need to be further negotiations. If he was smart, which I knew he was, he'd take this deal now.

He dipped his chin, staring me dead in the eye for a few tense seconds.

"Give her the room to the right of yours," he said.

"There's a room beside mine?"

"There is now." He nodded in Rabbit's direction. "Get her settled, but be ready in a half-hour. We've got work to do."

I grabbed Rabbit's hand and dragged her after me before he changed his mind.

21

Rabbit ran a hand along the wall as she followed me up the stairs.

"I can't believe you're really living here."

"You are too now, so don't sound so in awe." Coming from the factory and barracks, it was a step up, until she met Belinda. Rabbit might rethink her opinion after that.

"I am living here," she said, as if she couldn't quite believe it.

I glanced over my shoulder, smiling. "Still a lot of awe. Trust me, it's not all good."

"Yeah, I live in the broker building. No big deal," she said, swallowing back any awe she might've wanted to inject.

We made it to the platform outside my door, and there were now two doors. He'd said the room to the right, so my bedroom door had shifted left somehow. By the time I was used to this place, I was going to be gone.

Her room was exactly half the size my room was, or used to be, probably. It had the same setup, bed, and fireplace. She'd even gotten a bathroom that looked like it would've backed up to mine. I guessed even magic tried to use the easiest plumbing accommodation.

She walked in, and then spun around, taking in every little detail. "This is amazing. Is he really going to let me stay?"

I grabbed her half-empty bag and tossed it on the chest of drawers.

"He's going to let you stay. He wouldn't say it if he didn't mean it." I sat down on her bed as she touched everything in the bedroom, from the chest, to the walls, to the window. I bounced a little. The mattress felt exactly like mine.

"So what do you do here all day? Is there a job for me?"

I ran down the details of my normal day, including the practice for something yet to be determined.

"You don't know what you're practicing for?" she asked, finally done with her tour.

"He hasn't laid out all the details yet." I didn't even know the details and I'd committed. Before, I'd felt more tricked. Now I was in *this*, and I wasn't even sure what *this* truly was. I should've asked some more questions, but with Rabbit right beside me, smiling away...

Yeah, it was done now.

"So then...you're not really a Whimsy witch?" she asked.

"Turns out I'm not." Most witches would've been thrilled to say they weren't a Whimsy, and yet I was finding it hard to get the words out.

She sat on the bed staring at me. "What are you?"

"I don't know." Boy, was that the truth. I had no idea. I had magic, but it never worked right. Jasper called me evil. Nothing seemed to be going according to anyone's plan, least of all mine. Yeah, I was a big question mark at this point.

"But you really sent *that* newsflash?" She was staring at me like she was seeing me for the first time.

"I did." The way she said "*that* newsflash" made me wonder what had gone off. I might've asked if she wasn't staring at me like one of the witches at the factory who were cruel to her. "But it doesn't mean anything. We're still friends."

"Are you sure?"

"I don't care how much magic you have. *You're* my friend."

She nodded but still appeared to fear I'd wake up tomorrow and tell her all bets were off.

I glanced at the clock, also identical to mine, beside her bed. "I've got to get downstairs, but I'll come hang out as soon as I'm done, okay?"

At that point, I'd reassure her another ten times if needed. Right now, I had to go keep Hawk from kicking us both out.

I walked into the back room and something flew at me. I caught it, and the gem blazed in my hand. I'd begun leaving my necklace upstairs before practice after the last time I'd had to dig around in chipped porcelain to find it.

The same fiery rainbow of light shot out of it, like my fingertips were an electrical outlet.

"You're going to get calls soon," Hawk said, sitting on the couch and looking over at me. "When they do, I want you to go. But it's best if you can smother some of your magic. You need to learn to hold it in for at least a minute or so, at the bare minimum, so when they touch you, you don't broadcast how strong you are."

"Why can't I wear my necklace?" I asked, tossing the gem back to him. He didn't catch it, letting it drop to the couch beside him, robbing me of an opportunity to see what his magic did to it, which was surely not accidental.

"The person you're most likely to hear from is Raydam. If you were to say I had any opposition in Xest, he would be the ringleader of them. If you wear the necklace, he'll sense something off the moment he touches you, as I did. Considering the talk, he'll know there's something more."

I thought back to the first time I'd had skin-to-skin contact with Hawk, the day outside the factory.

"How did you sense it?" I asked, wondering if I'd get an honest answer out of him, or any answer at all.

He waved his hand to the other couch. I took the opportunity, hoping he was going to share, because as I remembered again, I was in this. It would be good to know as much as I could.

"The stronger the magic in a person, the more they can sense it in others. Raydam is one of the strongest warlocks in Xest."

Why was it that everything I found out ended up being bad? Couldn't I stumble upon good information every now and then? "Is he stronger than you?"

He smiled. "Not important at the moment."

The one thing I did know? The man before me might've had more secrets than all of Xest, and he guarded them fiercely. In a world of magic and oddities, most worn like badges, what was he keeping so undercover? Asking him was a waste of time, and maybe it wasn't any of my business. But some things definitely were.

I crossed my legs and rested my arm on the back of the couch, trying my best to look nonchalant. "What exactly is it that you think I can do for you?" I grinned in a warm and friendly way.

He grinned back. "I told you. I don't know yet. When I figure it out, you'll be the first to know."

Neither of us said anything else for a moment as we measured each other up from our separate couches.

Fine. Maybe he really didn't know what he needed, but there were other details he could be sharing. "Why is Raydam your opposition? How worried should I be?"

"We don't see eye to eye on a lot of things. He likes to bring powerful witches and warlocks into his fold. If you want to be in the fold, then there would be nothing to be worried about."

Into the fold. I'd never liked that expression, because I had no desire to be folded by anyone. I was either going to lie flat or be crumpled in the corner, but it would be of my choosing.

Hawk never tried to bring me into the fold. As much as Hawk kept his secrets and his distance, it was better. Yes, definitely better. A clean break was all I wanted from this situation, and that was tough when you were busy trying to iron out creases. I was going to be out of here the second I could be without any creases to remind me, or as few as possible.

"What if I don't let him touch me?"

"He'll find a way to make skin-to-skin contact. If you snub all his attempts, it will be the same as telling him how much magic you have. He'll know."

"How much do I have to manage to hold back?"

"A lot."

I remembered the categories Rabbit had explained to me, waited to see if he'd label me. When he didn't, I didn't ask, because it wouldn't matter once I was out of here. It didn't matter now, either. The only thing I would use my magic for was to get home, and I couldn't do that.

I toyed with the seam on the back of the couch as a soft thud sounded beside me.

"Well? Are you going to try?" he said. "Unless you're looking to keep your options open."

I looked down at the gem lying beside me. Once again, he'd managed to avoid touching it while I could see him. I hadn't seen a flare of light, either. Did he use something to throw it, or did he turn the gem black like his heart?

"What do I do?" I asked, looking at it, knowing there were only two choices: blunt my magic or deal with even more people who wanted things from me.

Hawk leaned forward, his forearms resting on his knees. "Before you touch it, imagine all the energy in your hand is gone, numb. The further you can shift it away from your hand, your wrist, even your lower arm, and hold it close to your core, the better."

I held the gem, focusing on pulling my magic back. The thing barely dulled. I dropped it back onto the couch. It was clear how tonight was going to go. Nothing I did magically went according to plan, ever. Maybe it was because I'd lived in Rest, or maybe I was too stupid. I didn't know, but it made me sure that I needed to get out of here. Nobody this bad at magic should be living in Xest.

"Try again," he said, not sounding any more optimistic than I felt.

I picked it up, knowing exactly what was going to happen. The thing might've been brighter. I dropped it onto the couch again and then stood, wanting to put some space in between me and my latest failure.

"We've barely started and you're taking a break?"

"I. *Am*." I moved to the window, crossed my arms, and

stared out at the alley instead of facing him. "We both know how this is going to go."

I expected him to rage and yell, tell me to sit back down and pick up the gem. That I was going to try all night until we both gave up.

Instead, he stood. "We'll try first thing tomorrow. Maybe you're tired."

Huh? I wasn't tired at all. In fact, I was as well rested as I'd been since I'd gotten here. The only fatigue I had was from failure.

Part of me wanted to call him out. Someone had plans and didn't want to share. The idea of five hours of being a loser changed my words to "Yeah, maybe after a good sleep."

A few minutes after Hawk walked out, I made my way upstairs. At least Rabbit was here. It was nice having another body in the building at night, someone I could go hang out with, talk to about my massive failures of the day.

It was still fairly early, but there weren't any lights shining underneath her door. I rapped softly, not wanting to wake her if she'd gone to sleep. No one answered. It was probably to be expected after what she'd been through. Might take her a few days to bounce back after the factory.

22

Rabbit was sipping the hot chocolate Zab had brought back from the Sweet Shop. She was wearing some of my hand-me-down clothes, since the only other things she had were factory uniforms. I'd given her the pick of my wardrobe, and she'd gone straight for the neon-green pants like it was her lucky day.

Belinda was even busier than normal today, having to split her glare between the two of us now, as if I'd multiplied in the middle of the night like a cockroach. Musso was his gruff self, with his lukewarm welcoming. All in all, it wasn't a bad introduction.

"What should I do?" Rabbit asked. "I want to earn my keep."

I grabbed her arm, pulling her into the back room as Belinda's eyes narrowed.

Rabbit's mouth dropped open and her eyes looked about to water. "Did I do something wrong?"

"No, not at all. I pulled you aside because you don't have to do anything. If you want to do something, that's different.

But even then, *don't ask in front of Belinda*. I told you about her." I'd spent a good chunk of the morning filling Rabbit in the best I could, the way I'd have wanted to be prepared for —well, mostly just for Belinda.

"But can I help if I want to?" Rabbit was studying my responses like her life depended on it.

"You can do whatever you want. But if you do help, ask Zab or Musso for stuff. Whatever you do, don't. Ask. Belinda. I think you've already been painted with the same brush because we're friends. She won't be nice."

Rabbit waved a hand, finally looking a little more relaxed. "I can handle hate. That I'm good at."

I walked back into the office and over to Zab. "Rabbit wants something to do. She should ask you, right?" I rubbed my neck as an excuse to point in Belinda's direction.

"Yes! Definitely ask me. I'm pretty sure Hawk told me I was in charge," Zab said, so loudly it was laughable. He turned to Rabbit. "Do you like to organize things? Or..." Zab's eyes went skyward as he tried to come up with something else.

"I can organize," Rabbit said. She waved toward the shelves. "Actually, I did happen to notice your books aren't in any order at all."

Huh? I'd organized them. What the hell was she talking about?

"Brilliant," Zab said. "I hadn't been able to figure out what Tippi did."

What the hell? Had no one heard of alphabetical order here? I didn't care enough to argue. I made my way to my table, knowing Rabbit had been spared Belinda.

Hawk walked into the office fifteen minutes later, barely glancing at Rabbit, who was waving at him in the midst of a pile of books she'd already pulled off the shelves. He stopped in front of the table I'd claimed as my own, evidenced by the little black cactus with a purple flower I'd found and the baskets I'd scavenged from other areas for my pass or shred piles.

"Back room," he said before walking away, completely ignoring my little setup.

That was it, and that was all I needed. I'd been dreading this moment since we'd quit last night. The normal Hawk had returned, the one who would want me to fail for hours on end and then ask me what I was doing, as if I knew. Guess what, Hawk? I didn't know! What came next was going to be a blaze of failure that would take up most of the day if I were lucky. Normally I wasn't tortured with my own inadequacies until after the office closed.

If I wasn't lucky, I'd be at it until late tonight, until the point that I could barely make it up the stairs from exhaustion. Failure had become such a foregone conclusion. My half-full glass had spilled all over the floor a week ago.

I walked past Belinda, who hated me even as I was being tortured, because I'd be spending time with Hawk. Yes, I'd be with Hawk, as he watched me in all my ineptness, failing, and failing again. Only a real psycho would be envious of me. Did she think this was enjoyable? Did she not understand I'd trade spots with her in a second?

Rabbit smiled and said, "Good luck," like she thought there was a chance in hell this would go well. I hadn't given her as many details on my magical failures as I had with the Belinda situation, but I'd told her enough that any optimism was wasted.

I stepped into the back room and saw the gem waiting on the table for me. Hawk stood, arms crossed, making it as clear as the finest crystal that the easygoing attitude of last night was over, a blip. Hawk the drill sergeant was back with gusto.

He gave me a look that didn't need any words. I took off my necklace and put it on the side table before picking up the gem. The thing lit up like I'd nuked it.

"Are you trying? We're running out of time. This should be simple. I'd thought we'd come to an arrangement," he said, looking to the door, reminding me of Rabbit's presence here and what he surely considered overpayment.

"Do you think I want to fail this much? Would anyone *possibly* want to fail this much? I'm *trying*." I didn't dare tell him that Zab was lighting the fire in my room every night. Or that he left a candle for me too.

If I wasn't so adept at destroying things unintentionally, I would've begun to think I was incapable of anything magical.

The more time that went by, the more I tried, the more I wondered if Jasper was right. Maybe my magic—or I—was evil. I shouldn't be doing anything with it. Maybe my mother had known too. It was clear she must've known about this place, at the very least. Maybe she'd lived here once and that was why she'd left and didn't want me to ever come? That was why I'd had to be hidden, had to live a life of lies. I might've appeared normal on the outside, but deep down, there was something wrong with me.

Hawk walked over and pointed at the gem. "If you were trying, it wouldn't be glowing."

My life had become a bad rerun. Failure was the only channel available, and I was the actor hired for the role who had to keep replaying the part. Forget that I'd already been paid. We needed to be canceled.

I put the stone down on the table. "You need to send me back."

There was a flicker in his eyes. I didn't know if it was anger or what, but it didn't matter. I was angry and past the point of worrying how he felt or what he'd do. I didn't care if he was going to kick me out into the cold. There had to be something better than this.

Instead of raging or getting mad, he walked closer. "You can do this."

His belief in my abilities in the face of repeated failures was bordering on lunacy.

"Maybe my magic is..." My words trailed off as Belinda walked in, making her way to the tea table.

"How's everything going?" She was all smiles and cheer, as if she didn't want to gut me and then salt my organ meat and store it in a dank basement for later feasting.

"It's fine," Hawk said.

She took her teacup and sipped daintily before asking, "Do you need any help? Is there anything I can do?"

"Actually, yes," Hawk said.

I looked at the floor, his shoes, my shoes, the wall, anywhere but at the two people talking. Was he really going to invite her in to witness my continual failure? Her? Of all people? That would be it. I'd walk out of here and be done. He'd have to drag me back in if he wanted me.

"Of course. What can I do?" she asked, so sickly sweet my stomach ached.

"Close the shop up early and send everyone home."

Don't smile. No one liked a gloater. I'd have to be secretly happy. Although I couldn't stop myself from glancing up to see the reaction.

She nodded, as if she weren't seething inside, and then took her tea and left.

The happiness and relief from that lasted a few seconds before it was time to deal with the truth again. I took another few steps closer to Hawk so that we were only a foot or so apart, in case Belinda was waiting outside listening. I was going to have to own it. I couldn't do what he wanted, and for a possibly bad reason. If he hadn't killed me when I called for Rabbit, he'd get over this too, hopefully.

"The thing is, maybe my magic is bad, like Jasper said. It's an evil thing that we shouldn't try to use. That might be the problem."

"I don't care what Jasper said." He nailed his stare to me. "It's not. *You're* not."

"You *don't* know." How could he be so sure? I wasn't. If I had to bet, I would've taken the other side of this one.

"I do."

There was a rap on the wall. Zab stood in the doorway, an awkward smile on his face, as if he didn't really want to interrupt.

"Hey, Belinda said we were closing, so why don't you take a break and let me give it a go? I might be able to work with her or explain things in a different way." Zab tucked his hands in his pockets.

"I'm game," I said, trying to encourage this. I doubted Zab was going to be able to do more than Hawk as far as making my magic work, but the bar was exceptionally low. And if I failed? He wouldn't lose his mind and accuse me of slacking.

"Fine. I'll be back in a few," Hawk said. He walked out, making me wonder if he was getting as exhausted as I was.

"Is Rabbit still working on the books?" I asked as Zab took Hawk's seat across from me.

"Nah, Rabbit said she wanted to go catch a nap."

More sleep? She'd gone to bed early and now already needed a nap?

"Did she seem okay?"

"Yeah, you know. Okay...enough." He was looking toward the door, and his foot was tapping a mile a minute. "We should get to work." He pointed to the gem sitting on the table.

If I asked anything else, I feared his foot might go through the floor.

I glanced at the gem, knowing I was going to fail. "I'm not sure you're going to be able to help me. I might be a lost cause."

His foot stopped tapping. At least he wasn't stressed about being part of my failure. "Just humor me. Hold the gem, and while you're doing it, focus on pulling everything inward."

There was no humor left in me. The constant failures had left me devoid of everything but wells of acid when I thought about failing again. Still, he was trying to help, so I picked up the gem. Every color of the rainbow shot out of the stone, and maybe a few I'd never seen before.

"Whoa, you really light that thing up," Zab said, leaning back and using his hand to shield his eyes. "Unusual pattern, too. I've never seen so many colors at once. I only shine lavender."

"Is that why you dye your hair that color?"

"I don't dye it. Sometimes the color of your magic leaks out in hair follicles. It's hereditary."

That was why so many people around here had weird hair colors.

"Are you focusing?" he asked.

"Sorry." I turned my attention back to the gem.

"Just focus. Imagine everything pulling back toward you. Like you're a black hole, sucking up all the light."

I did as he asked, pulling everything I had inward, toward me, imagining that I was sucking up everything into a small rock into the center of my chest.

The gem dimmed to about half lit.

"Ahh! I'm doing it!" I got up, jumping up and down.

"Yes, you are." Zab let out a little laugh, getting up with me. "I knew you could."

I stopped jumping, but kept staring at the gem, seeing if I could dim it a little more. It didn't seem to want to go lower, but that was okay. I officially hadn't failed.

Zab was still chuckling, and it wasn't because of overwhelming joy over my success.

"What's so funny?" I put the gem down, my fingers aching from the strain.

"You're not going to be able to practice this with Hawk," he said, laughter lingering in his voice.

"Why? Is it his fault I can't do it? It's his magic messing me up?" What a relief that would be. It was tiring to always be the idiot. Hawk could take a turn. His arrogance was a little too deep. It didn't help when people ran from him. Seriously? What did they think he was? Everyone here had magic. He wasn't any different—mostly.

Zab sat back down, still smiling, barely containing more laughter. "Not exactly his magic that's messing you up. More like his fine physique bursting with testosterone. Or his handsome face that I've heard way more about than I care to from Belinda. Which is it? What's making you crush enough that you can't pull your magic back?" He crossed his arms behind his head as he smiled.

"What are you talking about?" I glanced at the door, making sure we were still alone.

"I discovered a little-known fact a while back. I'd borrowed the gem, trying to impress a girl I liked. Your magic surges a little stronger when you're with someone you're attracted to. You can't pull back when he's with you."

"Hawk's attractive, but I don't want to be with *him*." I didn't even want to be here, let alone anything more. It didn't matter what that stupid gem did or what crazy theories Zab had. I didn't.

"I understand." He said it in a way that sounded like he didn't understand at all.

I might've left it there if the corners of his mouth would stay flat. "I *don't*. Your theory is wrong. Very wrong."

"And *I* believe you."

"I don't think you do."

"For the record, the more you protest, the more I don't believe you." He was barely holding back the laughter again.

"Then I won't say another word on it because I don't need to." I narrowed my eyes at him, making sure he understood how serious I was.

He smiled wider.

"And don't be sharing this crazy idea with anyone else," I said, not that Zab tended toward gossip.

"Oh, you don't need to worry about that. Do you think I want to have to deal with the Belinda hysterics? She's already bad enough. I won't tell a soul. There's nothing to tell." He shook his head, pressing his lips together.

"Right. There's nothing."

We both heard the front door opening again, and I gave him a last warning glare. He made a locking motion in front of his lips and then tossed the invisible key right as Hawk stepped back inside.

He walked over and held out a single folded card to me. "The invite is here."

The cardstock was incredibly thick, and I ran a finger over my name, neatly engraved on the outside. I broke the waxy seal holding it closed.

I'd be pleased to have you join me at my home tomorrow evening for drinks.

Raydam

Suddenly, it felt like everyone in Xest knew me or wanted me for something. My entire life, I'd been average. Average height, average hair, average everything, as far as what people saw. The way some people constantly maneuvered to place themselves in the spotlight was the way I cultivated my way into the shade. My hair had always been kept just long enough to work in a bun. My eyes were never lined, lashes never had mascara. My nails were always unpolished and short. My shirts were baggy, and my jeans flattened my curves, rather than flattered.

When you had a mother like mine, one who was a natural beacon for attention of the wrong sort, average was the greatest gift of survival. Average kept you alive while others burned in the harsh light.

Unfortunately, my days of average looked to be over, at least here in Xest. It was as if the spotlight had finally found me and I couldn't shake it loose, no matter how I cursed or screamed.

"Any luck?" Hawk asked, pointing at the abandoned gem on the table.

"She's starting to pull it in. It's not perfect, but it'll do."

Zab shrugged and shook his head. "I mean..." He threw his hands up. "She's just got too much to completely hide without a lot more time than she's got."

I walked to the window. The snow was falling, but my attention was solely on the invite. Hawk's attention was on me, as he watched with eagle eyes.

"I'm going to come with you. You're not ready to deal with him on your own," Hawk said, as if that made it so.

I waved the invite. "The invitation is for me alone. I don't think you're wanted." I turned and met his gaze. "Coming along isn't going to do anything but make it look like you need to guard me or I'll jump ship. Maybe that's what you believe or why you keep all your secrets so close to your vest, like there might be a traitor in your midst. Point is, you march in there with me, and they'll know why you're there. Then we'll leave. If they have any kind of determination, they won't stop until they get me alone anyway. All you'll do is prolong this and drag it out. Bottom line is, they know. Everyone knows." I was never going to be able to hide in the shadows again as long as I was here.

Zab nodded. "She's right. He'll just keep coming for her."

Hawk still wasn't talking. It was hard to tell if he was going to try to forbid me from doing it or accept it. Unfortunately, I couldn't read him as well as he read me.

"You'll have to take your chances that I can handle things. Let the chips fall wherever they may." I lifted the invite. "How does one go about replying to something like this?"

Hawk's eyes narrowed as I forced his hand. Then the tension seemed to ease.

"Take your finger, write 'yes' on it, and then fling it out the window," Hawk said.

I flipped the card open as if I was fully committed and determined. I was anything but. Agreeing to meet Raydam felt like I was digging in even deeper into this place, this mess. The reality was that I was standing in a ditch with no other option of getting out but tunneling under.

I scribbled my finger on the note, watching my name blaze to life in glowing blue. I cracked the window, tossed it into the air, and watched as it turned into a raven and flew off.

23

I sat cross-legged on Rabbit's bed, watching as she tried to stay awake, cupping her chin and furrowing her brow. She'd been waiting for me with her door open when I'd come upstairs.

She took another couple of breaths, letting out a little hum. She wasn't the best sounding board I'd ever had, but being one of my only friends here, the bar would need to be lowered.

"Just to clarify, as I want to make sure I'm not missing any details, we don't know exactly what Hawk wants, just that he thinks he needs you to accomplish it. And now, we don't really know why Raydam wants you either? Just that he wants to be good buddies and bring you 'into the fold,' as Hawk says?"

Maybe I'd been too critical. How could anyone be a good sounding board with so few details?

"That's pretty much the size of things. Plus, Hawk seems to not like Raydam."

She let out a yawn that lasted five seconds before saying, "Well, *everyone* knows that."

"They do? Do you know why they don't like each other?" They say you don't know what you don't know. Well, I was figuring out I knew what I didn't know, and it was astounding the *amount* I didn't know.

"*Nobody* knows why, exactly. Or nobody *I* know. The hatred is common knowledge, though."

The amount Rabbit didn't know sometimes seemed only slightly less, which was nearly as scary.

"What do you think? Am I making a mistake going alone? I don't know what I'm doing, Rabbit." I leaned back and thumped my head on the wall. How was I supposed to make any informed decisions with so many unknown variables? The sum of what I knew wouldn't fill half a shot glass.

I'd said I was going alone to that dinner, and the reasons I'd stated were more than legitimate. They just weren't the only ones.

I'd grown up with a mother who'd contradicted what all logic said was true. Up until I was four or five, I'd believed her. Then I started to see how other people lived and my life had been turned on its ear. For the next decade, I'd doubted all I heard. I'd trusted no one, not completely, ever again. I'd always believed that childhood truly ended when you lost your blind faith in your parents—or parent, in my case.

And now here was Hawk, with no answers at all and hardly an open book. Was there really any harm at this point in hearing this Raydam person out, considering what I was working with?

"The way I see it, it's the best way to figure out things," Rabbit said, then broke for another long yawn. "Like you said, if Raydam wants to talk to you alone, he's going to find a way. At least this is at your choosing. And if you disappear, I will find a way to get you, like you did for me."

"Thanks," I said. She'd try. The fact that Zab was now

lighting fires in two rooms before he left every night didn't bode well, but she'd give me her dying breath. That counted for more than anything.

"You get some sleep," I said, knowing I was torturing her with sleep deprivation.

Her head hit the pillow a second later. I paused at the door, listening to her soft breathing. Was she wheezing a bit? It was probably her head position or something. I paused for another second before I shut the door softly.

The door to my room creaked open an hour later and Hawk filled the door. Wide awake, I shifted until I was partially sitting up.

He didn't come in but rested his shoulder against the frame of the door.

"I haven't been holding back as much as you seem to believe. Magic isn't a precise art. I sent the finder out to locate a person who would be able to accomplish what I needed. I didn't expect it to go to Rest, and when it found you, it didn't tell me how you could help. I'm still trying to figure that out. The only thing I know is you've got the magical chops to do what I need."

"Then tell me what you need." I moved to the edge of my bed.

"Dress warm and meet me downstairs if you want to know more." He straightened and left.

All I'd wanted to do for the last hour was to fall asleep. Now you couldn't keep me in bed if you planted an elephant on my chest. I was finally going to know what he wanted, get some answers, know why I was still here torturing myself.

I layered two sweaters and pants. Xest was a cold place to

begin with, and I'd never gotten a warning about warm clothing before. Wherever we were going, it was going to be bad.

He was waiting on the bottom landing. Instead of walking out the door, and into the office, he began walking up the other set of stairs, the "die stairs," as I'd begun to think of them. Seriously? Was he screwing with me? I could've been lying in bed instead of looking like a colorful marshmallow.

"I had to dress warm to sit on a couch?" I was still following him because I was promised answers, and I was going to get them.

"You'll see."

We walked upstairs to the same sitting room we had last time. The die stairs really hadn't lived up to their reputation thus far, and I couldn't say I was anticipating them to be an overachiever this time either. Maybe the wood stove wasn't working in this portion of the building.

He opened the door and a fierce wind blew out. The sitting room was gone and a forest was there. Okay, the "die stairs" might've redeemed themselves slightly, but not completely unless I saw some monsters.

Although some things were making sense. That was why there was no third floor in the building when you looked at it from the outside. That door led to other places. That was why when I was listening to the fight he'd had with Belinda, they hadn't heard the blaring noise until the door had been open. He'd been in a different place altogether.

Hawk stepped into the snow, and I followed, glad I hadn't taken my jacket off in the midst of my doubts. If the fifth wind was typically biting cold, here in the forest it devoured you whole in one chomp.

"Where are we going?" I asked, raising my voice so he'd hear me over the whistling of the wind through the trees.

"You'll know soon," he said.

He was right—or sort of.

It was maybe five more steps when I began to feel it.

The closer we got, the more I didn't need an explanation any longer. The heaviness of it, the sinking feeling in my chest as I neared it. The closer we got, the more the stars in the sky dimmed, the sound of owls quieted, and everything seemed to hush to a foreboding quietness. I could still feel the wind, but the whistle was dulled. Nothing else had changed. The forest was still all around, but it didn't feel like that anymore. It felt like I was walking into a pit of despair, and with every step, I was losing all joy and happiness.

When we'd walked out of Jasper's and Hawk had told me he knew evil, this was what he'd been talking about. And now I knew it too.

Hawk's eyes were trained on me.

I stepped slightly farther in the direction the heavy feeling was coming from, and only because he was ahead of me. But then I stopped, afraid to go one more inch, terrified this feeling would suck me in whole and never let go.

He was waiting and watching to see if I'd continue.

I shook my head and took a step back, and then another.

"I want to go back," I said, turning and walking toward the door I could still see in the distance. It was closed, but damned if I wouldn't get it to open.

I'd had enough of this place.

He didn't fight me, and we walked back together. I opened the door, not waiting for Hawk and hoping I'd be back at the building. I was.

He shut the door.

I pointed at it.

"Is that still on the other side of there?" The "die stairs" had finally lived up to their name. I would've taken a sledgehammer to them if I could.

"No. It's farther away."

I would've sagged against the wall if it wouldn't make me look like a weak ninny. I mean, after all, I hadn't actually seen anything.

But what I'd felt...

A shiver passed through me as I walked down to the main floor without speaking. Something that I couldn't put into words seeped into my brain, my soul, and I wanted to evict the feeling as soon as possible.

I went directly to the setup in the corner and dumped some cocoa into a mug. It wasn't as good as the stuff from the Sweet Shop, but they were closed and I needed an emergency cocoa. Zab wasn't there to help me out. Hawk flicked his wrist and did the honors of heating my cocoa for me without a word. I walked to the couch and curled up into the corner with my favorite teacup and then dragged a throw over my lap.

I was three sips in and finally thawing out a bit when I asked, "What was that, exactly?"

"Nobody really *knows* exactly. There have always been rumors of a deep evil that lived in the forest. It's one of the reasons that land has never been developed or even explored much. No one knows for sure.

"But for the longest time—eons, even—it stayed in a small spot, not moving or shifting, so no one paid it much mind. The problem now is that it's growing."

I wrapped my arms around myself, wishing I had something that could shield me from what I'd felt in the forest. "You say growing. How big is it?"

"I don't know for certain, and it's not only size that I'm

talking about. The power. It's getting stronger."

I needed to get out of Xest before whatever that thing was grew any more. What the hell had I been dragged into?

"Look, I know your feather thingy told you that I was the one you needed, but that finder was wrong. I don't care if it's never been wrong before. This time it is. I mean, what exactly do you think I can do about that thing out there? Why even bother having me try to knock a book off the table? This whole thing is a joke. I can't do what you need."

"Yes, you can. The finder wasn't wrong. Your magic is just underused."

I put the cocoa down. "Look, you need to accept that there was a mistake and send me back to Salem."

"I'm not doing that."

"I can't help you."

"But you can. We just don't know how yet."

"I *can't*." I got up and stretched my legs. I'd never met someone more stubborn in my life. Even now, as I wanted to beat some sense into him, he remained calm, so sure in his rightness.

He leaned against the arm of the couch, watching me but digging into his position with an excavator.

"So that's it. You're not going to accept that I'm not your woman?"

"Interesting choice of words, but no, I'm not going to accept that because you, Tippi, are my woman."

He was looking at me with such confidence that I suddenly realized what my issue with him was. He believed in me like no one ever had in my entire life. It made me hate him and want him all at once.

I wanted him because, on some deep level, I *wanted* to be the person he thought I was. I basked in his belief.

And I hated him for it, too. I wasn't the person he

thought I was. If he thought I could help him with whatever was growing out there, the only thing that was going to happen was us both dead. And how dare he put that on me?

Instead of basking or raging, I walked out of the room, stunned over just how screwed I was at the moment. Worst was that he held all the power. I couldn't get out of here without him.

Or could I? It might be time to keep all my options open.

24

Rabbit brought me another cup of tea. She brought everyone tea, even Belinda, who might've been warming to her. I didn't blame Rabbit. She didn't know what else to do now that the books were sorted and Zab was out running errands. If I could've, I would've given her something else to do so I could stop drinking tea but not hurt her feelings. I was on my fourth cup, and the caffeine wasn't helping the nerves at all. Tonight's meeting with Raydam was going to be nerve-racking enough without having hand tremors and an eye tic.

Hawk walked into the office, and Rabbit sloshed the tea in her hands and then pretended she hadn't, even as her face turned a bright, rosy red. She faded back against the wall as he walked through the office, as if afraid he'd send her back if he noticed her.

If he did see her, it was hard to tell. He nodded at Belinda, who was with a client. She looked pleased enough until he continued to me.

"Come on. We're going out today," he said, stopping in front of my table.

"We are?" I was afraid to look in Belinda's direction because she might've turned into Medusa for the sole purpose of killing me.

I grabbed my jacket, while Belinda glared, hoping we could stop and get a cocoa on the way back. I'd already had one and needed another in a bad way. It was definitely a two-cocoa day.

"You need to tell Rabbit she doesn't have to leave," I said as soon as we hit the street.

"Why would I do that when she might?"

"You'd kick her out if I can't do what you need? It's not like I haven't been trying."

"I'm allowing her to stay for you. If you go, she goes."

I stopped walking. "Are you making me go?"

He stopped in the middle of the street. Luckily, Hawk had a way of clearing the path around us so we were in no danger of being bumped into or cursed at. "If you decide to go to Raydam's camp, you can't think I'd leave a spy here for you."

"You mean I'd have to leave the broker building? My room?"

"I won't fight you on going to that dinner alone. It's your choice. But there are other choices you'll have to make as well. If you're here, I have your loyalty. I can't have someone I don't trust staying in my place."

"But you already do have someone you don't trust staying with you."

"How so?"

"You don't trust me. You tell me the barest minimum you can. Even last night, you showed me, but how long did that take?"

"You're wrong. I trust the person in front of me. I'm just not sure I'll trust the person you are tomorrow. Sometimes knowledge and power corrupts. Sometimes it strengthens. I know who you are today. I'm just not sure who you'll become."

"I'll be the same person I've always been."

He smiled slightly. "That's an impossibility. Challenging times strengthen the strong and break the weak. You might be a better version after this is all over, but you won't be the same. That I can guarantee."

He began walking again.

I ran after him, realizing how often I had to do that and getting more annoyed by the step. "Look, let's go on the pretense that I won't be going anywhere until I leave for Salem. You need to tell Rabbit that she doesn't have to live in constant fear of being thrown out or ending up back at the factory."

"I had to pay twenty coins to smooth things over at the factory after your newsflash demanded her release. She might not be welcome with me if you switch sides, but after the scene you made, the factory won't want her either."

"Twenty? You paid *twenty* for her when you only paid fifteen for me. You didn't even want her and you paid five more?"

"She had a record of performance, and Marvin was unaware that she was about spent."

"I'm done with this little venture. I'm going back to the shop."

"Tippi."

I ignored him and continued to walk.

Unlike when Belinda and him fought, Hawk followed me. He needed me, but still, he followed me. He knew I was going back to the shop and he followed me anyway.

Then the big pain in the ass got in my way, and it wasn't

so cute and nice anymore. When he seemed intent on blocking me, I wanted to rip his head off his shoulders.

"Can you move?"

"No." He didn't continue talking, either. He waited for some acknowledgment I'd actually listen, which made me want to kick him.

Since he wasn't moving, listening seemed the only alternative.

"What do you have to say? Go ahead." It seemed there was no choice in the matter but to listen to him. Listen, listen, listen. Do this, do that.

"I had to negotiate for you. If I'd given in easily, if Marvin had any idea what I really would've paid to get you, I would've bled coin."

I stood before him, letting his words flow over me. Had to say, if I was going to be bought, it was nice to know he'd have bled. That had a really nice ring to it, if it were true.

"Really?" I watched, waiting for his reply.

"Yes." He tilted his chin down and made a point of meeting my gaze straight on, not that he'd ever shirked from eye contact.

I'd never been a good liar, but I'd been a decent lie detector. So far, he was passing with flying colors.

I turned a little bit, looking over my shoulder in the direction we'd been walking, debating if I could perhaps continue with our little field trip.

"I would've sold Helen to get you," he said.

I was glad I was still turned away from him so he couldn't see my cheeks warm. Helen, more formally known as the Helexorgomay that took up the entire back wall of the office, was the heart of his business. She had to have cost a pretty penny.

That all sounded good and well, except maybe my lie-detecting skills weren't so adept, because there was a huge flaw with what he'd just said. Now I had zero problems turning around and staring him down.

"If that's true, why are you so willing to step aside if I want to go work for Raydam?" I crossed my arms, tilted my head, and gave him my best skeptical look.

"Because if you did make that choice, which I don't think you will, you're not the person I need anyway. And you'd have been right. This was a mistake." Neither his words nor his attitude were meant to be biting. He was telling me his beliefs, plain and simple.

And yet to hear him say it was a mistake, even when I believed it myself, seemed to feel like someone gutting me. He was the one who believed in me, no matter what, right? Maybe not so much.

Although he had said he didn't believe I'd make that choice...

"So, where are we going?" I asked, turning and walking again.

"There," he said, pointing down the way to a shop I'd never been in, not that I'd been in many. The sign Potions, Powders and Perfumes hung on the shingle.

He took the lead again but was only walking slightly ahead, maybe less than a foot. It was progress.

"You don't make your own stuff? I don't know why, but I figured you did. Or at least had a hookup with all the people that come in and out of the brokerage house. You do get a ton of traffic, after all."

"We aren't shopping there."

My pace slowed for a second before I caught back up. "Then why are we going?"

"Introductions. It's time you met some people," he said, walking with determination even as I faltered.

What? No wonder I was constantly confused. The man had lost his mind. Did he have any idea what he was doing? Was there no plan at all? Was he winging it on a day-to-day basis?

"I thought I wasn't supposed to meet anyone? Wasn't that the deal?"

"Yes, but that was before your coming-out party tonight."

Before I could ask more questions, he had the door open, waiting for me, and damned if he hadn't done that on purpose.

There was a nice-looking older lady standing behind the counter with a tuft of white hair piled a good three feet high on her head.

"Hawk, what a surprise." The woman could've been an opera singer or a pop star with a voice that beautiful. Still, even with the beautiful tone, the dropped "nice" from that sentence and the way she stared at him and then me, made it all clear.

I stood still, not quite sure I should bother getting comfortable, since we might be kicked out in the next second. What kind of visit was this? Why introduce me to someone who clearly hated him? And would now hate me by association. Her sneer made me think I'd already been added to her shit list. Like I didn't have enough problems.

"Varima, thought I'd stop by and introduce you to my friend Tippi. Not sure if you've met." He put a hand on my back, pushing me forward as if he didn't understand my hesitance. Was this a Hawk problem? Had he not given a shit for so long that his social skills were so far gone he didn't know when people hated him?

"No. We haven't," she said.

I smiled, having a harder time figuring out what fake

formalities were needed. When the person you were introduced to was staring at you like you were vermin they'd
discovered crawling out from behind a basket, did you smile
and continue as if nothing were amiss here?

"Nice to meet you." Reflex made me lift my hand and
then yank it back, because the moment hadn't been
awkward enough.

She tipped her head, clearly out of fake formalities as
well. As she did, a chirping noise exploded from her hair
and a tiny pink bird burst out of the strands and flew across
the room to perch on top of the shelving.

"Dammit, you made me lose my songbird!" Varima
screeched.

"Well, we'll be seeing you," Hawk replied, going to the
door and holding it open for me, which was much longer
than the bird needed to escape.

Screams filled our ears until the door swung shut again.

"Why would you bring me to meet someone who hates
you?" I asked, and as we walked away I watched the songbird disappear into the distance.

"She doesn't really hate me. She simply dislikes me," he
said. "There's a vast difference between the two." He pointed
up ahead. "Let's stop there before we continue. I could use a
drink."

That I wouldn't argue about. I might need a few drinks if
the day's agenda continued in this way.

The door was wood with a marble surround, and the
restaurant looked inviting, with white tablecloths and little
flowers in the center. The place could've been in Salem, if
the people didn't look so odd.

We walked in and took a seat in the corner, and it was
immediately clear something was amiss here too. Everyone
in the place looked at us and were clearly wondering why

we were there. They whispered behind their hands. Some just whispered. Some spoke loud enough to hear.

A man a booth over leaned closer to his companion. "That's the Whimsy witch who wasn't. I'm not sure why they're here."

I was wondering the same. My anger grew stronger as the voices grew louder.

The waiter came to the table, stuttering as he took our order. He kept looking around the room, as if he thought he'd get stabbed for serving us.

As soon as he walked away, I leaned forward and grabbed Hawk's arm to get his undivided attention. That gesture sent a hush through the room, and I let go of him immediately, forgetting that these people didn't touch. I'd probably just made it worse, just as Hawk must've in the shop before. I'd *definitely* made it worse from the way they were staring at me. Now they didn't think I was an associate of his but *with* him.

If that wasn't bad enough, I was sure the story would get back to Belinda somehow. Now I really needed to take Raydam's invitation seriously or my daily life was going to be hell. This all compounded to make me shoot past anger to fury.

"Did you want to say something?" Hawk asked, as if he didn't have a clue how mad I was.

With the entire restaurant openly staring, I sat back and said, "No."

I wasn't giving them more of a show. I'd get him out of here first and then kill him.

Turned out that was going to be a good long while, as he ordered another round of drinks, then appetizers, main courses, and desserts. By the time we left three hours later, I was looking forward to meeting Raydam. Maybe it was time for a change. Maybe I was too flat and needed some folds.

I kept it together long enough to get out of sight of the restaurant.

"We're done. I'm not going anywhere else." That needed to be cleared up before he tried to ambush me anywhere else.

"That was probably enough," he said, walking behind me for once.

"I don't understand why you're doing this. The people here clearly aren't happy with you, and now they've all labeled me as an enemy. You might not care what people think of you, but you know this place. I'm new here. Are you trying to make me feel isolated and horrible?"

"Just thought you should know where the lines are drawn."

"You don't know where they all are because you walked right over mine."

I kept my pace brisk, not caring if he was behind me or not.

After three hours of meeting people who instantly disliked me because of the company I kept, I was ready to fly solo for a little bit. If I was going to be hated, I'd rather be condemned on my own merit.

The last thing I wanted to do was go for drinks at Raydam's, but I didn't have the luxury of having any more people hate me after what Hawk had just done.

I got to the office and flung the door open.

"Raydam's place is the large black house set off from the other buildings in the center of Xest."

I turned just in time to see Hawk walk off.

25

Rabbit's door was closed, lights out. It was probably better, since I was running short on time anyway. I'd need to go through my pile of hand-me-downs and find the least ugly thing.

Rabbit might've fallen asleep, but she and Zab had left me some gifts on my bed. It was a cute little black dress and woolen leggings, along with some snazzy black boots. As far as what I'd seen fashion-wise in Xest, this was straight off the runway.

There was a little card beside it.

Can't have an employee of the broker looking shabby!

Zab and Rabbit

I dressed quickly before dragging a brush through my hair, letting it hang free for a change. There wasn't much sense in hiding when I'd already been found. I made my way out, rushing because I only had ten or so minutes to get there.

When I first saw Raydam's house, I'd assumed it was a museum. It sat back from the center of Xest and yet still seemed to anchor the area. The iron gate swung open as I made my way up the walk to the sprawling house. Two large trees with black leaves framed a blood-red door. The windows were lit and there were a lot of bodies moving around inside. This wasn't drinks but more of a party of sorts. I'd have to fetch Zab and Rabbit a few cocoas tomorrow to thank them for making sure I didn't show up looking like a vagabond.

Knowing that some of the people inside must have noticed my approach, I took only a second to pause and catch my breath before I banged on the large iron knocker.

A gentleman in livery opened the door.

"Hello. I'm Tippi..." I stopped short of my last name. If he didn't know it yet, did I really want to hand over the information? Probably not. "I was invited by Raydam."

"Of course, madam." He stepped aside. "May I take your jacket?"

I shrugged it off quickly, hoping the frayed hem hadn't been noticed, and feeling that much more grateful to Zab and Rabbit.

"If you'll wait here," the servant said, and then disappeared.

Even though it was Xest, and therefore had a different bent to its aesthetic, grand was still grand in any flavor. It was dark, with blue and grey walls and accents of silver and gold everywhere. Stones dangled from a candelabra that sparkled like diamonds, nearly mesmerizing.

Other guests were peeking through the doorway into the foyer, where I stood, taking me in. More than one face was recognizable from the restaurant earlier. Pretending not to notice, I stared at the grand staircase, the walls, the mirror on the wall, and the gems—everywhere but them. It didn't mean anything if they already hated me. None of it mattered. I wouldn't be here long enough for it to.

A man walked into the foyer, his smile warm and his eyes direct. He had a full head of dark brown hair and amber eyes that suited a sculpted face of someone in their late twenties. His dark blue velvet suit seemed pretty fashionable for Xest, and he smelled amazing. Nothing about him screamed monster. Honestly, if I'd met him standing beside Hawk, I would've asked him for help first.

"Tippi, I'm Raydam. It's so nice to finally meet you." He gave me a once-over that wasn't creepy or weird or anything that made my skin crawl. "You're even prettier than they said."

"Thank you." Hawk never said anything this nice to me, ever. Actually, no one typically praised my beauty, but then again, I was hard to see in the shadows. This man didn't seem like a monster on any level, not the big, bad boogieman type or even the minor troll version.

"I'm sure Hawk has been filling your head with a lot of notions, or maybe not. He does like to keep his secrets. I hope you'll hear me out with an open heart and mind." He placed a hand on his chest.

Might've been a little dramatic, but perhaps Raydam was just a big old softy? What did I really know about him? Nothing. He hadn't even tried to touch me and gauge my magic the way I'd been warned.

"I wouldn't be here if I wasn't willing." That sounded like the truth even to my ears. After the show around town with Hawk this afternoon, it might've been the most genuine thing I'd said all week. I did want to hear Raydam out, even more so now that I'd met him. Maybe this man was my way out of Xest?

"I hope you don't mind, but there were others who are dying to meet you. Care to talk a little stroll and I'll introduce you?"

He nodded toward the main room, where they were all waiting for us but pretending not to. There had to be a good twenty people there, at least half of whom I'd already seen today.

"Of course."

If they remembered me, their expressions didn't show it. I was formally introduced to one after another, with names and vague generalities. This was nothing like the hostility in the restaurant. Maybe these people weren't so bad either. Maybe the real problem here was Hawk?

We'd barely made it halfway through the room when Raydam turned and said, "My, where are my manners? I didn't get you a drink. Wine?"

"That would be lovely," I said, not planning on having more than a sip or two. I didn't drink much, and this wasn't the place to start, surrounded by people who still might secretly think of me as the enemy, no matter how pleasant they appeared while I was with Raydam.

He waved a hand, and a servant immediately brought over a tray of white wine. Raydam handed me a glass, brushing my fingers for a moment as he passed it on. I'd been so distracted by everything and everyone that I hadn't expected it. I hadn't even tried to block my magic.

And he'd felt it, as I'd felt his.

His eyes were light with a shared secret as he looked at me.

I'd felt the sizzle of power from Hawk, and it had been

off the charts compared to what Raydam had just felt like, if that was truly the judge.

"Oh my, Tippi, you *are* impressive."

I nodded, not saying anything. The duplicitous way he'd touched me, the look in his eyes right now after he had, all the warning flares that hadn't gone off before were now exploding all at once, putting on a grand finale.

For all of Hawk's rough edges, when he'd wanted to know what I had, he hadn't made a secret of it at all. I'd just been duped.

"Let's talk somewhere quiet for a moment," he said.

I suddenly found myself wanting to remain with all the smiling vipers, but that wasn't an option. I'd come here. I'd accepted his invite and insisted on coming alone. Now it was time to see this out.

"All right."

He smiled and led me to a door off to the side of the room, all eyes on us as we walked through the crowd.

There was a spiral staircase that seemed to lead to nowhere, the candles lighting on the wall as we moved, as if motion-activated. The farther we got from the sounds of the other guests, the more my nerves frayed. I'd never felt this way with Hawk. He'd always been imposing, but never gave me the feeling that he was leading me to torture before he had me dig my own grave. Probably because half the time with him, he didn't seem to care if I was even there, which had been aggravating until right now.

Every step on the stone stairs seemed to echo more as we climbed. The only escape I had was if he thought I was going to play ball. If I disappeared, would Hawk come and look for me? Was I totally on my own now? Rabbit would. I wasn't sure she'd get too far, but she'd try. She'd recruit Zab as well. Even together, they couldn't fight this man.

There was a door at the top, and for a moment, I feared it would be the same type Hawk had, leading me to some unknown place I'd never be found. Instead, it opened to the rooftop of his home.

The wind whipped my hair around, and the cold felt like it was soaking into me, but the beauty before me was awe-inspiring. The sky looked like we had a view right into heaven with the way the stars sparkled and the land was immense. I'd yet to see a view of Xest like this, and it was massive and stunning. One view was the town, lit with warm, glowing lights.

But it was the land around it that really struck me.

"It's amazing up here." I leaned on the stone railing, looking at a forest the likes of which I'd never seen before. There were blacks and greys, deep violets and silver, rolling hills and lakes glittering in the distance.

Raydam's jacket landed on my shoulders, and he was suddenly growing on me a bit again. So, he'd brushed my hand when he'd given me wine. That might've been accidental. And he'd gotten excited over my magic. That wasn't a capital offense either. I was letting planted expectations skew my judgment, and that wasn't fair to him or me.

"Don't mind the wind. I know you're used to the four winds, growing up in Rest as you did. The fifth wind of Xest can be especially bitter to people unfamiliar with it." He leaned on the stone beside me. "It's quite stunning, is it not?" he asked.

"Most definitely."

We took in the scenery together in silence, Raydam seeming to be in as much awe as me, even though he must've seen this view countless times.

"I've heard from several of my associates and friends that

Hawk brought you around and made introductions," he said, finally breaking the silence.

"I'd asked him to show me about the place a little." The lie slipped from my lips naturally, as if I hadn't been able to stop myself from protecting him. I'd worry why I did that later.

Raydam nodded. "I hope you know, you don't need protection from me. Of course, it might've been nothing of the sort, but I felt it needed stating. I'm not looking to harm you, and neither are my colleagues. He didn't need to put out the warning."

"Of course not. You've been nothing but gentlemanly toward me thus far."

How stupid could I be? I might as well knock my head into the stone wall for as much as it was working. Hawk and my relationship had become so combative that I was oblivious to what he'd been doing. That he was going around and stamping me as one of his people and probably all that went with that. For as cold, arrogant, and all-around troublesome as that man was, he had my back. Only thing I wasn't sure of was did he do it to stack the deck in his favor or to drive a wedge between Raydam and me before we even met?

Hawk had respected my wishes and let me come here alone, but I might as well have walked in beside him. It was wrong to feel more at ease, but somehow, I did as I leaned a little more on the stone. Raydam smiled, as if he thought it were him. It was his words, though. No matter what happened here tonight, Hawk wouldn't hang me out to dry in this place, or he wouldn't have bothered with this afternoon.

Raydam moved an inch closer, not crowding me, but as if we were friendlier than we were.

"There's a power growing out there, in the Unsettled Lands." His gaze was on the far-off distance and his tone held reverence. "Some think we should fear it because we don't understand it. I don't believe that. I think we should try to get along with it. Be at peace with it. See what it wants."

"Have you encountered it?" I asked, trying to sound naive, as if the thing hadn't repulsed me. Hawk was wrong. This guy wasn't his opposition. He was an idiot.

"Yes, and if you felt it, you'd know immediately it's something good, warm, and beautiful. You get close to it and it swallows you in joy and warmth."

We couldn't possibly be talking about the same thing, but how many mysterious growing magic entities could there be? His eyes were glowing, but I wanted to shiver at the memory of the thing. What was going on here? How could two people feel something so completely different?

"That sounds wonderful," I said, trying to keep my eyes on the view off in the distance. This lie didn't fall off my lips as easily. Seemed my new talent was selective.

"I'm guessing Hawk told you all sorts of horrible things about it. I can tell by the skepticism in your voice, but you'd only need to feel it one time to know it's something truly wonderful. Would you let me take you there some time?"

No. Never. I'd die in Xest before I went to that place with him, and that might happen. He'd been my only other option, and it turned out he wasn't an option at all, if getting close to that thing was his angle.

I made a vague noise that could've been interpreted as a yes, if that was what you wanted to hear. It wasn't, but not knowing what words formed a contract of sorts in this world, I was sticking to grunts and groans.

"I'm hoping that maybe we can help each other. You

don't know this world, but I could help you navigate it," he said.

"What if I didn't want to remain in this world?" I asked, afraid even the question might cause me problems.

"You would. How could someone as gifted as you not? You just need someone to show you the way, is all, and then you'd never want to go back to Rest."

I nodded, trying to hide the hesitation until I got out of there. Even if he did sense my nerves, they would've been expected. A lack of cautiousness might've seemed more peculiar, or at least that was what I told myself.

"I'll have to bring you out to the Unsettled Lands and show you what I mean," he said, still trying to get that yes.

Talk about doubling down. I didn't only have nerves, I couldn't wait to run from this place. And the last thing I was going to do was say yes.

"May I think it over a little? I'm very hesitant to get involved with matters I'm ignorant of," I said, hoping he'd read that as my leeriness to do what Hawk wanted as well. This wasn't even a lie. I would help Hawk if I could, but I didn't want to help anyone. I wanted to get the hell out of there.

"Of course. Take your time. Think about it for a little while." He was smiling like a man who knew he was going to get his way.

The guy was a psychopath.

I'd half expected to find Hawk waiting outside Raydam's door when I left. He wasn't, but that didn't stop me from looking for him as I walked home, thinking maybe he'd be in the shadows somewhere, waiting. It wasn't that I wanted to talk to him. I didn't want to talk to anyone. I hadn't fully absorbed the events of the evening myself. Still hadn't by the time I got back to the office.

I walked in and saw a candle burning on the desk, and figured Zab must've come back and left it for me. Then I saw Hawk's dark shadow in one of the chairs, and my insides knitted up tight. He might not have been waiting outside Raydam's house for me, but he cared. The hard part was never forgetting that his caring probably extended as far as protecting his interests.

His gaze ran over me, and I was suddenly very conscious of my dress, the stockings, my hair flowing down my back. Most of my clothing was usually a size too big. I shrugged out of my jacket, as if I weren't self-conscious at all.

"How was your meeting with Raydam?" he asked.

Disgusting? Repulsive? The fact that Raydam liked whatever that horrible, evil thing growing in the Unsettled Lands made my skin crawl? If I told Hawk all that, I'd secure my position here, along with Rabbit's. Things would keep moving along smoothly, and hopefully I'd get back to Salem before too much more time passed, or at least somewhere near there. That was the smart move. Keep everything moving along.

There was one thing I was sure of: Raydam wouldn't let me walk away that easily, ever. I should tell Hawk I didn't trust Raydam and there was no way I was ever going to end up in the "fold."

No risk of being thrown out. No distrust because I'd laid it out on the table for him, all neat and packaged up for easy digestion. Then I thought about how he said he'd throw me out, kick out Rabbit, and the words didn't come.

"Gave me a lot to think about."

Would he question me on what I was offered? What I

needed to think about? Would he really kick me out? Would he throw me on the streets, with nowhere else to go? We weren't friends. We certainly weren't more than that, but still, I'd felt some loyalty toward him for reasons I couldn't fathom. I had to know if he'd be so callous and toss me out, if any of that loyalty was reciprocated.

Was he going to press me or tell me to pack a bag now and leave?

"Did you hold back?" he asked, leaning back, staring at me where he remained in the shadows.

There was a weird tension in the air, but with only the single candle, it was hard to read the expression on his face.

"No. He caught me off guard." Would that do it? Would he kick me out now? I shouldn't have explained.

He stood and walked closer, stopping a few feet shy of me.

"Maybe you can sleep on it," he said, a gleam in his eye before he turned and left

That was it? No "get out"? No ultimatum? Just "sleep on it"? Had I somehow shown my hand? I must've, but damned if I knew how. Worst was, why did I constantly feel like I was playing patty-cake with a pro boxer?

26

I walked over to the table I'd claimed as my own, as if yesterday's meeting with Raydam had never happened. It was business as usual, as far as I was concerned. I'd avoid answering Raydam for as long as I could, and I'd avoid telling Hawk my answer for even longer. And in that time? Hawk would eventually come to his senses, realize that there was zero I could do for him, and that would be it. I'd leave. I'd go back home and happily live in the shadows once again.

Zab put a mug of cocoa on my table with a smile. "Figured you might need it after last night."

I smiled. "More than you can imagine."

"Oh, I think I can imagine just fine. Was it as bad as I feared?"

"I'm sure it wasn't good," Musso said as he passed us on the way to his desk. "That slimy Raydam is never up to anything good. I'm sure our Tippi figured that out, though." Musso gave me one of his rare smiles, and I returned it, not confirming what he already seemed to know.

Our Tippi. I'd never been an "our" or even part of a

group. I'd always kept everyone at arm's length, even Loris to a certain degree. It had been easier that way. When you got close to people, they asked you things, and my entire life had been an awkward secret. No people meant no questions and no awkward explanations.

But here, there was nothing to hide. Everyone was like me, with weird in their veins. Here, I *had* people. My life was an open book. Somehow it felt like maybe I had a place. Of course, it was only temporary, and I couldn't let a hot cocoa and a smile make me crazy. This was not the place I should be.

"So?" Zab asked.

"It was okay, I guess," I answered, glancing around and wondering why Rabbit wasn't harassing me for answers, too. I'd thought she'd beaten me down here when I hadn't seen her upstairs.

"I think she's sleeping in," Zab said, reading my mind.

I caught a glance between Zab and Musso. Before I could delve deeper, Hawk walked in.

He nodded at Belinda. She stalked him with her eyes but didn't chase him around the office. She normally put on her running shoes when Hawk was around. Maybe she'd heard about the meet-and-greet, the awkward touch at the restaurant? Hard to know without crawling into her brain, but something had definitely shifted.

Hawk stopped in front of my table. "Go get your jacket and meet me outside. We need to go somewhere," he said before leaving without any further explanation.

Belinda's gaze met mine. Her eyes narrowed, and I could hear the list of mental curses that were being spewed my way. I went to get my jacket, all too aware that Belinda now stalked my steps.

I threw on my jacket, telling myself to not look Belinda's

way. That worked as well as expected, but what I saw threw me. Her stare had dropped to her desk as she sat there, slightly slumped over, not doing anything.

As much as I wanted to walk past her, something about her broken form stopped me. I'd been there. Maybe not over a man, but the hole she was in looked awfully familiar. Instead of walking out, I walked to her desk.

"It's only business between us. There's nothing personal," I said as softly as possible, hoping Zab and Musso wouldn't overhear.

Her shoulders stiffened and then she turned her gaze to me. It went to my shoes, traveled up my legs and the baggy green pants I was wearing. It continued up over my small chest until her eyes collided with mine.

Hers narrowed. "Of course there isn't."

She got up, nearly knocking me over as she walked past me to go into the back room.

I shook my head, lecturing myself internally for never taking my own advice. I had some good stuff sometimes. Not all the time, but this time I definitely had been right. She wanted no part of me, not even the kind and nice part. I should've left it alone.

Zab let out a sigh. "I don't know why she keeps hanging on. We all know it's not happening." He stood, looking at the back room and figuring the same as I. She'd gone back there like a wounded animal to lick her wounds.

It took another two head shakes before he followed to check on her, as I'd known he would. Zab only had the kind and nice parts.

"Sucks when you're not the one. Nothing to do about it but move on," Musso said, methodically going through his work as if nothing were amiss.

"You never know. Maybe it'll work out." I shrugged, lacking anything else constructive to say.

Musso snorted. "No one here, even her, believes that."

"Why do you think..." Stupid question. I knew why she hung in there. If I was dating him, I might too. He wasn't that nice, and he wasn't exactly adoring, but he was something else, had something that made you too aware of his comings and goings. I found myself doing it, watching the door for when he'd arrive. The only word for it might've been *addictive*.

At least he was nice to her. Me? He just bossed me around and needed things from me.

"You going to finish that thought?" Musso asked.

"Already forgot what I was going to say. Gotta go. Hawk's going to be yelling for me soon."

Hawk was staring down the road intently, looking at something I didn't see, when I stepped outside.

"What are you looking at?" I asked.

It took him a minute to respond. "Something feels off." He still wasn't looking at me but everywhere else. Up the street and down. Then he was staring at the sky and the rooftops.

I glanced around, wondering what he was sensing and not sure I wanted to know. This place was already a bit too much for me.

"Like what?" I asked, because I hadn't gotten any better at listening to my inner advice than I had with Belinda five minutes ago.

He shook his head, still looking about the place, as if something was going to pop up out of the air. Maybe it would. This was Xest.

"Let's go," he said, motioning me one way as he continued to look the other.

I wasn't sure if I was picking up on "something off" or his high alert was somehow contagious. Either way, the hair on my arms was standing at attention. I began looking over my shoulder as we walked, waiting for an attack.

"Where are we off to today?" I asked, looking for a better subject to concentrate on.

"Some people want to meet you."

"Oh no. Not more people." I stopped walking. I'd rather get attacked by the invisible threat than do another forced meet-and-greet. Every other one had not gone well. First I'd had a little troll fellow tell me I was evil. Then I had that screeching lady, and then a restaurant full of people who decided to hate me. I'd rather have my nails pulled out than meet another soul.

He turned around while I was crossing my arms and shaking my head. "I'm done with new people. I'd rather spend the night failing, if you don't mind."

He smiled, and it looked as if he might be on the verge of laughing. "This one will be more pleasant."

I didn't budge. "You've never taken me to anyone remotely pleasant, ever."

"It won't be bad. And if you want to leave after you've met them, we can go. It'll only take a few minutes."

A few minutes. I guessed I could handle anyone for a few minutes. Although I'd been proven wrong a bunch of times so far.

He raised a brow, silently asking if I was coming, seeming to give me a choice. I let out a long breath, dropped my arms, and walked in his direction.

"So who are these people who want to meet me now?" I asked. He was only about a foot ahead of me, which made it slightly easier to ask a question and not tell the entire street at the same time.

"I've got some friends and colleagues that have similar interests."

"And these people you call friends and colleagues, they like you too? It's a mutual thing?" This was sounding bad again.

He let out a soft laugh. "Yes, they like me too."

Had he just laughed? Up until this moment, I hadn't realized he was capable.

We only walked another block or so before he opened the door to what appeared to be a dark taproom. It hadn't had a fancy sign on the door, and there were drawn shades over the windows that made it look like it was nighttime inside instead of the middle of the morning.

The small crowd, some at the bar sipping on tankards and others sitting at the table, all turned to stare at us as we walked in.

We stopped in the middle of the room.

"Everyone, this is Tippi." Hawk nodded in my direction.

I waved at them.

Unlike the clamoring group that had tripped over themselves to pretend to greet me when I'd been with Raydam, this group barely budged. Maybe Hawk did have some friends here. These were the people I could see him being friends with. They all had a rough look about them, from the woman sitting at the table watching me over her mug, with narrowed eyes and a spiky red mohawk, to the guy leaning on the bar, glaring at me as if I couldn't possibly be the Tippi he'd expected. Yeah, this was making more and more sense. These might've actually been his friends.

Hawk had said they had "similar interests." Did that mean they didn't like the thing in the forest either? I'd have to ask later. Right now, silence seemed to be the thing.

If I was going to join a side, this would be the side I'd

pick. None of the frills of the group Raydam ran with. These people weren't here to socialize and tell each other how wonderful they were. They didn't even look like they wanted to be here with each other. They came because they had to get a job done. These were more my type of people.

A familiar face finally appeared from the back. Oscar walked toward us with two drinks in his hands.

"They're a little skeptical about you being able to deliver," he said as he got close.

"Yeah, so am I," I said, accepting the offered drink and then taking a healthy chug from it.

"I told them I'd bring her by. I brought her," Hawk said, turning to me and tilting his head toward the door.

"You're leaving?" Oscar asked, his brow furrowing as if he couldn't understand why we'd split the party early.

"Yes," Hawk said. "I don't care if they don't believe. I do, and I don't need to convince anyone. They know where to find me." He turned and walked to the door.

Dammit. Hawk was doing that thing that made me feel all special and gooey inside, like an under-baked brownie. This was not good.

I handed the drink back to Oscar. "Thanks. It was tasty."

I followed Hawk out the door, afraid to be left alone with these people, even if they were on our side.

Hawk didn't say anything, but our gap had narrowed to under a foot. Whatever his people had thought of me, it hadn't scared him.

"You know, they're probably right," I said, in case he needed a reminder of the possibility. Plus, I needed some skepticism to harden up my mushy center.

"They're not."

Dammit, he was a tough sell.

27

"There's nothing for me?" A guy with the platinum-blond hair sat slumped in front of Zab.

Zab's forearms were on his desk as he leaned forward, eyes heavy-lidded. "I'm sorry, man. It's just you have a very small skill set, at least what you're allowed to use. If you hadn't signed a non-compete clause, things would be a lot different."

The blond nodded as he rubbed his palm over his jeans. "What do you think would happen if I broke it?"

"I don't think that's a good idea, and I won't help you do that. We can't handle that kind of heat here." Zab leaned back.

The blond deflated again, rubbing his chin. "I know you're right. I've heard the stories. You know, they all said do it. It's a gold rush in Xest. You'll live the good life." He shook his head. "I never should've left. Now I can't go back without being ready to grovel for a decade. I'm not that desperate—yet."

Zab nodded. "Yeah, man. I get it. I'll keep an eye out for you."

214 DONNA AUGUSTINE

The blond took a deep breath, as if preparing himself. He stood slowly, like leaving empty-handed was too heavy a burden to bear.

"Make sure you call me if anything comes in, okay?" he asked.

"You know I will. You're my bro," Zab said.

The blond nodded, gave a weak smile, and headed out.

"Hang in there and keep on witchin'," Zab said, watching the blond's slow exit.

I rolled my chair closer to Zab, who was still looking at the door. The best and worst part of sitting so close to him was watching negotiations play out, and sometimes fail.

"What's his skill set? Maybe there's something in the stack."

"He came from..." He hooked a thumb toward the ceiling. "He can make certain appearances here and there, but man, the contract they sign when they leave is ironclad. They lock them up tight. They don't like defectors. Sometimes they forgo anything extra altogether and move to Rest. It's a tough situation either way when you're born into something that doesn't quite fit."

I rocked back in my chair. Boy did I know how that felt.

Zab jumped up from his seat and went to the coin box on the shelf behind him. He looked over at me with a big smile. "You game?"

"When do I ever turn down a cocoa?" I asked. I'd been two-a-daying it for a while. In the short time I'd been here, I'd quickly come to crave the Sweet Shop cocoa like a junky craved crack.

"Anyone want a cocoa?" Zab asked, gathering up coins.

Musso looked up from the client at his desk. "Yeah, I'll take one." He said it like he wasn't as into them as we were. That was bullshit. Sometimes he was a two-a-day-er too.

Zab and I had spied him stopping over for a second hit on his way home several nights in a row.

Belinda looked up, her gaze getting stuck on me long enough to remind me she still hated me. Then she turned to Zab.

"No. Thank you," she said.

The woman was incapable of being normal, not even for the two minutes it took to answer a question about something as generic as cocoa. If there was no Hawk, we still would've been doomed to not get along. She was way too much work, and that kind of maintenance was tiring to sustain for the long haul.

"Where's Rabbit?" Zab asked.

"I'm here," Rabbit said, walking out of the back room. "I think I'm good. I'm going to head upstairs soon." She leaned by the stairwell door, looking like she'd barely make the climb.

"Yeah, you should go up."

She nodded and disappeared.

I stepped closer to Zab, hoping Belinda would mind her own business. "I thought she'd get better after she left the factory. How long do you think it'll take?"

Zab was still looking at the door.

"Zab?"

He hesitated and then said, "Maybe you should talk to her? There could be more going on."

So he didn't think it was normal either. I'd been hoping for some excuse about her needing more time. I really needed that second cocoa today.

The door opened and a swell of people walked in. There had been a lot of calls going out today. It was definitely going to be a late night.

Zab cursed under his breath before saying, "I called half

of these people five hours ago. Now they show up? This is going to be a bit. I'll go as soon as I finish here."

"You always go. I'll go. I'm not exactly essential personnel."

Belinda laughed the loudest. She made it hard to even crack a joke.

"You sure?" Zab asked, looking out the window at the darkening sky.

"Zab, it's practically across the street."

"She'll be fine," Musso said.

Zab had the coins in his hand, except his fingers were still wrapped tight around them.

"Zab. Seriously, it's two seconds away."

He dropped the coins into my hand as the mob began descending upon his desk, all asking almost simultaneously if he had work for them.

"I'll tell them to make yours extra chocolaty," I whispered before I left.

I made my way to Sweet Shop, noticing that the streets were emptier tonight. Might've been that anyone with half a brain was hunkered down. Even for Xest, this was bad.

The Sweet Shop was empty too, except for the owner, Gilli, who knew our order and was quick to greet me with a smile. I was sure the steady flow of coin swayed her opinion of me. She had our cocoas lined up in a matter of minutes and added on a complimentary bag of soft sugars, known as marshmallows in Rest.

I shoved them in my pocket for equitable distribution later and juggled the three cocoas, yelling back to Gilli, "See you tomorrow."

As I stepped outside, it wasn't only the cold that hit me. It was my new reality. I had a desk—or a table, and that was close enough. I'd asked Zab today where he got his hair cut because I was going to need a trim. I had cocoas in my hand for my coworkers, and I *knew* Musso was going to somehow end up with extra marshmallows, no matter how well I divvied them up. I had a spot in my room where I dumped my laundry. I wasn't just *here* in Xest, visiting. I was *living* in Xest. When had that happened? How had a life here snuck up on me?

Glancing about this frozen tundra of a land, I realized if I wasn't careful, this might become home. The wind was bitterly cold as a flurry of snow blew across the empty street. The fifth wind whistled and then growled. I couldn't call a place with growling wind home, could I?

Whoa. Wait. What was that? Even in Xest, the wind shouldn't make a growling noise.

I looked around and saw the things that were hidden in the snowdrift. At first they'd blended with the snow. The longer I stared, the more I squinted, the clearer I saw. It looked like a herd of small animals, no bigger than mice but a lot of them, all with white fur. They had disproportionately large fangs that protruded from their little jaws. Then one stood on its hind legs, and it had extra-large claws as well.

Had to be at least fifty of them, all with beady eyes fixated on me, and they were between me and the shop. I took a few steps blindly backward before I heard a growl from that direction as well. I glanced over my shoulder to see another herd of them, in between me and the Sweet Shop, whose lights had been turned off for the night.

There was a small gap in between me and where I needed to go. I dropped the cocoas and ran for it, getting only two steps before teeth pierced my pants. I shook my leg, throwing the first attackers off, but they were replaced by twice as many on my other leg. I was surrounded by them. They crawled up my legs, biting and scratching. My screams were buried in the gust of whistling wind as I threw them off.

And then, suddenly, they were gone.

I stood there, the snow around me a circle of bright red that was growing larger by the second, as the blood was pouring rivers down my legs. My pants hung in shreds from my thighs. My hands were shaking, and it seemed to be spreading, as my entire body began to shiver.

Without thinking, I walked back to the shop, stepping on blood and cocoa-stained snow. I was woozy but couldn't tell if it was from shock or loss of blood. Maybe a combination. Hard to know when your mind was freaking out while you bled out. It could definitely be a combo.

Had to get back to the office. I couldn't think of anything beyond that. Not the warmth flowing into my boots or the pieces of either flesh or pants that grazed my legs with each step. I couldn't stop and think.

My hand slipped on the door, slick with blood from ripping carnivorous little monsters off me, as my hands shook and knees trembled. I stopped right inside. The place went silent. Belinda was gone, but Musso and Zab still had clients. Zab's mouth dropped open. There were several gasps. It seemed as if time was slowing, and then stopped, as I stood there.

Musso acted first, getting up from his desk. "Everyone out! Shop's closed." He waved the remaining clients to the door. They swerved around me, gaping as they did and getting a good look.

I opened my mouth to talk but found I couldn't quite speak yet. Zab tugged me to the nearest chair as Musso dropped the shades on the front window.

"What happened?" Zab asked, his hands reaching out to me but hovering in a lost sort of way.

I looked down, seeing the flaps of flesh, and understood his dilemma. Everyone with basic first-aid knowledge knew to put pressure on a bleeding wound, but what happened when the wound was half your leg and the skin wasn't attached anymore? It added some serious complications to the problem.

"I don't know exactly. These things..." I was shaking so badly that my teeth rattled. "I'm okay. I just need to stop the bleeding." That sounded right. I leaned forward. This wasn't that bad. It was probably all the blood. There was probably more skin than I realized. Yeah, not so bad.

I went to get up. I needed towels. Zab urged me back down with a hand on my shoulder.

"You sit. I'll get whatever you need."

But he didn't. He kept staring.

Musso walked over and knelt beside my legs. He made a signal of some sort to Zab, and then Zab crossed the room.

"I dropped our cocoas," I said to Musso.

"What happened, exactly?" Musso asked, staring at my legs.

Zab draped a blanket that felt like it had been sitting in front of a fireplace for three hours over my shoulders. It eased some of the shaking as I tried to get my scrambled thoughts together.

"I'm not sure. There was this herd of...things? Creatures? Mice? I thought it was a snowdrift, and then it wasn't. I don't know what I did, but they..." The shaking came back at the thought of them, and I pointed at my legs.

"And they appeared out of a snowdrift?" Musso laid a hand on the blanket, the heat growing.

"I don't know. I think so." It all seemed so unbelievable that I wouldn't have sworn to any of it.

"Zab, get me the magnifying glass."

Zab returned with it in seconds, along with some towels.

Musso leaned close, looking at my still-bleeding wounds.

I reached for the towels Zab was holding, but Musso swatted them away. He continued to look at several different spots on my legs.

"It was grouslies," he said softly, to me or Zab, I wasn't sure. Musso dropped the glass, sitting back on his heels. The wizened warlock was looking as rattled as I was.

"That can't be right. Are you sure? No one's seen grouslies in centuries," Zab said, turning a horrified stare at Musso.

"We don't want to stanch the flow. Better to let the wounds bleed. We need to get Hawk. He'll know how to treat them." Musso stood and went for the stack of newsflash papers on the shelf.

"Are you sure? How can that be?" Zab asked, stunned and kneeling in front of me, looking for himself.

"I study creatures. I know what a grouslie bite looks like," Musso said, jotting down something on the paper.

"I've had a tetanus shot," I said hopefully.

Zab laid a hand on the blanket in the vicinity of my arm. "I'm not sure what kind of human magic that is, but I'm not sure it will help with a grouslie attack."

Musso was walking toward the door when it swung open.

Hawk walked in. "Why is there a trail of blood leading..." He caught sight of me sitting in the chair behind Musso and Zab.

"Grouslies." Musso moved to the side, giving Hawk a clear view of my legs. Zab did the same.

Hawk's eyes went from my legs to my face. There was a flicker of emotion in his steely eyes as the room grew quiet for a heavy second.

I wanted to reach for the towels again, cover my legs, and pull the blanket more firmly around me, because when Hawk focused his attention on me the way he was now, I felt like I was lying bare before him. My entire life, I'd been able to blend into the background and hide. Not from him. The way he was staring at me now made me feel even more unhinged, like I wanted to run and hide, or run to him, and I couldn't figure out which.

Hawk walked over and knelt in front of my legs, calm and bringing a stillness with him. He took in the damage without a flinch. "It could've been worse. Most people don't survive a grouslie attack. I'll take care of Tippi. You and Zab take the cane and try to track them."

Musso and Zab immediately launched into action, digging through cabinets I'd never seen opened before.

Hawk bent over me to lift me.

"I can walk," I said.

"No, you can't. It'll increase your blood flow and spread the poison. Hang on to my neck."

"Poison?" I did what he said. He carried me almost in a sitting position so as not to touch where my flesh was mutilated.

"Don't worry. I can fix it. What happened?" He began climbing the stairs on the left. For some reason I'd assumed he was taking me to my bedroom. I didn't care where I went if he could fix me.

"I was getting cocoa. I left the Sweet Shop, and there

they were. I didn't do anything. I don't know why they came after me." I sucked in a breath as his arm grazed my leg.

He tried to shift slightly, righting the position as he continued. "How did you get them to leave?"

"I didn't. They just stopped. Oh God," I said as suddenly a wave of stinging pain swelled, feeling like a thousand bees were stinging me all at one. It ebbed as suddenly as it had come on.

"That's the poison beginning to work. Try to remain calm. I don't want your heart to beat too hard."

I would've argued over how stupid that suggestion was if my heart rate wouldn't have accelerated.

"Am I going to... Will I..." My biggest concern leaving the Sweet Shop had been making it back to Salem. Now I wasn't sure I'd make it out of this building again, let alone back to Rest.

"You'll be fine," he said.

There were many levels to what someone could think was fine. It could be right above horrible or right below good and anywhere in between. Fine was very open to interpretation, which was why I didn't ask him any more questions. This was one of those times I'd rather not know. Plus, another wave of stinging pain was spreading up my legs and stealing all my thoughts.

By the time the last wave of stinging subsided, we were at the door that had led us outside into the forest or to a sitting room. When he opened it this time, it was a bedroom. The walls were the darkest navy that seemed to blend into nothing. When I looked upward, I saw a night sky, except it wasn't cold as it should've been, and there was no fifth wind. That wasn't to say it was exactly warm, but more like a chilly spring evening.

"Are we..." I looked at the walls, then the sky again.

"It's an illusion—sort of," he said, placing me down on the large bed. He waved a hand and the fireplace roared to life.

There were no windows. Only the fireplace and the stars above shed light on some trunks and fur rugs scattered about a wooden floor. I wasn't sure where we were now, but we definitely weren't in the building. There was a feel to this place that was hard to define but much different, like it had some of the sizzle of Hawk's magic infused in the air.

"What's a grouslie?" I asked as he kneeled before me, took another look at my legs, and stood.

"A grouslie is a creature that comes from the Unsettled Lands, or so we believe. They haven't been seen in these parts for centuries, and even before then, we weren't completely sure where they came from."

"I guess I came when they were making a rebound."

He didn't laugh as he moved about the room, gathering bottles from different trunks and bringing them to a table, where he poured them together.

"And the grouslies just left?" he asked while he worked.

"Yes. Maybe I tasted too bitter for them." I laughed at my own joke, knowing it wasn't that funny.

His profile was toward me as he continued to work. "Did someone else come along? Were you alone the entire time?" His intensity seemed to increase as he waited for an answer.

"I was alone as much as I can recall." After the grouslies were chewing me up alive, there was definitely room for error. I sucked in a breath as another round of stinging began. It was worse than the previous times and felt as if it were crawling up my legs, working its way into my veins, and trying to spread farther.

He turned, a bowl in his hand, as he knelt in front of me. "Try to be still. It's going to hurt, but I've got to neutralize the poison before it kills you or your flesh blackens and rots off."

"Oh God," I said, and then closed my mouth, fearing I might vomit. I had to get out of this place. Had to. I couldn't live in a place that had killer rats that poisoned you. If I was stuck here too much longer, I was going to crack. I'd split open and my brains would tumble out, completely scrambled.

"Trust me, God has nothing to do with grouslies. Put your legs out straight."

I did as he asked, and he sprinkled them with an iridescent dust. It hurt, but not as much as the stinging. This was more like a splash of disinfectant on a very big cut. The longer the dust was on my skin, the more it began to numb, finally offering some relief.

"Flip over," he said, moving to the backs of my legs.

He was more than halfway done when I could think clearly enough to ask, "Is there something strange about the grouslies leaving on their own?" I looked at him over my shoulder.

His eyes met mine. "Grouslies don't attack and retreat. They attack and kill, unless you fight them off. Most witches and warlocks can't fight off a grouslie attack unless they're at least a lower-end Braw."

The evil in the forest was from the Unsettled Lands. These grouslies were from the Unsettled Lands. Raydam wanted to help the evil in the Unsettled Lands. I hadn't given Raydam a firm answer, but I knew how badly I lied. There were a few too many things pointing toward Raydam being behind this. Maybe they hadn't killed me because this had been a warning.

If I asked Hawk if Raydam was behind this, he'd know I was turning Raydam down. I wasn't willing to fess up to that just yet. I'd rather see how long Hawk's patience would last. How fast he'd be willing to throw me out. I wanted to know how much trust he really had in me or if we had a relationship built on facade only. But that didn't mean I couldn't ask at all. I just couldn't spell it out.

He was nearly to my knees, so I had a small window in which to try to slip the question past him. "Do you think that maybe the grouslies could've been controlled by someone who saw me with you and was afraid I was going to help you?"

He covered the last part of my leg. "It wasn't Raydam."

What was the deal? Did I blast every thought I had at him somehow?

"I didn't say it was Raydam. I'm just wondering if maybe someone else who saw us on your little tour might've done something." Why did I have to be the worst at duplicity? Why couldn't I have learned something about lying in my nearly twenty years of living?

He gestured for me to turn back over while he looked for spots he might've missed.

He sat back on his haunches, studying me. "It wasn't Raydam. I don't know anyone who's ever been able to command grouslies, and he certainly wouldn't be the first." He stood and grabbed some fabric strips he'd had laid out.

I kept my attention on him, too afraid to see my legs.

"If someone *other* than Raydam was in cahoots with the dark, evil thing, they might be able to control the grouslies," I said.

He made quick work of wrapping one leg and tucked in the fabric. "It's not Raydam and it's not one of his goons. This has nothing to do with trying to change your mind or getting back at you. I don't think he realizes you're declining him yet."

Did I still have to stay calm? I hoped not, because my heart was pounding.

"Of course he doesn't, because I haven't decided yet. I might *not* decline him. How could Raydam know my decision when I don't know it?"

Hawk looked up, raised his brows while saying nothing, and then went back to what he was doing.

"I *don't* know." I mean, I was leaning a certain way, but it might change. It probably wouldn't, but I didn't believe in saying never. There still might've been a fraction of a percent of me thinking of moving over to Raydam's camp, even if the thought did make my skin crawl. Weirder things could happen.

Hawk tucked in the last strip of fabric. "You do know, but if you want to keep it to yourself for a while, I don't have a problem with that."

"How is it keeping it to myself if you already know?" And he knew that as well. If he was really fine, like he said, why point it out?

"I didn't say you were good at it."

I'd been ripped to shreds and, in spite of it, been making jokes to a flat audience. *This* he found amusing?

"You aren't kicking me out because you think you know what I'm going to do?"

He stood and nodded. "Yes."

"Well, I hate to break it to you, but I'm leaning toward accepting Raydam's offer." I really hoped I didn't need any more of that dust stuff after this.

"No, you aren't."

It was illogical to be disappointed in that answer when I would've done the very same thing in his shoes. His logic had been sound. You can't live with someone you can't trust. Can't give them access to all your inner workings.

Still, I'd wanted him to say otherwise. I'd wanted him to trust me, even if I was going to jump ship. It was utterly irrational.

"What if I tell you that I was going to pack my bags tonight?"

"You can pack tomorrow, if you want. You're not going to be able to walk tonight, so it'd be a bit tough," he said with a wave to my legs, and the sound of swallowed humor in his tone.

"Why can't you take me seriously? I could defect. You're not the only game in town," I said, wobbling to my feet to prove him wrong about something.

He stepped closer.

"Tippi, I do take you seriously. Being a bad liar isn't the worst thing in the world." He looked at me like he knew me, like he knew what was inside me and it was all goodness and sunshine. It made me want to look anywhere but him. No one was that good. I might've been a bad liar, but I had other sins on my tally sheet.

I took another couple of wobbling steps, wanting nothing more than to get to my room and lie down. Exhaustion from the night was settling on my shoulders like a sunset hugging the coastline after a long day.

"You'll be able to take the wraps off by tomorrow, but try to take it easy for the next couple of days."

I looked down at my wrapped legs, wondering what they'd look like after this. I'd never been vain. Hadn't given much thought about my looks. Life had always been quick to hand me more important things to focus on, like food and shelter and an insane mother.

"Thanks," I said, knowing I should be grateful to have legs at all.

"You shouldn't have scars. I put something in the mixture to prevent it."

Scars? I was afraid I'd be missing chunks of muscle.

I wobbled again as I walked toward the door, and he reached out to steady me.

"I can walk. I'll make it," I said, slowly making my way for the door that would hopefully open back up to the hall.

"Not for long," he said.

"What's that supposed to..." I felt my legs start to give out first, and then the rest of my body followed suit. I was out for the count.

28

I limped down the stairs, feeling more stiff than hurt. My legs might've been a torn-up mess yesterday, but true to Hawk's word, they were fine today. Well, a bit pinkish, with a lot of regrowth, but nothing that appeared to be scarring. I'd been leery to look this morning and had toyed with leaving the bandages on and forgoing a shower. Then they'd begun to unravel as I got dressed, forcing me to address the situation.

"You sure you're okay?" Rabbit asked. She hovered on the step below me, as if she could stop my fall with her tiny arms and frail legs if I went down.

"I swear I'm okay," I said, wondering if this might be a good time to tell her I was more worried about her than me.

"You should've woken me last night." She took a few more steps, keeping an eye on me while gripping the banister.

"I didn't want to wake you. You've been sleeping so much lately that I was afraid you were getting sick."

She paused on the stairs, her chin dropping an inch or so, before shaking her head. "No. I'm okay." She turned toward me. "I want you to know how happy I am that I'm here. I need you to know that, no matter what happens. Even if things go badly, I'll be grateful until my final breath that I didn't die in that factory."

I didn't like the sound of that. Some people might've thought it sounded like a goodbye of sorts. What was going on here?

As much as I wanted to question her more, she'd said she was okay. Maybe she was feeling a little ill but didn't want to talk about it? The ways here were so different; maybe she didn't like to talk about sickness? Maybe she wasn't ready to tell me what was going on? Just because I'd divulged how badly I was mauled in disgusting detail didn't mean she wanted to tell me about every little ache. Still, that last part had really sounded eerily like a goodbye.

She had the door open before I decided which way I was going to go: pry or shut up. Guess it was shut up for now, because this was not a conversation others needed to hear.

Zab and Musso looked at me as I walked into the office, and both of their heads then dropped to my legs clad in pants.

"You okay?" Zab asked, Musso all ears beside him. Even Belinda's glare wasn't notched up to the normal hostility.

"I'm as good as new," I said, giving them a thumbs-up. The curious look at my hand made it clear that the thumbs-up wasn't a widely used gesture here. "Thanks for your help last night."

Zab and Musso both nodded as they continued to stare at my legs.

"Going to go get a tea," I said, waving toward the back room.

"I'll get it for you. You sit somewhere," Rabbit said, high-tailing it to the back room, like if I tried to walk another step, I'd fall over and die.

I made my way to my table now that Rabbit had stolen my chance to escape the awkwardness. Belinda deigned to nod to me as I passed. It wasn't a warm hello or anything, but it was a big stride considering the typical *I want you dead* stare. I guessed she'd rethought it and decided it was harsh since she'd nearly won. That was awfully nice of her. If things kept improving, I might actually try the apology again.

"Maybe you should take the day off?" Zab asked as he rested a hand on the table, watching me ease my way into a sitting position.

"They don't hurt. They're just stiff." Very stiff.

"She's tough. She'll be fine," Musso said from the other side of the room with a gruff wave. "Tough" was about the best compliment you could get from Musso, and it warmed my insides a hair.

"They looked really bad," Zab said, softly this time.

I smoothed a pant leg down, hoping the raw skin wasn't showing. "Whatever Hawk put on them healed them up nicely."

Belinda narrowed her eyes, as if rethinking her opinion on me breathing air and then deciding she'd let me off the hook too soon.

"I know you went looking for those things. Did you find them?" I asked, trying to switch gears so Belinda didn't try to finish the job. I was too weak for a fight at the moment.

"We tried, but the trail was gone. They're notoriously hard to catch. I'm sorry."

"No need to apologize. Thanks for trying." I grinned, trying to not look like I wanted to run and hide and maybe never set foot out of here again.

They were still out there. What if they wanted me in particular? It had felt like that. Like they'd been waiting for me. Hawk said it wasn't Raydam, but who else?

"We looked for half the night," Zab continued, and I realized that my face must've betrayed every emotion I'd been thinking.

"Sorry, kid. We really did try to catch them," Musso said, walking back to my table.

Belinda had her head down, so engrossed in her papers, but I could tell she was listening to every word.

"I'm sure you did. I don't blame you guys at all."

Rabbit walked back in, breaking up the little pity-fest everyone was having for me. It was just in time, too, because the more we discussed it, the more unhinged I was feeling about it.

She set a tea down in front of me. "Do you need anything else? Do you want me to get you something to eat?"

"I'm good. Really. I swear whatever Hawk did last night made a huge difference."

Belinda raised her eyes to glare. Dammit. We'd been doing so well for a couple minutes. That second mention of Hawk's help was one time too many.

The door swung open and a pair of men walked in. They had a burlier edge than I was used to seeing in the office, more like the two who'd nabbed me originally.

"Musso, you got any work for us?" one asked, but their attention was almost completely on me.

Musso must've noticed as well, because he brusquely asked, "Did I send you a notice? No. So then there isn't. I'll let you know the way I always do if I need the services you two offer."

The pair turned to leave, but the larger of them slowed

as he neared me. "You the witch who survived the grouslie attack last night?"

"Keep it moving," Musso yelled, getting up from his seat. I'd never seen Musso mad before. It transformed his older face into something less gruff and friendly to more of a hard edge. I suddenly realized Musso wasn't someone you'd want to mess with.

The guy who'd questioned me raised his hands. "Sorry! No harm. We'll be going."

They made sure to get a long look at me as they did.

"How does everyone know already?" I asked Zab the second they were out the door.

He was watching them pass by the window as he sighed. "There were the clients here when you came in. Then people saw me and Musso out hunting last night, plus there was a hell of a mess outside the Sweet Shop. We were asking people if they saw anything weird. We had to give some details. Word must've spread."

Three more people walked past the windows and went to open the door. Again, none of them were recognizable as the usuals that got work here, not that I knew all of them. Still, they had a different look about them, almost as if they walked a different path, a darker, shadier one. Proving my gut right, they scanned the office until they found me.

I had a few options: A. I could sit here and let them all have their stare. B. Go hide in my room or the back room, afraid to ever walk out of this place again. Or C. I could toughen up, go get some air, and let the entirety of Xest see I'd survived—the ones who knew who I was, anyway. I was starting to think that number was growing quite large these days.

"I'm going for a walk. I'll be back in a few." I grabbed my

jacket from the hook it always hung on, realizing it wasn't going to be that much of a walk with the stiffness.

Musso nodded. Even Belinda gave a little shrug.

Zab got to his feet. "You sure?"

"Yes. It's not like I'm never going to go outside again."

"But maybe you should wait until Hawk is around," he said, as if I'd be attacked by another herd of grouslies the minute I walked out the door.

That got Belinda's head up with a good healthy jerk.

"I can't stay inside unless I have Hawk to hold my hand. You said they were gone. It's broad daylight, with a lot of people around. I'll be fine."

"I'll go with her," Rabbit said, rushing to grab her jacket from the hook.

I wasn't sure I necessarily wanted company, but I didn't exactly mind it either. It would be nice to have someone to run for help if those grouslies came for me again. Rabbit might not be able to do much for me, being a Whimsy witch but she could sure scream loud enough.

"See? I have an escort," I said, smiling at Rabbit and then Zab.

"Hang on," Zab said. He dug into the petty cash box and flipped me a few coins. "If you're going out, you might as well have that cocoa you didn't get last night."

"Thanks. See you in a bit."

29

The shop window had an array of teacups and saucers, but I couldn't really see any of it. The only thing my brain would process was the need to get out of this place. How could anyone live in a place where monsters appeared out of snowdrifts to eat you alive? What if the next time it wasn't a warning?

And why was it that Rabbit was moving even slower than me when I was the one who'd gotten mauled?

"They're all getting their fill checking you out," Rabbit said, also not paying any attention to the teacups displayed in the window.

"I need to get back to Salem." If Salem wasn't an option any longer, I'd find somewhere else that was safe. Anywhere but here. The second I got comfortable, bad things happened.

"You will," she said, but she didn't look as positive as the words she'd uttered.

There was a pause as we both pretended to study the china display while everyone looked at me.

Rabbit put a shoulder to the window frame, a little less color in her cheeks than this morning.

This was a better time than any I'd had yet. I needed to know if something was wrong. Weren't we close enough for me to ask? To push a little?

"You know, Rabbit, I'm worried about you. Are you sure I—"

"Come on, let's go get that cocoa," she said, as if I hadn't been speaking.

What was I going to do? I couldn't drag the words out of her if she didn't want to tell me. Especially not when she looked like she was about to run away if I didn't stop with the questions, even if it were just in the direction of the Sweet Shop.

I followed her, letting the subject drop simply because I was too inept at figuring out a better approach. I'd grown up avoiding subjects. I had no experience in forcing issues. Maybe there was a book on how to do that on the shelves in the office. Until I could get some counsel on it, it might not happen successfully.

I fell into step beside Rabbit, in the direction I'd been avoiding since we'd left the shop. In order to get cocoa, I had to get past the bloody proof of my attack.

"What's Salem like?" Rabbit asked, as if sensing my unease and completely disregarding her own a few minutes ago.

I wasn't going to complain about a distraction.

"Calm and peaceful, quirky and flavorful. Most of all, homey, at least to me. Pretty much the best place ever. My main complaint used to be the cold, but that was before I experienced the fifth wind." The wind took that opportunity to kick up, and I pulled the collar of my jacket up. "It's like it's coming from every single direction all at once. Is there even a summer here?" I hoped I wouldn't be around long enough to find out.

"What's summer?"

"Does it ever get hot?" Maybe they had a different name for it, but that didn't bode well. *Please let them have a different name for it.* If this was their summer, I'd freeze before I made it back to Salem.

"Oh." She clucked her tongue a couple of times, clearly stalling. "What would you consider hot, exactly? It gets a little less cold, I guess, but only a few days here and there. Does that count as summer?"

Not even close.

"You know, not important." I shook my head and kept looking forward, avoiding the stares directed my way. My attention was focused on one spot—or where the spot should've been.

"It's gone." I slowed down, trying to find the big blood bullseye in the snow.

"What is?" Rabbit asked.

"Where's the blood spot?"

She looked around, as if trying to figure out what I was talking about. "Oh, that. Yeah, Zab was telling Musso that Hawk got rid of it," she said casually.

Why would Hawk have gone to the trouble of doing that? He must not have wanted to draw anyone's attention to it. Only plausible reason. He couldn't have realized how much I'd dislike seeing it. Even if he did guess, I doubt he'd care enough to do anything about it.

"Tippi!" Raydam's voice rang from somewhere behind us.

"Oh, shit. Keep walking and don't look back." I pushed stiff legs to a pace that strained my raw muscles. We walked past the Sweet Shop. Cocoa would have to wait.

The sugar sculptures and wall of candies would make a perfect trap.

"What's wrong? Are we avoiding him now?" she asked, forcing herself to keep up to my quicker stride.

"I think he had something to do with the attack," I whispered. The people who'd been staring earlier were now attempting to listen as well. Raydam chasing us down the street wasn't helping.

"But you said Hawk didn't think he did it."

I'd given her a full rundown this morning. I didn't know why she thought I'd adopted Hawk's opinion. Hawk didn't know everything Raydam was up to.

"I don't care what Hawk thinks. He's wrong."

"I just figured since Hawk was so strong, he might know."

"Tippi!" Raydam called again, closing the gap.

I grabbed Rabbit's arm and kept her moving when she slowed.

"Oh, uhm." She kept looking over her shoulder. It was clear that ignoring someone with more magic went against the grain for her. I was going to break her habit if it killed us both.

"Hawk doesn't know everything, and you need to stop thinking that people who have more magic know better. They don't. They lucked out with some genetics, or whatever it is that makes them that way. But it doesn't make them smarter."

"Are you sure?"

I gave her a stern look.

"Okay, I mean, I guess..."

I walked faster, urging Rabbit to keep up. My initial impression of Raydam was that he'd never run after someone on the street. It was too undignified and desperate.

I also didn't think he'd continually yell and wave his hands in the air like a desperado as he was currently doing. My initial assessment was way off the mark, as my name carried down this block and probably the next.

The outing's purpose of getting everyone past their curiosity was making things worse. The way Raydam was chasing us, they would never stop staring, wondering about the girl who'd survived the grouslies.

I could make a run for it. We were already becoming a spectacle, so no loss there. But was I really going to run like a chicken? I was sick of looking like a weak ninny in front of everyone. I was tired of running to someone else for protection, too. That hadn't helped anyway. I'd still gotten attacked.

"I don't think he's going to stop. He looks pretty intent on talking to you," Rabbit said. Raydam was nearly to us, walking as fast as he could without breaking into a jog.

I slowed and then resigned myself to wait.

"I can't believe he wants to talk to you this badly." Rabbit wrung her hands in front of her.

Raydam was smiling like he'd run into an old friend he hadn't seen in years. My expression was colder than the fifth wind.

Rabbit was picking at her cuticles, about to draw blood.

"Hey, this might go better if he gets me alone. Why don't you go get our cocoas? No reason we both have to deal with him."

"You sure?" she asked, her brow crinkling. I could see her twitching, as if she wanted to run even as her feet stayed put. Generations of an ingrained caste system showed in her eyes.

"Positive. I'll yell if things go downhill, and this will go better with fewer people." I dug out the coins, put them in her hand, and gave her a push in the other direction.

"I'll be nearby if you need me."

"I know."

Rabbit walked away as Raydam walked closer, not acknowledging her as he passed. To him, she was a nobody. Man, was I envious. I missed those days.

People were watching us, pausing farther down the street or walking past like they were wading through glue. Shopkeepers and customers were peeking out their windows, burning my face into their hard drives.

Raydam stopped in front of me with a sigh. His friendly expression persevered, even after the chase I'd given.

"I heard what happened and wanted to offer my condolences on the attack."

Be cordial and move on, that was what I should've done. I'd never been very good at that, though. Hiding in plain sight and evading, that had always been my thing. But he hadn't let me do that, so now we were here, me having to lie and pretend we were good. Which brought me to my other issue of lying badly.

"Really? You did?" I crossed my arms, and not because it was freezing.

His smile slipped. "You don't think I had anything to do with that, surely."

Shut up. Keep it pleasant and move on. Doesn't matter if he set the grouslies on you. Be smart about it. Lie low. Don't draw attention and declare war on someone who could eat you up and spit you out.

"Of course I do." *Shut. Up.* I had to shut up. Then I thought about the abomination I'd felt in the forest, the awe in his voice, and the dreams in his eyes. "Because I have no desire to become one of your co-conspirators and help you spread the evil that's growing. That's why." I'd once again ignored my inner voice. It was a wonder it bothered talking to me anymore. If it spoke again, it would probably just tell me to go to hell.

His face contorted as if he didn't know who I was anymore. He took a step back, looking me up and down, as if there was an imposter in my skin. I'd thought I was a bad liar, but I guess I'd done better than I'd thought the night we met. Or Raydam had seen what he wanted, another syco-phant waiting to do his bidding. That was more likely, since I was very aware of my shortcomings.

"Tippi, are you saying you felt the presence and thought it was evil?" He put his hand to his chest.

"Yes, that's exactly what I'm saying."

He shook his head, taking another step away from me as if I were some filth he'd accidentally gotten too close to that might sully his fine clothes. "Then worry no more. I won't be bothering you again. You're better off with him if that's how you feel about it. Good day to you both."

Raydam nodded to a spot over my shoulder before he gave me his back and walked off. I didn't have to turn around to know who was there, but I did. Hawk was leaning on the building.

"I really don't think he set the grouslies on you, but thank you for the entertainment. My day was getting a little dull." He smiled.

"Then why did they attack me? Who else?"

"I don't know."

"Well, I do. And how did you end up here? I was fine on my own," I said, not concerned anyone would hear us. I'd been laser focused on Raydam and hadn't noticed the street had cleared until now.

"Rabbit came and fetched me. Was afraid there might be trouble."

I took a step closer to him and tilted my head back until I looked him in the eye. "Why is it that you clear the street but Raydam doesn't?"

He made a show of looking around. "Guess most people are naturally skittish creatures. Since it seems you don't need me, I'll get back to my business." He nodded and walked away.

Rabbit swooped in with a cocoa in each hand as if she'd been lying in wait. "Hope you don't mind that I got Hawk. Thought I should go get these after he was with you. Figured you might need one after that."

"Thanks," I said, taking the cocoa from her and then sipping on it. Couldn't deny it hit the spot on a day like today, or a week like this week. Soon it might be a month like this month.

She sipped hers as she eyed me over her cup. "You're not angry with me, are you? About calling in Hawk?"

"Not at all. I would've done the same thing." And even if I didn't admit it, the thought that she'd run and gotten me help was a comfort—not that I'd admit that to Hawk.

We started walking again. "I do have to say, I'm surprised you got him and not Zab or someone." The stronger the witch or wizard, the more Rabbit had seemed to shy away. As far as approachability went, Zab had everyone in the office beaten hands down, including myself. The guy was like a beacon of friendliness. Even Musso with his gruff ways was easier than Hawk.

"If you got into a fight with Raydam, you would've needed Hawk. Not that Zab isn't great, but Raydam is an awfully strong warlock."

That tone of reverence was back, but I let it go. I had too

much on my plate at the moment to make any more progress in that department. But I would.

"I guess I just never figured you'd approach Hawk. You seem to avoid him."

She tipped her head a little and a smile played at the corners of her mouth. "I don't know. I guess I knew he'd want to come if he thought there was a problem. Plus, he's been growing on me. He never makes me feel bad, like I'm less than." She was still smiling as she sipped her cocoa.

Huh? I thought back to all the times Hawk had been around Rabbit and couldn't remember a single one where he'd gone out of his way to make her feel at home. This place was so odd, their ways so confusing. I'd never get used to it.

"I can see what you're thinking," she said, a hint of laughter in her tone.

"Well, it's hard not to find that a little curious. It's nothing against you. It's against him, if we're truthful. It's not like he's overly nice to people."

She smiled widely now, as if I'd just revealed everything. "That's it, though. Don't you get it? Besides you, he doesn't care who anyone is, or what they can do. Most people in Xest look at a Whimsy witch as if she's barely worth the air they breathe. Not Hawk. He treats everyone with the same disregard and disdain. It's *amazing*."

Luckily, we were back at the office before I had to hear any more about how great Hawk was for disliking the world.

30

After my initial attempt at letting everyone have a good look at me failed, I spent the rest of the day relaxing in the back room with Rabbit, where I didn't have to see anyone at all. She found some more things to organize, because she couldn't seem to help herself, while I flipped through magic books that didn't make any sense.

Zab came back to light the fire for us as the daylight waned without either of us asking.

"I'll get a light," Rabbit said, grabbing the nearest candle, trying to be helpful.

I'd given up on any pretense of my magic working. If I helped, we'd be in worse shape, so I sat there awkwardly, pretending to be intrigued in a book I couldn't understand. I must've grabbed some sort of advanced magic, because even the words were a muddled mess.

Hawk stepped into the room. I knew the second he did because I always sat up a little straighter. Then I slouched again, because I hated my reaction. I'd narrowed my sensitivity in his area down to either an inferiority complex on my part, because I continually failed in front of him, or the fact that he always noticed me and it made me self-conscious. It was definitely one of those two for sure.

He wasn't looking at me this time, though. His attention was on Rabbit. Out of curiosity, I glanced over my shoulder to see why she'd snagged his attention. Was there something brewing there I hadn't realized? I mean, she was a cute girl. Much nicer than Belinda. And if he favored her, then that was just wonderful. I'd be happy for them both.

Then I saw what she was up to and wanted to cringe for her. She was holding her fingers to a candle, but all it was doing was smoking. Mine didn't light at all, but I'd never seen one do that. From the deep red of her face, it wasn't a defective candle.

"I'm sure you had a long day. I got it," Zab said, walking over and lighting it for her.

She smiled and nodded, not meeting anyone's gaze and more interested in the floorboards.

I should've stopped looking sooner, but alarm bells were ringing and throwing me off my game. She caught my eye and shook her hand out before clenching it in front of her. "It's not a big deal. It always happens to me when my fingers are cold," she said, adding a little nervous laugh that sounded something closer to a siren blaring in my head.

I smiled back, pretending that I didn't realize anything was wrong and that whatever was happening with her magic was fine.

"Well, I'm beat. Going to head on to bed," Rabbit said, taking the candle with her.

I caught Hawk giving Rabbit's back another glance before she disappeared. Zab followed her out, and I knew he was going to find an excuse to go light her fire upstairs, the way he always did.

I waited until the sound of their footsteps on the stairs faded.

"Are you ready to practice?" Hawk asked.

For once, that question was not what put me in a worse mood. "What's wrong with Rabbit? I saw the way you were looking at her when the candle didn't light."

"It's not my place to say." He took a few steps closer, his brows a little lower and a solemn look about his eyes.

I shook my head and slumped farther into the couch. I was so tired of not knowing what was going on—not knowing what everyone wanted and not being able to do anything about it. I wanted to lean forward and crack my head on the corner of the wooden table in front of me and call it a day. I didn't have that luxury, since this problem wasn't about me. If there was something wrong with Rabbit, I wanted to know, and I was tired of sidestepping an issue everyone else knew about.

"We don't have an honest and open relationship. I get that. We're together because we have to be, and I understand that as well. But something is happening with her, and everyone seems to know what it is but me. Please, tell me. Maybe I can help her, but I don't even know what the problem is."

He shook his head. "Tippi, you're an outsider here. You have to realize it's not something that is discussed."

I didn't want to be here. I'd made no bones about it. So why did it feel like I'd gotten sucker-punched when he called me an outsider? It didn't matter, so I shook it off. I'd wallow another day when I could afford to care. This moment, I was going to get answers.

"It's clearly not a secret if everyone else knows. She's one of my only friends."

He looked the other way. When he finally turned back to

me, I could see the lines of his face had softened. "Her magic is fading. She won't be able to survive much longer."

What? I had to replay his words a few times as I put them together with what Rabbit had told me my first night there, about how Whimsy witches didn't last long in the factory. But she was out of the factory.

"Are you saying she's going to die? Surely that's not what you mean."

He walked over and sat on the opposite couch. "You can't live in Xest without magic. It's the equivalent of a human living somewhere without oxygen. Some people are born with regenerating magic, but most aren't. Rabbit was born with a low supply to begin with, and then working at the factory, it was bound to shorten her life span."

"But she's not in the factory anymore. She's barely using her magic. I mean, she's lighting a candle here and there, but that's it. How draining could that be?" I asked, feeling there had to be an error in his assessment.

"Even if she never used another drop, she's got maybe another couple months at best. She's fallen too low to be able to survive."

"Months? That's it?" For once in my life, I should've stuck with the secrets and mystery. Why did I have to know everything? Ever since I was a little kid, I'd had this problem. I could never leave well enough alone. Always had to get to the bottom of everything because I trusted no one. Had to know every nitty-gritty detail and find out who was lying. And where did it get me? I was sitting in some messed-up land, with a hot jerk across from me, telling me my only friend was going to kick it soon.

No. That wasn't going to be Rabbit's end. Work her entire life in a factory to finally get out and die? Not if I could stop it.

"What if she goes somewhere else? What happens if she gets out of the Xest? What happens if someone is born without it? It must happen once in a while."

"If they're lucky, they're abandoned outside one of your hospitals within an hour of being born or they die. She could live a normal life span as a human in Rest." He shrugged, as if this was an unorthodox suggestion.

"It's only here that she'll die?" I leaned forward, my gut telling me I was right. This time I listened.

"Yes."

"Then she's got to go."

He shook his head. "It's not that simple. Most people would rather live what time they have here than go somewhere with no family, no friends, a completely different way of life."

"A completely different life where she'll actually have one? That doesn't sound so bad to me."

"But this isn't you. It's her life and her choice."

No, it wasn't. Not anymore. Not if she made the wrong one.

"You said you were paying the rent on my apartment in Salem, right?"

"Yes."

"She could go there. She could take my apartment until she gets settled. Loris probably needs a replacement for me anyway. She has a hard time holding on to employees, but Rabbit would be a perfect fit." Loris was so outside the box, she wouldn't think anything if Rabbit seemed odd as well. And Loris could certainly use Rabbit's skills with organizing. "I could give her a crash course on normal. She's smart. She'll figure out everything else as she goes. Could you get her there?"

"If she wants me to, yes. Are you sure that's what *you* want?"

I didn't need to ask what he meant. In a sense, Rabbit would be stepping into my life, the one I'd been dying to get back to. I'd be handing it to her on a silver platter, all warm and toasty. It already hurt to think of her going back there without me, but there wasn't one part of me that didn't want to help her. The pain of her death would be a million times worse. It wasn't a question.

"Yes. And she will go. I'll make sure of it."

I got up, knowing I had to make her leave somehow.

"Where are you going? Time to practice." A book thudded loudly on the table.

Shit.

31

Rabbit walked over, grabbed the chair by mine and practically fell into it as she leaned her chin on her palm. "I know I said I'd go with you for cocoa after lunch, but I'm going to head upstairs early if you don't mind?"

Zab's attention shifted from the client in front of him to Rabbit, and then the clock above my head. I didn't need the reminder, even a silent one, that it was barely three and she was sputtering out. Not to mention that my plan had a better chance of going over well if she were loaded up with chocolate.

"Of course not. Go rest if you need to," I said, trying to hide the fact that she was messing up my schedule to save her ass.

"Thanks." She nodded, her lids drooping before she stood. She walked across the office as if she'd aged fifty years in the past week.

I went back to sorting requests but had to reread the one in my hand three times, and it still didn't register. I threw it on the pile and went in the back to get tea.

Musso followed me in a few minutes later, getting a cup himself.

He took a sip of his tea, watching me over the rim. "I might be the oldest one in this office, but I don't hold with all the old ways."

I waited to see where this was going. It might've been the longest sentence Musso had ever spoken to me.

"She's not going to be in this world much longer, one way or another. You're her friend. If you have a plan, you should talk to her. If you're going to try to help her, you don't have much time left."

Musso was a perfect example of never knowing where your allies might come from. "It's not that easy when she doesn't want to talk to me."

"Then you find a different way to do the talking."

I nodded, flopping down on the couch. "I just..." I shook my head. "I'm scared."

"If you're not terrified from time to time, you're not living life, kid. Good luck. Fight the good fight."

"Thanks, Musso."

He took his tea and walked out of the room.

He was right. I should've been taking on this fight as soon as I saw something wrong. I shouldn't have let this go on so long, but I hadn't wanted to see it. When I woke up in the morning, I liked having tea with someone who didn't care how much magic I had. Who'd liked me even when I was a Whimsy witch. When I went to sleep, I liked knowing there was a person in the room over if I woke up freaked out about something. I hadn't had that since I was a kid, and not even then.

When I'd woken with a bad dream as a child and gone to my mother, it had always turned into a full-out event that was worse. She'd tell me it was a premonition. No one

wanted to think their nightmares were what was to come. I'd
end up hiding under blankets in my closet afterward. But
Rabbit couldn't afford my selfishness.

There was one way I could disguise this that she might
buy. I just hoped she'd take the bait.

I put my tea down and walked out of the back room, but
instead of returning to work, I went to the stairs, hoping I'd
catch her before she was out cold. Musso gave me a nod of
approval. As silly as it was, that nod stiffened my resolve
more. I'd never known what having a father was like, but
Musso would've been a good one. He knew what was right
and wasn't scared to tell you.

I walked up the steps and knocked softly on her door.
"Rabbit?"

"Come in. Everything okay?" She was lying in bed, eyes
half-closed, as if I'd woken her up.

I sat down on the end of her bed. The irony wasn't lost
on me that the dying girl wanted to make sure I was doing
well. It galvanized my heart to do what was right, no matter
how it might sting.

I flopped back on the bed, letting out a sigh that
could've woken the dead. "Yeah, I'm a little homesick is
all."

"I'm sorry."

I bit my lower lip, like she often did when she was in a
bad way, and made sure she saw it. I'd bite right through it
and bleed out if I had to.

"The worst part is Loris. I told you about her. She owned
the shop I worked at?" I'd told her many times, thankfully,
and I was going to use it now.

"Yeah, I remember."

"I *know* she's having a hard time. I asked Hawk to stop in
there for me, and she's still alone in that shop." And if Loris

wasn't, someone was going to have to hire a ghost to scare them off.

"Oh," Rabbit said, with enough sadness in her tone to tell me my bull was working.

"She's getting older, and she's always been a little bit susceptible to being taken advantage of. I worry about her constantly. I wish I could go take care of her." I sounded so convincing that I was beginning to realize I wasn't actually full of shit at all. I was saying all the things I'd been feeling but swallowed back. I *was* worried sick about Loris. So much so that I found myself sniffing and afraid I was going to do something as ridiculous as cry.

"I'm sorry, Tippi. Isn't there anyone that could help her?"

"No. Not really." Another truth. I didn't know a single person in Salem that I'd trust. Not that Salem was full of bad people; I'd just kept to myself, and Loris had a way of scaring people away with her eccentricity.

Time for the big light-bulb moment. Acting as if this idea wasn't premeditated might really test my skills. Luckily, Rabbit wasn't used to seeing Oscar-worthy actors. The last thing she needed to know about was the conversations happening behind her back. She wasn't going out like that. She was leaving this place with her head high because she was saving me. And in a way, she was. The more I thought this over, the better I felt knowing someone would be with Loris.

I dropped my head, wiping eyes that hadn't actually teared, although they had gotten close. "You know, I did have a thought. This is a big ask, but do you think that maybe you could go stay at my place in Salem and help her out a bit? Just until I get done here? You know I'd never bring it up if I could go myself."

Her brows drew closer together, but she didn't seem

appalled by the idea. Just shocked? Stunned? Was there a difference? Whichever was worse, she was.

"Me? I don't know anything about Rest. How could I possibly help her?" She began to fidget with her blanket.

I launched into calming words before she went into full-blown panic. "Trust me, it's a lot easier than learning the ins and outs of this place. It will be cake for you, and you might like it. Plus, I know Loris would *adore* you." More truths. Loris *would* love Rabbit, and Rabbit was the exact type of person Loris needed.

The more I said, the more it started to sting. She'd truly be stepping into my life. It hadn't been the end all be all as far as lives went, but it had been mine. I'd worked hard for that life. Still, it had to happen.

"But how would I get there? Where would I live?"

"You could stay at my apartment. It's not much, but it's cozy and furnished."

Her jaw dropped and she leaned closer. Oh shit. Had I blown it somehow?

"All by myself? Like, my own place?" Her eyes lit up, as if I were offering her the keys to Buckingham Palace.

"Like I said, it's not much. All my stuff was bought used. My plates don't match. I mean, it's got some drawbacks for sure." She better not get too excited or this wouldn't end well when she got to *see* my place. By her expression, she either didn't understand what I was saying or didn't care.

"I've never gotten to stay somewhere all by myself, like— ever. But how would I get there?"

Okay, we were moving into logistics. This was a good sign.

"Hawk needs me here, so he'll have to get you there as a trade-off." He'd do it whether he liked it or not. As far as I saw it, my side of the scale had been piling up. Hawk would say my side was nearly touching the floor at this point but he'd be wrong. That grouslie attack had really evened things out.

Her brows dropped and her lips parted. She started chewing on her lower lip like it was an all-you-can-eat buffet. "What if I mess up?"

"I'm telling you, it's so easy. You can do it. I'll train you on everything you need to know before you go. And Loris *needs* you."

"I mean, you did save me from the factory. I do owe you this." She nodded more as the idea settled into a possible reality.

"Then you'll do it?"

She looked up at me again, not biting her lip this time, and with more strength and resolve than I'd seen since I met her.

"Of course I will. Like you said, Loris *needs* me. I'm not going to let anyone take advantage of her. You can rely on me."

"I knew I could."

I'd once heard the most important thing you could give a person was a purpose. I'd never realized how true that was until I saw Rabbit at this moment.

32

The office had closed hours ago. The only other person left was Zab, who was finishing up some paperwork. I sat on the couch in the back room, slowly stewing as I realized Hawk wouldn't be showing up for practice. Not that I cared. All I did was fail anyway. But still, would it have killed him to tell me he wasn't coming? A friendly *hey, you're off tonight*? It wasn't like I expected him to be super punctual. I'd grown accustomed to waiting until some undisclosed time for him, but now he wasn't bothering to show at all.

This could be good. Yeah, maybe he'd come to his senses and was going to finally send me home.

That would be good. Yeah. It *would* be.

"Hey, where's Hawk?" Zab asked as he walked in the back.

"Who knows?"

"You know, he does this sometimes. Don't take it personally."

"Nope. Nothing personal about it." After all, Hawk and I weren't on a personal level. Why *would* I take it personally?

It wasn't *me*. He was a rude man. He didn't think I was worth the courtesy of a note.

I sipped my tea, which felt lukewarm compared to the fire brewing in me, and smiled like I didn't want to rip Hawk apart with my teeth and set fire to his building. He was probably off somewhere banging Belinda and I was forgotten. I hoped they had a good time. They deserved each other.

And why was I angry? I had the night off. This was a happy thing. Happy, happy, happy.

The couch creaked across from me. My internal rage had blocked out the presence of my company for a few seconds. I glanced up, trying to suppress the hatred that was probably oozing out of every pore.

"Hey, I'm going to meet up with some friends for a snack and drinks. Why don't you come with me?" Zab asked.

"Nah, I'm fine. Thanks, though." Pity invites had never appealed to me, and I'd had a lot in my life. Although most had come from Loris and included muddling herbs and chanting through the night. They probably wouldn't appeal to a lot of people.

"I think it would be good for you. Rabbit's already fast asleep, and my friends are dying to meet you." He was leaning forward with hope in his eyes.

I recognized hope very quickly in others, since I was usually so devoid of it myself these days. It always made me a little green. It was splendid to be on the edge of thinking things might turn out well.

"Why would they want to meet me?" There had to be a catch.

One thing was for sure: this was definitely not a pity invite. It was almost as if he'd been waiting for an opening to bring me to meet people, which was more bizarre and so far out of my wheelhouse that this boat might as well have been a unicorn.

"They heard about Hawk taking on a new witch and, you know, the rumor mills have been grinding nonstop since you've been here. If that weren't enough, then they heard about the grouslie attack you survived."

"Oh."

His cheeks reddened. "I might've said how cool you are too, and added something about what a badass you were after the attack, not even crying or carrying on, but so stoic. It just came up in conversation, you know? The way things do."

"Yeah, sure." I hoped he hadn't talked me up too much. They'd be highly disappointed if they met me in real life.

His face was growing redder by the minute as he looked at the books over my shoulder. All I wanted to do was give him a huge hug. Instead of feeling like a loser, having been stood up, I was actually feeling kind of like a cool kid for once.

"Thanks, Zab."

He met my gaze. A grin spread and then grew into an all-out smile.

"You sure you want to go anywhere with me? I don't have a good track record these days."

"Of course you do. You're still alive, aren't you? That's a good record in my book." He stood. "So you're coming?"

I stood. "Yes, I'm coming. Lead the way." What else was I going to do? Sit here and stew, waiting for Hawk?

We both grabbed our jackets and were off a few minutes later. There was something liberating about getting out after the grouslies attack, and doing something as normal as going to a local hangout. There was something wonderful about not sitting and waiting around for someone else.

"Where are we going?" I hadn't asked until we'd walked a couple of blocks because the truth was that I didn't really care. Anywhere was good with me.

"It's called the Watering Hole. It's just down the way."

I remembered walking past that place and hearing the hum of music and laughter leaking out, wondering who was having such a good time. My pace grew a little faster.

"It's where most of the Middlings hang out. I wouldn't care who came, but any time we've invited a Whimsy, they never showed, and the Braws all think they're too good for us. That's the thing about Middlings. We're used to being thought of as lesser *and* better. Seeing things from both angles gives you a better perspective."

"But I'm a Whimsy. Are you sure I'll be welcome by everyone?"

He paused, hand on the door and a *you've got to be kidding me* look on his face. "Tippi, there isn't anyone left in Xest who thinks you're a Whimsy."

He swung the door open before I could ask what they did think I was.

Any jangled nerves quieted as soon as I walked in and saw all the smiles. They might've been directed at Zab, but they spread to me right after.

Zab waved at the crowd in general. He might've had plans with only a few people, but the entire place appeared to be waiting for him.

I followed Zab to a table in the corner, where I was greeted by four more smiling faces.

"Tippi, this is Ab, Berita, Doug, and Nancy."

"Tippi! We've been waiting to meet you," one particularly jolly redhead said.

"Thanks! Me too." I hadn't heard about them until today, and not even then, but I didn't want to be mean.

"Can't wait to hear how you fought off the grouslies!" a brunette with great cheekbones said as she poured a pale liquid into a mug and handed it to me.

"Thanks, but I really didn't. They just left."

A dark-haired guy sitting in between the two girls said, "That's even more interesting."

"Yeah. Sit! Tell us about it," another guy said, pulling out a chair for me.

They were all so excited about my attack and survival that it somehow wiped away a little of the lingering pain and fear. It felt a little more like it had been an adventure, especially as I sat down and regaled them with the finer details. Maybe one day, I'd think of it as another war story from my time in Xest. I might not have anyone to tell it to, but it would make a good book.

I wobbled to the left but righted myself before I hit the ground.

"I told you that ale was stronger than it tasted," Zab said, closing in on my side, as if he didn't trust my ability to remain upright.

"I'm telling you, I'm good. I can get back on my own. You don't have to walk all the way to the office and back."

It turned out that Zab had an apartment on the second floor of the building next door to the Watering Hole, which wasn't altogether shocking after the reception he'd received. Clearly, he pretty much lived in both buildings. I wasn't sure which had come first, the apartment or the Watering Hole, but it was a perfect pairing.

"Of course I'm going to walk you." He pointed to an alley. "We'll cut through here. It's faster."

"You should've warned me about those purple shots." I might've been tipsy when I'd left the place, but the fifth wind was sobering me up fast.

"You mean pixie breath? I did warn you."

I hiccupped, and a small puff of opalescent dust shot out of my mouth. It wouldn't have been that bad, except it was beginning to coat the front of my jacket, and my wardrobe was already odd enough.

"When is this going to wear off?"

"That one looked pretty tame. I'm guessing the next will barely sparkle at all."

I swatted at the front of my jacket, trying to determine if I'd made it better or spread the dust farther. I was going to have to leave this out for the cleaning crew. They'd know what to do.

"Tippi," Zab whispered.

If he hadn't sounded alarmed, I would've known something was wrong because he was grabbing my arm, tugging me behind him. Most people didn't touch here, for any reason. Whatever the cold hadn't taken care of, fear finished up as I looked around for a threat and found it.

Not even ten feet in front of us, right at the opening to the street, a silver-scaled creature that had to be at least thirty feet tall stood. Its green eyes were zeroed in on me as it craned its head forward, the only thing that could fit in the alley, as leathery wings expanded behind it.

"Is that a dragon?" This had to be a joke. Every time this damned place lured me into thinking it wasn't so bad, shit like this happened.

"It looks like the pictures, but I've never seen one in person before. They don't come to these parts." Zab took a small step back, forcing me to do the same.

Prompted by our movement, the dragon inched forward

until its body was pressed against the buildings on either side of it. We both stilled.

"Can it breathe fire?" I asked, hoping some of the basic knowledge I had was wrong.

"If it's a dragon, then yes."

Why couldn't I have been wrong like every other time? This time I had to be right?

"And we think it's a dragon," I said.

"Yes."

Great. It could breathe fire.

A tingling feeling in my gut told me that running wasn't an option. It was too close.

It leaned its head even farther in. I edged a step back, grabbing at Zab's coat, trying to pull him with me.

Its large eyes didn't budge from me as its nose flared, taking in my scent, not once but twice, as it sniffed in some pixie dust with it. It had been tracking me. Someone had sent it after me, and I had a bad feeling the pixie dust was the only reason I wasn't fried yet. If I made it out of this alive, Hawk and I were going to have a long talk about Raydam. First, I had to survive.

"Zab, you need to go. It wants me," I said, tugging at him.

"You can't work your magic. You don't have a chance."

From what I'd learned about magic thus far, neither did he, being a Middling. We were looking at one dead witch, or two. One trumped two by a long shot.

The dragon's nose flared again, as if it were trying to nail down my scent. If I got out of here, Raydam was dead. I didn't care what anyone said. Who else would do this?

"Zab, if you go, you might be able to get me help in time. If you don't, we'll both die."

Zab shook his head. "He's going to strike as soon as I run. I'll never get help in time."

It turned out *soon* was only seconds before it let out a killing screech. Its chest ballooned, its mouth opened, and all I saw were flames barreling down its throat, about to cook us alive. I didn't think. I just acted, jumping on top of Zab, shoving him to the ground and covering him with my body.

I felt a boiling heat around me, but neither of us were burned as the stream of fire parted around us. It went on for a few seconds that felt like a few decades before it stopped.

The second the dragon broke it off, I jumped to my feet, hauling a confused Zab up with me. My idea of trying to run the other way didn't pan out. We'd barely gotten up before I launched on top of him again, shoving him to the ground and shielding him from the next stream of fire. This time lasted only slightly shorter before it needed more air in its lungs.

We got to our feet again, and I shoved Zab forward. "Run," I said, hoping one of us might make it out of this alive.

I pushed him hard enough that he stumbled backward. It was a fatal mistake, because as the dragon reloaded, his aim was drawn to Zab's moving target.

The dragon geared up for another blast, and Zab was too far away. There would be no covering him this time. On pure instinct, I swung my arms wide, trying to block the attack.

A blast of purple light shot out of my hands, hitting the dragon in the chest, propelling it to the other side of the street. It cried out in agony, a stream of fire shooting across the sky as it was slammed back into the building behind it. The huge creature straightened, shaking its head.

We'd been frozen in shock, but that faded fast as it moved. I grabbed Zab's hand and made a run for it, but only got a few steps before the sound of massive wings beating the air filled the silence. A shadow covered us, and we both plastered ourselves to the side of the building, expecting the worst. Nothing came. The dragon flew off.

The dragon was nearly out of view when I caught sight of Zab staring at me instead of the disappearing monster, his jaw nearly on the ground.

"You kicked a dragon's ass. How did you do that?" he asked. He looked at me as if I'd actually have an answer.

"I don't know." I shrugged, lifting my palms.

He stared at my hands, the ones that had come alive with magic as I shoved the dragon away from us. I found myself staring at them too. What had I done? How had I done it?

"Do you realize what that means? To beat a *dragon*? A *dragon*!" Wide eyes met mine, trying to see if I grasped the depth of his question.

I turned my head, more interested in getting out of this alley than discussing what any of this meant. Being new didn't make me an idiot as well. Someone Middling wouldn't have been able to beat a dragon. That might be a good thing for someone who wanted to live here in Xest for the rest of their lives, but it didn't serve any purpose for a person who was leaving. Considering the attention I'd gotten for the small acts of magic I'd already done, this didn't bode well. What invites might show up tomorrow? Who would be coming for me next?

"We need to get back to the shop. That thing was sure to draw attention, and I don't want to be here when people come and find out what happened." I looked in the direction we'd been heading before the dragon. That place was going to be crawling with people any second. We had to go back the other way.

"Zab, come on. We've got to go." I urged him into a jog.

Zab shook his head, still stunned. "Yeah, we gotta get back to the shop and tell Hawk."

"You'll have to tell me later," Hawk said as we turned the corner of the alley to find him standing there. "Keep walking. I don't want more eyes on you than you already have."

For once, I didn't mind Hawk's longer stride. It took me away from the sounds of an audience gathering in the street, who might get curious and start looking down the alleys.

We took a few turns until we were at the back of the building. I didn't fully breathe until I was in the back room.

Musso walked in from the front, his hat and scarf on. "What the hell happened out there? I heard the commotion going on and rushed over."

Zab launched into the story before I could find the words. I was only half listening, too stunned. As soon as I did start zeroing in on what he was saying, I realized I should've at least tried to take the lead.

Zab's arms were flying around as he told the tale. "This thing came, and I jumped in front of Tippi, and then she lifted her arms, and I swear two lightning bolts shot out of her hands, and the dragon was propelled across the street into the building, so dazed and freaked out that it took off."

"Are you sure it was a dragon?" Musso asked, scratching his head.

"Definitely," Zab said. "It was huge and shot fire. Its skin was like nothing I'd ever seen before, and its wings were insane. When it took flight, I swore the ground shook.

"But you should've seen her," Zab continued. "She was amazing. Saved us both. I would've been burned alive if she hadn't parted that fire somehow."

The more Zab spoke, the more Musso looked at me the way Zab was, and I wanted to crawl into a hole. The only one remotely normal was Hawk, who didn't seem surprised at all.

"I'm not sure if I did anything." I highly doubted I'd be able to do it again if I had. And I didn't want to if I could. It hadn't felt like it was me. I was *just* Tippi, a nobody, a store clerk no one noticed, and I liked it that way.

"You didn't shield Zab?" Hawk raised a brow. "Because I saw the scorched area on the pavement where someone shielded him."

He'd been around the corner. How had he seen that? He couldn't have been bluffing, though, because I'd seen the mark myself.

He crossed his arms as he waited for my response. If I were a good liar, I could've thought up a convincing response on the spot. But I was me. So instead of something brilliant, I said, "Well, yes. That did happen, but I'm not sure I did it. The dragon might've had a quirk or something. A defect." This all might've been true. It was more believable than thinking my perpetually failing magic did it.

"And then you flung it across the street," Zab added, practically jumping up and down. If I didn't get a hold of him soon, he'd be writing the screenplay.

"She's a Protectorate," Musso said, scratching his beard. "Can't believe we didn't see it."

Hawk nodded. "There's not many of them around. Considering that less than one percent of one percent of the witch and warlock population is a Protectorate, who would've thought it?"

"Ooh," Zab said. "Now it all makes sense."

The three of them were discussing me like I was a new animal at the zoo, but no one was sharing what the hell a Protectorate was. "Can someone let me in on this? What am I now?"

I was getting whiplash with the changes lately. Once upon a time, I'd been a normal person, which was still my aspiration. Then I was told I was a Whimsy witch. Then I was the Whimsy witch who wasn't, but I wasn't sure what I was if I wasn't. Now I was the Whimsy witch who wasn't, who was a Protectorate. The entire thing was enough to tie my tongue into a knot and my neurons into tangles.

I turned to Hawk. "Can you tell me what that means?"

He smiled, as if he were taking pity on me. It was much better than the awe-struck gaping.

"Almost all magic in Xest is offensive in nature. Yours is defensive. That's why you couldn't toss the book or light the fire. Your magic works nearly opposite. You couldn't fling the book because once you focused on the book, your magic sought to safeguard it. Same with the logs. Whatever you focus on, your magic wants to protect."

"If that were the case, how come she couldn't fend off the grouslies?" Zab asked.

"Maybe she's still getting her feet under her," Musso said, scratching his cheek.

Hawk said nothing, not sharing an opinion he surely had. He had one, too, because he always did.

"Well, now that the excitement is over and everyone is alive, I'll be crawling back into my bed," Musso said. "I have a line of appointments tomorrow, and I'm not a young buck anymore." He waved and headed out. It seemed like any momentary awe he might've had over the dragon incident had gotten swallowed up by his innate gruffness. I'd be eternally grateful, since I was already afraid of Zab's awe-struck hangover lasting a while.

The room fell quiet for a minute, and I caught a look between Hawk and Zab.

Zab took a few steps toward the door. "Okay, well, see

you guys tomorrow. Thanks for saving me from the dragon," he said.

"And thanks for the drinks," I responded, as if they were equal.

Zab took another step to the door and stopped. "Shit. Almost forgot." He dug into his pocket and held a folded piece of paper out to me. "It's from Ab. He thought you guys were hitting it off but didn't want to put you on the spot."

He gave a final wave and was off.

Ab? *Ooh*, the dark-haired guy I'd been sitting next to. He'd been nice enough, but I hadn't really thought we'd hit it off. I tucked the note into my pocket for later.

With Zab gone, it was me and Hawk, and I was glad. I had several bones to pick with him, and they were going to be scraped clean. I wasn't waiting until it was convenient for him. I was done with his schedule. It didn't matter if he had somewhere else to go. We were having it out.

He was settling on the couch. Well, I'd already won one.

"Hitting it off?" he asked.

"Where were you? We were supposed to practice and I don't even get a note? A *go screw, I've got something better to do*?"

"So you liked Zab's friends?" he asked, steepling his fingers.

"Are you not hearing me? I'm trying to talk to you." I put my hands on my hips, shaking my head as he sat casually on the couch. Always his way, even with the conversation.

"I was curious how your night was. I'm assuming you went to the Watering Hole? I know most of those people. There are some interesting sorts," his voice huskier than normal.

What was wrong with him? Did he think someone was

going to try to offer me a job again? Was this Raydam part two?

"No one is trying to steal me away, so can we get back on track? Where were you? If you'd been here when you were supposed to be, I wouldn't have had a dragon incident at all."

"I was detoured," he said.

His tone normalized, even as his stare unnerved me. At least he was taking this situation seriously. We were now at two attacks.

I walked closer until I was looking down on him for a change.

"The dragon was coming for me. Someone wants me dead. You say it's not Raydam, but then who?" I asked.

Hawk shook his head. "I don't know, but I've got a question for you. How is it you can throw a dragon across the street for Zab, protect him so thoroughly that he doesn't have a scratch on him, and yet you let grouslies maul you nearly to death? Would you have let them kill you if they hadn't stopped? Is your own life worth that little?"

This wasn't a rhetorical question. He was staring at me, waiting for an answer with heat in his eyes.

"Stop trying to turn this into my fault," I said, walking to the other side of the room because I wanted some tea, not to get distance from him.

"It *is* your fault. You should've been able to get rid of them, and you didn't." His voice had dropped lower, angrier, accusing.

"You think I didn't try? I was screaming." The man was out of his mind. How did you fight with someone who was incapable of logic?

"You could've but you didn't," he said, pointing at me as if I'd betrayed him.

"You act as if I want to fail?" No. I wasn't getting dragged into this fight with him. I shouldn't even be here, and he was mad I hadn't acted correctly when I'd been attacked. That was his problem. "If I was back in Salem, none of this would be an issue."

I began making tea, because that was why I'd walked over here, right? He got up and followed me, clearly not as ready to move on.

"Do you think that this is only a Xest problem? That it will stay neatly in this world and not bleed over to yours? That you can go back and never deal with it?"

"Maybe..." Actually, that was exactly what I'd figured, but saying that now would make me feel incredibly stupid.

"Everything here bleeds over. Everything is connected. Xest has a problem, Rest has a problem."

He walked out, leaving me to stew over what exactly that meant for the rest of the world. For me? Did I even want to know? No. Not right now, anyway. I had a full mental plate at the moment.

33

Hawk had been in the back room for hours before he walked into the office, caught my eye, and waved for me to join him in the back room.

Zab raised his brows. Belinda dropped hers. Rabbit started piling up the notes she'd been taking of all things Rest. We'd been working on it all morning. The electricity situation was going to be a large hurdle, but we'd go back over that tomorrow.

I got up and made my way into the back, with no idea what Hawk wanted. He could've been calling me to yell about how it was my fault the grouslies had attacked me. It wasn't as if we'd left things on good terms last night. We'd simply gone to our own corners.

The table in the back was covered with large sheets of paper that looked to be a hundred years old. Hawk was sitting on the couch, leaning his arms on his knees, reading wording that was anything but English. It could've been hieroglyphics for all I understood. This better not be for me. Yeah, maybe we had a hint on what kind of magic I had, but

I'd yet to do something as simple as knock a book off the table.

"What's going on?" I asked, as if we hadn't had a huge fight last night and all was normal.

"This," he said, tapping his fingers on the papers.

"Which is?" I took a seat across from him and stared at the gibberish in front of me.

He looked up at me, and every cell in my body didn't want to hear what he was going to say. If I had any control of the magic in me, I'd use it to keep him from saying anything. Of course, I didn't and he spoke.

"This is a spell meant for someone who is a Protectorate. This is what's going to buy me some time. This is why the finder found you. *You* are going to do this spell. This is why you're here."

He might've thought this was why I was here. I knew better. I was here because a séance had gone wrong and some greedy jerk at a factory had hired bounty hunters to jump me over here. If I hadn't gotten dragged here, I didn't care what Hawk said about everyone having a price; I never would have agreed to any of this. Didn't seem like the time to rehash all that, though, since there were plenty of current issues to tackle.

"What does it do, exactly?" I asked, leaning over and looking at the endless rows of words I didn't understand.

"It'll contain that thing in the Unsettled Lands—for a while, anyway. As soon as that's handled, the faster we can get you out of here."

Well, that was something. At least he was acknowledging that there was something trying to get me, even if we couldn't agree on who or what. But if this was my ticket back to Salem, I had a feeling I was going to miss my ride due to insufficient funds. He was handing me a bill I couldn't pay, not that he'd listen.

Sometimes I wanted to rage and scream at him. Other times I wanted to give up and let him exhaust this situation until he finally saw the light, because he certainly didn't hear my logic. After what I thought of as the dragon incident, he was doing exactly what had made me dread our sessions from the beginning, setting me up for massive failure.

"You think I'm going to be able to do a spell that stops that thing I felt in the forest? The thing that made me feel like my soul was about to get ripped out of my chest and tossed around in the mud for a few days before all the good in the world was stamped out of it? I haven't been able to control the simple things yet." I pointed at the pages. "I don't care what you say, there is no way that thing is going to be simple."

My words were beyond logical, but they didn't seem to faze him. He sat opposite me with an expression that said that I was wrong and he was right.

"I know you can do it," he said, without the briefest hesitation. In his head, he believed it completely. He believed in me completely, even now.

I was never getting the hell out of here. I'd always thought delusions of grandeur were *self*-directed. Not Hawk's. He had delusions of *my* grandeur, and I had no grandeur to give. I was Tippi, a store clerk with a small apartment, with well-loved but well-worn belongings and zero big-picture ambitions. I was exactly what you saw, no makeup, no airs, plain Tippi.

Hawk looked at me like I wasn't that girl. He had more confidence than anyone else had ever had in me. When he stared like this, a part of me almost wanted to prove him correct, so I could bask in his approval. The sane part of me wanted to run from the room because I couldn't do what he wanted. This was going to lead to more disappointment when he finally figured out that I wasn't the person he thought. The dragon incident was a fluke, and I still wasn't sure if it had been me. I was a nobody. Beginning and end. I'd accepted it a long time ago. Why couldn't he?

"Look, if it would fulfill my end of things and I could do it, I would. But I still can't knock a book off the table. There's no way that I can do something as complicated as this looks." I stared down at the pages, something obviously written and created by a brilliant witch or warlock, and part of me felt a slight longing to be able to create something that grand. But I knew who I was.

He raised his brows slightly and digested my words for all of two seconds before saying, "Yes, you will, and you can."

I dropped my head into my hands, wanting to rip every strand of hair out. The man was more stubborn than a mule. Dragging in a few deep breaths, I tried to regain my composure before going in for the kill again.

He leaned back, resting an arm along the back of the couch as he waited for what I was going to say.

He wasn't going to believe me. He never believed me. He was always right and he knew best. Still, maybe one of these times he'd finally see some sense.

"As flattering as it is that you think I'm capable of this"— I waved a hand over the papers that were already giving me palpitations—"I'm not the person you think. I'm not capable of what you believe, and the sooner you come to grips with that, the better we both will be."

He nodded slowly. "And the other night?"

"It was a one-off fluke."

"No."

He leaned forward, piling up the papers he'd spread out. He'd said no, though. Was "no" some sort of backward agreement? Had he meant "no, you can't do it," and he agreed with me? Or was he seeing the light?

My answer came quickly as he moved the papers, brought a book over to the table, and placed it on the center.

"We're going to try things a little differently this time. Instead of trying to move the book, you need to focus on clearing the table. I don't even want you to think about the book. I want you to focus on not letting anything touch the table."

This was never going to end. I'd never get back to Salem because Hawk would never believe I couldn't do what he needed. Instead of finding someone who could, we'd all die of old age as I wasted my life trying to fling a book across the table.

"Tippi, clear the table," he said, dragging me back to the wretched night ahead.

I leaned back, resting somewhat, since this would be another long night and I'd need to preserve my energy. These sessions wiped me out, and this would be a long one judging by the look of determination on his face.

"Okay. You want me to clear the table? I'll try to clear the table." I raised my hand—

"No. That's an offensive gesture. Just concentrate on the table."

I put my hands on my lap and focused on the table, like he said. The *table*. Solely on the *table*. The *table* wanted to be left alone.

The book flew off the table and dented the wall, like it had been shot out of a gun, leaving a small crater in its wake as it dropped to the floor.

My jaw dropped. Hawk was smiling.

I lifted a finger toward the dent. "Did you..."

He shook his head. "That was all you."

"How did that happen?"

I wasn't sure if he was happy because I'd done it or because I'd proven him right. I didn't care. I *had* done it.

"You're a Protectorate. Your magic doesn't work offensively. It works defensively. Knowing you, I should've realized it sooner."

He should've? Why? I might've asked him if he wasn't already on the move.

"Let's try this." He walked over to the fireplace, placing his hand by the heat. The flames disappeared. "I want you to concentrate on warming the room. You need to think of the thing you're helping, not hurting."

I walked over to the fire, thinking of how nice it would be to light the fire in my room. Heat the water.

I didn't focus on the logs but the chill in the air. *Warm the room.*

The fire blazed to life. I reached out my hands to feel the heat, having a hard time believing that I'd made it. Hawk moved closer, standing right behind me, and I found myself drawn more to his heat.

"You can do this spell, Tippi. I know you can," he said quietly.

For the first time since I'd come here, I wondered if maybe he was right. Maybe I could.

34

"The green papers are dollars, and that's how you buy things?" Rabbit was sitting cross-legged on the couch next to me with a pad and pencil, wrinkles partitioning her forehead.

"Yes." I drew a star on my pad, which was shorthand for *needed more work.* I'd tried to keep it to the basics, but the list was still daunting, especially with all the stars spread out on the page.

Zab, who'd decided to organize the *already* organized books, was trying to glance over my shoulder. Musso was across the room, drinking his fourth cup of tea. It was a good thing the office was slow, because the only person helping anyone was Belinda, and helpful wasn't her forte.

Rabbit shook her head. "But you have coins, too. I don't see why you need both. Paper isn't worth anything."

Musso pointed his stirring spoon in Rabbit's direction. "She's got a good point."

"How's that tea, Musso?" I narrowed my eyes, making it clear he was going to get the boot out of this lesson if he made things harder.

He grunted but didn't leave as he continued to sip.

Him in line, I turned my attention back to Rabbit. "It's supposed to be backed by metal, kind of. Or it used to be. I'm not sure anymore."

"Then why don't they give you the metal?" Rabbit asked. "Wouldn't that be easier?"

"Because the economy is too large, and that would be difficult." This discussion was above my pay grade.

"What's the economy? Does that pay for things, too?"

"Look, you're going to have to accept that some things are very strange in Rest and it is what it is." I scribbled a line through "money." No way was I debating a financial system that I barely understood myself. Her current knowledge would have to do.

"It really is an odd place. I don't know how anyone makes any sense of this," Rabbit said, looking down at her notes. Musso and Zab nodded and grunted agreement.

I shot a glare over her head at the two agreers. They were really going to get the boot soon. Musso was already a two-time offender.

"I've known people who've gone to Rest and said it was so easy over there," Zab said. "Most of our clients go back and forth for work, so how hard could it be?"

Good. Now I'd only have to kick out the old guy if he acted up.

Rabbit looked up and nodded. "You're right. All those people that come in here, they do jobs in Rest?" The pencil tapping was slowing.

I grabbed on to the momentum. "See? You've got this. Now let's move to the other parts. Another week or two, you're going to have this down."

She nodded and tapped her pad. "And lights go on with

a twitch? How does one do a twitch? Is there a certain gesture or flair?" She was making swishing motions with her hand.

Zab leaned a little closer, studying her movements.

"Not twitch. They go on with a *switch*. And there's a few different types of switches. Some look like little bars on the wall. Some are round things underneath the glass ball or squiggly things that light up. You physically touch them and turn them on by moving them.

"But don't forget, you have to put the thing that looks like a fang into the matching holes in the wall or the switch won't work." I'd better draw some sketches, lots of them, maybe a notebook full.

"Because the magic is stored in the wall?" she asked.

Zab and Musso paused, waiting to see what I'd say, like they'd be making the trip with her or something. I tried to ignore them. There were too many things to cover.

Did I get into electricity after how well the currency conversation went, or did I do this in a way she'd understand? Was there even a debate to be had?

"Yes. That's where the magic is in the walls, but humans call it electricity. Calling it magic is a big no-no in Rest. And be careful, because if you try to stick your finger in the hole, the magic will get very mad and try to kill you."

Maybe I could get Hawk to bring me there before her, just an hour or so. I could make sure everything had fresh bulbs and that all the plugs were in sockets. I could child-lock the ones she wouldn't need. And maybe turn the gas to the stove off while I was at it. It would be safer that way, and I'd sleep a lot better.

Rabbit gasped. "Humans let bad magic that wants to kill them live in their homes?"

Zab and Musso walked over and sat on the other couch, all pretense of not partaking in these lessons over.

"It's not bad magic, because it does a lot of things for you. But if you poke at it, it gets mad. It likes to have its space, and no one likes to be poked. That's pretty reasonable on its part, when you think about it. If someone poked you, you'd get mad too."

Musso pointed at me as he spoke to Rabbit. "She's got a very good point. I don't like to be poked, so can we really fault this magic for not liking it? I don't think so."

At least when he was chiming in now, he was on my side.

"Don't sweat it, Rabbit. You still have until after Yule, maybe even longer, to learn all this stuff," Zab said.

Yule, what they called Christmas around here, was only days away. I'd never thought I'd be spending the holidays here, but it wasn't too bad, because at least I liked most of the people I was with.

"Can we get a tree?" I looked over at Zab and Musso.

Musso paused for a second before he said, "Yeah, we put one up in the back room every year."

It was a bald-faced lie, and I could've kissed him for it. "See? We can study this stuff as we decorate for Yule. It'll be fun."

"You're right. It'll be fun," Rabbit repeated, trying to gear herself up. "What other subjects did we need to cover today?"

I looked down at my pad. "Starting a fire. In Rest, there are these things called matches. You don't use your hands."

The lines on her forehead deepened. "Matches?"

"Rabbit, you're going tomorrow," Hawk said.

We all fell silent as all eyes turned to Hawk, who was standing in the doorway.

I was too stunned to say anything. I'd thought we had weeks.

"Okay," Rabbit replied as she chewed on her lip and looked at me.

"We should wait until after Yule. I'm not sure I've told her about everything yet." I couldn't tell him she wasn't ready. Then she'd know she wasn't ready either, and we were already working with a confidence problem.

Hawk glanced at me before turning his attention to Rabbit. "My schedule is too busy after Yule. It has to be now."

Rabbit swapped her lip out for the pencil. She'd never question Hawk. She was a Whimsy witch, and Whimsy witches took what they got without complaint. Luckily, she had me, who didn't give a shit what level witch she was. I didn't care what level I was, either. My magic could be wiped clean tomorrow and I wouldn't miss it.

He couldn't give her one last Yule in Xest? Her whole life was about to get upended. He might not know how horrible that was, but I did. It wasn't that hard to jump, from what I'd seen.

"How long is it really going to take that you can't squeeze it in?" I asked.

The room went from a normal quiet that happened when people stopped talking to the kind where you were all lined up in front of a ditch, waiting for the firing squad.

"Because that won't work for me," Hawk answered, giving me a look that suggested I accept it.

"And tomorrow won't work for us," I said.

Rabbit gasped. Good thing I'd thrown that "us" in instead of "her," or she might've keeled over.

"Too bad," he said.

I stood. "You're being a—"

"Give us the room," Hawk said.

They cleared out in less than two seconds, including Rabbit. Even though I was fighting her fight, I didn't blame her, or them. They'd been born into a caste system that had probably never been questioned. Ever.

The last body gone, with a flick of Hawk's wrist, all the surrounding sounds disappeared.

"Did you not stop to think that I might have a good reason?" he asked, more aggravation leaking into his tone now that we were alone.

"I find it hard to imagine what reason you have that would rob her of her last Yule here." He probably had a date night with Belinda. It was one thing to make me sit around all night waiting for him, but he wasn't doing this to Rabbit.

He made a humming noise. "I guess that's my answer, then. How about this? She couldn't light another candle this morning. Couldn't even get it to smoke."

She was almost out of magic?

I walked over and shut the door to the back room. It didn't matter if they couldn't hear us. I was afraid someone might walk past and see me. The way I was feeling right now, they wouldn't need to hear anything. I was sure one look at my pale skin and they'd know it all.

"You said she had months." I sat on the couch, resting my arms on my legs and letting my head drop forward.

"She should've, but she must've been using too much magic somehow. It *has* to happen tomorrow." The anger had been stripped from his voice.

When I glanced up, I saw the same feeling I was having reflected in his face, except maybe more composed and held together.

"Will this affect her life span there?" I asked.

"No. She'll be fine. Like I said, you don't need magic to live in Rest, even if you were once a witch."

"She won't be a witch anymore?" As much as I didn't care what my status of magic would be in the future, it was different. I wasn't used to having magic, and any I'd had so far had only brought problems. But Rabbit had grown up in Xest. Being a witch was her identity.

"The magic in her blood is nearly gone. She's barely a witch now," he said.

Barely a witch was still a witch, even if the difference seemed trivial to him.

I leaned back, coming to terms with her leaving. As selfish as it was, this wasn't all about Rabbit. I didn't want to be here alone. I'd been preparing, but now it all seemed so final. Before, I could put it off and focus on all the things that would come before it. Now it loomed large.

"Sorry if I, you know..." I rolled my hand, hoping he wouldn't make me spell out my assumption he was being his usual jerky self. It wasn't like he didn't bulldoze occasionally when he wanted something. After all, that was why I was here in the first place. Was it a stretch to think he'd trample Rabbit because he had a lunch date or something?

"Acted like an ass?" he asked.

I nodded, happy that my so-so apology was enough. Pulling myself together, I stood up. Then I jumped from foot to foot, hoping the color would land back in my cheeks.

"What are you doing?" he asked, watching as I hopped about.

I stopped. "Can she at least have the day? Can she make it until tomorrow night?"

He nodded.

I let out a breath and then took another deep one as I took a step toward the door. I paused again, another deep breath in order. How was I going to tell her she had to go because she'd die? A few more deep breaths. Maybe another few minutes on the couch?

Hawk was staring at me, where he leaned against the back of the couch. "Tell her you lost the fight. I'm being a jerk and insisting on tomorrow."

Sometimes I thought Hawk was the most controlling ass I'd ever met. Then he'd have days like today and I wasn't quite sure who he was.

"You're doing her a favor. I don't want to make you look like a jerk when it's for her benefit. It's not fair to you. You're helping her."

"I'd prefer it that way." He crossed his arms, as if he didn't like coming off as good as he was right now.

Yeah, I understood that.

We walked out of the back, and I made my way straight to Rabbit.

Belinda looked up as I walked past her. The green was showing in the brown of her eyes. I didn't have time for anyone else's issues. That was Hawk's problem. I had my own to deal with, and it was nearly as unpleasant.

Rabbit was watching me, and I nodded toward the stair door.

The second we were alone, I said, "I'm sorry, but he won't listen. He's insisting on doing it tomorrow. But not until late, so if there's anything you need to do, or goodbyes you need to say…"

Don't cry. Do. Not. Cry.

She shook her head. "My family is all gone, and my coworkers at the factory weren't friends. The only ones I need to say goodbye to are here." She hugged herself.

"I'll miss you too," I said, taking her into a bear hug. To my shock, she returned it. It was only the second time she'd hugged me. Once when I'd broken her free of the factory and now this time, and this one was bittersweet.

She nodded. "It's for the best. I know it is."

She knew. She had to. Not once had she mentioned coming back. She'd known all along.

35

If this were to be Rabbit's last day in Xest, it was going to be the best day I could make it. Unfortunately, my resources meant I couldn't make it *that* good. I needed to work a few things out, which was why I got up earlier than Rabbit and rushed into the office.

Zab was usually there first, and he didn't disappoint today.

"Hey, you're here early," he said.

"Yeah, I have something to talk to you about, and it's a little awkward." More awkward than I'd imagined last night when I thought of it in the wee hours.

"What is it?"

"Is there a way I could maybe borrow a few coins? There are some things I need to do today."

He jerked his head back, and my stomach dropped. Was this another thing people didn't do here? Ugh. Talk about awkward.

"You know, forget it. I shouldn't have asked."

"Why would you have to ask to borrow coins? You've been earning coin. I've been wondering why you haven't asked for a payout yet." He walked to the coin box. "Do you want it all or a partial?" He was waiting for me to answer with a bag in his hand.

"All, please?" I didn't know what I was being paid, but I couldn't imagine it was much. If this was going to be the best day of Rabbit's life, I'd need every coin I could get.

He handed me a sack of coins that felt heavier than I'd expected. I didn't know the coin system here. Maybe the cheap coins were heavier than the good coins? That could be a problem. A single cocoa was not going to make this the best day of anyone's life, ever.

I weighed the bag a few times before asking, "Can I afford a cocoa with what's in here? I wanted to take Rabbit out and treat her to a nice day."

"I set the wage. You can do a whole lot more than a cocoa," he said, smiling. Then he laughed.

"Thanks."

"If you need more, tell them to charge it to the office. If you come back by six, I'll have a little surprise set up for her, you know, to say goodbye."

"We'll be back."

I grabbed a tea and brought it up to Rabbit's room, where she was just opening her eyes.

I put the tea down on the stand beside her. "You need to do your hair and get dressed. I'm taking you out today."

"You are?"

"I am. We're going to get cocoa, then breakfast, then we're going to go eat somewhere fancy."

"We are?" she asked, her voice growing louder.

"Yes, now get up and let's go."

I'd hated the restaurant Hawk had taken me to, but Rabbit would be in love. And if I had a coin left over after all of that, I was taking her shopping for a new outfit so she felt pretty on her trip to Salem, even if it did only consist of a puddle jump.

This was going to be a good day if I had any control over it.

I'd had to do a little charging to the office, but Rabbit looked amazing in new clothes from head to toe when we walked into the office at six. Hawk, Musso, Zab, and even Belinda were all there waiting with a cake in the back room.

There were jokes about who was going to follow Musso around, keeping him organized after she was gone. Who'd overdose Zab on caffeine during the day so he'd be awake for his dates later on that night. Even Belinda was trying to be pleasant, if quiet.

There was a lot of laughter, and I faked a good share of it, not feeling any joy as I did. Rabbit was leaving, and not because she wanted to. She left or she died. She'd be going back to my life, without me. I'd be staying in her world, where I didn't belong. We were celebrating to lighten the situation and say goodbye, but this wasn't an occasion full of joy for anyone.

It was only an hour or so in when Rabbit sat on the couch, her laughter fading, her skin pale.

Belinda left first without saying much.

Musso nodded. "Good luck, kid! I'm sure I'll be seeing you again soon."

Rabbit nodded, but everyone in the room knew it was a lie. She'd never be back. She couldn't.

"I'll miss your teas," Zab said. He didn't drag it out because he looked like he was going to cry himself. Then he was gone, his eyes watering as he passed me.

Rabbit leaned an elbow on the arm of the couch, propping her head up, and I knew it was my turn to take the lead.

Hawk was watching from the other side of the room. His head dropped a notch, as if he knew exactly how much this was costing me, and his cold, hard heart might've actually melted a little.

"Are you ready, or do you want to hang out for a while longer?" I asked. At least she'd have the illusion of some control over her fate, even if it was a lie.

She sucked in her lower lip and then stood. "I'm ready."

We walked out of the back of the building, somber and quiet, as if we were approaching a deathbed. I was hoping this wouldn't be our final goodbye.

Hawk opened a flask, creating a puddle big enough for the three of us before sprinkling it with some salt. That was it, a little water and some salt and he'd have Rabbit in Salem. So simple and yet impossible.

"It's ready," he said, stepping into the puddle and waiting.

Rabbit and I met each other's gaze, and then took a step together.

The landing was a lot easier than it had been going to Xest. I barely wobbled as I landed in the middle of my kitchen and living room area back in Salem, with Rabbit on one side and Hawk on the other. My worn couch had never looked so good. I breathed in deeply of the scent of the candles I'd scattered about the place. Loris always gave me the defective ones that came in the order.

"This is your home?" Rabbit asked, awe in her voice.

I nodded as I tried to keep the tears from coming.

"It's lovely," she said in a breathless tone.

It was a modest hodgepodge of a place, but I loved it. It was filled with worn items that were all handpicked by me.

"How much time do we have?" I asked Hawk.

"I'll give you a few," he said, walking to the door and leaving us in the apartment alone.

"Let me show you a couple things before we go," I said, walking to the wall and flipping on the switch.

"Wow," she said, following me and then turning it off and on a few times herself.

"Eventually it will stop working. When it does, you need to go to the store and buy more light bulbs." I pulled the pad out of my pocket and put it on the table. "I wrote this all down for you, okay?"

She nodded, still staring at the switch. I ran down a list of things in the apartment, went through all the appliances in the kitchen, and tried to explain the TV, then motioned her into the bedroom.

"There's clothes in the drawers. Use whatever you need." I looked about the room, trying to think of anything I might have forgotten. I'd pored over the notes for her at least five times and was sure I'd still left holes.

Rabbit was looking out the window, running a hand over the curtains.

"Don't forget the letter I gave you to give Loris," I said.

She patted her pocket. "I've got it. Are you sure she's going to believe the story?"

"Yes. Loris will, and she'll recognize my writing." I kept looking around my room, knowing I wouldn't see it again for a while.

Rabbit was still looking out the window. "It's so different."

I walked over, looking down at the familiar street, remembering my first look at Xest. How lost I'd felt. "You'll get used to it."

The door in the other room opened. Hawk was back.

"You know, you can always write to me in the meantime, even if I can't get a letter back to you," she said.

"I will. I definitely will."

"And maybe Hawk will be able to pop you in to visit once in a while until you come back?"

That was a lot less likely. He might not be the horrible person I'd thought he was, but bringing me back here? No. I wasn't sure that was going to happen again until I finished up what I had to do for him. At this moment, I understood why. Visiting was almost worse.

I lay flat on my back, staring at the ceiling of my again large room, hating the size of it. Rabbit was gone and today was Yule. Soon it would be New Year's.

The worst part was that I didn't know if I was more upset about being here alone on the holiday or the fact that I had nowhere to go back to after this was over. Hawk had told me a while ago that Salem wouldn't be an option for me anymore. I was finally accepting that I was homeless, like I'd been when I was a kid, after the men in white coats took my mother away. Homeless, like I'd promised myself I'd never be again.

Too rested to be tired and too awake to continue to lie there, I got to my feet. I made my way downstairs, finding the office empty. It was Yule, and although I hadn't been completely sure, it wasn't surprising the office was closed for the day.

I made my way into the back room and stopped short. It looked like Christmas had exploded in here. There was garland, dripping with pine cones and berries, draped along the bookcases. A large wreath hung over the fireplace and a tree stood in the corner, decked out in glittering candles with bird ornaments that were so realistic they could've been alive.

"Rabbit said you had a thing for Christmas. Asked if I'd put up a tree for you before she left," Hawk said from the couch.

"It's beautiful."

"She left you something. It's under the tree."

I walked to the tree and saw a small box underneath it. I pulled the lid off and found a letter and a pouch. I didn't even care what she gave me. I wanted to read her words.

Dear Tippi,

I want to thank you for giving me your knowledge and lending me your home. You gave me a chance at a full life, and I will never be able to repay you for that. I've never had a sister, but I had parents. When I lost them, I thought I'd never have family again, but you gave that back to me as well. Just know I'll always be there for you the way you were there for me.

Love,
   Rabbit

I folded the note back up and tucked it into my pocket for safekeeping before opening the pouch.

There, hanging from a gold chain very much like the one my mother had given me, was an almost identical necklace. This one didn't have a coal pendant, but a warm stone that reminded me of an opal, but warmer somehow.

I walked to the couch, letting the stone dangle from my fingers.

"You can't buy that. She must've made that with the last of her magic," Hawk said, watching me.

This was why she'd gotten weaker. I never should've told her about exchanging gifts. I wrapped my hand around the gem, holding it close to me, the gift bittersweet. I would've rather had her here for another few weeks.

"Don't feel bad. You gave her a new life, one in which she'll be able to live until she's old and grey. She never would've had that if not for you."

I nodded, hoping he was right.

I looked up, and he was staring at me in a way that made my insides warm.

"Well, thanks for doing this."

He nodded, still staring at me.

Then he stood abruptly. "I'll be back tomorrow to start on the spell," he said, then left out the back door without a last glance.

36

We were standing in the middle of the forest, and I felt like I was about to freeze to death. The fifth wind was cutting right through my jacket and I would've sworn we were out here because he was mad at me for something.

"Why do we need to be out here?" I tucked my hands under my arms because my gloves, jacket, and hat weren't cutting it. Sometimes I wondered if Xest was actually in Antarctica, but they didn't like to fess up. That didn't sound as cool as east of East and north of North, or whatever bull-shit they said. I was probably in some stupid no-man's land that had been rejected by sane people.

"You can't do this part in the office or town. It's too strong if you screw it up."

For someone who seemed to think I was the answer to all his problems, he didn't hesitate to let me know all of my shortcomings.

"Maybe if you were a better teacher I'd be further along," I shot back. I didn't know what his issue was, but he definitely had a problem with me right now.

He ignored my jab, handing me a sheet of paper. I took it

begrudgingly, angry about having to remove one hand from under my arm.

"Can you read it?" he asked. "Don't try aloud until I tell you."

I looked at the sheet of gibberish. The letters looked familiar, but not the words. "I don't know how to pronounce any of this."

"Point to the ones you think you can't manage and then try with the rest."

I pointed, or tried to, as my finger shivered over the first word that was so crazy looking that I wouldn't know where to begin.

He shrugged out of his jacket and slung it over my shoulders. It was like all his warmth had come with it.

"You're going to freeze out here," I said.

"I'll be fine. I run hot. Now point to the word again."

I did, all too aware of his proximity and the way it was making my breathing shallow. I didn't like Hawk, but I felt myself getting a little jumpy whenever he was around, like my brain or body went a little haywire. Considering what he expected me to be able to do, it was probably natural. Who wouldn't get nervous?

He was standing close to my side as he looked over my shoulder. For someone from Xest, he didn't have the same aversion to closeness most Xesters did. Was it a him thing or was it a me thing? If it was me, how come Zab hadn't shaken my hand? Musso didn't touch me either. Even Rabbit had been weird. It had to be a Hawk thing.

"That's pronounced choc-co. Like the first syllable of chocolate and co from company. What else?" he asked, pulling me back to the spell.

I scanned the page that was only about two paragraphs long. "What's this?" I asked, while my brain wandered. If it was a Hawk thing, why didn't he touch anyone else? He was dating Belinda, and I'd never seen him touch her either, although there was probably plenty of touching in private. The thought of them together made me want to gag, but that was definitely a Belinda thing. I shouldn't have let my mind wander to her.

"Francolean. Frank, O, and then lean. Anything else?"

Pretty much every word written, but I was having a hard time concentrating as he leaned over my shoulder, his breath tingling at my ear.

"I think I've got it." I backed away, putting a few feet between us as the thought of him and Belinda still lingered.

"Good. Read it. After you're done, take a deep breath, as swift and deep as possible, and then drop to your knees, laying your palms just so as you exhale." He expanded his chest and then dropped to the ground himself, demonstrating the movement. "That shuts it down."

"Shuts down what, exactly?" There were two paragraphs on the page. What exactly was I going to open that would need to be shut? Being out in the middle of nowhere was suddenly more forbidding than it had been a minute ago. I'd thought the cold was going to be the only problem tonight.

"The spell you're going to do isn't easy. In order to do it, you need to open certain channels of power. Because we aren't doing the entire spell, you're not going to have anywhere to direct the magic you aren't using. I'm having you channel it back into Xest, in a sense."

"Wouldn't it be easier to practice the entire spell than having to open and shut things?" I didn't know what to do with the magic I had. I didn't want any more lying around, causing trouble.

"No. You're going to need to work up to this one." He

shook his head, appearing to be patient, but I knew him better.

I didn't like this. Not even a little. It felt like I was repeatedly drowning and Hawk kept throwing me in the deep end. He kept telling me I was an Olympic swimmer while I choked on water.

I pulled his coat a little snugger, feeling the warmth that seemed to exude from it. For someone with a lot of neat tricks, I still couldn't quite wrap my head around why he needed me.

"You're strong. Why can't you do this spell?" You didn't have to know Hawk that long to know he would've if he could've. He wouldn't have hunted me down with a feather and then bought me from the factory if he hadn't needed me. Still, I wasn't looking forward to whatever this was, and I still needed to hear the why before I jumped in with both feet, or even one.

"This spell is meant for a Protectorate. My magic is offensive. I *can't* do it. It's the same as when I tell you to push and you pull."

"Then this spell is going to protect something?"

"Yes. You're going to do exactly what you were meant to do. Protect. In this case, it's going to be Xest."

I nodded and then met his eyes. "So, this isn't to hurt anything. It's going to protect Xest from that thing I felt?" Something about that felt right, checked some inner box inside I hadn't known existed until right now. Maybe I was a Protectorate, the way he kept saying. If this was the kind of witch I could be, maybe being a witch was something that I was meant for?

"Yes," he said, as if he sensed the gravity of the question and the precipice I stood upon.

Something flurried inside of me, calling from deep

within. It felt like something was clicking into place, as if I were supposed to be here somehow, in this moment, and I had no conceivable reason why, other than maybe some part of me had come to like this strange place called Xest. I didn't want whatever that evil thing was in the forest to ruin it, not for Zab or Musso or Hawk. Not for Rabbit, either. And when I left here, it might be nice to know I could come back someday if I wanted.

I straightened my shoulders, holding my head high. "I can do this."

It wasn't a question anymore. I *believed* it. I could do what was needed to fix this world.

"I know. I've known for a while, but it's nice to finally have you on the same page." He took a step back, giving me room I hadn't known I was going to need. "Once you start, don't stop. Just keep going until the end and do what I told you."

I held the paper in front of me, skimming the words once more. I could do this. The paper held eight sentences in total, two average paragraphs. This was not a big deal. Only a fragment of the spell. And it felt right. This would be okay.

I spoke the first sentence, words that seemed like gibberish, tripping over half of them. There was a sizzle in the air, like right before a storm, but nothing crazy happened. The second sentence was said and the air began to warm around me.

I looked at Hawk, who nodded, encouraging me to keep going. As long as he wasn't freaking out and thought this was normal, I wouldn't freak out either. By the third sentence, there was a power that felt palpable around me, and the hair on my head began to blow about. After that, I stopped counting. I focused on gripping the page and reading the rest of the sentences. My hands shook like I'd mainlined adrenaline, and the air pulsated around me as if it had become a creature of its own, with a heartbeat that throbbed through the air and I was in the center of the beast's chest.

By the time I was done, terrified was an understatement. Hawk, who was standing close but not touching me, nodded, but I could see the urgency. I needed to finish, the way he'd said. I tried to take the quick, deep breath and then release. I dropped to my knees, placing my hands on the ground.

Nothing happened. I felt like I had an atomic bomb building inside of me and I couldn't get my finger off the detonator. I tried to take another deep, hard breath and release it, but it didn't do anything. I slapped my hands on the ground until I was beating the snow with my fists. The power was burning inside of me, around me, building until my thoughts felt scattered, and it was going to burn me alive from the inside out.

Arms wrapped around me as Hawk pulled my body snug against his. His magic shivering against mine, he bent over with me, placing his hands on mine and holding them to the ground.

"Force it out. You can do this."

I didn't speak. Wasn't sure I could. I just gasped.

"Feel my energy. Mimic it."

His heat and stillness enveloped me. I'd never thought of Hawk in terms of calm before, but his energy was like a beacon I clung to in the center of chaos. I could feel the waves of it coursing through his body, flowing down his arms and into his hands. His magic was calling to mine, coaxing it to follow like a tornado being pulled along a low-pressure front, riding the ridge of power.

At first, there was a hint of the pressure releasing, following the flow of his. And then it seemed to happen all at once. With a swoosh, all the built-up magic flooded out of me.

I sank forward, as if all my energy had gone with it. My hands shook, this time from weakness. Hawk curled his arms around me, pulling me against him as he fell back on to the snow, as spent as I was. He was lying underneath me, as if he'd used every ounce of himself to guide the magic out of me.

Neither of us moved or spoke.

37

I'd woken in my bed in the same outfit I'd gone into the forest with, minus the jacket, hat, gloves, and boots. I wasn't sure how long we'd lain in the snow, or how I'd gotten into bed.

I walked into the office at noon the next day, after sleeping what had to have been a very long time. My legs felt weak and my hands were shaking like I hadn't eaten in days. If half a page had done that to me, how was I ever going to make it through multiple pages? That feeling last night, the delusional one that must've come from Hawk, where I'd thought I could actually do what he needed, was flopping all over the place like a half-dead fish on a pier.

Sometimes the faith Hawk had in me made me feel like I was this special person. Then shit like last night happened and I remembered who I was and knew we were both doomed. Yesterday had proven that. Hawk and I were going to have to have yet another talk. After last night, even he'd have to realize I wasn't capable of what he believed. Maybe I could assist with the spell, but I couldn't take lead.

"Sorry I'm late," I said to Zab as I passed by. He gave me

a half wave and a smile then went back to dealing with his client.

I ignored Belinda's glare, which seemed to be jacked up to a ten today. Considering it was usually at least an eight, I wasn't overly worried.

Showing up late went against the grain for me. I'd opened up the shop for Loris since a week after I'd started. After I'd seen someone talk her into discounting some herbs by fifty percent, I'd begun showing up early. I wasn't a slacker. I was a caretaker, like I had been for my mother and for Loris. Skulking in at noon felt wrong.

There was a white bag with purple squiggles on my table that I recognized immediately. It was that weird meat sandwich with the purple sauce I loved. I was still missing Rabbit, but thank God for Zab.

Musso's client got up and left, and I took the opportunity to lean toward his side of the office.

"Sorry I'm late, Musso."

"Don't worry about it, kid. Knew you had a rough night."

"You did?" Did everything that happened in Xest spread like wildfire?

"Yeah, Hawk told us when he dropped off the sandwich and said you might be sleeping in. He didn't want anyone to wake you."

He'd left them orders not to wake me? Now I knew why Belinda was at a ten. That must've made her morning perfect. If the bag wasn't taped up, I might've feared she'd slipped something in my food. And how had Hawk known I loved these sandwiches? Zab must've told him.

Zab's client left, and as soon as the office was empty, Musso asked, "Well, what happened last night?"

Zab was listening now too, waiting to hear more about my long night.

Belinda looked up from her desk. "Yes, what happened? What was so *exhausting*?" Her glare scale, which used to go up to ten, had now broken through the ceiling and was definitely closer to fifteen.

As much as I wanted to hate her, I still couldn't quite do it. If I'd been dating Hawk, him being with another woman all night wouldn't sit well with me either. Forget about the fact that I'd passed out on him and he'd obviously put me to bed. Innocent or not, it wasn't going to go over well. But she didn't need to know about that.

"Nothing much. Practicing. Pretty boring stuff," I said, directing my answer at Zab and Musso.

Her lips pressed into a flat line. There was no pleasing this woman.

Luckily, I was saved from further interrogation by more clients walking in. A young brunette walked up to Musso, saying something about getting his call.

Another two women, with about a twenty-year age gap separating otherwise identical faces, made their way in and took a seat at Belinda's desk.

"Hi, Bonnie. Hi, Gil," Belinda said, shooting a last glare at me that made it clear she wasn't done with me.

"Do you have any jobs for us?" the older woman asked as they both took seats at her desk.

"Any particular genre or religion?" Belinda asked.

"No. We need the work. We'll take whatever you have."

Belinda flipped through the papers on her desk, plucked one up, and held it out. "This looks interesting. She's Greek and asking Dionysus for a good crop for her wine. Says she'll give up gambling forever if she could get a good batch. I haven't vetted it totally, but I think I can get you a good price."

"What's the conversion rate on gambling? I haven't done one of those in forever. The rate used to be horrible."

"It's pretty good now. With all the online gambling, lots of demand. I'd think we could get you at least ten coins for it."

"Okay, I'll take it. Do you have some—" Bonnie, the older woman, coughed loudly. "I'm sorry. I have the worst tickle in my throat. Could I bother you for something to drink?"

Belinda lifted her hand and snapped in my direction. I stopped sorting slips, knowing what was coming next.

"Tippi, go fetch Bonnie something to drink."

She couldn't send me out anywhere, but she was going to get her pound of flesh out of me somehow, someway. Still, I'd play nice because it wasn't worth the fight. If Bonnie needed a drink of tea, I'd be the fetch girl.

As I stood, Bonnie took a look over her shoulder at me and began waving her hand. "No, I'm fine," she said, but her voice went nearly hoarse before she finished.

"Are you sure?" Belinda asked, only caring that she'd lost her opportunity to boss me around.

Bonnie got to her feet. "Really, we're going to go get something across the way," she said, still intermittently coughing as she waved her daughter to follow her. She plucked the card from Belinda's fingers. "I'll take care of this right away."

She waved at everyone, and then stopped as she faced me. "I'm sure your drink would've been lovely. I hope I didn't offend."

"Not a problem."

She gave me a half wave and a nervous smile, while her daughter fidgeted beside her, shooting me stares. They nearly ran to the door.

Right before they left, I heard the daughter ask her mother, "Was that her?"

Bonnie gave a quick shake of her head and pushed her daughter outside.

Belinda narrowed her eyes at me before getting up and walking to the back room, as if she couldn't handle my presence anymore.

I turned to Zab. "What was that about?"

He didn't look at me right away, and when he did, he didn't speak for a second. He took in a breath, parted his lips, and then paused.

He did that two more times before he said, "I don't want to say people are..." He stopped and shook his head. "It's not that you've got a..." He sighed.

"They're all scared of you," Musso said loudly, not having the same delicacy issues.

I turned to him, having to confirm he was speaking to me and not to someone else who might've walked in. No one was scared of Zab, and Belinda had left the room. But still, that made no sense. No one was afraid of me. Ever. Even the vendors I'd fought with on behalf of Loris would get irritated but never frightened. I wasn't scary. I was Tippi.

"Me?" I said, pointing at my chest like Musso wouldn't fully grasp the question otherwise.

"Yes."

I turned back to Zab. "And you think so too?"

"It's not a thought. It's a reality," Musso answered for him.

"Is it?" I asked Zab, wanting to hear it from his lips.

"Just spit it out, Zab," Musso said. "Don't lie to her. It's nothing to be ashamed of. Hell, when I was a kid coming up, people were proud to be feared."

Zab slumped a bit. "It's true. They're scared of you." He

threw his hands up as if he wished he could tell me differently.

"They're scared of me?"

I got a nod from both Musso and Zab.

Zab shifted his chair a little closer to me, bending forward a bit, like we were about to have a heart-to-heart. "Look, it's nothing personal and a bit understandable. First there was the shopping situation where your magic started to slip a bit. Wasn't a huge deal, but it caught some attention.

"Then you did that newsflash, and that was one large flash, from the sounds of it. The glass in the windows of every building in the center rattled when that thing went off. Even though Hawk tried to claim it, there were suspicions, since he was in the center when it happened, and that's not typically the way things are done. That still could've been overlooked.

"But, of course, it got worse from there. You fought off a herd of grouslies on your own. And still, you might've been able to fly under the radar, but people saw you arguing with Raydam in the street and hanging out with Hawk all the time. So, you were developing quite the reputation—"

"And then the dragon incident happened," Musso said.

Zab let out a loud sigh and shook his head, lifting a hand in a sign of defeat. "And like Musso said, then the dragon incident happened. You can't kick a dragon's ass and not get something of a reputation around here. That's life."

Everyone knew about the dragon? "But we were alone. How'd they find out?"

Zab shook his head. "Apparently not as alone as we thought. There were people watching the whole thing play out through their windows."

I slumped into my chair as this newest update stole another little piece of hope that I'd ever have a normal life again. I was running out of pieces as it were. My entire childhood, all I'd wanted was normal. When my mother passed, the silver lining had been, okay, at least now I can be normal. *Now* I'll have an average life. It was looking as if I'd never get the chance. If people like Marvin would hunt me down when they thought I was merely a Whimsy witch, what would they do now? If Hawk was right, I'd be hunted down forever, wherever I went.

"This is bad. This is really bad." I might've let a groan out before I could stop it.

"People think you're a badass. Own it! It's a good thing," Musso said in his short, gruff way.

"I was afraid it would upset you, but it's not that bad. So what, they're a little scared? It's not the end of the world." Zab leaned forward, tapping my table with his big fake smile in place.

"Hawk said the stronger people think I am, the more likely they won't leave me alone when I go. I'll never be able to go back to Salem, not even ten years from now."

My head went down, my forehead planted firmly in my palm while I waited, hoping someone would say I was wrong. The silence stretched out until it was clear that wasn't happening.

"You know what? I'm going to go get you the triple-sized cocoa. What do you think about that?" Zab asked, getting up before I said yes.

I leaned back, about to ask him if he really thought that cocoa would fix losing my home for good. But then he might not go get me that cocoa. If I was losing my home, cocoa wasn't going down with it. I could only handle so much loss in one day.

"I think that's a good idea." If nothing else, I'd drown my sorrows in a well of chocolate.

38

Belinda leaned a shoulder on the door of the back room, twirling a piece of hair in her fingers as she feigned confusion.

"When was Hawk supposed to be here? An hour ago? Two?" She squinted hard, pausing while she tapped a finger to her lower lip. "Maybe he's not coming?"

"Possible," I said in the blandest tone, sipping my third cup of tea on the couch where I'd planted myself hours ago.

I could swear she'd stayed late hoping I'd be sitting here, stood up for practice with Hawk. Normally being stood up was irritating, but having her as an audience? Belinda was like having a multiplier of pissed off by a thousand.

"I guess if you wait around long enough he'll show up eventually. I mean, *I* wouldn't wait, but you have nothing else so why not?" Her smile was sickly sweet. "Well, I'll be leaving for the night. Have things to do and all." She waved and turned to leave, giggling as she walked in the other room, knowing I'd hear her.

I shouldn't hate her. I did anyway, but I shouldn't. She was right. It wasn't like there was a long list of other things for me to do. Rabbit was gone, busy living the life I couldn't return to. Even if she were here, she would've been fast asleep hours ago. Zab was probably busy on a date or out with his friends, the ones I'd probably scared off after the dragon incident—no judgment. If I heard I'd kicked a dragon's ass, whether I claimed to know what I was doing or not, I'd still be a little leery of me. No, I wasn't expecting any invites to that crowd anytime soon. Musso was home with his family, not that I'd know what to say to him if we did ever hang out. Belinda was dead on. I had nothing else to do but wait around.

The door opened in the other room thirty minutes later. It was unfortunate for Hawk, since I'd gone full circle since then. I'd gone from being a loser back to boiling angry. If he needed me that badly, he shouldn't leave me sitting around for hours.

He strolled into the back room as if nothing were amiss.

I cleared my throat, raising a brow.

"You ready?" he asked.

I remained seated. "You're late and there was no note. Clearly you weren't being mauled somewhere. You appear to be perfectly healthy." Too healthy. Too broad. Too handsome. Why couldn't he be scarred or something? Bent over and a hundred years old? Smelled like mold?

He smiled only enough to raise the corners of his mouth slightly. "I'm very sorry. I should've left a note. I didn't realize I'd be interrupting your schedule. Now are you ready?"

Why did everyone have to keep bringing up my lack of plans? It wasn't my fault people were scared of me. The dragon incident was not my fault.

"I'm not ready. I need to talk to you about something."

He sat on the opposite couch, leaning back as if he were settling in to placate me. "And what would that be?"

The list went on and on, but I had to pick my battles.

I leaned back, mimicking him. "After our last practice, I'm not overly enthusiastic to try again." He'd nearly killed me, or it seemed that way.

He slowly nodded. "I wasn't anticipating how strongly you would hold on to magic. Now that I know, I'll factor it in so we don't have that same problem again."

"That same problem? So you anticipate *different* problems?" It was bad enough I expected this to blow up in my face. He did too?

"No, I don't, but that doesn't mean there won't be any."

Even though the answer sucked, there wasn't much to be done. There was no way out of this but through. And as I sat there, the more it became clear that my agitation wasn't just about the spell. What happened after I got through with it? I couldn't go back to Salem. Could I go anywhere and be safe?

"Was there anything else you needed to discuss?" he asked, leaning an arm on the back of the couch as he waited.

He was asking. I might as well get it all out.

"If I do manage to achieve what you need, will I ever be able to go back to a normal life? Everyone here knows of me now. Will I be hunted forever?"

"I'll ensure you are left alone, although a change of location is going to be essential."

He gave the impression of someone who'd thought this through, but that wasn't good enough. I needed details.

"How can you guarantee that?"

He got up from the couch, making his way to the tea stand. The fire in the hearth flared, casting his shadow across the rug. Something about its wavering form caught my eye. At first it was the form of a man, but then it grew until it was cast out long behind him in a shape that was altogether unfamiliar to me. It continued to enlarge until the outline was blurred into the wall and I couldn't make out the outline at all. I didn't need to see it to know it wasn't human.

My breath got caught in my chest, trapped for a few seconds as I examined the creature in the shadow, ignoring the man. When I moved my gaze back to compare the two, he was watching me.

He didn't move. My gaze left the strange shadow that took up half the room to look at his face. We stared at each other for a moment. Then his lips softened into a slight smile, as if he'd remembered something that had happened that amused him.

Did he think I'd go running from here? Running from him? Even if he was a monster, where would I go? Back to the factory? I had nowhere to run.

"Like I said, I'll guarantee it," he said.

For the first time, I had to acknowledge that whatever Hawk was, it might not be entirely human. That was what Rabbit had been trying to warn me of the first time we'd discussed him. She'd heard enough to know he was someone or something to be avoided. She just hadn't known enough to know what, only passed down whispers and hints of something more.

He went back to pouring himself a drink and sipping on it, as if nothing amiss had happened. As he stood drinking, his shadow morphed again, shrinking back into the shape of a man.

"Are we good?" he asked, not looking at me.

Did he think that I'd cower now that he'd shown me that? I wasn't sure what I used to be made of, but the girl who'd been living in Xest for weeks wasn't the same girl who'd lived in Salem. I *might've* had a little something to do with the dragon incident.

Was he a shifter of some sort? Had to be. Did it matter? No. Not anymore. When I first got here? Maybe. Now? I didn't care what or who he was as long as he was on my side, which I believed he was—for the moment.

I was curious enough to ask. But I didn't, because again I wasn't the same girl from Salem. Hawk only shared what he wanted, and I wouldn't waste my energy on non-answers. And did it matter? No. I was doing what I had to, and so was he. Nothing else mattered.

"Whatever you are, I don't care if you're human or the worst monster to walk this world. The only thing I care about is that you hold up your end of the bargain, and what you say you'll do."

"You know, with very little work and practice, you wouldn't have to fear being hunted at all." He looked over his shoulder at me, and the intensity I saw there made me shiver.

It always did. It was as if he saw who he wanted to see. Perhaps who I might've liked seeing, too, but not who I was. I might've grown, but I'd never be the person who deserved that look.

"I think I'm getting all the practice I can stomach for now." I stood and grabbed my jacket before walking over and getting in his space, just to make sure he knew I wasn't afraid of him. "And one more thing: if you tell me to be here to practice at a certain time, make sure you're here too."

He smiled, a soft laugh following.

———

I read the page again.

"You're saying it wrong."

"I'm saying it the way you told me." I dropped onto a

fallen log. It didn't matter how cold it was. Most of my body had lost feeling an hour ago.

"That's not how I said it."

I plopped my chin on my palm. Nothing too scary had happened thus far, but man, was this particular page wiping me out.

"Tippi," Hawk yelled.

I jerked a little, realizing I'd almost fallen asleep out here.

"Let's go," he said, standing in front of me.

"You sure? I might be able to do another round." I punctuated that with a yawn.

"I'm sure. Come on."

I got up, and we made our way back to the door, the distance feeling twice as far on the way back.

"I don't know why I'm so tired tonight." I yawned again as soon as we were back in the building.

"This part of the spell is going to make you tired doing a partial."

"Oh. Good to know," I said, then made my way down the stairs and headed back up the other, toward my room.

"Night, Tippi," Hawk said from the landing below.

"Night, Hawk."

I threw off my jacket to the side on the way to the bed. I kicked off my boots after I face-planted into the pillow and tugged the blankets over me, still fully dressed.

A cool breeze entered the bedroom. I shifted farther underneath the blanket for a few seconds while I debated how bad it might get if I didn't go check the window. If I didn't shut it now, would I be able to sleep, or would it get so cold that I'd wake up freezing?

I stumbled out of bed, tripping on my hastily discarded boots. I had one eye half-open as I made my way to the window and tried to push it down. It didn't budge. I squinted up at the top pane. It was already sealed up tight. Maybe when the walls shifted back and forth, it had created a crack. I'd have to mention it to Hawk tomorrow. For tonight, I'd have to burrow under a bit deeper.

I crawled back into bed, my eyes closing as soon as my head hit the pillow. Practice tonight hadn't been nearly as bad as it had been the previous night, but it was still exhausting. My words hadn't done much of anything other than warm the air around us, but it had still knocked me out like a two-ton elephant had stampeded over me. I sank a little deeper into the blankets, trying to forget about magic and evil for a little while.

Ice-cold hands circled my throat, choking the air from me. My eyes popped open, but there was nothing to see. I grabbed at air. The grip on my throat tightened to where I wasn't sure if I'd die of strangulation or a broken neck. I thrashed about, trying to dislodge the hands, my headboard banging against the wall.

The door crashed open, Hawk barging into the room. The grip released immediately.

I rolled on my side, coughing and choking as I dragged air back into my lungs. The window blasted open, smashing glass everywhere.

Hawk ran across the room as if he could see whatever had attacked me. Hawk took one look at me. I nodded, letting him know I was fine. He leapt out of the window and was gone.

I shoved my feet into my boots, dragged the blanket around my shoulders, and left the room. Whatever that thing was, I wouldn't wait for it to come back.

I was curled up on the couch in the back room when the door in the office opened.

"Tippi?" Zab yelled.

"I'm in here," I called out, my voice hoarse.

He was in the back room a second later. "What the hell happened? I got an emergency flash to get over here."

I shook my head. Like always, I wasn't quite sure.

39

I was sipping on the cocoa Zab had made me as he tried to drop yet another throw blanket on my shoulders.

"Zab, I'm fine. I was attacked, not left out on the tundra for a week."

He sat down on the other side of the couch, fiddling with the throw I'd just shrugged off. His eyes went to my neck again, and I could tell he wanted to throw the blanket back on, as if that would fix everything.

"I'm fine. Don't worry." I pulled the blanket tighter so my neck wasn't visible anymore. I wasn't sure if I was hiding it for him or so I didn't see his face blanch when he looked.

"I still don't understand why your magic didn't kick in. You'd think if you were a Protectorate, you'd be able to protect yourself." Zab rested an elbow on the back of the couch and then perched his chin on it, as if it was going to be a nice, long stare that his neck alone wouldn't be quite up to.

"Me neither." It was the third time he'd brought it up since we'd been sitting here. I hadn't wanted to talk about it the first time. But his stare continued. At least Hawk had only sent notice to Zab. I wasn't sure I could've handled Musso's blunt approach to this subject. It might've been worse than what Hawk was going to say, and he'd surely say something.

"Maybe I'm only a Protectorate to other people? It doesn't work on me? I mean, there's not a lot of Protectorates. This might be normal." Hawk hadn't thought so when he'd questioned me about the grouslies, but that didn't mean my hypothesis was wrong.

"Maybe. I guess."

Zab clearly wasn't buying it either, but at least he'd stopped staring. There was a limit to what I could handle in one day.

Two sets of footsteps sounded in the office. My heart jumped right before Hawk and Oscar walked inside.

Hawk immediately scanned me, as if he'd thought I might've been stabbed twenty times in his absence. He had cause.

Oscar nodded in my direction, with a curious look, as if he were still trying to take my measure but his ruler was broken in a million pieces.

"You find it?" Zab asked.

Hawk shook his head, his gaze landing on me again. "No. And if Oscar couldn't, nobody will. He's the best tracker around."

"How do you think it got in?" I asked. All I could think of was going back in that bedroom, and it made my whole body tremble. I pulled the blanket up to my neck, as if it were chilly in the room.

Hawk walked closer, his gaze still on me, like maybe he'd missed a stab wound. "I think it came in through the flue. It's the only thing that wasn't warded. Only way it *could've* gotten in."

"What was it?" I asked.

"I'm not sure," Hawk said.

Oscar gave Hawk a glance, as if something wasn't being said.

"You still don't think it's somehow connected to Raydam?" I was beginning to doubt it was Raydam myself. The only thing I did know was Hawk and Oscar knew something they weren't saying.

"No, and neither does he." Hawk tilted his head toward Oscar. "Trackers can sense magical signatures. Raydam could've pulled this off, but it wasn't him."

Oscar nodded. "Like I told Hawk, I couldn't pick up on a signature of any sort, and hiding a magical signature is definitely something that Raydam *can't* do."

"Can it get back in?" I asked. How was I ever going to sleep again?

"It won't come back again, not tonight. And I won't let it have another opportunity."

It. Why not a *he* or a *she* or a *they*? Hawk did know what was after me. He just didn't want to say it, and I knew why.

"You keep calling whatever attacked me 'it' like you know it's not a he or a she? And now Oscar is doing the same. What do you think keeps coming for me? You might not know, but you have a guess." I watched his face, waiting to see any signs of evasion.

He stared straight at me, not a secret to be found, as he said, "I think you already know."

I hadn't, not until right then, and was still hoping I was wrong.

"The evil in the Unsettled Lands," I said, hoping someone would disagree with me. Hawk didn't. He looked like I'd read his thoughts. Oscar didn't look shocked either.

I turned to Zab.

He shrugged. "It does make sense."

Everyone knew, including me now.

I wanted to scream, cry, and groan, to completely and utterly lose it. Instead, I leaned back on the couch and didn't move a finger or even breathe. If I did anything, I might explode.

Zab fidgeted. "Can I do something for you? Get you something?"

I took a long, slow breath, focusing on looking sane. "No, I'm good. Thanks for coming, but you should go get some sleep." My voice was so calm that I must've still been in shock. I certainly didn't feel that way on the inside.

"We're good, Zab," Hawk said.

Zab turned to me, his eyes going to my neck again, even though it was still covered. I was afraid to see what it looked like myself, the way it he couldn't stop staring.

With a wave and a last pause by the door, Zab was gone.

Oscar cleared his throat, crossing his arms over his chest. "Maybe I should stay here? This way, if it does come after her again, I can track whatever went after her?"

"No. It'll be a little crowded. I'm moving her into my place."

"Your..." Oscar nodded and took another couple of seconds before he said, "Oh. Okay. Well, I'll take a last lap around, just to make sure I didn't miss anything before I call it quits."

With a wave, he was gone as well.

I didn't move off the couch.

"That thing is trying to kill me. It felt me, the way I felt it, and wants me dead."

Hawk wasn't talking, but his eyes said he agreed with all of my statements. So this was real. I'd liked it better when Raydam was my biggest problem.

"Come on," he said, getting up and waiting for me.

I'd thought his comment about staying with him had been a ploy to get rid of Oscar. He didn't really mean we were going to share his place, did he? Would Belinda be there too? This was going to get seriously weird. I might've been better off going it alone.

He stood waiting by the door.

Okay, so we were doing this. Not that this was anything but awkward. But it *was* happening. I followed him but then paused on the stairs.

"I need to get a few things," I said, motioning in the direction of my room.

"I can get you whatever you need," he said.

If he was feeling any of the awkwardness I was, he didn't show it. He climbed the stairs to the door that led everywhere. I took one glance backward before following him.

The evil thing wanted me. I'd never be able to sleep there alone right now.

He opened the door, and we were back in the room with the stars above. Was there more to this place? When he shut the door, would it lead to more rooms?

But one thing struck me: there was one bed. It was a big bed, but only one.

"I'll crash on the floor," he said.

"It's big enough for us each to take a side."

"It's fine."

Of course he wouldn't share a bed with me. Belinda. She'd be livid. Maybe they'd worked out their problems? He'd changed his mind and wanted something more? She was already probably going to be furious we were in the same room. If I was dating him, this would be a no-go for me too. It wasn't as if I was going to jump all over him or anything. A lot of women might, but I wouldn't.

"Is Belinda going to be okay with this? I'd be fine back in my room." Every fiber in me was hoping he'd tell me no and insist. *Please insist.*

"We can't risk it. Belinda will be fine."

I wasn't sure fine was accurate. That was a stretch, considering she didn't want me in the same building, same world, or breathing the same air.

I didn't speak, but my expression must have said it all.

"This is the way it needs to be for now." He moved to the side of the room, reached behind his head, and pulled his shirt off, tossing it on a nearby trunk. He unbuttoned his pants, the muscles in his abdomen flexing as he did.

Belinda disappeared from my thoughts. I turned so I didn't gawk and moved to the other side of the room. I dropped the blanket from around my shoulders onto the top of the bed.

"Why the hell didn't you do something about it?" His voice was soft, but raspy.

I jerked my hand to my throat, where I could still feel the bruising grip.

He stared at my neck and then crossed the room. His hand went to my throat, grazing gently over the area.

"I couldn't." All I could manage was a pathetic whisper, my vocal cords sounding like they'd been run through a cheese grater.

"What is it, Tippi? Why are you so convinced that you aren't worth saving? Why can you protect others, but when it comes to you, you're not worth it?"

It would've been less painful if he'd kicked me in the gut.

"My magic doesn't work like that." Although I couldn't fault him on his logic. It did seem to look that way, whether I liked it or not. Whether it was true or not.

"Oh, I bet it does," he said, anger now tinging his voice, as if this were my fault.

"Fine. Maybe it does or doesn't. Either way, it's none of your business. I'm doing what we agreed upon."

I grabbed the blanket off the bed, finding I'd rather risk sleeping alone than dealing with him tonight. He didn't try to stop me as I went to the door. The knob wouldn't turn.

"Let me out," I said, not looking at him.

"Whatever happened in your life, wherever you got this baggage, you need to see it for what it is. You need to let it go."

He walked toward me until I abandoned my spot by the door and moved back toward the bed. If he thought this was when we were going to have a heart-to-heart, he was way off the mark. This was the point in the conversation where we went our separate ways because too much was being said. Except he wouldn't let me go anywhere.

If I couldn't get away from him physically, I'd do it mentally. I turned, giving him my back, cutting him off as best I could as I crawled into the bed, pulling the blanket around me.

"I don't understand how you can't see yourself the way everyone else sees you, the way *I* see you. You're worth saving, Tippi. You're even worth killing for."

A breath shuddered out, but then I pulled it all in and locked it down tight, closing my eyes.

40

I woke alone, a stack of familiar clothes piled in the corner. At least he wasn't here. Waking up in his room was too much after the night I'd had. This way, when I saw him later, we could both pretend things were still normal between us, in spite of the fact that something weird had changed last night. I didn't know what, exactly, but I'd felt it.

The second I stepped into the main office, I wanted to run right back out. The tension was sizzling in the air. Everyone was there but no one was talking. Belinda was stalking Hawk with her eyes as he looked over some paperwork by Musso's desk. Zab and Musso were looking everywhere but at her.

Did Hawk tell her where I'd stayed last night? Nothing had happened. There was no reason to lie, but it felt like it right now. I walked over to my table to start sorting, afraid to say anything, even a bland hello. My voice might trigger someone's attention, and if this didn't have anything to do with me, I didn't want to get pulled into it.

Belinda was looking over at Hawk until I walked past, and then turned her energy to trying to stab me to death with her eyes. From what I knew, she wasn't a strong enough witch to pull that off, or I'd have been a bloody mess already.

Zab turned my way, giving me a fast shake of his head, reinforcing my gut instinct to stay silent.

"Well, here's the little princess that needs protecting. Why should we even work anymore? We should all sit around and wait for her to need us."

Staying quiet when no one was speaking to me was one thing. This was another. Those were fighting words.

"Excuse me, but I—"

"Bel, I said that was enough." Hawk turned his gaze from what he was looking at to stare at her.

And now I knew why no one was talking and wished I hadn't. How much had been said before I'd gotten here? My hand went to the high-necked pink and green striped sweater. It had been one of the uglier items I'd been avoiding. It had suited today's purpose because it hid my neck, and I hadn't wanted to look like a victim. *Thanks, Belinda.*

Did I say something more? And what? After the current events, it was hard to call her out on her assessment. I was feeling the same myself. Plus, Hawk had shut it down. That was probably for the best.

"It's ridiculous that she—"

"Back room," Hawk said.

Nope. That wasn't shut at all. It was gaping open.

She looked at him, and it was clear what she was thinking: did she want him enough to continually sacrifice her pride? I could've answered that question for her ten times already. What pride? She'd thrown out what scraps she had ages ago, from what I'd seen.

I wasn't sure if anyone was to blame for it. She was utterly in love with him, probably one of the worst cases I'd seen. To him, she seemed more of a convenience most of the time. I'd heard the conversation, and worse, I'd been watching closer than I'd ever admit. He cared a fraction as much as she did. She knew what she was getting and kept waiting for more, and everyone but her knew it wasn't coming. It was like she kept showing up at a bar that only served appetizers and repeatedly ordered a twelve-course meal. She was never going to be full, not with what he was willing to give.

Belinda, as anyone here could've predicted, walked into the back.

Hawk moved a second later, pausing to give me a very pointed stare before he said, "No listening."

"It was a little blip. It's not like I listen to *every* conversation you have." Although how interesting would that be? To know all of Hawk's secrets? Would he still be as sexy if I had it all laid out? Not that he was irresistible or anything. But yeah, I had a feeling if I knew every little nitty-gritty detail, he might be even sexier.

He kept staring for another second before he walked into the back, shutting the door.

Dammit. I really would've liked to hear this particular conversation, especially as it was about me.

"There should be some sort of rule that if more than fifty percent of the subject matter is going to be about you, you get to hear," I said.

Zab nodded. "Completely agree with you on that."

Musso shook his head at both of us.

Ten minutes later, a calmer Belinda walked out of the back room. Not a *happier* one, but she avoided looking at me. I took that as a sign that she'd be avoiding me entirely, and that was a very good thing as far as I was concerned.

She took a seat at her desk, not glaring or throwing anything. That was a big achievement, considering.

Hawk came out a moment later, walking back to Musso, resuming his perusal of a document and then shaking his head, saying something about not wanting the office to take on the job.

Things seemed to be calming down. I flipped through my cards, placing them in piles of accept or reject as the office resumed its usual grind for the day. I'd just about been lulled into a false sense of tranquility when Zab turned to me.

"Forgot to ask, did you see the thing I left hanging over your bed last night? I ran it back over after I left," Zab said.

Oh shit. "No, I didn't. I must have missed it. I was really tired."

I flipped through some more requests, hoping that would be the end of the conversation.

"You hang it over your bed. It won't protect you, but it'll make a little sound to alert you if someone or something bad is coming near."

"That's amazing. Thank you." It would certainly help me sleep.

"You didn't notice it? When you weren't in your room, I put it up for you. Didn't you see the note? It was right on your pillow."

How did I tell him I hadn't been in my room after what happened? Did I lie? My life had been built on lies growing up. I'd lived a life of pretend ever since I was a child. Pretending my mother was something she wasn't. Pretending I was something I wasn't. That I didn't hear and see things. That I was normal. It had gotten me nowhere, but I could already feel Belinda's eyes on me again, and I didn't need more problems. If I didn't give it a good try, this situation was going to go from calm to disaster.

"I didn't notice. I'm sorry. I'll make sure to check when I go upstairs." *Now please shut up.*

Zab nodded, but I could tell he was still trying to piece together how I'd missed both. In the short time I'd known Zab, I'd grown to love him, but he was being awfully thick right now.

Belinda's gaze of death was fully centered on me, and she was about to lose her shit completely. Someone had figured it out. I didn't know what had upset her before, but she hadn't known I'd spent the night in Hawk's room until now.

Hawk stepped closer to me and Zab. "Tippi didn't see it because I moved her out of her room last night."

He hadn't said where. Maybe Belinda would leave it be? Nah, that wasn't her way.

"Oh, yeah, I can see that," Zab said. "You know, after the attack, that's reasonable. Anyone would've done that." Zab's cheeks were glowing and the boy was finally catching on.

"Moved her where?" Belinda asked, like a shark smelling blood in the water. If she found out, I was fairly certain it would be my blood about the office.

"I took her to my place," Hawk said. There was something laced in those words that sounded a little bit like an apology, as if he didn't relish the thought of hurting her. But his tone was firm enough that he didn't regret his decision either.

Or maybe I was just reading way too much into one sentence and had no clue what I was talking about? That was a good bet, too.

She slumped back, as if she'd taken a sucker punch that

had caught her hard and off guard. "Your place? You don't even bring me there."

He didn't? What I'd thought about wanting to hear every word? I changed my mind. I didn't want to hear any of this, but I was pretty sure I wouldn't get that opportunity. It looked like Belinda was going to blow, and there wouldn't be any back-room option on the table. We'd all be dodging shrapnel in a moment.

"I explained this to you. There are things beyond your concern that need to be handled." Hawk dropped his papers and walked across the office. I didn't know if he was planning on leaving or going in the back room, but wherever he went, Belinda tailed him.

"You didn't explain anything," she replied.

She was talking to Hawk, but her eyes were burning me at the stake, like the bad witch she claimed I was. Actually, she wasn't the only one claiming that either. She had to get in line behind Jasper. He got the original credit for labeling me "evil."

Shit, what card had I just sorted? I picked up the last one off the accept pile.

Destroy the world in a fiery blaze.

Definitely a shredder. This was what happened when you pretended to work when there was no possible way you could. Hopefully it wouldn't have passed the negotiations, but right now, Belinda would gladly work out a deal to set the world to blaze if I was on it.

"Because it's none of your concern," Hawk said, walking away from her again.

I glanced up and locked eyes with Zab. He made a whistling face, minus the sound.

I gave a little shake of my head.

Musso wasn't as subtle about the situation, groaning as he looked over at the scene. If they heard him, no one cared.

Hawk walked to the front door.

"Where are you going?" Belinda asked.

He left without answering.

Hawk now out of reach, she switched targets like a seasoned sniper, the bullseye planted firmly on me. She stalked across the office.

"You think you're so special, don't you?"

Me? If she was going to lay on an attack, this was definitely the wrong approach. I wished I was special, but I certainly didn't think I was. Opposite, in fact. The only thing I seemed to be adept at was stepping in shit and making the wrong decisions.

She stood, arms crossed, waiting for an answer. I sorted another card, and another, all the while cursing Hawk in my head for leaving me to deal with her.

It became clear she wasn't going to move until she got her response.

I looked up. "No, not really." I went back to reading the slips, hoping she'd move on to something else.

"You think you're going to get him, don't you? That luring him into bed with your victim act is going to make him want you? He pities you. That's all. That's what you are. A pity case. He might need you for something or other, but he could never *want* you. You're a mess."

I clenched on a slip as my breathing became a little ragged. She wasn't worth it. Just let her have her fit. She was a scorned woman, and the man who'd left wasn't available to scream at. This had zero to do with me.

"Belinda, you're out of line," Musso yelled at her from the other side of the room.

"What? Can't even defend yourself?" she asked, not budging from her spot in front of me.

"Belinda, you need to back off. Whatever is going on with you and Hawk has nothing to do with her," Zab said.

"Can't even talk. Pathetic, like I said." Belinda continued to stare down at me.

I was trying to stay calm, to not get into it with her, but everyone fighting this battle for me was not helping.

Zab ran a hand through his hair as he looked over at me. He slowly shook his head, as if to apologize for her.

That was it. I couldn't take it anymore.

I leaned back. "I told you I wasn't trying to steal Hawk from you. I'm not trying to lure him into my bed. If I wanted him there, I'd invite him. The reason he doesn't love you is the same reason he isn't in this office right now. You, Belinda, are a *des-per-a-do*." I dragged out every syllable, hitting as low as I could, as low as she had. "You cling to him like a bad stench. But to be completely honest, even if you decided to take a step back and regain some of your long-lost pride, he still wouldn't want you, because you're a bitch and an ugly person. It oozes from every pore, just like the stench of desperation."

I heard a throat clear, so in the moment of rage, I looked over just in time to see Hawk walk back in. Great. He might've mentioned he was coming right back to deal with his problem, which Belinda surely was. Nope. He had to walk back in while I looked like the lunatic.

He'd surely only heard my part.

He shot me a look that said *cool it*.

I held my tongue. That was easy, as there wasn't anything left to say.

I turned back to Belinda, who had gone from looking like she was going to blow smoke out of her ears to a trembling lip. Oh yeah, great. Now she was going to cry and really make me look bad. To be totally fair, my biting words might've contributed slightly to her being upset, but boy was she stepping on the gas pedal.

She turned to Hawk, big, fat tears running down her cheeks now. "Do you see how she treats me? You need to send her away. I told you, she's not a good person. This is who she is."

Good. I'd been dying to leave. Absolutely couldn't wait to get out of here. I crossed my arms, not looking at Hawk because I didn't care if he sent me away. He could go to hell. This whole place could. Well, not Zab and Musso. They were awesome. And not Helen. I enjoyed reading her slips, very entertaining, if somewhat disturbing. And not the Sweet Shop, either. I'd miss my cocoas and the people who worked there.

Point was, parts of this place could go to hell. Definitely significant parts.

"She's not going anywhere," he said.

I swallowed so loudly that I was afraid everyone in the office heard. My fists unclenched.

"Then at least send her somewhere else so I don't have to see her."

"No," he said, with zero give in his voice. I took my first tentative glance at him. He wasn't looking at me right now. He was looking at Belinda. If there was anyone in this office he pitied, it was her. He'd never once looked at me the way he was staring at her right this moment, and I was glad for it. I might've shriveled up and died in shame if he had.

"And I'm telling you I'm not having it."

Did she just stamp her foot? It was slight, but it *had* happened.

"I'm sorry you feel that way," he said.

He *was* sorry. She might not have realized it, but he seemed like a man who finally realized he had to end something that he'd barely realized was happening.

"So that's it? You're picking her over me? She's more important?"

The silence was deafening.

If the tears were fake before, the stuff flowing now was made up of pure agony wrapped in the sorrow of crushed dreams. It was so genuine that it was tough to see. If I could've rewound the clock ten minutes, I would've taken every word back, because to watch someone's heart break was not fun, and my part in this stung.

"I've told you, she stays," he said, sounding tired, as if he'd repeated himself one too many times.

Belinda turned back to her desk then grabbed her jacket and her bag. We all watched as she walked out, pausing in front of Hawk.

"I..." She shook her head, not finishing her thought.

She didn't have to. We all knew. She loved him. When she left this time, I didn't think she'd be back.

Hawk didn't say anything else as he turned and walked into the back room.

Zab blew out a breath. "That was..."

I leaned back in my chair. "Yeah."

Musso was looking down at the work on his desk, as he shook his head in silence.

Zab stood. "I think we need some cocoas."

No one argued with him as he grabbed some coin and left.

Guilt was weighing me down like a two-ton anchor. I'd never liked her, but that last scene…

"Maybe I should try to get her, explain things to her? I think she thinks Hawk likes me more than he does. I don't know if she understands that he just needs me. That's all." She seemed to think it was more. It would never be. Hawk didn't want me in that way, and I had a life I was going back to. I wasn't meant for this world.

Musso scoffed. "Nah, kid. Leave it be."

"You don't think it might help?" I asked, realizing how much I'd begun relying on Musso's wisdom.

"I think that situation was going to end badly whether you came along or not. It's best if it ends now instead of dragging out any longer."

I looked at the door she'd walked out of, knowing Musso was most likely right. Hawk had never looked at Belinda the way a man in love looks at a woman. Still, some part of me felt a little ache in my heart for her loss. She hadn't wanted to see it, and now it probably hurt all the more because of how hard she'd avoided the truth. I knew what hurt felt like. What it was to not be loved by people you loved.

I looked down at my slips but couldn't read anything.

"It's not your fault. Don't beat yourself up about it," Musso said.

"Thanks." I would anyway. I'd been on the other end of many painful words and knew how they could haunt you. I'd added a couple of ghosts to Belinda's closet today, and that would stick with me.

41

"You sure you don't want me to stay?" Zab asked for the fifth time.

I'd been telling him to leave for the last hour as I watched him flit from place to place in the office, all in an effort to look busy.

"I'm telling you, I'm fine. Go on your date." I'd been curled up on the couch for the last few hours, pretending that I wasn't looking for company, that I was really interested in reading a book that might as well be upside down for the amount of attention I'd paid it.

Hawk hadn't shown up for practice, and for some stupid reason, I'd assumed he'd come tonight. Belinda's words about everyone sitting around to protect me earlier today haunted me now. She wasn't the only one with a few ghosts hovering around. Maybe that was where Hawk had gone? To make amends with Belinda? I'd heard enough stories of men finally seeing the light after the woman left. Didn't matter what he'd thought before. After she walked out, a blazing high-beam could've hit him in the face and he realized he wanted her. Shit, how many love songs told that same story about wanting the girl to return? Only thousands. He might come back tomorrow and tell me that I had to get out.

If that was how things worked out, it would be good. Definitely. I didn't have to think on all the pluses for very long at all. I'd get to go back to my world and everything would be right again. I should *hope* Hawk was reconciling with her right now. I wasn't meant to be here anyway, not with this craziness.

Yep. I'd be happy. *Really* happy. So happy that I'd be annoying to others. They'd want to tell me to quit it with my fake happiness, but it would be all real. Happy, happy, happy.

"What's wrong? You thinking about Belinda again?" Zab asked.

I hadn't even noticed he'd been staring. Clearly it was the resting bitch face I didn't know I had, because otherwise he would've seen my glowing happiness over going home soon.

"Just daydreaming a bit. Why are you still here? You need to go to your date already. You told me how excited you were at least five times today. What was her name?"

"Alice." He smiled. The boy was cooked and didn't even know it yet.

"Well, I will not be the reason for two breakups in one day, so you better be off with yourself." I threw my blanket to the side, knowing I'd have to get up and go to my room if I wanted to get Zab out of here. "Plus, I'm pretty tired. All the drama I'm causing is wiping me out. I'm going to go to bed."

"You sure you don't want to hang out a little while?"

"No. I want to go be boring, and I want you to go on your date." I grabbed the book off the couch and the candle from the table. I wasn't ruining everyone's day today. I'd already done enough of that. "I'm good. See you tomorrow. Have a good time." I gave him a wave before I disappeared and headed toward my bedroom.

I paused on the landing, my heart ratcheting up a gear. I gave myself two seconds to get a grip before I continued. That was all I could afford, since these stairs creaked like gunfire and Zab might catch on that I didn't really want to go to my room. Then he'd never leave, Alice would be mad, and I'd have broken up another couple. I made my way up the stairs, hoping somehow Hawk was already there waiting for me, even though I knew he wouldn't be.

I opened the door to my bedroom to find myself still alone, as expected, the note and the ornament Zab had left me clear to see.

I got ready for bed, not looking toward the window that was now fixed, and curled up on my side under the blankets.

The door opened ten minutes later, and I shot up, gripping the blanket while my heart played a dirty game of dodge ball with the rest of my organs.

Hawk stood in the door and my heart slowed, as my self-worth dropped into the gutter. What kind of wimp was I to fear sleeping alone? He'd said the building was protected last night, that he'd sealed off any possible entrance. It was safe.

Worse, I was more afraid of what he'd say. Was he here to send me back? Why did I care? It was what I wanted. Was I losing my mind? Why would I want to stay here? Didn't matter. If he told me to go, I'd go. I had no other options here. He was my landlord and my boss.

He looked about the room, pausing on a couple piles of my things. I wasn't the neatest person to begin with, and this recent lifestyle of danger and intrigue hadn't helped that situation. Either way, I wished he'd get the words out and get it over with.

He took a few steps in, looked about the room again, and said, "I don't want to stay in this room. Come on."

Relief surged through me, and the true amount of dread I'd felt about leaving hit me. I didn't know why I wanted to stay, but feelings didn't lie. I did. Maybe it was becoming habit to be here? I'd stayed so long that it felt normal?

He stood, waiting for me.

I got out of bed, wishing I hadn't worn the sleeping pants with all the stains. I took a few steps, feeling pathetic for more than my pajamas.

"You know, I can stay here alone. I'll be fine. I know it's causing you issues." If he did want Belinda, had spent the night chasing her down, then I wasn't going to get in between them. No. That wouldn't be me, ever. I didn't want to be the end of anyone's relationship.

"I'm not taking any chances," he said, waiting.

"I don't want to be the—"

"You're not."

That didn't tell me much at all. I wasn't what? The thing that ended them, or had he been late tonight because he'd smoothed things over? Were they officially done or not? Another thing I shouldn't want and definitely shouldn't care about. It would just be nice to know if Belinda would be back at work tomorrow, trying to stab me. That was the *only* reason I wanted to know.

He didn't have to wait long this time. I was done giving him an out. I'd tried. If this ruined his relationship, that wasn't my fault when he was insisting.

We made our way up to his room, or the door that led to wherever his place was, and I knew it wasn't actually in this building.

"Where are we, like, exactly?" I asked as I walked in and climbed into the bed, happy that Belinda had never been in it before. I reminded myself I didn't care even if she had.

"It's nowhere," he said.

Nowhere was a safe place to be.

I cuddled deeper under the covers as Hawk stripped out of his shirt. I turned away but then glanced back a second later, watching the way his muscles flexed. Of the few men I'd messed around with, none had looked like him. Maybe I would've been more interested if more of them had. He turned, and I closed my eyes and rolled away slightly.

He was moving about the room again, and I was wide awake, feeling guilty. What if Belinda was right and I was the problem? They might not have had a perfect relationship, but it must've been better before me. And now look at me, sneaking glances while I slept in his bed. Maybe I was the desperado?

"I really didn't mean to cause issues for you and Belinda," I said.

"It wasn't you. It's been done for a while."

It was done? Done for a while? Like, how long? Was it because of her, or was he just not the sort that would end up with any woman? A bachelor for life?

It didn't matter. I couldn't ask anything else without it getting weird, and he wasn't offering anything else.

Maybe there was a simple reason anyway. Relationships didn't work for people with a dump-truck loaded with secrets, and Hawk definitely had his fair share.

Now I needed to go to sleep and stop fixating on him and his relationships. I had big problems, like the evil in the Unsettled Lands that wanted me dead.

I was never getting any sleep tonight.

42

All good things must come to an end, and that seemed to include my magic. We'd been at it for hours. I'd repeated this paragraph so many times that it was going to haunt my dreams, and it still wasn't working.

If it had, Hawk wouldn't have been able to wrap his hand around my arm the way he was right now. He let go, shook his head, and walked away.

"Again," he said, his voice so sharp that it could've drawn blood.

At least we were in the back room this time and I wasn't freezing while I failed.

I got through one sentence and there wasn't a single stirring.

"We need to try this a different way. Maybe we need to leave this part out altogether." I was sick of rolling over every time he insisted. Did he think I was purposely screwing this up? He could insist as much as he wanted, but it wouldn't change anything.

"If you can't enact the Protectorate part of this spell, you leave yourself open. You need to be able to do it." His eyes shot to the discarded paper on the table and then back to me.

"I would do it if I could, but that's not how I'm made. It's not how my magic works." As green as I was to this world, and this way of life, I'd learned enough. This spell was falling flat.

"Do it *again*."

Hawk stared at me as we fought a mental tug of war. This time I wasn't budging. He'd have to drag me into a mud pit before I'd bend, and maybe not even then.

Zab walked in, and I dropped onto the couch, not caring who witnessed my failure. In fact, I was so past caring that Hawk could sell tickets to the event and I wouldn't lift a brow. My dearest wish was that Zab would stay long enough to buy me a few minutes of rest on the couch. He should stay a while. Have a tea and a nice, long chat.

"I was just finishing up. Wanted to poke my head in and say goodnight," Zab said.

I groaned inwardly. That was it? Barely a minute?

Zab smiled and nodded in my direction, giving me the impression I'd groaned more outwardly than inwardly. He waved and turned to leave.

Hawk stared at the door for a minute before shouting, "Zab, hang back a second."

Zab came right back in with a smile. At least someone was happy in this room, because neither Hawk nor I was.

"Go sit by Tippi for me," Hawk said.

I sat up a little straighter. "Why? What are you planning?"

Zab didn't hesitate to take the seat next to me, the trusting fool.

Hawk walked over, smiling at the both of us, as if we were right where he wanted. "You're a Protectorate. You need someone to protect. We already know you won't step up and protect yourself."

There it was again, the same underlying anger, as if I were doing this to spite him or something. Hawk could be as mad as he liked at *me*, I could handle it, but Zab was not getting dragged into this mess.

"Absolutely not," I said, anger dripping from my tone.

Hawk didn't flinch. "Yes."

"Zab, you need to leave," I said, switching tactics.

"No, you don't," Hawk said.

Zab was leaning forward but still sitting, torn between the two of us. Zab looked back and forth and then sat back again. He gave me a little shrug of defeat. I'd lost the tug of war. Hawk must have had a better stare.

"Try not to make it hurt too bad?" Zab asked, forever the right-hand man, willing to do whatever it took.

Hawk gave him a noncommittal shrug.

"No, this is not happening." I stood and stepped in between Zab and Hawk.

"Well, that doesn't bode well for Zab, now does it?" Hawk asked, leaning on the arm of the opposite couch crossing his arms.

All the occasional nice thoughts I'd had about Hawk being secretly kind were gone. He was evil to the bone.

"Maybe you should just try?" Zab asked.

If Hawk said he was going to do something, he was going to do it. He'd missed school on the day they'd taught bluffing. Sometimes it was good, because you always knew where you stood with him. Sometimes it sucked, because that place you stood might be a swamp.

"If you do this, I will never speak to you again."

"That's fine. I don't need you to talk to me. I need you to do the spell the way I know you can." He picked up the paper with the portion of the spell we'd been working on, grabbed my hand, and put it on it.

Zab cleared his throat. "Tippi, it's okay if this gets it done."

"It's not okay, and I'm not doing it." I walked from the room. Without me there, hurting Zab would serve no purpose. I left before there could be any further argument, hoping Hawk didn't try to block the door. If he did, I might bulldoze into him. He wanted to see me get Protectorate? I'd toss him like I did the dragon. We'd see just how Protectorate I could get.

I made a right on the landing and headed toward my bedroom. I'd sleep by myself tonight, too. Hawk could go to hell. I was done with his authoritarian run. Things were going to change.

Footsteps sounded on the stairs behind me. I turned to lace into Hawk and found Zab instead.

"I'm sorry," he said, as if the fiasco a minute ago was his fault.

"You don't need to apologize. This was all him," I said, opening my bedroom door as I still looked at him.

A cold wind sucked me inside, dragging Zab along with it.

I crashed into the freezing snow in the middle of the forest, Zab landing beside me. I was on my feet a second later, spinning, waiting for an attack.

"What the hell? Did the doors get screwed up?" Zab asked, getting up a bit slower, not sensing the urgency.

He didn't feel it. He didn't know that *it* was here. Whatever it was, that horrible soul-sucking feeling of evil, *it* was definitely behind this. *It* had come for me—again.

I couldn't see whatever *it* was, but I could feel *it* everywhere. *It* was watching me. Hawk had been right. It hadn't been Raydam with the grouslies or the dragon or the invisible creature that had tried to strangle me. It had been this thing. *It* had lost too many times. Now *it* had brought me to *its* turf to finally finish me off.

I had to get Zab out of here, away from me, and now.

"Let's get back," I said, walking to the door that was still there, not wanting to waste a second. Zab walked beside me. "Maybe you should open it. Who knows what my magic might do to it." I waved to the knob, afraid to touch anything in case it was somehow me.

He looked at the door and laughed, still having no sense of urgency. I didn't tell him, either. *It* was probably listening to every word, and I didn't want to acknowledge *it* yet, for fear that I'd force *its* hand somehow.

Zab stepped forward and swung the door open. It didn't lead to the hall or anywhere in the building. It opened like a plain doorframe had been dumped into the middle of the forest. Zab let go of the knob, staring, and then stepped around it to look on the other side.

The door began to turn black, and he jumped back. It continued to darken until it looked charred. It crumbled, becoming a pile of dark ash on the snow.

"Well, that's odd. I've never seen that happen before." Zab took a step forward, about to kick the ashes with his boot.

I grabbed his arm, tugging him back. "Best not to touch it in case it's something you can catch."

He nodded and, finally, really looked at me. "Are you okay? It's probably just a glitch. It's not like anything is here," he said, looking about the place. "I've been in this neck of the woods before. It's pretty safe."

It might've been once, but it wasn't now. "That's good to

know," I said, wondering how I was going to get him away from me before *it* struck.

"Maybe we should start walking?" Zab said, rubbing his arms and looking around. We could see the far-off lights from the town in the distance.

I wanted him to run, not walk away from here, but if I said that, Zab would die with me. This wasn't his fight. Whatever *its* problem was, it was with me.

"I should wait here and you should go. Hawk will realize that something went wrong and open up another door," I said, nodding to where the last door lay like a stain in the snow.

"You think it's a good idea to split up?" Zab's forehead was creased.

"Definitely. You'll get back faster without me, and if Hawk doesn't show, I'll follow your tracks." It was swelling around me, and it took extreme strength to smile and nod as Zab watched on.

"I don't know, Tippi. We might be better off staying together." He looked around as if finally sensing something wasn't quite right about this place.

It was lying in wait, as if *it* were giving me this one thing. *It* was letting Zab leave. Or maybe *it* had learned my weakness—or my strength, depending on the perspective. *It* knew that taking me on alone was an easier fight after what happened with the dragon.

If I kept Zab here, I might have a chance. Or *it* would kill him too. Zab was one of the kindest people I'd ever met, and the decision was easy. If I was going down, I'd be doing it alone.

"I'm telling you, it's better if you go. I'll wait for Hawk. Zab, trust me. You'll be able to get back to town faster alone.

I'm not much of a jogger, and Hawk might pop through another door in five minutes."

I could feel *it* getting impatient.

"Yeah, I'll run," he said, as if that would fix everything.

"Good. Go."

I watched Zab leave, disappearing into the trees. I'd wanted to say so much more, but if I did, he wouldn't have left. If I could've, I would have told him how much I appreciated his help and his kindness, from the first moment I met him. How he'd kept me afloat with his cocoa and company. I squinted, waiting until I couldn't make out a trace of his yellow shirt.

I turned, not sure if I was trembling from fear, cold, or both. This was it. I was alone, fully awake and not sure how I was going to get myself out of this. I glanced back at the ashes of the door again, not so delusional to think someone was going to save me.

"What do you want?" I spoke to nothing and everything. I could feel it all around, wanting something from me. If I was going to die, it would be nice to know why.

There was no answer. The wind had stopped blowing. The birds had stopped chirping. The area felt abandoned by all life except me, and maybe it, if *it* were alive. If a dead thing could have a presence, I'd imagine it would be something like this, cold and soul-sucking, like it were about to drag me straight into the depths of hell.

"That's it? Nothing?" I asked, forcing a bravado that was built on a platform built of desperation and death. If I was going to die, I'd at least like to know why.

The wind blew around me, but *it* gave me nothing else.

"Give me an answer!" I screamed into the air, desperation turning to something else.

A wind curled around me, swirling, kicking snow up in

its wake. It finally struck, *its* tendrils of evil whipping at me, lashing my arm and leaving a wound six inches long. It was deep enough to hurt like hell and weep blood. I spun, trying to find my enemy and knowing I wouldn't. I pressed a hand to my wound, circling around, waiting and watching.

Another slash, this time on my leg. I bent with a gasp, only to be attacked on my back and my ribs. Then another, and another, until there wasn't a part of me that hadn't been slashed open. It was shredding my skin, tasting me and then retreating and trying a different spot, as if it couldn't find what it was looking for. It wanted to kill me. I could feel *its* bloodlust and yet it was struggling.

I stood, dripping blood, feeling as if my life was spilling out into the snow, but the fear receded.

"What's wrong? Can't beat one little girl?" I screamed, egging it on, trying to force *it* to show *its* hand.

Its power, palpable in the air, swarmed around me like a tidal wave, but it couldn't kill me. I knew it on some deep level that was beyond words or logic. This thing, for whatever reason, despised me. It wanted me dead but it couldn't kill me.

Images began to dance around me. My mother stood over a playing toddler, looking at the child who was crying and reaching out for comfort. Her lips formed the words I knew so well. *You have evil within you. You must learn to be better.*

Children taunting a girl, throwing rocks and mud at her while she stood in a corner. I could hear what they were saying in my head. *You're a weirdo like your mother. Go away!*

The looks of the bystanders as my mother was dragged away to the asylum. The pity and disgust as they all appeared around me, pointing, scowling.

It wasn't only the memories it was plucking from my

mind and replaying—it was the magnifying of all those feelings. It was doing something to my psyche that made me wonder if I could stand one more minute of the mental agony. I'd lived through this, and yet it felt a thousand times worse.

A knife appeared at my feet, begging me to finish the job it couldn't, as waves of depression surged through me. I clenched my hands, knowing the heaviness and desperation would end as soon as I was away from this thing.

The images changed. I was standing there in the middle of Xest as it burned down around me. People were running through the streets, screaming for help and crying in agony. I turned, taking in the destruction all around me, and I was in front of the office. Zab was pounding on the windows, unable to escape as the building burned. Hawk lay dead in front, as Musso leaned over his body.

It was a threat, a warning of what was to come. It was me or them. I was in the forest again, my mother standing in front of me, holding out the knife.

"You have evil within you. You shouldn't be alive."

She, or *it*, thrust the knife in my direction.

Whatever this thing was, it had made a fatal mistake. Did it think I would kill myself out of fear of what it would do to them if I didn't? The only thing it was inciting within me was a boiling rage. If I took that knife, what would happen to them then? Did it imagine I'd believe it would leave them be?

I could feel the power surging inside of me and I began to recite the first part of the large spell we'd practiced, the one that had almost killed me. The wind shifted from bone-chilling cold to burning hot as the power surged to me.

It could have me, but it would never have them. And if I didn't do something to stop it, *it* would. I let out a scream of agony over everything it had shown, raising my hands as I did, clueless to what would happen, if anything, as I unloaded all of the horrible things I felt inside outward.

Pure white light blasted out of me, shooting straight ahead in a surge that was unstoppable. I fell to my knees as it continued and dropped my gaze as the light burned my eyes. The wind howled around me as if in agony as the power continued to pour out. This might be my end, but I wouldn't go out alone. Everything I had and more seemed to be spilling out into that white-hot heat as I continued to bleed.

I crashed to the ground, knowing that whether or not I woke, I'd given everything I had. There was nothing left in me to give. My cheek in the snow, I was too spent to move. A wall of crystal, sheer and humongous, lay twenty feet in front of me, extending farther than I could see on either side. If *it* was still here, I couldn't feel it anymore.

I had to get up but couldn't move. My eyes wouldn't stay open. I might end up dying here after all, but I'd saved them. Or, at least, bought them time.

I didn't know how long I'd lain there when fingers grazed my cheek, moving my hair away from my face and stirring me awake.

I knew the tingle of Hawk's magic immediately.

"She's okay. She'll be okay," Hawk said, picking me off the ground and cradling me against him.

The sunlight was streaming in the window of my bedroom in the broker building when I woke. I was in a fresh t-shirt that I didn't recognize, my wounds all bandaged.

The soft murmur of a crowd outside drew me to the window. There had to be twenty or thirty people gathered outside. Some were still, some were leaving and some coming, but they all took a moment to pause and look at the building, talking and pointing. A man in front looked up, saw me, and nudged his buddy. Soon the entire crowd was staring back at me, their expressions hard to read. I went to take a step back but paused. It didn't matter anymore. I was officially out of the shadows, and there wasn't any way back in. I leaned on the sill, letting them get their look.

The door opened a few minutes later and I tore my gaze away from the crowd.

Hawk stood inside my room. He did a perusal of my many bandages before meeting my gaze.

"You did it," he said.

It wasn't until then that I fully believed what I'd seen last night. I remembered the wall of crystal, but I'd been so spent from exhaustion and blood loss that it could've been a hallucination. I guessed not.

"How did you find me?"

"I heard you and Zab go up the stairs. When neither of you returned, I followed you up here, but there was no one in the room. Then I saw this." He held up something that looked like it had been charred.

"It's the token Zab left in your room, except this one Zab had never seen. It was identical except for a single bead. The one he'd left is gone. This is a dark token. It acts as an entryway of sorts."

"Where did it come from?" I wasn't going to blame Belinda, not yet. But if I ever found out it was her, I'd hunt her down and kill her myself.

"I'm not sure." He clenched his jaw, as if he had the same hunch but was also refraining. "It doesn't matter now, at least not for you. You held up your end of the bargain. I'll take you back to Rest. I'll handle things here."

No. *No, no, no.* I was screaming it on the inside as I stood silently. I didn't want to go back. I was supposed to be here. I'd never felt so sure of anything in my life until right now, as I was on the verge of leaving. I had to stay.

"I'll take you back tomorrow." He turned to walk out.

Nooooo. Say something, you idiot!

"That might not be a good idea," I blurted out before he'd gotten through the door. He turned, waiting to hear what I would say.

"I might need to do it again," I said. "I'm not sure how well I did the spell. It might fall apart. I should probably stay for a bit, just to make sure." There. I'd said it. I'd pretty much told him I wanted to stay. I'd made the first step. I could do it. I could make this place home. In truth, it was already home. The idea of leaving, even with everything that happened here, left me feeling like I was gaping wide open, worse than last night or the grouslie attack.

Hawk would want me to stay. He'd forced me to be here this whole time. Plus, the way he looked at me sometimes, like I could do anything I put my mind to? Why wouldn't he want me to stay?

Why wasn't he saying that, though? Why was he standing there so quiet?

"What if it gets weak? Maybe I should stay another few days to make sure," I said, aiming a little lower.

Hawk still wasn't saying anything, and he wasn't looking as happy as I'd hoped. Not that he was the jump-up-and-down type, but there was usually some sign of pleasure, and I was getting none. If anything, I was picking up on some of the *I'm sorry* vibes I'd caught from him when he booted Belinda. Except this time they were aimed at me, and it felt even worse than I'd imagined.

He finally spoke. "It'll hold long enough. You held up your end. It's time for you to go. It's for the best."

And there it was. It didn't matter if I wanted to stay here. This wasn't my home, and there was no invitation on the table. Worse, he *wanted* me to leave. That was it. The job was done and so was I. He didn't need me anymore, and that was the end of the road.

I broke eye contact, looking back to the crowd. It felt like if I looked at him now, some part of me would start to unravel until I was just a big knotted heap on the floor.

He didn't move, and I kept staring at the crowd. When I eventually looked back, he was gone.

44

I slept for most of the day. Zab stopped by, bringing me a cocoa. Musso came by to check in. By that night, I wasn't sure if I was still tired and weak or just dreading what was to come so badly that I didn't want to get up and face reality. I'd spent so much time trying to get out of here that the idea of lying in bed to avoid leaving seemed absurd.

I'd tossed the ideas over and over again in my head, trying to find some other logical reason why I dreaded leaving this place. There was only one. This felt like home. These people had come to feel like family, even if not all of them wanted me here.

I got up and walked downstairs, knowing this might be my last night in this place. There wasn't a soul in the office. I walked about the room, ran a hand over my table, my baskets, my weird little plant. I looked up at Helen.

"It was nice working with you," I said, feeling like I was speaking to a coworker.

A slip flew out and tumbled in the air a few times before landing right side up in front of my feet.

. . .

Don't leave.

I picked up the slip. No one had ever told me Helen could talk.

I looked up at the giant machine. "I have to go. I'm not welcome here anymore."

Another slip flew out and landed in front of me.

You'll be back. You're meant to be here.

The message ripped at my insides. Even Helen thought I should stay, but she wasn't calling the shots, and I had nowhere else to go. There was no choice but to leave.

"I have to, so please, don't make me feel worse about it."

Another slip shot out. It landed at my feet, upside down. I flipped it over, and there were no words on the other side either.

"I know. I don't know what to say either."

I took the slips and brought them to the shredder, destroying them, as if they'd never been suggested.

The front door opened, and Hawk stepped inside.

"I didn't want to wake you, but since you're up, we should probably do this now."

"You mean leave? I was hoping to say goodbye," I said, looking around the room again, thinking I'd have until tomorrow at least. I'd been here for months and been so determined to leave the entire time. Now I didn't know what I'd do in the morning when I couldn't have tea with Zab or laugh when Musso was being a grumpy old man.

"I'll make the needed explanations, or perhaps you can

leave them a note. It's better if you don't hang around here too long, especially considering you want to go back to Rest and have a normal life. The longer you stay, the more entangled you'll become in what's going on."

I was starting to think this was more about Hawk wanting me gone than anything else. He couldn't wait to get rid of me. And if that was the way of it, then fine by me. I wouldn't beg. I never had.

"That's probably a smart idea," I said, faking a smile.

"I set up a place for you in—"

"No. I don't need you to make arrangements for me. I'll be fine on my own and I'll figure it out. I'll be going back to Salem for now."

"What about finances? It's not cheap to move, and you can't stay there."

"You don't need to worry about me. I can take care of myself."

"I know you can. Tippi, this is for—"

"I agree. It's for the best."

I sat at my table with two sheets of paper and tried to jot down a quick goodbye note to both Zab and Musso. Nothing seemed adequate, and Hawk silently staring at me wasn't helping. In the end, it was a simple goodbye and thank you to them both, though I hoped they knew how much they'd both come to mean to me.

I laid a note on each desk and turned my attention to Hawk.

"If you don't mind, I'm pretty tired already, so if we can get this going?"

I'd never seen Hawk indecisive until right now. He was staring at me like he wanted to talk, to say something, and maybe would if I gave him an opening. But I didn't need a lecture on what was best for me. What I needed was to go to

Salem, and now. I walked and didn't stop until I was out the back door, figuring he'd want to do this in the alley instead of making a puddle on his floor. Plus, I needed the brisk air to hide the red of my cheeks and cool the burning in my eyes. He wanted me gone so badly that he wasn't even going to let me say goodbye to my friends.

When I'd come here, I'd known I was going to be stuck until I could do his spell. I hadn't realized that it would be just long enough for me to care about this place, these people, to begin to believe I belonged here. Long enough to shift my entire paradigm on life. Long enough to crush me.

Water spilled behind me. I turned and saw him sprinkle salt. I stepped into the water first, without a word, waiting for him. He hesitated for a second and then followed suit.

I thought I'd find myself in my apartment. Instead, he'd landed us behind my building, perhaps for a private goodbye. My goodbyes were done. I'd said them the best I could in a cheap note to the people who'd miss me.

I gave him a nod, intent to give as good as I got. If he could send me away, I certainly wouldn't show him how deeply it cut.

"Thanks for the lift. Good luck with your—problem."

"Tippi..."

"It's a little chilly out." It felt like a warm spring day compared to Xest. "I'm going to go get settled. Again, thanks for bringing me back here so quickly, a man of your word. You said I could go as soon as I was done, and you held up your end of things. I appreciate it."

He nodded, as if he was beginning to understand how much I didn't appreciate it at all.

"After everything settles down, it might be possible for you to come back and visit occasionally."

Visit occasionally. Wow. As if I thought this whole

scenario couldn't get any worse. Did he think I'd pop back over, do some spells for him, hang out with the friends I'd made, before telling me I had to leave again? I didn't think so. No. This was it for us.

"I think staying here is for the best, like you said." I nodded slowly.

I turned away from him. A hand on my arm stopped me, but I didn't turn around, wouldn't look at him.

"Tippi, you don't understand. This is the way it has to be."

"Yeah, sure. I get it. You've got your reasons." He always did, didn't he? They might've been great reasons, too, but who would know when he never bothered to share them? Stay when he says stay and then leave when he says it's time.

I tugged on my arm. When he didn't let go, I finally turned to look at him.

"What do you want from me? Do you want me to say you're right? I said it already so if you don't mind..." My gaze went to his grip.

Instead of releasing me, he yanked me back to him. His arms closed around me, one wrapping about my waist as the other dug into my hair, tilting my head back as his lips found mine, and then his tongue delved within.

I should've pushed him away, but instead I melded to his form, feeling how perfectly we fit. The smell of him swallowed me, and the taste of him was intoxicating. Nothing had ever felt so perfect in my life, so right, so meant to be. All the times I'd watched him, curious, wondering why I couldn't seem to escape his presence—it was all so clear now. Maybe he felt it as well, would ask me to stay. Tell me to come back with him and say how wrong he was to force me out?

His mouth finally broke from mine, even as his arms

remained wrapped around me. I could feel his stare as I kept my lids lowered, waiting for him to tell me how wrong he was.

"I shouldn't have done that," he said, not sounding contrite at all. His arms dropped and he stepped back. "You should go."

My body, which had molded to his, stiffened. I was a fool, and even more so now. From the second he embraced me, I'd acted like an idiot. The hands that had wrapped around him now wanted to choke him. I'd behaved just like Belinda. He'd forced me out, and then I'd stood here and kissed him back like my life depended on it. I'd stood here and taken his scraps until he was finished with me. At least when he ended things with Belinda, he'd seemed almost sad about it. With me? He was acting as if I'd done something to him.

"You're right."

I turned and walked away, refusing to look back even though every part of me wanted to. I'd been a fool to get comfortable in Xest. I'd been a bigger fool for believing I had any choice in staying. I'd been the biggest fool for letting him kiss me, thinking he'd change his mind.

I wasn't sure if he stayed standing there watching me or left right away. I didn't look and didn't want to know. He'd played me for a fool once too many times.

I walked into my apartment building, happy there was no one about to ask where I'd been. I made my way to the second floor and paused outside my door, wondering if I should test the knob or knock.

I hit my knuckles on the wood. Even if it was open, it didn't feel like it was my home anymore. Not really.

Rabbit shrieked as soon as she opened the door, pulling me into the apartment and then into a huge hug.

She'd barely been here and Loris had already taken her down with her hugging ways.

"You came back!" Rabbit said, jumping up and down while she continued to hug me.

"I'm back!" I said, trying to match her enthusiasm, which was impossible.

She pulled back immediately. "What's wrong? Did something happen?"

"No. It's all good. Just finished up what I needed to do there, and now I'm done, ready to get back to normal." I smiled as wide as I could, even as I knew my eyes wanted to flood the apartment.

Rabbit looked at the door and then back to me. "Hawk didn't want to say hello or anything?"

She knew Hawk well enough to know he wouldn't come and say hello to nearly anyone. I knew what the real question was.

"I guess he's too busy getting on with his life now that the situation is under control."

She nodded, her smile dropping.

"And you'll get on with yours," she said, patting my shoulder, another Loris thing.

45

Two Months Later

"What's that?" I asked, not liking the way Rabbit was looking at the letter in her hand.

"It's another one from him." She held it out to me.

Hawk again. We never said his name anymore. I wasn't sure when that had started. Probably when the first letter had come and I'd cursed him, saying I never wanted to hear his name again. Who knew Rabbit would take that so literally?

I hated the way I wanted to rip the envelope open. How my heart thudded as I wondered if he was going to ask me to come back. That he was sorry that I left, that he'd forced me out.

That my fingers nearly trembled as I read it.

.   .   .

You haven't moved into the New York apartment.

I dropped the letter to the table in front of me. Every time I got one, I hoped it was him asking me to come back. Telling me I should be there, in Xest, and he'd been wrong. It never was. It was always about when I was moving. I needed to get out of here. It left me too vulnerable. He'd even leased me a place in New York City. I'd googled the address, and he'd spared no expense to try to lure me to safety. I was daydreaming of returning while he was terrified that I would.

"You still want to go back, don't you?" She took a seat at the table across from me.

I'd been lying to Rabbit, saying I was happy to be back in Salem, knowing she'd never be able to return to Xest herself. How could you pine about a place you'd barely lived in when the person who'd grown up there, had called it home her entire life, could never return?

"It's okay to admit it. I don't miss Xest. I'm happy here, and it's okay if you aren't."

I looked up, saw the smile in her eyes, thought of the way she hummed every morning before she went to work. She'd even hung new curtains in the living room and had painted. She liked it here. I had too, once upon a time. That was back when this place had felt like a sanctuary, a place I could spend the rest of my life hiding. In Xest, I didn't need to hide. Now all I thought about was going to Xest and actually living the life I might've been meant for.

"Sometimes." Confessing, even slightly, made the pain worse somehow. As if giving the thought some air to breathe also gave it a sharp edge with which to stab me.

"Is it him?" Rabbit motioned toward the letter.

"No." Not that part of me wouldn't have liked to see him, maybe just once more, on a day that I was looking my best and making sure *he* knew I didn't care. "I just..." I missed the place. I missed being able to be the me that I never had been able to here. Being around people that didn't think I was a freak for what I could do. I wouldn't say any of those things, though. I couldn't handle giving any more ideas room to breathe and then stab me.

"You know, there's probably a way to go—"

"No. There isn't." This was my life. I'd learn to like it again if it was the last thing I did. I'd find a place to go that wasn't New York. It would be okay.

"Are you going to be okay?"

"I'm fine. I really am." It was the most honest question she'd asked yet, and I'd answered it with a lie. How skilled I'd become at them. "I'm going to go take a walk. I'll get dinner while I'm out, okay?"

I grabbed my jacket, heading for the door before there was a chance for any more honesty.

"Oh, I can't. I told Loris I'd help her with a séance in an hour."

"Yeah, okay."

Rabbit and Loris had clicked just as well as I'd hoped. Knowing eventually I'd have to leave, there wasn't any point in dislodging Rabbit from the position. Plus, as it turned out, my bank account had ballooned exponentially since I'd returned. Zab had written a letter, letting me know he'd deposited back pay. Turned out that the conversion rate from coin to dollar was mighty good.

I'd walked for over an hour until I finally gave up and headed home. Walking wasn't fixing what was wrong. This was my life. It was the life I wanted and that I'd died trying to get back to.

I stopped and looked at the shop I'd planned on working in for the rest of my life. Loris was laughing with Rabbit inside. I was happy for them. The only thing I was envious of was how content they seemed. I'd been that way once. I could be again.

There were some very good things here in Rest. I could build a new life. So why did every step feel like walking through wet cement? Who needed magic or Xest—or him?

I tried to pull in a deep breath while my chest felt like it was caving in. I ducked into the alley to the side of the building, slumping against the wall, alone in the shadows as I tried to pull myself together.

Rabbit had moved here and felt immediately at home. I'd come back and found I couldn't breathe in my own skin anymore. I didn't feel like I *belonged* anymore. But I didn't belong in Xest either, so where did that leave me? I leaned my head back, closed my eyes, and forced a few more breaths down deep until it felt like I was alive again.

A hand wrapped around my arm and dragged me off the wall, and a burlap bag was shoved over my head. I swung, kicked, and screamed, but there were definitely two of them, one on each side, and one of me.

"Get her wrists."

"I'm trying."

I knew these voices. The two idiots who'd dragged me to Xest the first time. This had to be a joke, right?

"You've got to be kidding me. You're doing this again?" I asked as I stopped fighting. I should still be fighting, right? I mean, they were going to drag me back to Xest. Any second, I'd start fighting. I had nothing to go back to in Xest. This wasn't a good idea, no matter how badly I craved it.

"Why's she holding out her wrists?" Spike asked.

"I don't know. Just tie them," Braid answered.

Rope was looped around them and then tightened.

"Who wants me now? I didn't call in any jobs."

"What?" Spike asked.

I felt the burlap on my head shift.

"No, don't take that thing off her head. They say she's dangerous."

The burlap sank back into place, and I didn't care. I was going back to Xest. I really needed to fight. This wasn't a good thing. No one wanted me there. It wasn't like I could get a job with Raydam.

"But I can't hear her when she talks," Spike said.

"Doesn't matter. She's dangerous. You shouldn't try to talk to her. Remember? No talking. That's what he said. Now help me get her ankles. She's supposed to be tied up tight before transport for safety reasons," Braid said.

"But this is the same girl we picked up last time. Why do we got to do all this work?" Spike asked.

"She's *dangerous* now."

"She's not doing anything. How's she dangerous?"

"Just help me sit her down so we can finish!" Braid was really losing his patience now.

I sat for him and put out my legs. The sooner they took me wherever they were supposed to, the sooner I could deal with this. That was really the only reason I was cooperating. If this was Raydam, I was going to kick his ass, or I would as soon as he threatened someone else who needed protecting. Maybe I could trick him into it? I surely could.

The rope looped around and around so many times that I wondered what they thought I could do. I wasn't even putting up a fight.

"Hurry up. Make the puddle," Braid said, dragging me to my feet.

"I *am*."

I heard splashing, and then the fifth wind was blowing. Once you felt the fifth wind, you never mistook it.

"What the hell did you do?" Braid asked. "This wasn't where we were supposed to jump!"

"I did it right. Maybe it was that weird salt you bought on discount. Even I know you can't use bath salts and they call me the dumb one."

A loud growl broke the air. It could've come from a lion if you could find one that was about three times the size of normal, which maybe they had in Xest? If I'd been moving, I would've frozen. As it was, my two captors did.

"What was that?" Spike whispered.

"I don't know. Let's hurry up and get out of here. You got more salt?"

"No."

There was a pause, and then I was lifted, an arm under each of mine.

There was another growl, and if possible, it was even louder. Whatever this thing was, it was close, big, and angry.

"We gotta go! Leave her. We're not getting paid enough to die," Braid said.

Both my supports were gone as I stumbled and ended up on the ground, their footsteps disappearing.

I maneuvered myself into a sitting position and tried to wriggle my hands free, all the while waiting for whatever creature had made that noise to come and eat me. This was a fine ending. Dinner for a monster in Xest. When I had daydreamed about coming back, this was not how it went down.

Suddenly the sack was tugged from my head.

"I thought you had no interest in visiting?" Hawk asked, kneeling in front of me, smirking.

I turned my head, screaming after my two abductors who had hightailed it out of there.

"It's safe! Come back! Take me with you!"

Read The Nowhere Witch, *the next installment of Tales of Xest now.*

SCAN THE QR CODE WITH YOUR CAMERA BELOW TO JOIN MY MAILING LIST:

Or, follow me on one of these platforms:
http://www.donnaaugustine.com
Twitter handle: @DonnAugustine
https://www.facebook.com/groups/223180598486878/

ACKNOWLEDGMENTS

The writing a book can be a lonely process, but finishing a book definitely isn't. Over the years, I've come to rely on a lot of people to help me get over the finish line. Many of them drop whatever they're doing to help me put out the best book possible. Donna Z., Lisa A, Camilla J., Lori H., Tammy K., Christine J. and Ashleigh M., you each bring something unique and priceless to every project we work on. I'd be lost without all your help :)

ALSO BY DONNA AUGUSTINE

Ollie Wit

A Step into the Dark

Walking in the Dark

Kissed by the Dark

The Keepers

The Keepers

Keepers and Killers

Shattered

Redemption

Karma

Karma

Jinxed

Fated

Dead Ink

The Wilds

The Wilds

The Hunt

The Dead

The Magic

Born Wild (Wilds Spinoff)

Wild One

Savage One

Wyrd Blood
Wyrd Blood
Full Blood
Blood Binds

Tales of Xest
The Whimsy Witch Who Wasn't
The Nowhere Witch
The Most Wanted Witch